*From the battlefield to the homefront,
they were the proud
and passionate inheritors of a glorious frontier,
their fates linked to the star of one ambitious,
enigmatic—and tragic—man*

LIEUTENANT COLONEL GEORGE ARMSTRONG CUSTER

Driven to succeed at any cost, his destiny was bound inextricably to the savagely beautiful Great Plains—and to the very people he came to conquer.

GENERAL PHILIP SHERIDAN

A seasoned commander and Civil War hero, he'd witnessed firsthand just how fierce the "Boy General" could be—and tried to protect his friend Custer from himself.

D0049704

TOM CUSTER

An incorrigible lady's man, rogue, and hero in his own right, he worshipped his famous brother to a fault and would take his stand beside him no matter what.

ROMERO

A half-breed scout, his loyalties were divided between his Mexican and Cheyenne heritage—and the white man's army he was paid to advise.

LIBBIE CUSTER

As Custer's beloved wife, she understood the soldier in her husband—but not the complex man who yearned for the one thing she could never give him.

MONASEETAH

Daughter of a proud people, she lost her family to the pony soldiers only to lose her heart to the fiercest and most famous of them all—Custer.

Terry C. Johnston's triumphant new novel
LONG WINTER GONE

General George Armstrong Custer as he appeared in the Washita Winter of 1868–1869. Photograph courtesy of the Custer Battlefield National Monument

SuN of ThE pLAINS - VoLUMe 1

LONG WINTER GONE

TERRY C. JOHNSTON

BANTAM BOOKS

NEW YORK · TORONTO · LONDON · SYDNEY · AUCKLAND

LONG WINTER GONE

A Bantam Book / November 1990

ISBN 0-553-28621-8

PUBLISHED SIMULTANEOUSLY IN THE UNITED STATES AND CANADA

Bantam Books are published by Bantam Books, a division of Bantam Doubleday
Dell Publishing Group, Inc. Its trademark, consisting of the words "Bantam
Books" and the portrayal of a rooster, is Registered in U.S. Patent and
Trademark Office and in other countries. Marca Registrada, Bantam Books, 666
Fifth Avenue, New York, New York 10103.

PRINTED IN THE UNITED STATES OF AMERICA

OPM   0 9 8 7 6 5 4 3 2 1

Dedicated to my friends,
Charlotte and Jory Sherman—
for all your time and tears, work and worry . . .
I'll never be able to repay what you both have
given me from the heart and core of your beings.

Indian women soon got to know the white men very well indeed. Many became wives, mistresses, casual bedfellows. The relationships that evolved were about as intimate as human contacts could well be. Yet, there was a gulf that was never bridged: a chasm, not just of race but of archaeological time, that perhaps no civilized white man has ever succeeded in closing between himself and a primitive woman.

WALTER O'MEARA
Daughters of the Country

"I was wondering," an Arikara chief mused, "whether you white people have any women amongst you." I assured him in the affirmative. "Then," said he, "why is it that your people are so fond of our women? One might suppose you had never seen any women before."

HENRY M. BRACKENRIDGE
Journal of a Voyage Up The Missouri River, in 1811

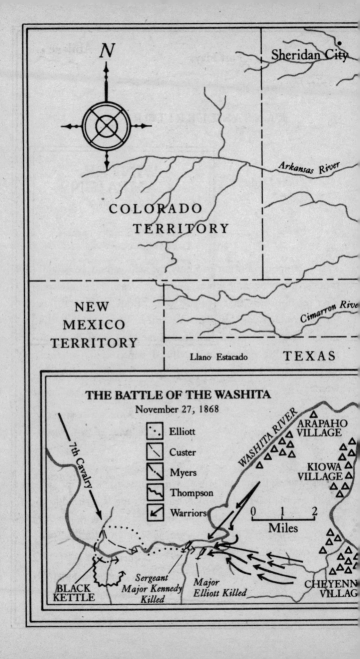

N

Sheridan City

Arkansas River

COLORADO
TERRITORY

NEW
MEXICO
TERRITORY

Cimarron River

Llano Estacado

TEXAS

THE BATTLE OF THE WASHITA
November 27, 1868

- Elliott
- Custer
- Myers
- Thompson
- Warriors

WASHITA RIVER

ARAPAHO
VILLAGE

KIOWA
VILLAGE

7th Cavalry

0   1   2
Miles

BLACK
KETTLE

*Sergeant
Major Kennedy
Killed*

*Major
Elliott Killed*

CHEYENNE
VILLAGE

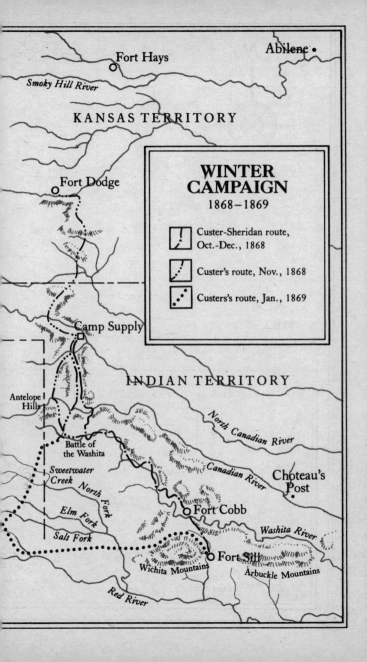

Abilene •

Fort Hays

Smoky Hill River

KANSAS TERRITORY

Fort Dodge

WINTER CAMPAIGN
1868–1869

Custer-Sheridan route,
Oct.-Dec., 1868

Custer's route, Nov., 1868

Custers's route, Jan., 1869

Camp Supply

INDIAN TERRITORY

Antelope
Hills

North Canadian River

Battle of
the Washita

*Sweetwater
Creek*
*North
Fork*

Canadian River

Choteau's
Post •

Elm Fork

Salt Fork

Fort Cobb

Washita River

Fort Sill
Wichita Mountains
Arbuckle Mountains

Red River

PROLOGUE

"THE hell of it is . . . I can't seem to put my finger on what's gnawing in my goddamned gut," Philip H. Sheridan growled.

As he tore the moist stub of a cigar from his thin lips, a bit of dead ash fell on the lapel of his dark blue army tunic. He brushed off what he could with a quick swipe of a hand, smudging the gray into the uniform like a street beggar. Lieutenant General Sheridan studied each one of his staff in turn.

Lieutenant Colonel Michael V. Sheridan was the first to speak, answering his older brother's question. "I don't understand what's eating at you, Philip. Custer won the victory we were certain could be won."

"And a stunning success it was at that, General," echoed Major Nelson B. Sweitzer of the Second Cavalry.

"No mistake about that, Nelson." Sheridan used his cigar to jab home the point. "Still, a voice inside troubles me."

In stony silence, the commander of the Department of

the Missouri turned back to the wide window behind his massive oak desk, his eyes gazing far beyond the bustling Topeka, Kansas, street below. Though he stood shorter than most of the officers gathered around him, Sheridan somehow conveyed a greater stature than most men of the day. Here stood a confident man, every inch of muscle rippling with the martial fervor that had made him the hero of countless cavalry battles in the late war between the states.

But that rebellion lay some four and a half years behind him. Today he had a new war to fight.

The leaden skies dropped a wet, icy snow that turned the Topeka streets into a barnyard slop. Sheridan turned back to his staff and sank heavily into his chair at last. "Sandy, tell me what you're thinking."

Major George A. Forsyth cleared his throat. "Undoubtedly, Custer did more at the Washita than my command of frontier scouts ever hoped of doing, pinned down on Beecher's Island, General. I can't fault him his success."

"He damn well could have gotten himself wiped out!" blurted Lieutenant Colonel James W. Forsyth, Sandy's brother. "Himself . . . along with a good piece of his regiment. But we all know that, don't we? That's something no one in this room has had the guts to mention. Begging the General's pardon—"

Sheridan waved his hand; flakes of ash littered the papers scattered across his desk. "No offense, Tony. We all know—don't we, gentlemen—that Tony's right. But that's not all that bothers me." He rose stiffly, the cold in this office penetrating to his marrow more of late. At the nearby hutch where the ever-present bottles and glasses waited, Sheridan poured himself a few fingers of amber liquid.

Without ceremony or inviting the others to join him, he tossed the fire down a throat more parched these days with the burn of long hours and too many cigars.

"Is this damned Custer doing a single thing different than he ever has in his military career, sir?" Michael Sheridan asked.

With the back of his hand the general wiped some lingering drops of whiskey from his bushy mustache after a second drink. "Near as I can tell, Custer's still the same cavalry magician he was at Gettysburg, Shenandoah, and Appomattox Wood." He slammed the empty whiskey glass down. "And frankly, gentlemen—Philip H. Sheridan isn't a man to argue with success."

"All of us need reminding that those victories were exactly why we wanted Custer brought out of that year of his . . . unofficial retirement." Major Morris V. Ashe uttered the words the rest of Sheridan's staff wouldn't admit to. "All of us asked for him back before his court-martial was over . . . simply because we all knew he was the *only* one who could march into Indian Territory. Any man here who says he didn't believe Custer was the *only* one who could slash his way through the hostile tribes last year is a damned liar."

"Strong words, Major." Michael Sheridan sank into his horsehair-stuffed chair, hands steepled before his bearded chin.

"But true, sir," Ashe said. "Wasn't a one of us didn't know what Custer could accomplish . . . what Custer *is*."

"Sounds like you agree with his tactics, Morris."

Ashe glared at Michael Sheridan. "He won, didn't he?"

The younger Sheridan turned away without a word, lighting his own cigar.

"Goddamn it, that's what we're all about, isn't it?" Ashe prodded the rest of them.

Philip Sheridan finally filled the aching silence. "Yes, Major. I suppose you are more than right. You're damned right. We are army. It's not just what we do. It's what we *are*."

"General, again I beg your pardon," Tony Forsyth said, "but Custer's success last winter don't hide the fact that he blundered twice in winning his startling victory."

"His lack of reconnaissance," Michael Sheridan added. "The lack of intelligence before attacking Black Kettle's camp is more than appalling, Philip. It could have cost him—us—the entire campaign!"

The general rose. "We're all aware my brother has never shared a high opinion of Custer. What I want to know, Tony, is what was Custer's second blunder."

"Elliott, sir." Ashe allowed the death knell of that name to hang in the cold air of the room. "Major Joel H. Elliott, Seventh U.S. Cavalry."

Philip Sheridan turned back to the smudgy window, peered out into the gray of early winter battering the plains. "With Grant in the White House and Sherman replacing Grant as commanding general of the army, we can now focus our attention elsewhere, gentlemen." Sheridan's breath clouded the window before him. "If Custer's done nothing else, he's brought peace to the southern plains."

"And the Southwest, sir?" Major Sweitzer inquired.

"Quiet for now."

"The Northwest?"

"Nothing stirring there either." Sheridan sighed.

"All that's left is the northern plains, sir," Sandy Forsyth said. "Command have someone in mind?"

The question hung like day-old smoke in the room. This staff that was the cream of the officers corps of Sherman's "New Army of the West" could only stare at General Sheridan's back.

"Short of me going personally," the general replied, "there isn't a man in this room who's up to taking on the likes of those Sioux and Northern Cheyenne. Short of me, there remains only . . . Custer."

"That sonuvabitch charges without knowing his enemy's location, strength, or desire to fight!" Michael Sheridan fumed.

"It's not Custer's reconnaissance that wins his battles for him, Michael," Philip Sheridan said. "It's Custer's bold, daring charge into the face of any enemy no matter that enemy's strength. It's always been his damnable Custer's Luck."

"You'll reassign Custer to the northern plains?" Tony Forsyth asked.

"Not yet. That'll come soon enough. Look around you, goddammit. The whole country's clamoring for him. He's even more of a hero now than he was at the end of the war. Back east they've all heard how he wiped out Black Kettle's village—what the Republican papers called a nest of vipers. And with that reporter Keim accompanying Custer on his winter campaign last year, the public damn well knows how Custer himself brought the Kiowa, Arapaho and the rest of the Southern Cheyenne back in to their reservations, single-handedly putting an end to their bloody forays into the Kansas settlements . . . all without firing another goddamned shot."

"A stroke of genius?" Michael Sheridan asked.

"Damn right it is," the general growled. "For those who

want a peaceful resolution to the Indian question, Custer has conquered five bands of hostiles without firing a single bullet. And for those who desired a bloodier close to the problem . . . well, gentlemen—they got the Washita."

"You make him sound like a publicists' dream," Sweitzer said.

"I'm beginning to think that's what he is," Philip Sheridan admitted.

"So you'll assign him to Terry's Department of Dakota?"

Sheridan glowered at his younger brother. "Not just yet." He turned back to his window, watching the drizzle becoming a wet snow. Soggy flakes layered the sill outside. The silence in the room turned as cold as the snow lancing down from the heavy cloud underbellies stalled over eastern Kansas.

George Forsyth finally cleared his throat. "General, I can't shake the feeling that something's still bothering you about this whole matter of Custer's success with the southern Indians."

Without turning, Sheridan said, "You've hit it right on the head, Sandy. Something's kicked around inside me ever since I rode north, leaving Custer at Fort Sill to finish that winter campaign on his own. And the bastard did better than I expected him to. He even followed my orders, for a change."

The general wheeled on them, his Irish eyes grave. "So somebody tell me why I can't sleep at night. Why I drink more than I should . . . why I have the dread feeling that even I, his commanding officer, can no longer check or restrain George Armstrong Custer."

BOOK I

WASHITA

MASHUTA

CHAPTER 1

"I'LL be back."

Those lips below the shaggy, wheat-straw mustache barely stirred. Yet none of the eight officers strung out on either side of him had trouble hearing the soldier's determined declaration. The chill November air across the parade ground echoed with clatter: low rumbling voices, the incessant roll of drums, the occasional snort of a horse.

"And when I do get back, I'll show each and every one of these . . . *men* who claim to be soldiers how to fight Indians."

"On those counts of courts-martial—" Fort Leavenworth's adjutant sent his voice crackling across the dusty parade, "the first, disobeying the orders of a superior officer, dereliction of duty, and misappropriation of U.S. Army property."

Across the chilly parade shot an electricity every man sensed. Here in the waning weeks of 1867 stood the darling of the army, the youngest man ever breveted a major general, a soldier never found wanting in courage who had seen eleven horses shot out from under him during the recent war of rebellion. Now they watched that same officer sit ramrod stiff astride his favorite mount, his pale face a mask to the tempest raging within his soul.

I'm just like some old bull, he brooded behind those shocking blue eyes of his. *Protecting the herd. Fighting off the wolves that nip and snarl at my hamstrings. Here I sit, guilty of protecting the sanctity of this army of our Grand Republic.*

"—Guilty of a second count, that of ordering his subordinate officers to summarily execute deserters escaping from his command without the process of trial."

Didn't those bastards throw away that very right as they deserted in broad daylight? Taking their government mounts and weapons with them?

"—Refusing to allow proper medical attention to be given to those same wounded deserters he had ordered summarily shot for their infractions of army code. To this count and this count alone the board attaches no criminality."

"Bloody good of the bastards," he mumbled, running the pink tip of his tongue across lips drying in a cold breeze that foretold of a harsh winter soon to grip the southern plains.

"—The court found guilt on the charge stating the lieutenant colonel did in fact order the shooting of one Private Johnson without process of trial as deserter, causing same Private Johnson to suffer mortal wounds inflicted by order of the lieutenant colonel."

A stiff breeze tugged at the blood-colored plume atop his ceremonial helmet emblazoned with an American eagle.

His red-blond curls fell over the glittering gold epaulets that crowned his blue tunic. More gold braid and tassels spilled down his chest while broad gold stripes gleamed at his cuffs. Freckled hands encased in white kid gloves gripped the pommel of his McClellan saddle.

"I'll be back," he muttered once more, watching the young adjutant square his shoulders. "By then I'll be—"

"—Sentenced: to one full year of suspension from rank and command, along with the forfeiture of pay for that rank and its command during the same period of suspension."

Slowly, his breath whistled past his dry lips. Almost imperceptibly he shuddered with the weight of it finally torn from his shoulders. As the adjutant across the parade finished reading, the drums began their stirring roll once again.

By heavens, he thought, *it could have been much worse. What with the weight of all those arrayed against me . . . their testimony having the ears of—*

"—The Court herewith has ordered the reading of its verdict in regard to the case of Lieutenant Colonel George Armstrong Custer, U.S. Seventh Cavalry . . ."

I'll bet the court realized this southern department can't do without me for all that long. The corner of his lip turned up and he scanned the quiet knot of civilians, locking on Libbie's eyes once more. *She knows too.*

The drum rolls sank into a staccato cadence. His march to the far edge of the parade ended among a cluster of friends and supporters. The distasteful ceremony was over at last.

Again his pale blue eyes surveyed the assembled cavalry

and infantry that symbolized this expanding New Army of the West.

"I'll be back," he said, clear and strong, turning the heads of soldiers ambling back to barracks or officers' quarters. "This country out here needs a man like me. I'll be back . . . to take things in hand."

So many times since that frosty November day in 1867, Custer had ruminated on his brief, explosive tenure in that new land of the West.

Chasing Sioux and Cheyenne up and down the Platte River Road in Nebraska Territory with General Hancock, sweeping down into the Kansas country, whipping his young soldiers along behind him, wishing they would ride as hard and as fast as the young warriors they chased—an enemy who eluded his plodding cavalry. More often lately Custer turned his gaze of a late afternoon to watch the sun setting low and lonely, like his own private ache, upon that far land.

That's the arena for a true gladiator, he brooded, tearing his eyes from the west, tramping back across the wide lawn toward the massive house where lived the family of Judge Daniel Stanton Bacon, pillar of Monroe, Michigan, society.

It was here that the judge's only child, Elizabeth Bacon, had yielded to Custer's proposal of marriage in the middle of the bloody conflict that had ripped south from north. Only natural following his court-martial that the young couple would return to Michigan, here to hearth and home for both Bacons and Custers alike, to endure that awful year. Still, each night like this at supper time, Custer drew

ome small measure of satisfaction knowing one more day
f private torture had drawn to a close.

"What day is it, Autie?" Libbie threaded her arm
hrough his as he stepped into the kitchen. She used the
ickname he had given himself as a tiny lad as yet unable
o pronounce Armstrong.

"Thursday, Rosebud."

"No, dear," she replied, patting his arm. "What date?"

"The twenty-fourth, I believe. September."

"There, now. I can't allow you to wear that droopy face
f yours to supper. Thank God it won't be long until this
readful year is over."

"I suppose you're right after all," he said, sliding a chair
eneath her while the rest of the bustling household noisily
at down to a supper of roast beef, summer corn that
napped in your teeth, crisp pickles, young potatoes burst-
ıg fluffy from their skins and biscuits that melted on a
ıan's tongue.

Custer's younger brother Boston and nephew Autie
Reed both hungrily eyed two fresh-baked apple pies sitting
n the sideboard nearby.

With a clearing of throats, everyone's attention drew as
ne to Libbie as if she held marionette's threads in her tiny
labaster hands folded before her. The family bowed their
eads.

"Our most gracious and heavenly Father," Elizabeth
rayed, "we gather here before you, beseeching your
lessing upon this bounty you provide for us all. Here
vithin your sight, our Father, we again ask your
orgiveness . . . and ask that you help us forgive those
vho have trespassed against us."

Custer felt the gentle, insistent pressure of Libbie's leg

against his own beneath the mahogany table. *Why*, h
thought, *does she toy with this fire I suffer?*

This last year of enforced separation from the army ha
taken its silent toll upon the Custers in many subtle ways
Worst of all—for him—there was no more intimacy share
between them. Barely controlled beneath the surface
Custer burned with a raging desire for this pale-skinned
auburn-haired beauty. Yet even before the sentencin
at Fort Leavenworth, Libbie had begun to refuse him
Gently, lovingly . . . yes. No longer able to submit t
his insatiable hunger. For too long now she had bee
unable to give him what they both so desperately wanted
a son.

"We ask that all things be made right in your kingdor
on earth, as they are made right in heaven above. Amen.

On cue, male voices around the table echoed "Amen" a
they hurriedly stuffed napkins in their collars.

"I'll get it!" young Autie Reed shouted. He leapt u
sending his chair clattering across the hardwood floo
heading to answer an insistent rap at the front door. .
moment later the towheaded youngster tore back into th
dining room, flagging a telegram addressed to his famou
uncle.

"It's from Sheridan." Custer gripped the envelope as
afraid it would fly off on its own.

"Open it, dear," Libbie prodded, her heart alread
sensing that the envelope would take her beloved Auti
from her, a parting she had come to dread more tha
anything on earth.

Custer ripped at the envelope, sending it fluttering t
the rug beneath their feet. Between his trembling finger
Sheridan's words leapt from the page.

Hd.Qrs., Dept. of the Mo.
In the Field, Ft. Hays, Kans.
Sept. 24th, 1868

GEN'L G. A. CUSTER
Monroe, Mich.

Gen'ls Sherman, Sully & myself, and nearly all the Officers of your Regt., have asked for you; and I hope the application will be successful. Can you come at once? 11 Cos. of your Regt. will move about the 1st of Oct. against hostile Indians, from Medicine-Lodge Creek toward the Wichita Mts.

P. H. SHERIDAN
Maj. Gen'l Comdg. Mil. Dept. Mo.

"Ca-can I come at once?" Custer choked on the words with a characteristic lifelong stammer. He rose from his chair as family members pounded the daylights out of his back.

"I must go wire Philip." He slipped the telegram to Libbie, the mist in his eyes answered by the tears clouding her own.

"Yes, dear Autie," she said quietly. "Tell Philip you're coming as quickly as you can."

"My regiment . . . my men."

"I know . . . we all know how you feel about your men," she said before turning aside, blinking back the tears. All too well Libbie understood the army came first in his life, first in his heart. Back on that ninth day of February in 1864 she had readily accepted second place in his life. Elizabeth Bacon had become Libbie Custer—till death do they part.

"Go now, Autie," she said bravely. "We're all so happy for you."

Bending to kiss her pale, upturned cheek, Custer then

dashed from the room. The ground flew beneath him as he leapt from the porch, tearing down the brick walks to the telegraph office.

Giddy with excitement, he shook hands with everyone he met along the way, breathlessly telling them of the coming campaign and that he had been selected to lead his gallant Seventh into action again. He wildly pumped the arm of the telegraph operator before setting the old gentleman to work pounding out the message to his friend Philip.

> Will start to join you by next train.
>
> CUSTER

As a rusty sun came up in the east that very next morning, Custer boarded the first express train out of Michigan heading south and west toward the frontier and the shining destiny that beckoned him. He knew he would ache for her from time to time, but reminded himself: *No, Libbie chose to remain behind. It is the right choice. This is to be a winter campaign. No telling how long I'll be out. The fighting could last all winter long.*

That evening he stared into a sky dripping like coal oil across the western horizon, scratching the ears of his favorite pointer, Blucher. Dear Blucher and Maida, two staghound pups, were Custer's only companions now. Dusk became night and the locomotive spit cinders into the sky.

At that very moment out on that aching expanse of the western prairie those same bloody atrocities committed by the roving bands of Kiowa, Arapaho, and Cheyenne warriors coupled with the army's blessed clemency for their own marvelous, curly-headed "Boy General" both conspired to set in motion the gears of a crude bit of machinery that would grind slowly, inexorably slowly, over the next eight years.

★   ★   ★

Nipped by the cold frosts of lengthening autumn nights, the tall grasses across the prairie turned and dried withering in the incessant winds. Deer and elk grew restless, fought, and mated in their own ancient ritual of love and combat. Ponds slicked over with ice each night until the morning sun came to break the grip of so many things dead and dying on the land.

Near midmorning on 9 October 1868, a large band of painted, feathered warriors swept off the sandy hills, tearing down upon a civilian caravan of wagons returning to Kansas from Colorado Territory along the Old Arkansas Road. The Kiowas and Cheyennes caught the white farmers by surprise some ten miles east of the mouth of Sand Creek.

Blankets flapping, war cries splitting the air, they scared off the loose livestock herded beside the settlers' train. What few oxen and cattle the first rush left behind were hitched to the wagons. Before the first sun went down on those farmers, the warriors finished off the harnessed animals, leaving the oxen to die a slow and noisy death while the battle raged around their bleeding carcasses.

The siege lasted for days with little hope for relief. Early the third morning the Indians captured Mrs. Clara Blinn and her two-year-old son Willie. When the warriors decided they'd had enough of these farmers, they hoisted their booty and two captives atop war ponies and spirited them over the low hills. Only Mrs. Blinn's seriously wounded husband and the wagon master were left behind to send their prayers heavenward before limping to Fort Lyon.

It came as no surprise that before long those same young warriors sent word to the pony soldiers and Brevet Major General William B. Hazen, commander at Fort Cobb down in Indian Territory, stating their desire to ransom the white woman and her son.

Still, no one in the army's higher echelons would wager on who the captors were—Cheyenne or Kiowa or Arapaho. An unfortunate ignorance, for at the same time, from his winter camping grounds along the Washita River, Cheyenne Chief Black Kettle began to mediate the negotiations between the army's General Hazen and those warriors holding the captives. Just when it looked like Black Kettle and the white general would make some headway in ransoming the white prisoners, General Sheridan himself learned of the negotiations and squashed Hazen's peace machinery in midstream.

"I may not have learned much in my short tenure as commander of the Department of the Missouri," the general snorted to his aide Lieutenant Colonel J. Schuyler Crosby, "but now, by God, I can connect Black Kettle's bloody band of Southern Cheyenne with some of the white captives."

"You've got them red-handed, sir!"

"And an old horse soldier like me knows where there's that much smoke, there's bound to be fire!"

"This is your winter to crush them, General."

"Damn right it is, Crosby!" From his office he watched some infantry at drill across the parade of Fort Leavenworth. "It took us too damned long to realize the army was inadequate to catch mounted warriors fleeing across the plains. The only way to stop those warriors is to find their villages, then hit the bastards where they're content to sit out the winter."

"Sherman agrees?"

"Damn right he does. That's why we're pressing ahead with this winter campaign to wipe out—once and for all—this Indian problem down here. In fact—" he shuffled through papers on his desk until he located what he wanted, "in Sherman's reply of fifteen October, the old warhorse says it is up to the Indians themselves to decide whether they are to live or suffer extermination. These are Sherman's own words, Crosby:

'. . . we, in the performance of a most unpleasant duty, accept the war begun by our enemies, and hereby resolve to make its end final. If it results in the utter annihilation of these Indians it is but the result of what they have been warned again and again, and for which they seem fully prepared. I will say nothing and do nothing to restrain our troops from doing what they deem proper on the spot, and will allow no mere vague general charges of cruelty and inhumanity to tie their hands. . . . You may now go ahead in your own way and I will back you with my whole authority, and stand between you and any efforts that may be attempted in your rear to restrain your purpose or check your troops.'"

"Every man in army blue hungers for a decisive victory, General."

"The cold weather this coming winter will keep those marauding sonsabitches home by their lodge fires, won't it? Damn right, it will. Home in their villages—where Custer's Seventh Cavalry can find them."

"But, sir—what about General Sully? He'll expect to head the expedition you send down into the Territories, won't he?"

"I'll handle Sully when the time comes, Crosby. I owe Custer that much."

CHAPTER 2

"THE buffalo are plenty," Chief Black Kettle said with satisfaction. "Here we will stay the winter." His band of Southern Cheyenne spread out along the Washita River just east of the Texas Panhandle. One by one their browned, buffalo-hide lodges yearned toward the autumn-blue skies. Smoke from many fires rose to join the clouds dancing across the blue dome, pushed by the eager fall winds that foretold a taste of winter.

Black Kettle's people did not camp alone this robe season. His village of fifty Cheyenne lodges had been joined by one lodge of visiting Arapaho and two Sioux lodges desiring to winter a little farther south than they normally did. Small as it was, Black Kettle's village stood on the western border of a grander encampment spreading itself some twelve to fifteen miles along the looping river. Arapaho, Kiowa, Comanche, along with other bands of Southern Cheyenne and even a small village of Apache—in all, some six thousand strong—had erected their winter lodges in that ancient valley.

"Here to this valley dotted with hills that will break up winter's icy blasts has the Earth Mother herself invited us. Here we will laugh and sleep, hunt and dance—safe for the winter."

He smiled in that gentle way of his, watching his wife waddle off to unload the single travois of their simple possessions. Medicine Woman Later, his lifelong partner, gurgled in the back of her throat, a sound she used whenever she wanted to tell him he should do less talking about the trees and the land. A little less talking and a little more work.

It gave his heart a fierce pride to watch this raising of the few lodges left to his small band, smaller now after the slaughter at Sand Creek four winters ago. These few had survived, clung to life like ticks on summer buffalo. They had moved across the plains and along the river valleys with the seasons, persisting in life as The People had lived it for centuries already. They knew nothing else but to go on as they had lived for time beyond any one man's memory.

In the heart of this river basin the southern tribes had long visited, the Washita wound its lazy trail in tight twists before it finally looped northward to form a large horseshoe. Black Kettle's tribe selected that same bend in the river for their winter home. Here they were protected by the sandy red bluffs to the north across the river and the shaded knolls rising behind them. Here they would find no end to fresh water and abundant grazing for their pony herd of nearly a thousand animals. For fires to ward off the chill of autumn mornings and the numbing cold of winter nights, timber grew thick along the bottoms choked with plant life of all description ablaze in color.

One clear, frosty morning, the Cheyenne awoke to find

a thin slick of ice coating the water kettles. It was a magical time of year along the Washita. The buffalo hunted by the young men who left camp each day had already grown fat from a long summer grazing on the rich grasses carpeting the southern plains, their curly coats grown thick—a sign of an early and cold winter.

Chief Black Kettle sighed as he bent to retrieve a bundle his wife expected him to bring to her in their lodge. His heart swelled with happiness.

The Cheyenne will sleep here for the Time of Deep Snows.

"Good to have you here with us," Major Joel Elliott said, dropping his salute. "You belong here, sir. At the head of your men."

"Thank you, Major." Custer flashed that famous peg-toothed smile and shook Elliott's hand.

"Damn good to have you back!" First Lieutenant Thomas W. Custer shouldered his way through the crowd clustered about his older brother.

"Tom!"

"Can't begin to tell you what it means to us having you leading us into this one, Autie."

"Trouble?" Custer asked.

"Nothing we can't handle *now!* Right, boys?"

Custer waited until the cheering died. "So, tell me. Something's afoot. I can smell it." His eyes moved from man to man, watching each of his old friends and fellow officers avoid his look.

"Tom?"

"It ain't been a pretty sight here," Tom replied. "Under siege practically every day . . . small bands of warriors wandering past here heading north out of the Territories. Some bands not so small."

"That's trouble?" Custer rocked back on his heels and smiled beneath the corn-straw mustache. "You worried about a handful of roving warriors?"

"They've proved us idiots so far," Elliott answered grimly.

"Buck up, gentlemen!" Custer said. "A new day is coming. We'll soon show them a force to be reckoned with—our own beloved Seventh!"

"Hear, hear! To the Seventh!" Tom roared, slapping his brother on the back. "To the regiment that will pacify the plains!"

On the morning of 30 September, George Armstrong Custer had arrived at Fort Hays, Kansas, new duty station of the Seventh Cavalry. There he reported to General Sheridan, who had moved his departmental headquarters farther west to station himself closer to the main theater of hostilities.

After less than a day of rest and some final instructions, the young lieutenant colonel pushed west with a small escort, arriving at Fort Dodge on 4 October. There he had learned his regiment was encamped some thirty miles southeast of the fort along Bluff Creek, a small tributary of the Arkansas River. Into this besieged camp the regimental commander had galloped on the afternoon of the fifth to find brother Tom, Major Elliott and the others relieved that he had arrived at last to lead the regiment into the winter campaign.

Along with orders to reorganize the Seventh, Custer brought new ideas for some specialized training he and General Sheridan had designed for troops unaccustomed to winter warfare. Although General Alfred Sully commanded this District of the Arkansas, Sheridan had devised an operational force of eleven companies of the Seventh Cavalry to ride under Custer, along with five companies of infantry and twelve companies of the Nineteenth Kansas Volunteer Cavalry that had yet to march south from Topeka. This massive force would then push out of Kansas Territory due south a hundred miles from Fort Dodge to establish a supply base from which Sheridan would begin his strikes against the hostiles. . . .

"You haven't wasted any time getting the regiment shaped up, Autie," Tom said one cold evening as he slipped through the tent flaps. His brother sat hunched over a lap desk. "Orders? Or another letter home to Libbie?"

That smile flashed again. Custer could keep nothing from his little brother.

"Orders first, Tom. Then, yes, I'll get another letter off to Libbie tonight."

"All work and no play. You've heard me say it many a time."

"You! Preferring the cards or the bottle—even the ladies—to your soldier's work."

"By the heavens, Autie! Your brother? Wouldst that I prefer the feel of a perfumed breast beneath my hands or the sting of strong whiskey upon my tongue to drilling and target practice?"

Laughter came easily to them both, laughter rooted in a bond nurtured from childhood, a closeness now mellowed like aged Kentucky whiskey.

"Be gone with you, then." Custer shooed with his left hand, the right bringing the nub of a pencil to his tongue once more. "I've too much work to be done and so little time to do it. Go off and play then while your poor brother works his fingers and his pencil to the bone!"

Tom's easy laughter rang through the tent flaps as Custer returned to his sheet of foolscap atop the small lap desk. *So bloody much to do,* he thought. *All of it riding on a perfect execution of Philip's plans for this winter campaign.*

First, fresh horses had to be purchased. Not an easy task on the western plains of Kansas along the Arkansas River. But once accomplished, those horses had to be wrangled in and drilled with their new riders. And through the ordeal the regimental blacksmiths had been pushed beyond all endurance, beginning their hot work before dawn every morning, toiling into the dripping black of twilight, fitting each and every new mount for its journey into Indian country.

Infantry marched on the feet of its men while cavalry depended on the hooves of its horses. For every mount headed into Indian Territory he had ordered an extra fore and hind shoe fitted and carried in the trooper's saddle pocket. An unshod horse would be worse than useless on this campaign through ice and snow.

Every clear day Custer had his men practice signaling cross-country with small mirrors from the top of nearby hills—"nature having formed admirable signal stations over this part of the country," he explained, writing to Libbie.

At the same time he held a competition among his troops to determine the best marksmen in the regiment. With the dual promise of a separately marched unit of sharpshooters along with his order that the marksmen be exempted from mess details and picket duty, the competition grew stiff for those forty slots placed under the leadership of young Canadian Lieutenant W. W. Cooke. With the best selected, an intensive regimen of target practice with repeating Spencer rifles began for this elite corps.

Custer sat the lap desk on his crude bunk and rose, stretching the knots from the muscles along his back. *So much riding on the success of this venture, Libbie.* He would write her later when the camp quieted and his only companion would be the night wind bringing with it a promise of early snow.

If this winter operation fails, Sheridan alone might take the blame. And, if the operation smacks of a massacre, why, Philip alone might stand court-martial . . . considering the nasty mood of those Quakers in power at the Indian Bureau back in Washington City.

Rubbing his palms together eagerly, he stared out at the glowing fire points of red-orange, cooking fires along company rows allowed to burn themselves out in the blackness of night. *But, if the winter offensive proves even a moderate success there'll be a hungry mob of army brass clamoring to claim paternity for Sheridan's brainchild.*

He turned back into the chill of his tent. The smoky heat of two coal-oil lamps held some of the prairie cold at bay. Somewhere close a horse snorted and stomped. Custer smiled again. Things were going well. In the waning days of October he had instituted another innovation of his own: "coloring the horses" by troops, in which every man in a company rode a similarly colored animal. Each company would ride a different color horse into Indian country.

A few hours later, with his long, sentimental letter to his wife finished, Custer blew out the smoky lamps. Only then did the silence around him grow suffocating. Almost as if he couldn't breathe . . . . then the weight of it disappeared, as quickly as it had smothered him. In the overpowering silence, he barely heard the first smattering of hard, icy flakes against the side of his canvas tent.

The cold settled along the valley of the Washita like old ash settling under a persistent rain.

Monaseetah, daughter of Cheyenne chief Little Rock, second only to Black Kettle himself, moved back to her father's lodge, leaving her cruel and abusive husband.

In the cold chill of her father's lodge she awoke each night, staring at the dull red glow of the dying coals, feverish in the frosty air as the sweat of fear rolled from her copper flesh. The brute she had married had treated her no better than a camp dog. No better than some piece of property he could abuse and discard . . . until she shot him.

His pride wounded more than his bleeding leg, the shamed husband had divorced this fiery girl of seventeen summers—in the Cheyenne way, sending her back to the lodge of her father.

Trembling now as she remembered his shaming her, Monaseetah caught her breath, then slowly calmed, listening to the reassuring snore of her father. They were without others, alone. It had been four winters now since the terrible day of black cannon smoke in the air and red smearing the snow. In a place the Southern Cheyenne knew as Little Dry River—a terrible day along the white man's Sand Creek where Monaseetah saw her mother fall beneath a slashing cavalry saber. No more than a cowering child, she watched young soldiers defile her mother's bloody body.

Monaseetah knew the remembering would always be with her, bringing the all-time pain. There would be no losing of that pain the way she had rid herself of the beast-man.

Her eyes stinging with tears, Monaseetah blinked and blinked again. There had been no blood-that-comes-with-the-moon since the shortgrass time. Now she could believe only one thing. She carried the beast-man's child in her belly. Monaseetah clenched her eyes shut with fierce resolution. Though she carried his child, she knew she could not return to the cruel one who had bought her away from Little Rock.

Eventually she lay back against her father's curly buffalo robes once more. *Let him find another wife*, she consoled herself. *Another woman to rut and abuse. Perhaps a wife like that pale white woman they hold prisoner in the Kiowa camp downstream.*

Why anyone would want such a pale-skinned creature, with hair so thin, and the color of winter-dead grass?

General Hazen's negotiations for the release of the captive white mother and her son dragged on through the fall, getting nowhere with the Kiowas down at Fort Cobb during the Moon of Leaves Falling and into the Deer Rutting Moon.

Monaseetah herself was visiting the Kiowa camp that first day Hazen's half-breed scout, Cheyenne Jack, rode into the center of camp to declare he came from Army Chief Hazen with a plea for the release of Clara and Willie Blinn.

Cautiously, Jack dismounted and sidled over to the terrified, beaten prisoner. "Listen to me, lady," he whispered harshly when the others weren't looking. "These Injuns don't know no English. Take what I got in my hand.

Write your name for the general at Fort Cobb. So he'll
know who you are. He can tell your people."

"You have to—"

"Shut up!" he growled. "Not a word, or your life ain't
worth the time it takes for one of these bucks to spit! Now,
take what's in my hand."

Clara Blinn pulled a scrap of paper and a pencil stub from
the scout's dirty palm. As Jack conferred with the tribal
leaders, she hunkered in the shadow of a nearby lodge and
scribbled her hasty note to the outside world:

KIND FRIEND—

Whoever you may be, I thank you for your kindness to me
and my child. They tell me, as near as I can understand,
they expect traders to come and they will sell us to them. If
it is Mexicans, I am afraid they would sell us into slavery in
Mexico. If you can do nothing for me write to W. T.
Harrington, Ottawa, Franklin County, Kansas—my father.
Tell him we are with the Cheyennes and they say when the
white men make peace we can go home. For our sakes, do
all you can, and God will bless you. If you can let me hear
from you again let me know what you think about it. Write
my father; send him this. Goodby.

MRS. F. R. BLINN

I am as well as can be expected, but my baby is very weak.

Little could Mrs. Blinn know at that time what fury
would soon be released in securing her freedom from the
hostiles. Little could she know that even as she wrote her
plea for help, General Philip H. Sheridan had ordered
Hazen to break off his negotiations, reasoning that his

winter campaign would secure the results every white man desired: an end to Indian raids along the Kansas frontier and a return of those captives held by the savages. Negotiation, Sheridan informed Hazen, accomplished nothing.

"Don't need me to hang around the post no longer?" the half-breed scout and interpreter asked before he took another long pull on the cheroot General Hazen had given him, filling Hazen's tiny Fort Cobb office with blue smoke.

"Sorry, Jack. Can't use you anymore." Hazen turned so that the half-breed could not read the worry etched along the thin features of his well-defined face. "Sheridan doesn't want us trying to make peace anymore."

"He got something else in mind?"

"Guess so." Hazen used his words sparingly.

The commander of Fort Cobb knew he would have to send for Black Kettle. He watched Cheyenne Jack rise from the creaky, straight-backed chair, then cleared his throat as the half-breed reached the door.

"Jack," Hazen said, "there is one last thing you can do for me. If you would. I'll pay you regular wages. Per day."

"Yeah?" Jack answered, something in Hazen's tone snagging his interest.

"Want you to find Black Kettle. I'm told he's wintering his band on the Washita with Satanta, Medicine Arrow, and the others."

"Just Black Kettle?"

"Just Black Kettle. Tell him it's very important that he come see me."

"General, you know that ol' boy. He won't come without you giving him good reason to see you."

"Tell him we need to have an important council."

"Council?"

"Just tell Black Kettle he's in danger."

"In danger from what?"

Hazen's eyes leveled on the scout. As a soldier he could say no more. "That's what I will discuss with Black Kettle myself."

Cheyenne Jack opened his mouth to protest, but then thought better of it. Instead, he said, "General, I figure since you don't need me after this, I'll winter with the Kiowa. But I'll see you get to talk with Black Kettle. Start tonight, you want me to."

"Daylight will be soon enough for me, Jack."

The half-breed swung the door open wide and stepped into the night, his buckskinned form swallowed completely by darkness.

On 12 November the Seventh Cavalry pulled out of their training camp south of Fort Dodge, marching toward Indian Territory at last. Time and again on that long march Major Joel Elliott turned beneath a glaring winter sun to behold those troops arranged by color: companies of chestnuts, blacks, bays, sorrels and grays, browns and tans—every man trained and ready. Not a raw recruit among them.

And rumbling right behind them came better than four hundred wagons loaded to their bulging sidewalls with forage, rations, tents, blankets, and winter campaign clothing.

"By glory," Elliott whispered under his breath, "I ride at the head of the finest mounted cavalry in the entire world!" A Civil War veteran with an impressive record of victories, the major's chest swelled with pride.

By the fifteenth the weather turned on the glorious

Seventh. A blue-norther swept down on the regiment, a storm so bitter it could only have come straight out of the maw of the Arctic itself. That prairie blizzard persisted all night and right into the next day before it gave out. Three more difficult days followed, the cavalry breaking trail through snowdrifts left in the storm's wake.

But by noon on 18 November, Custer's command stopped a mile above the confluence of Wolf Creek and the Beaver River, some hundred miles almost due south of Fort Dodge.

"We'll establish our base for winter operations here, Major," Custer informed Elliott. "Have the company captains establish pickets and pitch their tents across the prairie. We'll meet at my tent at sixteen hundred. Dismissed."

Custer watched Elliott trudge away before he turned to the civilian scout beside him.

"Smith, you've done well. Found us an admirable spot."

"Knowed you'd like it, General," the scarred old trapper answered.

"Where you off to now, if I might inquire?"

John Simpson Smith tore a corner off the tabacco twist before he stuffed it back into the pouch on his belt. "Aim to track my family, General. Least what's left of 'em after Chivington butchered a bunch down to Sand Creek."

"You married a Cheyenne?"

Smith spit into the snow at his feet before answering. "Many robe seasons ago. Time was, I was trapping the headwaters of the Arkansas long afore you and the gray-backs got into your big argument back east. Best damned woman I ever knowed, that one. Cheyenne, she is."

"Children?"

"Only two now. Both growed, I s'pose. Rest killed at Sand Creek. I aim to find those two, and their mama."

"You heading south?"

"Likeliest place, seems to me."

"You aim to warn the hostiles I'm coming?" Unconsciously, Custer shifted his pistol belt, a move not lost on the old mountain man.

"Tribe my wife runs with ain't causing no trouble in Kansas. They're real peaceable. Not the sort you army boys're hankerin' for."

Custer cleared his throat. "Your wife's people won't have a thing to worry about."

"That's what the agents and army both said when the tribe went to camp on Sand Creek."

"By God, I'll not be compared with the likes of that butcher Chivington!" Custer barked. "He and his Colorado militia . . . amateur soldiers. Why, this regiment is hunting warriors, and warriors only."

"S'long, General." Smith stuffed a moccasin in his stirrup, lifting himself to the saddle.

"Smith." Custer suddenly snagged the reins to prevent the old scout from pulling away. "What band is your family with?"

"Why, ol' Black Kettle's. He's always been a peace Injun. Always will be. That ol' buck's a smart one. He sees the writing on the ground clear as I read trail sign. Figures it won't do him no good to make war."

"Black Kettle, eh?" Custer released the scout's reins. He watched Smith lope off, pointing his pony north, back toward Kansas rather than steering south into the Territories.

CHAPTER 3

EVERYWHERE he looked he saw the activity of men preparing for a wilderness winter, men preparing for war.

Correspondent De Benneville Randolph Keim recorded each scene with a journalist's eye. His boss, publisher James Gordon Bennett of the New York *Herald*, had sent him to accompany Custer's winter campaign. Keim's dispatches would be carried north to Kansas and the civilized world in the oiled leather pouches worn by the army couriers riding between Fort Dodge and this new military base, which Sheridan himself had christened "Camp Supply." Keim even dreamed of one day writing his chronicles telling the story of riding off to war with the "Boy General" and his gallant Seventh Cavalry.

From daybreak to well past sunset, he watched herders drive horses in or out of camp, grazing the mounts on the excellent pastures surrounding the site. The animals needed every ounce of strength they could muster for the task ahead. In addition, one of the frontiersmen along for the campaign showed Keim a seed from a mesquite tree that grew in the area, claimed to be every bit as good for fattening the big army horses as the oats the soldiers relied on.

Good sweet water flowed past the camp. Ample firewood could be found in the groves along both waterways. Enough timber for a stockade. First the soldiers muscled trenches out of the frozen soil some 126 feet square in which to bury the upright timbers. At the same time water wells were dug and the nearby meadows mowed for emergency hay. From the time Keim crawled out of his blankets in the morning until well past dark, cursing civilian teamsters whipped their plodding mules up and down the course of Wolf Creek or the Beaver River hauling logs for the cantonment and hay that the soldiers piled into huge windbreaks along company rows.

Almost daily the young reporter accompanied Custer's hunting party into the surrounding woods in search of game of all description: deer and elk, buffalo and turkey, rabbits and quail, pheasant, dove, and prairie chicken. Yet as the hour for the regiment's departure in search of hostiles drew near, Custer realized the time had come to sift through the herds in search of a special animal.

"He's a beautiful horse, General," Keim said, admiring the sorrel with excellent spirit.

"Quite an animal." Custer turned to his brother. "I believe I'll call this one Dandy, Tom."

"A fine configuration!"

"I'll ride him this winter. Then give him to Libbie as a present when the campaign's over. She will rejoin me come spring."

Keim self-consciously cleared his throat and stepped

away before Custer spoke again. "We've not had a good year, Tom."

"That dalliance with Mrs. Lyon down in Texas bothering Libbie again?"

"That and the young wife of an officer on Sheridan's staff when we passed through St. Louis two years ago. More and more it returns to haunt me."

"You two will make up and things'll be as they were during the war—when you were inseparable. Always remember, dear brother, there's never a winter so long that spring doesn't come."

"General?"

"Come in, Lieutenant. I've been expecting you."

James M. Bell, regimental quartermaster, ducked through the flaps of Custer's wall tent, kicking the ice from his boots. It had begun snowing just before supper, right after Bell had finished issuing each soldier his weapons for the coming fight: a magazine-loaded Spencer carbine and a Colt revolver using paper cartridges and caps.

"Every man has his buffalo greatcoat and hip leggings General Sheridan had made for the campaign."

"A capital idea, wasn't it, Bell? Nasty as it's beginning to look out there. Were there enough to go around?"

"Yessir. Along with a fur cap and fur-lined mittens for every soldier who'll saddle up in the morning."

"By a stroke of divine providence itself, Lieutenant. My troopers will have their furry protection . . . like veritable beasts plunging into this wilderness. Thank you for reporting, Mr. Bell. We'll talk again before departure in the morning. Get some rest now. Lord knows you can use it."

"Thank you, General. Just wanted to do my part . . . see we really hurt the savages this time out."

Late that night Custer finished supper and set his plate aside. Tonight's would be the last hot meal he or his men would remember for some time to come.

The snow continued to pile up outside as the camp settled into that restless peace of soldiers on their last night before departing into the unknown. A solitary tent glowed with lamplight. Well past midnight Custer continued to push his numb fingers across the sheet of paper, scribbling a final letter to his wife.

MY DARLING ROSEBUD,

Your handsome beau is thinking only of you at this hour. We stand on the precipice of something great. Perhaps all we have dreamed of, my sweet. With one stroke I can right the wrong done me. Continue my career climb. And put our lives back together. I so need you. All others are as toys compared to you. That you must believe.

The snow grows deeper outside. Already I find more than six inches on the ground, and it's falling rapidly. Problem is, in this corner of the world, the wind blows every bit of it into icy drifts. Do not worry for me, my love. Destiny awaits me down this wilderness road.

It snowed all night.

When reveille sounded at four A.M., yanking soldiers from their warm blankets, the Seventh Cavalry found better than fifteen inches on the ground; and the storm wasn't letting up. Still more snow pushed angrily through the bone-bare trees.

Despite his wool blankets and buffalo robes, Sheridan had found it hard to sleep through the icy night. Now he lay alone in his tent, listening to the familiar, reassuring sounds of men and animals preparing for departure. Surprised at himself, the general suffered a momentary pang of doubt in sending good men out in such bitter weather. His melancholia was just as quickly interrupted by a sturdy rap at the front pole of his huge wall tent.

"Yes?" Sheridan demanded.

The buglers were blowing "The General," that familiar call ordering troopers to strike their tents and pack the wagons for the march.

"It's Custer, sir. May I have the honor of saying farewell to an old friend in person?"

"Of course, Custer. Come in."

Clutching a blanket around his trembling shoulders, Sheridan stood to turn up the wick on his lamp, its feeble, flickering saffron light wind-dancing on bitter gusts that sneaked in on Custer's heels.

"Damn this infernal thing!" His numb fingers were unable at first to adjust the wick roller.

"May I be of some help?"

"There." Sheridan got the lamp to respond. "That's better, now." He pointed to the corner by his trunk. "Grab one of those stools, Custer."

The young cavalry officer settled on his perch, clumsy in his bulky buffalo coat, looking like a portly blackbird balanced precariously atop a delicate branch. His thick mustache dripped melting hoarfrost into the beard framing his face.

"Warm enough, Custer?"

"Yes, sir. What's more, I'm happy to report the Seventh is prepared for what may come in this campaign."

"I see." Sheridan rose from his cot and paced to the front flap, where he allowed the cold to slice in at him as he peered out at the men and animals, dark smudges across the new snow. "Seems the storm has moved east at last."

Custer stood, stepped to the flap beside Sheridan. "It's a good sign for us, pulling out just as we are."

Sheridan trudged back to his cot, where he sank heavily. "I had forgotten how you look at things sometimes. Searching for a good omen in every turn you make in life."

"But, of course. I've been blessed with what many of my men have come to call Custer's Luck."

"You're the first to believe in it, too, eh?"

"If I didn't, how could I ask my men to believe in me?"

Sheridan studied the bushy eyebrows of the taller man. "You damn well go out there and make your own luck, don't you? You did it with General McClellan when you recklessly waded the Chickahominy. Then you impressed General Pleasanton with your daring charges, and by jingo you were on your way to capturing the cream of the Confederate cavalry at Appomattox—right when Lee himself saw fit to hand his flag of surrender to no one else but you."

"I was the only one there to take his flag, sir."

"That's bullshit and we both know it, Custer. He wanted to hand that flag to the one man who had repeatedly stymied the cream of his Reb cavalry under Stuart."

"I learned from the best, sir. Philip H. Sheridan."

"Perhaps I am the only one better than you, goddammit." Sheridan knocked his boots together to shock some warmth into his frozen feet, "Still, I'm having some second thoughts about campaigning in the jaws of winter. Perhaps that old scout Bridger was right after all. I'm not so sure we won't suffer casualties to the goddamned weather you'll encounter on your march."

"On the contrary, sir—begging your pardon." Custer stuffed his hands in his coat pockets and glanced down at the squared toes of his tall black boots. "This deep snow is exactly what I had in mind. It could not come at a more opportune moment. My men are ready, capable of marching through that snow. By the same token, the hostile warriors we seek won't even consider moving out of their villages for days to come."

"You are one of a kind, Armstrong."

"Shall I take that as a compliment, sir?"

"Of course, my eager young friend." Sheridan rose to his feet and clapped his hands on Custer's broad shoulders. "I'll buy your optimistic estimate on this weather . . . and your men."

Sheridan shook Custer's hand. "I made you what you are, Armstrong. I can't ever forget that."

"General!" Custer saluted and wheeled toward the tent flaps.

"Custer?"

The young officer turned, one of the canvas flaps still clutched in his buffalo mitten, admitting a cold slash of winter into the tent. "Sir?"

"Take good care of your troops, my friend. They are your backbone."

"Understood, sir. They've never let me down."

Custer saluted smartly before he tugged the buffalo cap down on his forehead and plunged into the cold. To his side leapt his beloved Blucher and Maida, the two splendid

Scottish staghounds he had brought from Monroe. At the Bluff Creek Camp south of Fort Dodge, Blucher had run down and killed a young wolf during one of his master's frequent hunts.

Custer knelt to pull at their ears playfully. Lieutenant Myles Moylan stomped up through the calf-deep snow.

"How will this do for a winter campaign, General?"

"Just what we want, Moylan," came Custer's swift reply. "Exactly what the gods ordered for me." Custer stood, squared his shoulders, then stomped off, stiff-legged.

With Custer's words fading into the darkness, other voices hung just beyond Sheridan's tent, strong voices come stinging to his ears. Familiar voices, some of them, familiar to an old soldier. Other wars, other battles, other campaigns . . . different names but soldiers just the same.

Sergeants ordered their men to "Prepare to mount!" followed by a rustle of frozen, squeaky harness, jangling bit chains, and cold black leather as the officers called out, "Mount!"

The coughing and wheezing of a few of the troopers slithered through the oiled canvas of his tent as Sheridan stood framed in the cold flickering light of his single hurricane lamp, eyes fixed on that patch of ground where snow threw itself beneath the tent flaps.

Rhythmically plodding with the creak and swish of cold harness and frozen buckles, two columns of shivering pony soldiers lumbered past, their broad shoulders smeared upon the taut canvas wall of his wind-whipped tent. Sheridan recognized the shrill voice of handsome Major Joel H. Elliott as Custer's headquarters staff rode by.

"Goddammit all, but I wish I was home right now!"

Elliott's was a voice full of youth and mirth and a soldier's camaraderie.

"I'll bet you do, Major!" Sergeant Major Kennedy replied. "And we know just what the hell you'd be doing at home right now with that pretty wife of yours you've kept tucked away back at Leavenworth!"

A cruel gust of wind flung open the flaps of his tent, shoving Philip Sheridan back against his cot. Snuffing out the oil lamp with its icy breath. The solitary gust brought with it such a blast of cold that the general scurried beneath his blankets, pulling them just below his eyes.

"Get a goddamned hold on yourself, Philip."

Shuddering with more than the cold of that icy gust, the commander of this Department of the Missouri glanced anxiously at the extinguished lamp. A ghostly wisp of purple smoke climbed out of the glass chimney in that pale light of predawn gray seeping into his tent.

Outside in the snow and darkness the regimental band began to pump out that Seventh Cavalry favorite, "The Girl I Left Behind Me":

> The hour was sad I left the maid,
> A ling'ring farewell taking;
> Her sighs and tears my steps delay'd—
> I thought her heart was breaking.
>
> In hurried words her name I bless'd;
> I breathed the vows that bind me,
> And to my heart in anguish press'd
> The girl I left behind me.

Once more Sheridan's mind replayed those orders he had written for Custer like some broken telegraph key:

You are hereby ordered to proceed south, in the direction of the Antelope Hills, thence toward the Washita River, the supposed winter seat of the hostile tribes; to destroy their villages and ponies; to kill or hang all warriors, and bring back all women and children.

It was the coldest time of day on the prairie, now when night was undecided in yielding it's place—harsher still with the cruel battering winter gave the defenseless plains each year.

Sheridan closed his eyes, shut out the gray light awakening the frozen world outside. The band continued to play.

> Full many a name our banners bore
> Of former deeds of daring,
> But they were of the days of yore
> In which we had no sharing.
>
> But now our laurel freshly won
> With the old ones shall entwin'd be;
> Still worthy of our sires each son,
> Sweet girl I left behind me.

A somber Black Kettle returned to his Washita camp two days after the great snow had buried the land.

The sun finally broke through the gloomy overcast and shone over his little village. The news their chief brought from General Hazen at Fort Cobb was nowhere near as bright and warm.

"Black Kettle, I wish I could find something to say or do

to persuade you to stay here at the fort," Hazen had told him. "I'm sticking my neck out to offer you personal sanctuary."

Silent for a long time, a bewildered Black Kettle finally said, "Why would I need sanctuary, Soldier Chief, if my people are camped far south of the Arkansas River, deep in Indian Territory where we are supposed to live according to the very words of the talking paper I put my mark to for the white Grandfather back east beyond the rivers?"

Again and again Hazen had attempted to tell this old Cheyenne that because of the young warriors raiding into the Kansas settlements, his tribe might still be in danger of some wandering patrol of mounted cavalry. Problem was, how to warn Black Kettle without directly informing him of Sheridan's winter campaign plans?

Seemed nothing got through to Black Kettle.

The aged Cheyenne nodded sadly. "It would be a dishonorable thing to stay here at your fort for my own personal safety. Black Kettle belongs with his people."

Those words were the last he had spoken before beginning his cold, melancholy return trip northwest along the Washita's icy course.

"What?" Medicine Woman Later's voice rose shrill across the camp as she trundled after her husband, following him to their lodge, where she would build up the fire and set some meat to boil.

"Keep your voice down, woman!" he grumped as she shuffled along beside him through the snowdrifts that had gathered in crusty, wind-sculpted ridges between the old lodges.

He was weary of the travel. Weary too of her harping at him. Most of all, Black Kettle felt as drained as an empty water skin, trying to keep the peace with the white man while keeping his people alive at the same time. Again he wondered if he was up to the task. Perhaps he should step aside as leader of his people.

"I do not like this news you bring us!" She was as hoarse as the creaky lid on an old rawhide parfleche box.

"I am not deaf, woman!" Immediately he was sorry for snapping at her and turned to find that she had ground to a halt in her tracks.

Medicine Woman Later stood with snow piled up to her knees. Her gray head hung, and as she began to weep, Black Kettle came back to her side. He put his arms around her, gently encircling her within the curly warmth of his robe.

"Why is it that you cry, woman? Was it that my words were cruel and cutting—sharp like your favorite knife?"

"No," she sobbed. "I suddenly realize you truly are deaf, my husband."

He snorted. "I hear you perfectly."

"Why is it you cannot hear the agent Wynkoop and that soldier chief Hazen when they warn you of danger coming down upon our heads?"

She scurried through the opening in the lodge cover, seeking the warmth of their fire.

"I am not deaf, woman," Black Kettle muttered softly, hoping the argument was over.

For too long he had hoped to make all things right for his people. He had listened to both the Indian agent and commander at Fort Lyons some four winters ago, taking his people to camp where the white men guaranteed his people would be safe from harm. There in the grassy, shaded meadows along Sand Creek a few miles above its junction with the Arkansas River his Cheyenne camp had awakened that November morning to the rumbling roar of cannon tearing through their hide lodges, iron shrapnel scattering blood and gore across the snow. They were peaceful Cheyenne. Black Kettle had seen to it that the agent's flag of white stars and red stripes flew above the camp to show any soldiers who came that they were Indians protected by the Grandfather in far away Washington City.

His flag had not turned the bullets and cannonballs, sabers and bloodlust of Colonel John M. Chivington's enraged Colorado militia.

"If you are not deaf," his wife grumbled, offering him a bowl of hot meat and broth, "then surely you must be crazy."

"Perhaps I am touched by the moon." He chewed on the softened meat with what he had left of teeth.

She turned away, muttering to no one at all. "My husband, he is a crazy man." Pulling a small morsel from the kettle, she plopped it on the end of her tongue. "He is told we should move our camp. He is warned the pony soldiers are roaming this land where we camp for the winter—pony soldiers looking for the white prisoners taken by the foolish young men downriver. We could have moved long ago when Hazen and Wynkoop learned where we raised our camp. Their skin is white. Surely, Hazen will tell the pony soldiers where we camp . . . here where we wait like possums for the pony soldiers to ride down on us again."

She sat back atop buffalo robes and blankets, drawing her knees up against her withered dugs. "No, my husband. If you are not deaf and truly can hear Hazen's words of warning, then you must be crazy."

Her clucking slowly faded as she carried on the angry tantrum all by herself. Eventually her tirade was replaced by the sweet, rhythmic melody of the great honkers swooping overhead. What pretty music to Black Kettle's soul their flying-talk had become through the many seasons of his life. Melody birds, flying south this time, far away from this cold land where the white man had plunged a knife deep into the heart of the Earth Mother.

Black Kettle ached to be far away to the south where he did not have to worry about the snow and the cold and the pony soldiers searching for a Cheyenne winter camp while the rivers grew slow and icy.

He wanted nothing more than to listen to the mournful song of the last departing geese.

CHAPTER 4

O NCE the sun ducked its head back in its hole far behind the western edge of the earth, the air itself chewed on an old man's bones. Kiowa chief Lone Wolf wrapped the thick winter robe tightly about his shoulders. Once more he was glad his youngest son had chosen to kill this fat cow almost two moons ago when the shaggy hides grew thick for the coming of winter.

Lone Wolf smiled as he watched more of the lodges in his village begin to glow, warmed with the cook fires of his people. Earlier each afternoon darkness slithered down this valley of the Washita. Already the shadows ran deep among the villages by the water. To the west lay the old one's village, as that cold, creeping tongue of night snaked its way up the icy river. Black Kettle's small band of Cheyennes.

Turning with a shudder, the Kiowa chief started for his warm lodge and hot supper when what seemed the thunder of half a thousand pounding hooves stayed his feet. Shouts of greeting and cries of congratulation rang through camp.

Lone Wolf grinned, wrinkling his leathery face. It must have been a good hunt for the two riders who pulled up beside their chief.

"Where is Hump Fat?" Lone Wolf asked with chattering teeth.

"That one, *aieeee!*" The young warrior Rabbit Way rolled his head back, laughing as only youth can. "He is looking for a Cheyenne bride this night, I think!"

"What do you mean?"

"He stays over in Black Kettle's camp. They invited us to a dance they will hold with the falling of the sun. But Sees Red and I decided we best bring these Ute ponies home to our camp."

"You found many horses in the land of the Utes, yes?"

"Not as many as we would have liked to find, Uncle!" All three laughed. "We had to travel far to find the Ute villages. By my count-stick, forty-three suns have come and gone—so Hump Fat wants to do nothing more until he finds a maiden to warm his robes tonight. He cannot wait!"

"Does he not know the Cheyenne guard their chastity with more than just a buffalo-hair rope tied about a woman's loins?" Lone Wolf asked.

"They guard the chastity of their women with the same vengeance they use when they go to war!" young Rabbit Way exclaimed.

"I am glad it was a good hunt for you," Lone Wolf said. "To bring back so many fine Ute ponies without the loss of a friend—it was a good journey. I am happy you did not have to leave your hair along the way! Our village can celebrate when you have given the horses away. Do you think the Utes will follow the wide trail all these new Kiowa ponies made in your travel across the snowy land?"

"No, Uncle," Sees Red answered. "The Utes did not follow us after the fourth day of hard riding. They turned back like frightened women, afraid to reclaim their ponies. But we did see a very large trail that worries us both."

"Yes?" The older man looked back and forth between the two young horse thieves. "Tell me of this trail."

Rabbit Way answered: "A trail far wider and deeper than all our new ponies together would cut in the snow."

"There is more you must tell?"

"Yes, Uncle," Sees Red added. "The trail spoke to us of horses wearing the white man's iron on their hooves."

"Pony soldiers?"

"Perhaps," Rabbit Way admitted. "Any man could read the wide, deep trail, seeing many hundreds of iron-shod horses that cut deep into the crust of the old snow near the Antelope Hills. They drag the big wagons behind them—pointing their noses into the land of the south winds."

"Did you tell the Cheyenne of your discovery when you stopped in their camp?" Lone Wolf asked, growing uneasy.

"We told them of the trail of hundreds," Sees Red answered. "But they talked only of our new ponies. They were not interested in hearing our stories of pony soldiers—only our ponies!"

"That is the Cheyenne for you!" Rabbit Way stopped laughing as soon as he saw Lone Wolf staring off to the west, toward the Cheyenne camp of his old friend, Black Kettle.

"Did you tell their camp police of the great iron-shod trail?"

"Yes, Uncle. We told Medicine Elk Pipe of the horses and wagons. But he and the others just laughed at the idea of pony soldiers coming to fight us in the cold of winter.

They claim the soldiers are harmless sun-birds, chasing warriors around the countryside only after the shortgrass comes in spring."

"So I reminded Medicine Elk Pipe about the great sadness of Sand Creek four winters gone," Sees Red added. "He grew angry with me, saying I was no more than a boy wetting my cradleboard when his people escaped from the Sand Creek soldiers. Another man, Red Shin, laughed and claimed we three children got lost and double backed onto our own trail."

Lone Wolf shivered with something more than the deepening cold. "You did not get lost and double back on your own trail, did you?"

"No, Uncle," Rabbit Way answered. "We saw iron shoes on those hundreds of hundreds of pony tracks. Saw deep cuts carved in the snow and mud near the foot of the Antelope Hills—meaning but one thing—the white soldier wagons."

"Near the foot of the Antelope Hills?"

"Yes, Lone Wolf. On the north side of the hills."

"Perhaps it will be all right," the chief said.

"Do you want me to warn the other villages?" Sees Red asked.

"No, Nephew. The tracks reach only as far as the Antelope Hills. The sky grows dark. It will be very cold this night. If there are any pony soldiers near the Antelope Hills, they will not move far from their own fires now. No, you have been on the trail for forty-three suns already. Go, get something warm in your bellies and put these many fine ponies in our great herd."

"You believe us, Uncle?" Rabbit Way asked.

"Yes," Lone Wolf answered. "I will go at first light to

convince my old Cheyenne friend that he too should be on the alert for soldiers. Black Kettle will believe me."

Out of the inky twilight loomed three shadows: horsemen. Scout Jack Corbin first recognized the young standard bearer who carried Custer's personal banner. To the right rode Myles Moylan, Custer's adjutant. Between them, Custer himself.

"Major Elliott sends his compliments, sir!" Corbin announced as the trio halted before him.

"Jack! Elliott has some news for me?"

"Good news, General."

"We can use it."

"Them Osages of Pepoon's found you a trail."

"How big?"

"Best news of all. Better than a hundred ponies."

Custer whistled low with approval. "Good-sized war party."

"Nary a one of 'em wearing shoes."

"What direction?"

"South, by east."

Custer slapped his thigh. "By jove! Just where we counted on them gathering all along!"

"Wintering on the Washita, General!" Moylan agreed.

"How old's the trail?" Custer inquired.

"Less'n a day now."

"Beautiful! That means they can't be far ahead now. How long till we join with Elliott's detail?"

"Twelve, maybe fourteen miles. What with all the snow—"

"Fine job, Corbin!" Custer cut him off, appraising the young man atop a strong gray charger. From beneath

Corbin's worn mackinaw coat poked a pair of revolvers. And across his left arm rested a Sharps carbine—short-barreled and easily handled by a man on horseback.

"Moylan. Ride back and inform the command. Give them my apologies—there will be no sleep for us tonight."

Myles realized the moon had been up for more than an hour already. "We've been driving them hard already, sir."

"Lieutenant, I've got a trail to follow. I want to be sitting right there on the Washita before dawn so I can awaken that village myself."

"As you wish, General." Moylan reined away, his mount kicking up rooster tails of new snow.

"You bring me good news, Jack. Four days out of Camp Supply now. Some of the men beginning to grumble with the cold—and the rations. But it reminds me of the sacred meaning of this special day."

"Special day, General?"

"Yes, Jack. November twenty-sixth—Thanksgiving! And we have much to be thankful for now. Lead on, Mr. Corbin. Troops forward! Ho!"

A glorious day! Custer cheered himself.

Twenty-four hours ago they had crossed Wolf Creek itself, climbed into snow-capped ridges, then descended into the valley of the Canadian River. After beating their way through quicksands and floating ice snared along the river, the regiment had crawled around the five towering embattlements of the Antelope Hills, each piled deep with new snow.

But Custer's Luck has returned in spades!

They had tried to strip him of his dignity, his rank and office. But he had shown them he could take the drumming, like some bitter medicine he was forced to drink.

With the courage he had shown in the face of court-martial, Custer let them know who alone the brass could count on in all the West. Now he would give the hostiles a taste of cavalry steel.

By glory! These Cheyenne will not soon forget the name of George Armstrong Custer!

His old bones began to warm at last. For so long now, Black Kettle had sensed the coming of this winter's cold. Each night it took longer to chase the icy knots from his chest. Age had made a prison of his body. No more could he deny that it had.

Still, he had felt this eerie chill clamp its icy fingers around his heart but once before. As it took hold of him, he suffered the painful visions of long ago: the brittle white of winter snows littered with death, blood oozing to fill Sand Creek until the stream overflowed its banks and washed away his little band . . . as the flag of the Indian commissioner fluttered overhead in an angry wind.

He filled his belly with none of the big meal his wife had prepared for his guests. Instead, the old Cheyenne slewed his eyes around the warm lodge, touching each of the tribal chiefs and counselors he had called to join him here this night. They had finished their supper and the pipe had completed its solemn rounds when Black Kettle remembered that many of his friends frequently called him Sour Apple because he rarely smiled anymore.

Ever since Sand Creek and all those people gone. A long winter. And all his people gone.

With the pipe still in hand after he had emptied the burnt tobacco and willow bark into the fire pit, Black Kettle began his hushed story in words so quiet that the guests had to lean forward to hear of the lonely ride their chief had just made from his council at Fort Cobb with the pony soldier chief Hazen.

Medicine Woman Later finished passing out cups to their guests, each brimming with the scalding sugared coffee her husband had brought back from the fort as a gift from Hazen. She nodded farewell after she pulled a robe over her shoulders, then slipped out the door.

"What could be so important for the soldier chief to bring you a hundred miles to Fort Cobb?" Black White Man demanded in his own characteristically brusque manner that always drove right to the heart of a matter.

"Hazen says there are pony soldiers roaming about the country this winter," the chief answered with a flat voice, his eyes staring at the faint ghost trails of steam rising from his coffee.

"Pony soldiers?" Heap of Birds squeaked, his warm belly suddenly grown cold.

"The white chief wants to have a joke with you, Black Kettle?" asked Slim Face.

"He did not smile while I was three days at Fort Cobb."

"Then surely you are the one who is the fool for listening to his words," Red Shin growled.

Red Shin had never been much of an ally to Black Kettle. It was even common knowledge that while the old chief did much to promote peaceful coexistence with the white man, young Red Shin led war party after war party north to the white settlements of Kansas, killing, stealing, carrying off the captives who were at this very hour scattered among the other camps along the Washita.

Black Kettle's old rheumy eyes climbed over the lip of

his tin cup. "A fool is one who will not listen to what the insistent winds bid him."

"Hah! A fool is one who listens to Hazen!"

Immediate agreement with Red Shin's words rumbled through the lodge. Black Kettle patiently waited for quiet before he spoke again.

"When has Hazen told us something not the truth?" he said.

Red Shin spat contemptuously into the fire. "He is a pony soldier, old man! A white pony soldier who sits in his little fort, robe season after robe season, and knows nothing of the life lived as our grandfathers hunted these plains."

"It would be a mistake for us to stop believing in his counsel."

"The only mistake we have made, old man, is that we listened to your counsel . . . coming to winter on the Washita with you."

"You say that? While our brothers and cousins—Kiowa, Cheyenne, and Arapaho—spend the winter here in this valley with our people?"

Several of the older chiefs and warriors grunted their approval of Black Kettle's point.

"Foolish old women too!" Red Shin rocked back on his haunches, glaring at his chief. "Still, a few of their brave warriors ride north with me to attack those white settlements that spread like dung fouling our ancient buffalo lands. A few young men with brave hearts beating beneath their breasts."

"Black Kettle is not an old woman!" Medicine Elk Pipe howled in protest across the fire.

"You agree that we must believe in the word of a soldier

chief?" Red Shin demanded of the man who many times had accompanied him on his early scalp and pony raids.

"I do not often agree with Black Kettle. Yet I, Medicine Elk Pipe, agree that Hazen has done nothing to harm the Cheyenne people."

"Hah!" Red Shin roared. "Because we have never given him the chance!"

"True, my friend," Medicine Elk Pipe said calmly. "We must never give him the chance to hurt our people. Yet what harm comes in listening to what he now warns us?"

"Has your heart grown old and—"

Red Shin's head drooped. He could not bear to look at the powerful warrior who had for years been his respected mentor. He looked at this man now as a coward.

"My brother *Tsistsistas*—" Medicine Elk Pipe filled the silence in Black Kettle's lodge, "Red Shin is young but you know he does not lack courage. Long have I been proud to have it known that Red Shin learned his courage in battle from Medicine Elk Pipe. But what Red Shin failed to learn is the danger that comes from words too quickly spoken. I know Red Shin is sorry and wishes the council to know this."

From most of the council arose quiet assent, for this above all else was a great thing for Medicine Elk Pipe to do. Instead of lashing out to challenge the youth who had all but called him a coward, Medicine Elk Pipe had jumped to the young man's defense, seeking to explain Red Shin's emotional outburst.

"So it must be in Red Shin's heart as it is in mine to wonder what General Hazen seeks to accomplish by warning Black Kettle of the pony soldiers marching in Cheyenne country this very night."

Every head in the lodge turned from Medicine Elk Pipe to the old chief.

"Perhaps Hazen does not wish to have the coming war carried to his doorstep," Black Kettle responded. "If he warned us of the soldiers heading our way, and we were able to avoid conflict, matters for him would be all the more peaceful."

"Perhaps you are right," Medicine Elk Pipe replied.

"But if there are soldiers in our country, who is it they look for?" Little Rock inquired. He sat at the chief's left hand, a place of honor as the second in command and one in charge of tribal matters during Black Kettle's frequent absences from camp. No man among them could forget that Little Rock had lost his wife at Sand Creek.

"They are looking for the warriors who raid north of the Arkansas," Medicine Elk Pipe admitted when everyone else remained dumb, slow to accuse. "Those who have killed whites along Walnut Creek and Pawnee Fork, north into the settlements that daily sprout up along the Saline and Solomon rivers. Soldiers look for Kiowas who took scalps and burned the settlers' wooden lodges. They look for Kiowas and our own Cheyennes who rode with them these last six moons of blood-spilling!"

Medicine Elk Pipe looked at Red Shin, waited until the young man's eyes met his across the leaping flames of Black Kettle's lodge fire. "These soldiers who come, they are looking for Kiowas and Cheyennes—are they not, little brother?"

Red Shin nodded once, unable to meet the accusing eyes of all about him.

"Did you not ask Hazen for safety from these soldiers?" Little Rock asked Black Kettle.

"Yes, my friend. It was the first thing I thought to ask of

him. Because our band is so small, I asked the soldier chief if we could camp near the walls of Fort Cobb, to winter there in safety."

"What did he say?" the ancient one, Heap of Birds, asked.

"Hazen, my old friend and counselor, said he could not give us sanctuary at the fort."

"Why not?"

"He told me if he protected us in the shadow of his walls, his chief would take him away because he had helped us. You see, if he allowed us to come to the fort, he would have to allow Satanta and his many Kiowas. Hazen does not trust Satanta."

"We cannot rely on the help of a soldier chief," Medicine Elk Pipe said. "What we do from here on out, we do because we are *Tsistsistas*."

"Long have I thought on it during the journey home," Black Kettle explained. "I cannot instruct any of you what to think in your minds, what to feel in your hearts. All I can do as chief is ask that each man sees that none of our young men leaves camp during the next few weeks while pony soldiers search for our winter villages. We must give the soldiers no reason to follow a war party back here."

"And what of the others?" Little Rock snapped. "What if the other tribes along the river draw us into trouble?"

"We will talk to the elders of these other tribes with the coming of the new sun," Black Kettle suggested.

"Surely we can do more than talk!" Bark Face squeaked in dismay. "We are not strong. We must move closer to the others downstream!"

"Perhaps even better," Little Rock said, "is to send out

a party to find these soldiers. We should parley with them. Tell the soldiers we are not at war with them."

Black Kettle chewed on that for a moment, his eyes studying the somber faces of his friends. "There is agreement on this matter. It is a good idea, Little Rock."

"It is decided?" Medicine Elk Pipe inquired.

"Yes, young friend," Black Kettle affirmed. "In the morning I will send runners to the other camps, inviting their chiefs to come with the falling of the sun and council with us about these soldiers who hunger for a fight. More runners will go out to find these pony soldiers—to tell them we wish to parley and want no trouble. We are on land the Grandfather far away said we could keep as long as the buffalo roamed it. We will be safe here, my brothers."

"I am sure Red Shin will volunteer," Medicine Elk Pipe said. "As I myself volunteer to go parley with the soldiers."

"Red Shin?" Black Kettle turned his tired eyes toward the young warrior.

"Yes. I will go with Medicine Elk Pipe. His council has never brought any man harm that I know of."

"It is good." Black Kettle spread out his arms, signaling an end to the council. "You each must send one of your young men to my lodge when the sun rises one hand out of the east. Some I will send to the other camps with news of a council tomorrow night. The rest will ride under the leadership of my wise and thoughtful friend, Medicine Elk Pipe."

Through the doorway the leaders filed into the night. Small, frozen flakes lanced out of the sky. Black Kettle watched his wife shuffling along between the lodges, coming back home to their warm robes. She would have spent an evening with friends, singing at the dance and gabbing of woman matters.

It was good she did not have to worry about the concerns of men. Still, she alone was able to cheer his gloom when the burden of leadership grew too great. Black Kettle sucked at the cold air, wishing he had pulled a blanket around his shoulders as he waited for Medicine Woman Later.

Tomorrow the riders would find the soldiers and his tribe's safety could be assured. After all, his old friend Red Cloud of the Sioux had recently touched the pen on another treaty with the white Grandfather. After a long and bloody conflict, the plains both north and south could be at peace.

Peace would burst across the prairie as surely as the spring grasses rose to flower after the hard, dark days of winter. Pony soldiers would come no more.

"You are tired, my husband?"

"Yes," Black Kettle answered as his wife ducked back inside the warm lodge. "Tonight I can once again sleep the sleep of peace."

And dream of the great birds flying south.

CHAPTER 5

IT was close to nine o'clock, long since dark, before the regiment finally rendezvoused with Elliott's scouting detail.

Adjutant Moylan nudged his mount close to Custer. "Sir?"

"Pass the word. From here the troopers will take only what they need for battle. And Myles, that means only what a man can strap behind his saddle."

"I'll pass the word, General."

Moylan loped back into the freezing darkness to give the details of the order: Every trooper was to carry a hundred rounds of carbine ammunition and twenty-four loads for his pistol. In addition, each soldier was to be rationed some coffee and hardtack, along with an equally scanty bit of forage for his mount.

From here on out their buffalo coats would have to do. Blankets and tents would be left behind with the wagons. Not knowing the exact location of the hostile village, the men must be ready for battle at any moment. Word had it that at least five hundred warriors awaited them on the Washita. Earlier that evening the scouts had run across a "small" war party of over a hundred braves moving south with the smell of home fires in their nostrils.

For a few minutes the men slid from their saddles after better than fourteen straight hours in leather. A short break to rub some semblance of life back into their numb, cold rumps. One hour and no longer to chew on the crackerlike hardtack, to sip at the scalding coffee Custer allowed them to brew over small fires built beneath the overhang of creek banks.

A good site had been chosen by Elliott's chief scout. He had worn the same droopy sombrero for years, a bushy mustache and dirty beard spilling across his chest. Christened Moses Embree Milner, the scout came to call himself Joseph, and later took the nickname California Joe during his gold rush days. A Kentuckian by birth, Milner had escaped his farming home to end up scouting for Kearny's forces during the Mexican War. After peace had been gained in the southwest, Joe had moseyed to the California gold fields. Until Nancy Emma Watts came along to temper some of his wanderlust. She was all of thirteen but every bit a woman when he met her; she would bear him four children before Joe figured out domestic life really was a scratchy suit. Milner owned up to what he was—a wanderer—taking Nancy Emma and their children north to the ranch of some friends in Oregon.

Once again on the plains enjoying a man's freedom, Joe cut quite a figure atop his cantankerous mule Maude.

Learning of Milner's qualifications, the Seventh Cavalry's young commander had snatched up Milner to become his chief of scouts.

"One thing 'bout a prairie winter," Milner growled to anyone who would listen, "it don't stop reminding a man he can never wear enough clothes."

He huddled with the rest of the scouts, both white and Indian, around a small fire. They warmed feet and hands, then turned for a moment while they pulled up the tails of their long coats, exposing some weary rumps to the welcome warmth of the flames. With a little rubbing, a rosy sensation of life began to seep back into this single most important part of a cavalry soldier's anatomy.

Joe chuckled privately at the thought. He wasn't all that different really from these numb-ass troopers. Just better paid. The dozen or so Osage trackers and the handful of white guides were all paid about $2.50 a day. In addition, they had Custer's promise of a $100 bonus paid in gold to the man who led him to the hostile village.

Milner's young partner Jack Corbin glanced at him over the lip of his tin cup as he sipped at the boiled coffee. Stiff, Milner eased himself down on his hams beside Corbin. He shared his joke on himself with the other scouts. The white men chuckled, frosty halos engulfing their heads. The Osages drank their coffee, not making a sound.

A few minutes before ten o'clock, Moylan brought orders to resaddle their mounts. Custer wasn't taking any chances blowing "Boots and Saddles" on the tin trumpets. By now a milk-pale moon had broken through a thin overcast. What little heat the earth had held would quickly disappear now with no cloud cover to speak of.

"Damn," one of the men grumbled, "this next haul could be the coldest stretch yet."

Out here in the wilderness, a man had only his dreams or his fears to keep himself warm tonight.

★   ★   ★

"Found something, Ben?" Custer asked the scout who materialized out of the inky darkness up ahead. Custer and Moylan had left the rest of the column a quarter-mile back, hundreds of weary horses plodding along the frozen river.

"One of them Osages thinks he smells a fire," Ben Clark said.

"Anyone else smell this fire?"

"No, General. Just the old tracker."

"Lead on. Mr. Moylan and I are right behind you."

Around the next loop of river the trio loped up on a cluster of forms looming dark against the snow. Overhead a brightening sliver of moonlight splayed across the land. Custer dismounted and handed his reins up to Moylan, motioning for Clark to follow him. A few steps across the crusted snow brought Custer to a circle of trackers squatting out of the wind. Corbin and Milner stood nearby.

"Clark tells me one of the trackers smelled a fire," Custer said to the Osages.

"Me smell small fire." One Indian rose stiffly, old joints crackling like rusty buggy springs, his heavy wool blanket capote slurring across the crust of snow where he had hunkered out of the keening wind.

"What's your name?"

"Osage name, Paw-Husk. Second chief of my people."

"Paw-Husk means what?"

"My moccasins are tired." He grinned toothlessly. "You soldiers call me Little Beaver."

"Well, Little Beaver, let's pray your nose is not as tired as your moccasins."

Custer judged Paw-Husk to be in his early sixties, skin the color of well-worn gloves, and just as wrinkled. Spare and thin, but with the sinewy muscles of a younger man. This Osage might prove a savvy tracker.

"So tell me what you found."

"Small fire. This night." He peered into the sky and pointed. "Moon was here."

"Something like two hours old, Joe?" Custer asked Milner.

"Close enough, General." Milner spit a brown curd of tobacco onto the snow.

"You smell this fire too?"

"Not me."

"Jack?"

"Me neither, General."

"Well, Little Beaver, looks like you don't have a soul to back your story up."

"Paw-Husk don't need soldiers to tell him he smelled fire. You come smell yourself." He walked off across the crumbling snow.

Custer muttered to himself about it being hard to smell anything with sweaty saddle blankets and bear grease in the Osages' braids. Hard Rope and the younger Osages rose from the snow to follow the soldier chief.

Behind him drifted the snorts of horses stomping over the crusty snow as his columns inched up the river. Once a wolf howled in loneliness from the hills. And at his feet the Washita slurred its icy gurgle along its banks. Sounds . . . but no smell of fire on the wind.

"Sorry, Little Beaver. I don't smell a thing like smoke." He went back to the head of the march.

"Joe . . . you and Ben and Jack move these trackers ahead again. We'll stay right on your heels. And Joe, be sure we stop for something important next time. No pipe-smoke fire. Understand?"

Milner and the others were mounted and gone without another word.

"Didn't smell a thing, sir?" Moylan asked.

"No, Myles. What worries me isn't what I didn't smell—but what I heard with my own ears. This regiment's making one helluva racket tramping downstream. I bloody well don't want to alert that enemy camp to our approach. To steal this close to my quarry only to flush them from the brush like frightened quail—that's what I fear the most, Mr. Moylan."

Less than a half hour later, Custer slid from his horse and stomped up to the little knot of Osages hunkered down in a circle on the snow.

"You smell anything now, Joe?"

Before Milner got a chance to open his mouth, Little Beaver stood. "White man's nose no good. No matter how big it gets." He pointed at Milner's face with a childish smirk. Several of the younger Osages snickered.

When Milner waved his arm the Osages rose and stepped back. In the middle of a small area cleared of snow lay the remnants of a tiny fire. A handful of coals still struggled, glowing against the falling temperature hovering close to zero. A gray wisp of smoke circled up from the red snakes, vanishing on the chilly breeze.

"The fire you smelled, Little Beaver?"

He nodded. "This old nose never wrong."

"Paw-Husk likes to eat too much," declared a middle-aged Osage who ambled up. "If he ever missed a fire, he might miss out on a meal."

"Who are you?"

"Hard Rope. Old Paw-Husk rides with you, for his is the best nose. We have the best eyes here too. I have the best ears. All to hunt the Cheyenne."

"Then tell me—have we found Cheyenne? Was this the fire of some of the hundred warriors returning home?"

"No." Hard Rope pointed to the snow leading toward the trees at the river's edge. "No warriors here. Small tracks only. Pony boys."

"Pony boys?"

"Young'uns watching the herd, General." Milner stepped beside Custer.

"Boys guard the Cheyenne ponies?"

"Not rightly," Joe answered. "They watch, warn the village if there's trouble."

"Have they gone to alert the camp?" Custer asked.

"Not from the looks of things. Appears they moseyed on back to camp. No rush a'tall."

"Camp guards?"

"None we've run across."

"Seems you've found nothing conclusive in this tiny fire," Custer said. "Perhaps we're as far away from an enemy village as we have been all night."

"Soldier chief can't smell Indian fire, but fire still here." Hard Rope pointed off to the southeast. "Soldier chief can't see Indian village, but village still there. Close. You come with Paw-Husk and Hard Rope. You scout with us. We show you village, Custer."

"Capital idea!" Custer exclaimed. "I will go with you. Let's be off!"

From the top of each knoll the trio encountered, Little Beaver made a careful inspection of the winter countryside below. Hard Rope and Custer shivered in the snow back among the oak and hackberry until the old Indian crept up to the tall white man.

The toothless scout announced, "Whole lot Cheyenne now."

"You see the village?" Custer asked.

"No. See whole lot Cheyenne ponies." Little Beaver motioned for the others to follow him to the top of the hill. "Look for worms." He pointed where Custer should look.

Try as he might, Custer couldn't make out anything. "I'll take your word for it, Paw-Husk. I can't make out a thing in this darkness."

"Come, soldier chief. We find."

"Yes, by God. You best find me something better. Not a fire. Not some worms. Find me the *village*."

Two hills later, Little Beaver motioned for Hard Rope to join him at the crest of the knoll. A finger to his lips, the old Indian demanded silence. "I want Hard Rope hear," he whispered hoarsely.

This way and that, his head up in the air, then close to the ground, Hard Rope listened to the night. Cold, freezing minutes crawled by until Custer could take this sitting in the snow no longer. He struggled to his feet. "I'm going back. When you have the village located, come fetch me. Seems I might as well be looking for this blessed village with a compass and a map all on my bloody own!"

"You hear?" Little Beaver whispered, paying no attention to Custer.

"Yes, Uncle. A dog. There."

Hard Rope stuck out his woolen mitten, stretching his arm toward the river course below. Here and there in patches the Washita silvered beneath the moon's pale light like bands of polished metal.

"You heard a dog bark?" Custer asked. "Not in this wind, you didn't!"

"Man who wants to hear, he must first listen, General." Hard Rope clamped Custer's bearded cheeks roughly within his mittens and pointed his face in the general direction of the enemy camp he had located.

Then he heard it! A dog!

"How're we sure?" he whispered. "Not a wolf?"

Litter Beaver shook his head. "Soldiers never learn the difference."

With each pause in the whining chorus of the wind, Custer listened with all that was in him. Then . . . he heard the dog bark again. Answered by another, different voice.

Custer muttered, "If only I could be sure—"

With Custer's next doubting heartbeat, an infant's cry rose above the trees lining the silver river course.

"By all that's holy, boys!" Custer whispered harshly, flush with excitement and pounding the trackers on the back. "The Cheyenne are here!"

"We find your Indians for you, soldier chief. Get your hundred dollars ready. Pay your Indian friends," Hard Rope reminded him.

"Of course I'll pay!" Custer said, turning to race downhill.

Nothing would stop him now. The village was at hand and the enemy hadn't been warned. The cry of the infant confirmed that much.

"By glory!" he exclaimed. "I've got them now. They'll learn not to sleep so soundly when Custer's nearby!"

CHAPTER 6

CUSTER countermarched his troops a mile upstream to guard against their discovery by Cheyenne guards. Only then did he send his three civilian scouts to read the lay of the land and size of the village. Corbin reported first, Milner on his heels. Ben Clark finally appeared out of the ice-rimed trees, his story confirming what the other two had seen in their search.

"They chose a good spot on the south bank of the river," Clark continued. "Fifty-some lodges, all sitting on level ground in a wide loop of the river—something like this."

Clark dropped to his knees, pulling out a knife. The scout scratched the river's meandering course in the snow, with that big loop where the troops would find the village sleeping.

"Where are we now?" Custer inquired.

"Right about here, sir." Clark's knife point jabbed the ground. "On the far side of the village is a steep cutbank. Fifty feet high. Noses almost straight up, following the course of the river. Plenty of—"

"Splendid!" Custer interrupted, slapping his thigh as he stood. "They surely can't make their escape that way, can they, now, Clark?"

"Why . . . not at all."

"I expect them to run, you see. Indians always do when we attack." Custer's smile faded as his eyes scanned the officers and scouts.

"They'll skedaddle, General. Like hens with a weasel in the yard." Milner spat into the snow. "Make no mistake about it—Injuns always run."

Custer grinned beneath a winter-bright quarter-moon. "I'm counting on that, Joe. I must have all the exits sealed—if you catch my drift, gentlemen."

"General Custer?" A swarthy scout named Romero rose on creaky knees. "Some of your Osages think your soldiers will be outnumbered by that village."

"That so?" Custer turned it over in his mind like a man would inspect something in his hand. He figured this Romero ought to know. Born of Mexican parents. Kidnapped by Indians, growing up a Cheyenne. "What else my Osage got to say?"

"They're scared."

"Scared of those warriors in the village?"

"Not scared of Cheyenne. Afraid of your cavalry . . . and you."

"Afraid of us!" Custer exploded. "Insane! Why in heaven's name should they be afraid of us?"

"Way they see it, the Cheyenne in there will give you a real fight of it. So when things turn out a draw, they figure you'll parley with the Cheyenne to save your men. And to save your men, you'll hand the Osage over to their old enemies, them Cheyenne."

"That's the most preposterous—"

"There's more. These Osages aren't all that impressed by what you soldiers done so far out here in Indian country. These trackers got their doubts, you making good your attack on that village."

Custer glared at Romero. "Seems we're just going to have to educate these Osages on how the Seventh Cavalry fights Indians. Won't we, gentlemen?"

A murmuring of assent arose among the officers before Custer continued. "By General Sheridan's orders we'll level the village and kill or hang every man of fighting age. I wasn't sent here to show these hostiles any mercy at all. So tell your Osages that Custer won't stop until Sheridan's orders are carried out—"

"General?"

Custer's eyes snapped to Jack Corbin, youngest of the scouts, who had earned the respect of many frontiersmen on the southern plains. "What is it?" Custer barked.

"Don't know what the others think," Corbin began, toeing the snow as nervously as a schoolboy stammering before a pigtailed, freckle-faced girl. "But I don't see a way there can be a big war party down in that village. That camp's just too damned small."

"Not a war camp?" Custer's voice rose an octave. "Why in Hades did these Osage trackers follow Indian ponies here? You remember those ponies, don't you, Jack? Better than a hundred or more—you all told me that!"

Corbin shook his head in exasperation. "Something just don't fit right, General."

"Better than fifty lodges, I'm told!" Custer roared.

Corbin's pleading eyes darted to Milner, then implored Ben Clark. Joe looked away, studying his dirty fingernails.

Clark eventually stepped up to Custer. "Might be Jack's put a finger on something."

"Which is?" Custer growled, glowering at Clark with eyes that could frost a man's mustache.

"Doesn't read right. That village ain't got fifty warriors in it—much less a hundred fifty."

"What are you saying?" As it did every time he got excited, Custer's voice was on the verge of stammering like a buggy spring hammering over a washboard road.

"I figure what we've bumped into ain't a hostile camp, General."

"You agree that's not a hostile camp, Corbin?"

"General, I don't figure we'll find but a handful of seasoned warriors down there."

"So where did all the rest of them just off and disappear to?" Custer hissed.

"I suppose it's my job to find out where the warriors disappeared," Corbin answered sheepishly.

"Well, now." Custer hammered his fist into the open palm of his left hand. "That's just what I intend to do, gentlemen. We're finally in agreement! About time you found out where they went—the ones that you and the Osage trackers followed into that village down there."

"We figured better than a hundred warriors," Clark said.

"Those odds will make for a pretty fair fight of it. We've got the hostiles pinned against that cutbank behind the village. Unable to reach their pony herd for escape. We'll charge across the river from the north. So their only route of escape will be downriver." He stabbed his toe into Ben Clark's snowy map. "Right about there."

Custer ground his heel into the snow and mud. "And that's where I'll be waiting for them—with Cooke's men!

That's it!" Custer wheeled suddenly, stomping off deep in thought. "Deployed up the south bank. By the stars, that's good!"

Corbin looked back at Clark and Milner. "You think that's the camp we're looking for?"

Clark squinted, appraising something unseen. "Don't think so, Jack."

They both looked at Milner for his confirmation.

"I don't reckon how neither one of you got anything more to say 'bout it now. We found a village for the man. And no matter what Injuns they be, Custer's going on in there and carve 'em up. Just like Custer's been intending all along. Was only a matter of time before we found what he wanted—any village a'tall."

Corbin turned away, stung by the certainty of Milner's words. With his own eyes he had seen those browned, smoke-blackened buffalo-hide lodges, hunkered sleepy and silent beneath the winter sky. Almost forlorn—all squatting in slumber on pewter-bright snow aglow beneath a quarter moon splaying itself through thin, pony-breath clouds. The haunting vision of that sleeping village clung to Corbin's mind like old smoke in his clothes.

That wasn't a war camp.

Corbin wheeled on Milner. "I tried to tell Custer about—"

"You've done all any man can do, son," Milner consoled. "When the army brass gets high behind and ready to plunge ahead without listening to his scouts . . . it's just a waste of time trying to talk sense to him."

"I gotta make him see—"

Milner grabbed his young partner, yanking him around. "Best just shut up! And see you got your rifle and pistols loaded afore the peep of day when Custer rides down on that village."

Corbin watched Milner turn toward his mule Maude.

Joe's right, he brooded. *I've already done my damage. I've brought that hungry wolf stalking up on that sleeping winter village.*

Time to watch my own goddamn backside now.

Down in a gully behind a brushy hill north of the Washita, Custer gathered his officers. In the snow he scratched a diagram of the river, where the village stood and the horse herd grazed.

"We'll surround the village, deploying the regiment along the river," Custer explained. "My plan will make for a rapid encroachment of the village, securing it within minutes. Only in that way can we effectively seal off any chance for escape."

"And lessen the odds of losing any of our own men?" the deep, familiar voice prodded him.

Custer measured Frederick W. Benteen, an experienced Civil War veteran. "Yes, Captain."

Custer glanced over his men, most of whom had been with him for better than a year, not counting his temporary absence. He knew what he could expect from each of them. Still, it disappointed him that there were some in this group who had grown to despise him, losing no chance in letting Custer know it. Benteen stood at the center of the opposition. Though he could be a mean, sniveling complainer, Benteen remained every bit as good a leader of cavalry under fire as Custer. Now, as these two decorated veterans prepared to plunge into battle, perhaps each realized he had to count on the other.

"Saving lives is, after all, a main thrust of this campaign, isn't it, gentlemen?" Custer waited, looking into the expectant faces encircling him. "Let us begin. Major Elliott?"

"Yes, General?" He stepped forward, saluting.

"You'll take your command and ride wide left. To the east."

"Splendid, sir!"

For some time, Custer had been aware of the contagious power in Elliott's unbridled enthusiasm. "Should any of the Indians escape the trap we've laid for them, they'll be running your way, Major. Right into your arms."

"We'll be ready for them, General. They won't get past us."

"Good. Now, Captain Myers—you're to move your troops off to the right." Custer traced a ragged line in the snow. "By backtracking west a short distance, the scouts tell me you'll find a wide bend in the river where you can attack from southwest of the village. Station your two companies in the timber after crossing the river about a mile above my command here. You won't have to ford the river at the moment of attack. Understood?"

"Perfectly, sir,"

"Captain Yates?" Custer gazed at the tall blond yankee from Monroe, Michigan, who for a short time during the Civil War, George W. Yates had served as an aide to Custer as part of General Pleasanton's staff. A hometown boy, and a natural for the Custer inner circle. "General?"

"Your F Company will be assigned to Captain Thompson."

Custer watched Yates's steel-gray eyes flick to William Thompson. "Yessir," Yates responded, nodding.

Custer turned to Captain Thompson. "Will, you're to

take your two companies with Yates's men to the crest of the knoll directly south of the village. If possible, link up with Elliott's command, sealing the escape route the hostiles might use."

"Certainly."

"Sweep around the village and establish yourselves to the south of the village to await the attack."

"As you've ordered, General."

"Good. Now, I suppose you're all wondering what my four troops will be doing as you flank the village on the east, west, and south. Frankly, boys, I've saved the point of the lance for myself. I'll lead my companies across the river. While the four company commanders secure the village in concert with your actions, I'll oversee the attack from a knoll south of the village."

"Sir?"

"Mr. Cooke?" Custer turned toward the tall, handsome lieutenant, just recently awarded his bars. Billy Cooke, his men called him. And with respect. This dashing, bearded Canadian had migrated south into the States at the beginning of the Civil War simply so he could become a soldier. Some called him a patriot. Others, a soldier of fortune. A few went so far as to call Billy Cooke a mercenary. Little did it matter to Custer what made the Canadian tick, for he had recognized the makings of a fine officer and a close friend in W. W. Cooke.

"Will my corps of riflemen ride across the river to engage the hostiles, sir?"

"No, Lieutenant." Custer stepped over to Cooke. "You are the final, crushing blow I plan for these murderers who have plundered the southern plains for the last time. Your sharpshooters won't cross the river at all."

Custer waited for Cooke to nod. "I've sealed the village up from left and right, from north and south. The only way the warriors escape is to use the river itself. The banks are high enough to use the terrain for cover in an escape—but we don't want one of these murderers to flee. So I'm sealing my trap with your forty sharpshooters—right there." Custer pointed to his snowy map, showing Cooke to station his marksmen in the timber high along the north bank of the river. "Up there you will command a wide field of fire when the hostiles attempt to flee down the Washita."

"We won't let you down."

Custer smiled, giving Cooke a hearty slap on the shoulder. "The scouts will remain with me." He gazed down at the crude, muddy drawing in the snow near his feet and paused. "I suspect these warriors will be all the harder to bring down because we're striking them in their homes, with their families. Be sure your men understand we'll have a real scrap of it on our hands."

He waited for them to nod.

"Good. From here on there must be no talking. Nothing above a whisper will be allowed. Warn the men against stamping their feet. An Indian sleeping on the ground might hear our troops. We'll attack at first light—which gives you less than four hours to circle into position. Just prior to dawn, the men are to strip to battle readiness. I'll signal the attack from here."

He stepped from the center of the group, turning so he could face them all at once.

"Gentlemen, we're about to spell an end to those bloody depredations committed on the southern frontier. Until now, an operation such as this hasn't been possible—for there had been no Seventh Cavalry. That makes us, very simply, the spearhead of destiny, gentlemen! It is our Seventh that will always ride the vanguard of glory and honor. To that glory and honor, gentlemen!"

"Glory and honor!"

It stirred a fire within him hearing the chorus of their strong young voices echoing the courageous sentiment that would bring the Seventh Cavalry fame across the years ahead. Soon enough they could cross the river. Dawn would bring him what destiny had promised.

He repeated it in a lead-filled whisper that could raise the hairs on the back of a man's neck. "To glory and honor."

Two hours of freezing agony ground past for the men waiting huddled in the freezing mist of the Washita.

Officers repeatedly checked their watches as time dragged by. Eventually the moon slipped behind the western hills, throwing the countryside into complete and eerie darkness.

"Gotta be your mind playing tricks on you," Milner, the man they called California Joe, muttered to himself. "Feels colder what with that goddamn moon sunk." He carried his old Springfield across an arm as he prodded his mule in Custer's direction. "Morning, General."

Custer nodded. "Joe."

"What I've been trying to get through my old topknot all night is whether we'll run up against more Injuns than we bargained for."

He watched Custer raise an eyebrow, concerned. Milner realized he'd handed the general a thorny problem.

"You don't figure those Cheyenne down there will make a run for it, Joe?"

"Them Cheyenne skedaddle? How in the Good Lord's Creation can Injuns run off when you'll have 'em clean surrounded afore first light?"

"Precisely my plan. I don't want a one to escape." He chewed thoughtfully on the corner of his droopy mustache. "Supposing we are able to bottle them up—you figure we can hold our own against the warriors in that village?"

"That is some handsome dilemma, now, ain't it?" Milner ground teeth on the stub of his unlit pipe. "One thing's sure as sun. If them Injuns down there don't hear a squeak out of your soldier boys till we open up our guns on 'em come crack o' day, they'll damned near be the most astonished redskins that's been in these parts lately! If we do for certain get the bulge on 'em . . . why, we'll sweep their platter clean!"

"I'm relieved to have your confidence in my plan, Joe."

"Well, General—I like to deal the cards face up. We're holding aces high over them Injuns down there."

"I've got the feeling that something still troubles you."

"I've played enough cards to know that both Lady Fate and Lady Luck often sit 'cross the table from a man—and it's them two whores what might have something to say about what a man draws from his deck."

"You think those Cheyenne still have a draw at one of our aces?"

Milner ran the tip of his tongue thoughtfully across winter-chapped lips. "I've fought me plenty Injuns, and damn if they don't always find a draw at the cards. Hang me but they've got a play even at the bottom of some god-damned played-out deck."

Without another word, Milner plodded pulled Maude away into the roiling mist, quiet as cotton through the calf-deep snow until the mist had swallowed him completely.

Custer shuddered. Some parts of this Indian fighting sat in his craw. Cursed with scouts so ofttimes somber and ghostly. Turning into the brush, he decided to find himself a quiet spot and stretch out on the snow for a nap.

Until time came for the bugles.

Here and there small knots of men congregated, waiting for that opening note of the coming fight. Enlisted men complained of the bitter cold or talked of the warmth of their hard haytick bunks back at Fort Hays. Some dreamed of the pleasure brought a man by those fleshy sporting ladies in Hays City, friendly kind of gals who followed soldiers to every post and fort and fleshpot dotting the western frontier.

Talk of anything now . . . but no talk about the coming battle.

Instead of talking at all, most only leaned against their mounts, using the horses' warmth to ward off some of the foggy cold that stung a man to the bone, chewing away at the core of him. Many of the battle-hardened were long used to eluding prefight jitters. They snored back in the snowy rabbit brush.

Custer himself awoke refreshed from a long nap about the time a ghostly light climbed out of the dense river mist. Nearby the scouts murmured among themselves. A few Osages began chanting their own eerie melodies as the bright light emerged from the thick fog bank, ascending into the lamp-black sky.

"It's the Morning Star, sir," Moylan whispered at Custer's side.

It loomed close. Huge, and shimmering with life.

"A good omen for our victory, Lieutenant."

Nothing short of powerful medicine to the Osages, this appearance of the celestial light above the river, here on the precipice of battle. As the brilliant globe climbed above the southwestern horizon, it seemed to ascend more slowly, its light radiating prismatically from color to color. An imperial stillness settled over this wilderness in these last moments before dawn, causing something deep within Custer's being to assure him this star was destined to shine on this valley, his command—on he alone.

Custer smiled, certain to the core of the outcome of the impending fight. The heavens had ordained the star to shine upon him.

He vowed to do nothing to disappoint the gods of Olympus with the coming light of a new day.

Stiff with cold, the Cheyenne sentry who stationed himself atop the knoll south of camp had no appreciation for the celestial light glowing above him in the river mist. Half Bear settled in the snow.

Not much longer before he could return to a warm lodge where his woman would build up the fire, put some breakfast meat on to boil. His stomach churned, angry with him, a hunger enough to keep a sentry awake.

Yet he decided he could nap a bit before the sky paled in morning-coming.

Half Bear slumped over. By the time he had curled his legs up beneath the heavy robe, his breath had begun to warm his frozen face. His breathing grew more regular. Before he realized it he was no longer merely napping. Half Bear slept.

Down he plunged, deep and sound, unable to yank himself back out of that warm, liquid pit. In the midst of its welcome darkness he was sure the ear he laid against the ground caught the warning of iron-shod hooves scraping across the frozen breast of the Mother of Them All.

Half Bear's eyes refused to open. He heard horses circling to the backside of the knoll where he slept on. Horses clattering up from the river. Creeping south of the village behind him. That unmistakable jangle of pony soldier saddle gear! Still he tried to convince himself it was only a dream.

Hah! That pony soldiers would come in the cold of a winter dawn made bright beneath the Morning Star—this could only be a dream!

Curled deep within his robe, Half Bear dozed . . . warm enough to dream on.

With the growing light, Custer sent Lieutenant Cooke's detail far to the left, deploying his men among the tall oaks along the steep northern bank of the Washita. A quarter-hour later, Custer led his four companies down the gradual slope that sank away to the river. There he halted the troopers in a dense copse of trees shading the north lip of the Washita as it circled the sleeping village in a lazy loop of icy water.

To his left, astride a broad-backed gray, sat the regimental color guard, his guidon dancing stiffly in the fog. Staying near Custer and refusing to wander far from that colorful cavalry standard sat the twelve Osage trackers. In a mad charge against Indians, they had decided, there could be no safer place for them.

Like warm milk from a cracked bowl, the gray light of a new day eventually began to leak out of the east.

The twenty-seventh of November. One day after Thanksgiving. That thin band of growing light caused Custer to send Moylan to carry word among the four companies shivering behind him.

Troopers shed their warm buffalo coats. They dropped their haversacks holding rations of hardtack and coffee. One soldier from each company was assigned to stay behind to guard the coats and haversacks. All eyes focused on the coming light of dawn.

"Moylan, bring the band up. I want them to play at the moment of attack."

Officers pulled pistols from mule-eared holsters, reins gripped anxiously in the other hand. Hundreds of troopers sat shivering in the brutal cold, not knowing what awaited them in that sleeping village on the other side of the frozen Washita.

Across the river a dog began to bark, its call soon taken up by another.

Murky light spread behind the hills like alkaline water strained through a dirty pair of trooper's stockings.

A few more minutes. A few more anxious heartbeats, and he would lead them splashing across the Washita, victory assured before that new sun ever rose above these ancient hills. Wrapped securely in winter's cloak of deep hibernation, the Washita valley slept on.

Little Rock stirred and listened again. Now he was certain. The dog he heard wasn't snarling at another in camp.

He sat up, straining at the thick blanket of silence laid over the sleeping camp. In his dark lodge he quickly pulled on his clothing and wrenched up his old muzzle loader, checking the priming in the pan.

For a heartbeat the old Indian gazed down at his young daughter, peacefully cocooned in childlike slumber. Wisps of last night's fire hung like skinny ghosts refusing to depart, suspended beneath the dark smoke hole. Up in the narrow opening he could make out a growing light in the sky, knowing dawn would come to the valley in little more time than it took a man to eat his morning meal.

Slipping quietly through the doorway, he stood. Listening to all the air told him. Again the two dogs barked from the far side of camp where the sun rose each morning. Something told him they didn't bark at each other. Perhaps at something across the river—some predator roaming through the horse herd.

He moved east, through the cadaverous lodges and around those hard, frozen droppings left behind by more than ten times ten ponies three young Kiowas had driven through the Cheyenne camp late yesterday afternoon.

It did not matter. He had not truly been asleep anyway. Little Rock never was able to fall back to sleep each night after his daughter awakened him with her nightmare screaming.

In minutes he found himself down at the sharp slope of the bank. The river lapped quietly beneath a thin scum of ice within the webby red willow nodding in the breeze above the slow-moving water.

Again the dogs barked . . . moving to his left now. He crept back along the bank toward camp. Perhaps the dogs tormented a hungry wolf, wandering about with an empty winter-belly, hoping to drag down a poor, weary, winter-old mare.

With his breath freezing his cheeks, he stepped from the cover of some overhanging oaks. The dogs lurched back and forth in the shallow icy water, barking at the anonymous north bank.

Little Rock's eyes crawled across that short span of the cold river collared in fog. His old eyes strained to penetrate the swirling gray mist. Still the dogs yipped and howled, barked and splashed, snarling at the far side of the stream. The fog slowly danced and cavorted . . . lifting momentarily.

He could not be sure.

Little Rock crept down the bank. Cracking through the ice at water's edge, he found his footing shaky on the slippery rocks. Three more greasy steps brought him out to the river's main flow. The stinging mist lifted fully for the first time. Only then did the dark trees on the steep northern bank relinquish their frightening secret.

Pony soldiers!

"*Aieeee!*" That frantic sound clutched his throat as surely as the icy current clawed at his spindly legs. Tugging, making it hard for him to turn and sprint out of the river. Struggling against the Washita's icy flow, he raised his rifle in the air and slipped an old finger against the trigger.

Make it to the bank now! If I cannot . . . must fire a warning shot.

The fog that momentarily swirled off the river to expose the cavalry to Little Rock had at the same time revealed the old Indian to the troopers.

Major Joel Elliott's mind seared with the dilemma dropped in his lap. He wasn't sure if he should stop the old man. But the Indian had a rifle held up in his hand. No mistaking that. And no mistaking that the old man had seen Elliott's men waiting like a long ribbon of black ghosts picketed among the icy trees.

With a damning frustration Elliott understood he would be alerting both the camp and the rest of the regiment to his predicament if he fired at the old man. Yet that was exactly what it appeared the old man himself was about to do.

Only one way to get the jump on that goddamned village. . . .

"Sergeant Major Kennedy!" he barked.

"Yessir!"

"Kill that Indian!"

Without dropping his reins, the veteran trooper answered by throwing his carbine to his right shoulder, pressing his cheek along the frozen stock. The deep rumble of the Spencer tore through the low-hanging mist. Kennedy rarely missed.

The bullet caught Little Rock squarely between the shoulder blades. With both arms flung wide, his old muzzle loader went tumbling across the frozen mud at the river's edge. A gaping hole blown in his chest where his heart once beat, he stumbled two more slippery steps. Then took one last lunge as his wet, gut-slimy moccasins fought to hold the rocky bottom. It no longer mattered. He could walk no more.

As the old man crumbled into the skiffs of snow at the water's edge, the village disappeared from view behind the gentle slope leading to the water. Little Rock pitched face down into the frozen crust lapping at the edge of the icy Washita.

An old man robbed of time to sing his death song.

CHAPTER 7

Sitting a quarter-mile away, Custer recognized the roar of an army carbine. No throaty boom of an Indian muzzle loader. What he heard had been the report of a Spencer.

Custer knew his troops had been discovered. Better to plunge ahead now that the whole camp had been alerted. His troop commanders would be anxious and confused. It set his gall to boiling having his hand forced.

Whirling on his bugler and the regimental band behind him, he waved his arm. "Sound the advance!"

As Custer had planned, young John Murphy, the bugler, began first, blowing the charge that would send the regiment dashing into the village. As those initial stirring notes of the charge faded over the river, the band struck up the first strains of the rollicking, stirring drinking tune "Garry-Owen."

Custer burst from the trees. On Dandy's heels galloped his four companies. Left behind, the regimental trumpeters broke off raggedly in discordant notes as moisture from their warm breath froze in the brass instruments. The fighting men plunged ahead.

The battle of Washita was on.

Downstream from the main command, past the high slope where Cooke's sharpshooters stood, Elliott's cavalry had to struggle down the same steep embankment that Custer's companies plunged over. A slope high and steep enough to preclude an immediate charge. Instead, Elliott's grumbling troopers had to lead their horses down the vertical bank by leaping the animals off the lip of the slope into the icy unknown of the river below. Once the first soldiers made the water and were able to spur their staggering horses toward the village, wave after wave of troopers dived into the Washita. That very delay in the charge allowed the Cheyenne a precious few seconds of breath to sort out the nightmare of the attack: time only to draw a blanket about their naked shoulders, a heartbeat allowing some of the women and children to run while the men covered their escape.

Myers's troops were practically in the village before they fell under the eyes of an old woman out gathering some deadfall for her breakfast fire. Busy scouring through the snow and ice that coated everything, she wheeled to hear the horses an instant before the black forms loomed from the blood-thick mist. With hundreds of hooves they thundered on over her. One young trooper aimed his carbine at the solitary, blanket-wrapped figure. A lead bullet tore through the center of the old woman's chest.

Calls Twice at the Moon was dead as she hit the snow, her frail body sliding backward before she was trampled beneath iron-shod hooves. The back of her blanket a patch of bright crimson across the dirty snow beside her scattered bundle of tiny sticks.

With the soldier's charge, the warriors, their women and children, and with the old ones, of many winters, all came clawing out of their sleep-warm robes and blankets like so many grass beetles scattering in panic from beneath an overturned buffalo chip. Scurrying in all directions. No direction at all. Warriors shouted, directing the old and weaker ones as each fighting man searched for some route of escape.

There was nowhere to run.

In those first few seconds pure bedlam whirled around the charging, slashing soldiers. Thompson, Elliott, and Myers reached the shrieking camp within seconds. Custer's four companies galloped up from the Washita as the lieutenant colonel himself pressed on into the heart of the hostile village with Captain Louis M. Hamilton at his side.

What few Cheyenne camped in the center of the village were more fortunate then those who had pitched their lodges near the horns of the camp circle. They alone had a few precious seconds to decide what to do, where to go. That is, until Elliott pulled in on the east side of camp, plugging the last escape route south of the river. Custer's crude noose tightened around the village, strangling those who had escaped slaughter in the initial charge.

Everywhere the Cheyenne turned, rifles spit yellow fire, and long, slashing knives sang a wheezing death song through the frozen air. No chance for the warriors to stem the blue tide and turn the avalanche already burying their sleepy village.

. Women and children and old ones died in the mud alongside their fighting men.

Like a deafening thunder, the roar of thousands of rounds from the Springfield swallowed the keening cries of the dead and dying. Curses of frightened soldiers mingled with the war whoops and valiant death chants sung by young warriors standing their ground, ready to die.

"There!" Custer pointed, showing Captain Louis Hamilton three warriors disappearing behind a lodge.

"Got 'em!" Hamilton replied, his throat raw from barking orders, cheering his men across the river.

Custer knew Hamilton as a fearless, proven leader. In the young captain's veins coursed the blood of colonial patriots. Grandson of no less than Alexander Hamilton himself.

"Go that way! I'll flank them over there!" Custer drove his spurs into Dandy's ribs with brutal urgency.

Custer swept around the side of the lodge, searching for three warriors. He saw only two. Hamilton had disappeared.

As the young captain galloped after the warriors, he twisted to the left to aim his pistol across his body. His frightened mount strained against the bit. Too late Hamilton realized he was vulnerable, presenting a broad and inviting target to the solitary warrior who wheeled on him, raising a rifle.

Funny, he thought in that blink of an eye as he watched the ragged puff of blue smoke blossom from the Indian's weapon, *looks just like one of those old rifles the peace commission gave the Cheyenne for putting their marks to the treaty at Medicine Lodge Creek. Damned old muzzle loaders never were any good—*

Hamilton never heard the weapon's blast. His chest burned with a sudden fire. His body snapped rigid, legs clamping around the gaunt ribs of his wild-eyed mount. As Hamilton's convulsive corpse rode the terrified horse another thirty yards through the village, the warrior Cranky Man ducked behind a lodge to reload his trusted weapon.

Hamilton tumbled from his horse. Cranky Man's bullet had penetrated his twenty-four-year-old heart. He never got a good look at the wrinkled old man who had killed him.

After shooting the other two warriors, Custer spurred on toward the knoll just south of the village. To his right he watched a young trooper savagely yank his horse's head to the side as he slashed at a stocky warrior. The mount reared in protest as the soldier clung to the bucking animal. A Cheyenne trained his old rifle on the young pony soldier.

Custer fired on instinct. Beneath a puff of blue smoke he watched the warrior crumple to the ground like a sack of wet oats, a bullet through his head. With his mount once more under control, the young soldier darted off to continue his fight, not realizing his life had just been saved by his regimental commander.

Eagerly Custer wheeled Dandy hard to the left, charging to the knoll, knocking down another warrior beneath the huge animal's pounding hooves. Aiming his pistol at the same time, Custer fired point-blank at the trampled Cheyenne.

"That one won't fight again," he said aloud to himself.

Reining up atop the low rise, he brought Dandy sharply around as the first smudge of gray light splashed across the battle site. From the knoll he would watch the rest of the skirmish raging below. Glancing at his pocket watch, Custer saw it had taken barely four minutes for him to cross the Washita, charge through the village, and reach the knoll.

★   ★   ★

Down with Elliott's command rode Captain Frederick W.
Benteen at the head of Company H. Finding himself near
the center of the village, he worried how many shots he had
left in his pistol. He was about to find out.

A young, owl-eyed warrior jumped from behind a lodge,
his bowstring taut. Benteen fired. The warrior dropped as
another dashed in front of the same lodge, tearing off at a
full sprint. The captain pulled the trigger. No bark, no
familiar buck in his hand.

Benteen jammed his empty weapon in his holster and
secured the mule-ear while the other hand yanked his
carbine from its boot beneath his right leg. He wheeled to
find another target.

Benteen caught sight of a stocky youth bursting from a
lodge near the center of camp, grabbing for the single
rawhide rein of a lone war pony tethered there. Judging the
boy to be no more than fifteen years of age, Benteen
decided against killing him. Following at a hand gallop, he
signaled the boy to give himself up.

But instead of surrendering, young Blue Horse wheeled
his pony smartly and fired at the pursuing soldier. As the
nephew of Chief Black Kettle, he realized a warrior must
either escape or die trying. Though short of youthful in
appearance, this warrior had lived twenty-one summers,
fighting Pawnee, Osage and Kaw many times. His choice
was simple. He would kill this pesky soldier.

Like the whine of a persistent mosquito, Benteen felt a
bullet slice the air by his face. He heard the familiar crack
of a carbine as the youth raced off again, only to wheel a few
yard away and fire a second shot. Then a third.

That one hit something with a loud, wet smack. Before

he could react, Benteen's mount pitched headlong, spilling him across the snow.

"That's about enough, you damned rascal!" he growled, scrambling to his feet.

Up ahead the young warrior bellowed his victory song. He had unhorsed a pony soldier!

By now Benteen couldn't care less how young his enemy was. He shouldered his Springfield and fired as Blue Horse again raised both his rifle and defiant song to the dawn sky.

An army-issue bullet caught him square in his bare chest, tumbling him heels over head off the rear of his war pony into the dirty snow.

Unhorsed, Benteen crouched, slashing his ammunition pouch from the dead mount, then darted back into the village.

Second Lieutenant Algernon E. Smith, who had crossed the river with Custer's four companies, galloped knee to knee with John Murphy, the bugler who had signaled the attack. Just ahead of them darted a Cheyenne cloaked in a dirty red blanket, scurrying toward a cluster of keening women. Smith slid to a halt beside Murphy as the young bugler threw his carbine to his shoulder.

"Murphy! Don't fire!"

Flashing a quick Irish anger, Murphy glared at Smith.

"Can't you see it's a woman, son?" Smith hollered, waving his left arm, wounded so badly in the Civil War that he could barely raise it above his shoulder.

"Yessir! Now I do!"

"By damn—find yourself a buck to kill!" Smith blared, spinning his horse around and dashing into the fray once more.

Murphy whirled suddenly at the hackle-raising howl coming from one of the Cheyenne women who had by now been herded by the troops. His eyes must be deceiving him—for now that old squaw he had seen running had dropped her red blanket. The Cheyenne was not a woman.

The old warrior drew back on the bowstring of a weapon he no longer concealed beneath the dirty blanket. He raised his thin, reedy war cry as Murphy ducked off the far side of his mount—a move that saved his life.

Instead of taking the arrow in his chest where it had been aimed, Murphy sensed a blinding flash. The iron point grazed the young soldier's brow, entering above one eye, tearing the flesh and scraping the bone before it ended its flight just above the ear. Yet with all its force, the point had not penetrated Murphy's skull.

Stunned, he flopped from his horse like a hooked fish brought to the bank, certain he was a dead man. An arrow fluttering above his eye, Murphy rolled across the ground, feeling his empty stomach lurch. In his hand he recognized the comforting feel of the carbine. The old warrior shot a second arrow. Murphy squeezed the trigger, rolling out of the way.

Murphy's bullet knocked the Indian backward into the knot of shrieking, screaming captives. The warrior was dead as he sank to the ground.

The bugler caught his breath, swallowing hard, choking down the pain of the arrow still hanging in his scalp. After he had broken the shaft and pulled the arrow out by himself, Murphy daubed at the oozing wounds with a dirty bandanna he yanked from his own greasy neck. The next task was to rip the graying scalp from the old warrior's head. He stuffed the dripping trophy in the folds of his blue tunic, smearing his wool shirt with the Indian's warm, sticky blood.

Damn, but his feet were cold.

For seasons without count, Black Kettle had counseled peace with the white man. So many times he had been promised his people could live where they wanted and hunt where they must. Despite the repeated broken government promises to all tribes roaming the southern plains, the chief remained sure that a way would be found allowing red man and white to live side by side.

With those first early-morning blasts of rifle fire, shouts of soldiers joining the valiant death songs of angry warriors and screams of women and children, Black Kettle yanked his wife from the warm robes of their bedding. Stumbling from their lodge, the couple plunged into the terror.

Nearby stood some war ponies Cheyenne warriors always staked in camp. Black Kettle frantically tried to lift his woman onto a pony but found he didn't have the strength left in his cold, tired bones. He crawled atop the nervous, mule-eyed animal, grasping its mane in one hand. The other he extended for his wife to grab, and held stiff his naked foot for her to use as a step. Together they struggled to get her seated in front of him on the prancing, skittish pony, frightened by the shrill noise and gunfire, made madder yet by the smell of gunpowder and fresh blood.

Ahead of them dashed a ragged line of troopers heading east toward the edge of camp and the horse herd—some of Major Elliott's men charging toward the open plain.

There seemed little choice for the Cheyenne chief. Simply a matter of running the gauntlet to cross the river.

From there to race south for those Arapaho, Kiowa, and Cheyenne camps downstream.

"Be of strong heart, woman!"

Her only reply was the squeeze she gave his old hand.

"I am with you always, old woman!" *Hep-haaa!*" he sang out to the stouthearted little pony beneath them.

A simple matter for the old man to jab the little pony in its ribs, driving the overburdened mustang toward the icy river. Crashing straight through the shredded line of confused, blue-shirted troopers.

"Holy—"

"What the hell?"

"Look out!"

"There goes one . . . behind you, Kennedy!"

Black Kettle found himself near the crossing at the bank of the Washita. Several soldiers wheeled with a jangle of saddle gear, training their carbines on the old Cheyenne's wide back. They did not notice the old woman nestled within the arms of the chief like a tick clinging for life itself.

They fired a ragged volley.

Black Kettle stiffened as the hot lead tore deep into his body, piercing both lungs and shredding his abdomen. Shuddering with the first throes of death, he clutched both arms around Medicine Woman Later.

If only I can make it to the river . . .

A second wild volley crashed into the old warrior's body. For winters without count the heart of the grizzly had beat in his chest. Yet it was not enough against the soldiers' carbines.

A third volley riddled the little pony. In a death spasm the animal stumbled, lunged valiantly, pitched the old couple to the edge of the icy river. Black Kettle was dead before he hit the water.

Like angry hornets the soldiers' bullets buzzed and stung. It was nothing short of miraculous that Medicine Woman Later found herself alive. Though bleeding from several wounds, she struggled to her hands and knees, crabbing across the rocky bottom of the stream. Her husband was dead. She must plunge into the river alone, without him for the first time in more years than she could remember. But before she could turn, red blossomed across her chest and belly, the side of her face. Numbing impact drove her backward several stumbling steps. Through the water grown red around her, Medicine Woman Later dragged herself a yard at a time, back to Black Kettle's side. She collapsed, breathless, unable to crawl any farther. She reached out with the one good arm left her, and clutched his hand in hers.

She moved no more.

"C'mon, boys! Here goes for a brevet or a coffin!" Major Elliott hollered enthusiastically to the squad of soldiers close on his heels.

Elliott's troopers leapt their horses over the bloodied old chief, galloping southeast from the village along the Washita's course, chasing a band of Indians scattering on foot. None of those soldiers or their commanding officer realized they had just killed the peacemaking chief of the Southern Cheyenne. Few would have thought it mattered much at all.

In less than a hundred yards Elliott watched the fleeing Cheyenne break into two groups. To the left scampered older women and men, along with young children. To the right darted the warriors and fleet-footed young women. They turned to taunt the soldiers, urging them in the chase, as a sage hen lures the coyote away from her young.

"Simmons! Take a squad with you—there! Follow that group!" Elliott pointed toward the old ones. "Kennedy! You and the rest, follow me!"

The major whirled his horse, kicking up the untrammeled snow as they tore after the Cheyenne disappearing around the brow of a hill.

"We'll rout them, Major!" Kennedy shouted. "Like the cowardly Johnnies they are!"

Around the hill, through the trees and brush. One young woman stumbled and fell. Elliott saw her disappear in the snowy bramble, watching a trooper rein up to capture her. The major galloped on, accompanied by sixteen troopers who followed him across the deep gash of a dry wash. They were gaining on the warriors, who scurried this way and that through the trees like rabbits.

Another hundred yards now . . . and you'll have them trapped in the middle of that open meadow ahead!

—Surrounded! In the open!

"Sunuvabitch! Where'd all them come from?"

"Major!"

Elliott reined up so savagely his mount went down in the snow. Kennedy and the others clattered up, crashing into one another, pitching two men from their horses. The men cursed. They were surrounded by more Indians than any of them had ever seen in his short life. And in this last heartbeat, the Indians had turned the winning card.

"Back, goddammit!" Elliott ordered. "Retreat!"

Bouncing against one another, the troopers started a ragged dash, reining up as soon as they had started. The neck through which they had galloped into the meadow closed up. A hundred warriors or more plugged all hope for escape.

"Dismount!" Elliott was already on the ground. "Skirmish formation, dammit! Pull your ammunition off— let the horses go! They'll do us no good now."

"Sir!"

It was his sergeant major. Gripping the bridle of Elliott's horse.

"Yes, Kennedy! You'll ride. If any man can make it—" Elliott laughed almost cheerfully. "I know you can!"

The troopers freed their horses now, squatting in the tall, frozen grass, taking their positions in a circle, guarding each other's backside. Elliott shook Kennedy's hand quickly, shoving him aboard his horse. The major slapped its flank, sending it on its way up the side of a snowy, tree-lined hill where two dozen warriors raced to head the pony soldier off.

"Ride, you sunuvabitch!" Elliott cried, fighting back the tears. "Ride!"

CHAPTER 8

Lieutenant Edward S. Godfrey had crossed the Washita with Custer at daybreak, leading his K Company into the village. His orders dictated that he not stop for any reason. His men were to drive on through the hostile camp and capture the enemy's most prized possessions—their herd.

Less than a mile from the village, where Custer's scouts supposed they would be, Godfrey located the ponies scattered among the frosty meadows. After he had detailed a platoon to drive the herd toward the village, Godfrey loped to the top of a hill overlooking the timbered countryside. From there he saw a handful of escaping Cheyenne scampering across the north side of the valley.

"Damn!" he muttered. "Must be a trail of some kind after the bastards ford the river."

Godfrey raced off the hill, gathering his command to pursue the fleeing Cheyenne. In the growing light of day Godfrey located the shallow river crossing. Without slowing he plunged his force across the Washita and up the icy north bank.

"Trail sure as hell shows a lot of use, sir," Sergeant Quinton O'Reilly commented.

"I aim to find out the reason," Godfrey replied.

Minutes later, they understood the beating the narrow trail had taken. In a large, wooded draw they bumped into a second pony herd. A herd bigger than any a young soldier could imagine.

"Pony boys," he muttered softly. Last night the Osage scouts had found a small fire on the north bank, a fire that pony herders used to warm themselves through a subfreezing night. Only hours ago he and a few officers had speculated why that herder fire was found on the north side of the river, while the village was found nestled on the south bank. Now it all made sense.

"Seems the hostiles figure their precious horseflesh might be that much safer if kept some distance from their village."

O'Reilly pointed. "Lookee there, Lieutenant!"

Across the meadow the Indians he had spotted fleeing on foot were leaping atop ponies. One by one or in pairs they darted off into the broken timber leading toward a series of rolling hills. Two of the riders drew up at the top of that first hill while the rest of their party disappeared over the rise. The pair circled their ponies.

Godfrey reined up, more than surprise crawling the pit of his gut. "Halt! Dammit, halt!" he bellowed over the jangle of saddle gear, yelling soldiers and whinnying horses.

"What the hell you stopping us for, Lieutenant?" O'Reilly demanded. "You ain't 'fraid of a lil' bunch of—"

"Best have yourself a look up there!" Godfrey pointed

uphill. "Two will get you ten they're signaling someone beyond that ridge yonder. Whoever's over there is being told an enemy is down here in pursuit."

"Why, who the Sam Hill's gonna be on the other side of that ridge, sir?" the sergeant asked.

"Hell, I don't know for sure, but I've got a suspicion."

He twisted in his McClellan. "Reload if necessary! File out at a gallop—sergeant on the point! Forward, ho!"

Near the top of the ridge, Godfrey and O'Reilly signaled a halt for the men charging up the slope on their heels.

"You keep the men here. I'll have a look over it myself," Godfrey said.

"But sir!" O'Reilly protested. "Why the hell should you expose yourself?"

"I damn well won't expose my command, Sergeant!"

"Yessir!"

Godfrey dug his heels into his mount, tearing up the rise. Peering over the crest, he stared at the winter landscape below. Across it raced the black, beetlelike forms of the Cheyenne escaping on horseback. As his eyes scanned the white plain below him, following the direction the escaping Cheyenne were taking—

What he saw would chill the blood of even the most fire-hardened veteran Indian fighter.

Below him the Washita oxbowed its way north for several miles through a heavily wooded river glen. Down in that valley stood a camp of several hundred lodges. Beyond that camp, another. Farther downstream, still another. Already more than a hundred warriors had spilled from those lodges, scurrying like maddened black ants across the snow.

For a few cold moments he watched the advance force

spur straight for him. Half-naked warriors ready for battle and screeching for blood.

Savagely he kicked his lathered mount downhill, hollering at O'Reilly. "We've stirred up a damned hornet's nest!"

Godfrey got his men headed back down the slope toward the meadow in a ragged retreat about the time the first warriors howled over the top of the rise on their heels. The sight of those screeching demons was all his men needed to understand what all the yelling was about as their lieutenant tore pell-mell down the hill toward them.

It was a footrace to the river.

Lieutenant Godfrey could not know that these warriors were Arapaho, Little Raven's band, several thousand strong. Riding fresh ponies, the Arapaho under War Chief Left Hand began to overtake the rear of Godfrey's disorderly retreat, intent on making things hot for that squad of soldiers forked atop played-out army mounts.

Godfrey realized his men didn't stand a prayer in a footrace. They'd have to turn and fight.

Yelling, he ordered his men to form a skirmish line. With pride the West Point graduate watched his men perform the drill by the book. As they dropped from the saddle, three troopers threw themselves down behind cover after handing their reins to a fourth soldier retreating to the rear with four horses.

"Make damned sure of a target before you fire!"

That command sent a return of solid, deadly fire smashing into the face of the attacking Arapaho. Though the first blast spilled only three warriors, it drove the rest retreating to a stand of oak, dragging their wounded. From that thick cover the Indians began to pour their heavy fire into the troopers.

More Arapaho poured over the top of the ridge. With every passing moment Godfrey's squad grew more outnumbered.

"Sergeant! If we're not careful, these goddamned savages will pin us down."

"By Gor, Lieutenant, not enough ammo left to make a fight of it."

"Pull back—in skirmish formation!"

"Damned right, sir!"

"Keep the men together. Hold your defensive perimeter as we retreat. Make it orderly!"

"We'll give 'em hell on the way!" O'Reilly dashed off, spreading the word among the troopers pinned down in the brush and timber.

Step by step they began their retreat. Those with the horses pulled back first. The others, low on ammunition, fired only enough to keep the warriors at bay. Close on the sunrise shadow of every trooper darted ghostly forms— Arapaho who continued to advance, made bolder as the soldiers retreated. Tree line by tree line, ridge by ridge, Godfrey urged his men back toward the Washita, fighting for every foot of ground they could hold until it came time to fall back a few more yards. At last they reached the heavy timber at the river's edge. With hoarse shouts of relief the soldiers plunged into the icy water, leading their horses with them.

And with their relief, something even more miraculous happened. The Arapaho fire slackened, faded, then died off. As quickly as they had been attacked, Godfrey's men found themselves alone.

From the moment the soldiers had reached the thick timber at the river's edge, they had heard heavy rifle fire coming from the rolling meadows across the Washita, southeast of the crossing. Godfrey couldn't be that sure, but from the sound of things he thought it could only be one outfit—Major Elliott's. The Arapaho had discovered Elliott while forcing Godfrey's retreat to the river.

"Into the came, men. Now!"

Out of the icy Washita, into the captured village. Godfrey felt he must find Custer, make his report on Elliott's predicament with the Arapaho. The major needed help in the worst way.

Custer held the village. Thompson's and Myers's troops held the ground to the south.

For those Cheyenne still alive in the village there existed little chance for escape from the blue-coated terror—only the riverbed of the icy Washita itself.

"When we reach the river," Clown whispered to the warriors at his side in the brush, "we can fight our way down to the high banks of frozen red clay. Protection there."

"We must chance it," Roll Down agreed.

Scabby said, "Pray we make it downstream to our Arapaho and Kiowa cousins."

Unknown to these retreating Cheyenne warriors was that Custer had figured the hostiles would seek just this avenue of escape. He had positioned Lieutenant Cooke's sharp-shooters among the bone-bare trees atop the northern bank. When the first of the women and children and old people burst from the lodges into the trees at the water's edge, Cooke ordered his hidden platoon of forty marksmen to open with a deadly fire.

Their first volleys left many dying and wounded in the icy water or scattered across the frozen bank. Down they crumpled, their blood seeping into the crusty red mud. A few riddled bodies washed into the main channel, to be carried downstream toward those camps the fleeing Cheyenne had sought to reach alive.

Scabby, Clown, and Roll Down witnessed every moment of the horror at the river. Their only choice was to retreat so they might battle these soldiers another day. This last fistful of warriors decided the time had come to fight their way to the river crossing.

Clown was the first to spot his old friend at the water's edge. Black Kettle's body lapped against the frozen shoreline, a captive now only of the river. Medicine Woman Later lay at arm's length from him.

Scabby and Roll Down crabbed along the muddy bank, firing behind them, holding some of Thompson's troopers at bay. Afraid of Beaver slipped over the edge of the frozen bank to join them. Only then did they notice Clown kneeling over the bodies sprawled in the water.

"You will see to them," Scabby ordered Clown. "We will protect you."

The three wheeled as one to provide cover for Clown while he tore the blue blanket from his back. Over the bank clambered more warriors retreating to the river crossing. Time to bid farewell to this battle. They would fight another.

Most knelt beside their dead chief for a heartbeat as they crawled by, touching Black Kettle before they plunged into the water, dodging a lead hail from the north bank.

Clown called out. Afraid of Beaver crabbed over to help pull the two old people from the river onto the frozen bank.

Bullets slapped the water around them, smacked the trees overhead.

Tears of anger coursed down Clown's cheeks. Wrapping the bodies in his blue blanket was the least he could do for the dead ones.

"No more will Black Kettle mourn the passing of the golden days of the *Tsistsistas*," Clown cried out. "The sun has begun to set on our people."

The fighting had taken less than twenty minutes.

In less time than it takes a Cheyenne to eat his breakfast, the Seventh Cavalry controlled the village, despite several pockets of heated resistance. Custer had his long-needed victory. He wasn't about to let it slip through his fingers. He ordered all resistance crushed, no matter the price.

While Clown and his companions fought their way yard by bloody yard from the river crossing, upstream another small group of warriors, women, and children was nowhere near as lucky. When they sought to escape north across the Washita, they found themselves instead trapped in a deep gully. Behind a lip of that narrow coulee eaten away by erosion each spring, the little band of Cheyenne took their final refuge, there to fight like cornered animals.

Cooke's platoon directed a brief but murderous fire into the gully.

Within minutes every warrior, woman, and child lay dead . . . save one Cheyenne mother and her tiny, light-skinned infant. Her nostrils stung with the stench of the offal of dead friends. She watched the warm steam puff from wounds riddling her family's bodies on the muddy embankment all about her.

A terrible fate waited her and the child should they be captured alive by the soldiers.

Walks Last struggled to her feet when the trooper fire died. By the back of the infant's doeskin gown she held the last of her children aloft.

"We go the way of our ancestors!" she screamed in defiance.

"Sarge! She's got a white baby!"

"White?"

"That ain't no white child. It's a Injun nit!"

"A *white* baby, I say!"

"She's gonna kill it! A knife! Watch that knife!"

With one swift motion, the Cheyenne mother yanked a knife from her belt and raked it across her child's belly. The infant jerked spastically as its entrails spilled onto the reddened snow.

Before her next breath, Walks Last vaulted backward, driven into the ravine by a hail of cavalry bullets.

"That was a *white* baby, I say," the trooper claimed, still shaken. "One of them captive babies."

"She ain't shoutin' no more." The sergeant felt last night's hardtack in the back of his throat. When he had gulped a few cold swallows of air, he ran in a crouch to the snowy ravine and cautiously stuck his rifle barrel over the edge. He placed the muzzle against the woman's head and fired one last, needless bullet into her brain.

Accompanied by Ben Clark and Little Beaver, young Jack Corbin wandered through camp.

He watched as the old Osage tracker grew more angry. With a private rage Little Beaver inspected every slashed, bullet-torn enemy body. Able to control his fury no longer,

Little Beaver fell upon one dead warrior, yanking the body over so that it lay face down in order to take the scalp. His skinning knife ready, Little Beaver found the scalp gone. Not taken by an Osage. Not taken by one of the white scouts. Jack could tell this kind of crude butchery could be done only by some young soldier hankering for a trophy of his first battle.

Little Beaver cursed, hacking the warrior's head from the body. Splattered in blood and gore, Little Beaver smashed the head into a pile of lodge poles until all he held at the end of his arm was a lumpy, bloody mass unrecognizable as anything human.

Unable to tear his eyes away, Corbin fought down the gall threatening to gag him. Little Beaver dropped the bloody head in the mud. Corbin tried but couldn't talk, stuttering, the question in his eyes.

The old Osage tracker understood. "My uncle's wife . . . killed by Cheyenne many winters ago. Far too long he waits to wear Cheyenne blood on his hands. I do this for him."

Corbin dared not speak. Unable to control his gagging any longer, his cold, empty stomach lurched.

In another part of the village Ben Clark, adjutant Myles Moylan, and Captain Frederick Benteen, after counting the dead, reported to their commander. Custer learned that a total of 103 men had been killed by his troopers.

"I don't know what you're thinking . . . but most of the dead aren't fighting men," Benteen whispered to Clark as Moylan reported to Custer.

"Fighting age for Indians means anything between eighteen and forty," Clark said. "You're right. I count only eleven warriors. And two of them were the old chiefs of this camp: Black Kettle and Little Rock."

"You recognize any others?"

"A few."

"This one?" Benteen asked.

"Blue Horse. Black Kettle's nephew. Why?"

"I had to shoot him."

Clark pointed out Cranky Man, White Bear, Little Heart, Red Bird and Tall Bear, Red Teeth and Bear Tongue as more of the warriors he had known. As for the ninety-two other bodies scattered through the village or in the snowy ravine west of camp . . .

"Squaws and kids. Goddamn," Clark whispered.

"General Custer!"

Clark and Benteen both turned at the sound of riders led by Lieutenant Edward Godfrey galloping up, showering snow as they slid to a halt.

"What is it, Lieutenant?" Custer asked. "You can plainly see I'm busy with a count of the plunder—"

Godfrey flushed as he leapt to the ground next to Custer. "We were driven across the river, close to where Major Elliott's men rode east out of camp while we were chasing—"

"What's the point of this?" Custer snapped.

"My unit was pressed hard, General. But, of a sudden, the hostiles pulled back. At the same time, we heard a shitload of rifle fire from the direction the major led his men."

"Meaning what?"

"It's my belief Major Elliott's trapped and needs our assistance."

"To the east, you say?"

Custer listened to the distant rifle fire.

He smiled. "Can't you see, Mr. Godfrey? All that racket down below is Elliott giving your savages a hot time of it."

"Beg pardon, General." Clark stepped up. "If you listen close you'll know that isn't Elliott's men."

"How the devil are you so certain?"

"Hear all those high-pitched cracks?"

"Yes, I do. That means Elliott's—"

"Got his ass in a jamb," Benteen interrupted. "The sharp cracks are Indian guns. Our Spencers have a deep roar."

Custer ignored his captain, turning to the scout. "Spit it out for me, Clark."

"This time I'm afraid you've jammed your saber into a real hornet's nest."

"Come now. We've secured the camp. It belongs to us!"

"The camp may belong to us, General. But we don't control these hills. Those warriors who chased your lieutenant here back to camp? I'm worried where those warriors came from."

"Escaped Cheyenne, I'd imagine."

"Begging pardon, General." Godfrey shouldered up between Custer and Clark. "What'll we do about Elliott's command?"

"I'm unconvinced the major is in any serious danger."

Godfrey said, "Sir, permission requested to lead a detachment and reconnoiter for the major."

"Request denied. You and your men will assist the clean-up of the enemy camp."

"General, I must protest—"

"Protest registered! Now, you'd best be moving your

men into the center of camp where I need your help, or you'll be placed on report!"

"General?" Benteen said.

"Same goes for you, Captain!"

Godfrey saluted and remounted, signaling his men to follow him into the village.

"I know just how he feels," Benteen whispered to Clark. "Ordered not to go to the aide of a fellow soldier."

"Aiyiiii!"

They wheeled at the screeching war cry. A warrior dashed toward Custer. Feathers tied from his scalp lock fluttered in the cold breeze as he yanked back on his pony's halter, sliding to a stop beside the startled soldier chief. Custer was unable to recognize the Indian's face. But he recalled the clothing.

An Osage warrior whose face was smeared with savage stripes of yellow, black, and bright vermilion.

He held up a dripping souvenir of battle for the cavalry commander to admire. Custer gulped. From the warrior's hand hung an entire Cheyenne scalp, still heavy with blood and gore.

"Aiyiyi!" Shaking the scalp and slinging blood on Custer, the warrior whirled and tore off through the village to share his joy with his kinsmen.

Custer turned as Romero, the Mexican scout, trotted up on horseback. The swarthy scout herded better than a hundred head of Cheyenne ponies before him, assisted by two captive squaws.

"Romero!"

"Looking for me, General?"

To the trained ear, Romero's accent sounded more like a Cheyenne speaking English than a Mexican speaking the gringo's tongue. He had grown to manhood with the Southern Cheyenne.

"What's all this?" Custer asked, irritated.

"Found these war ponies hidden off a ways." Romero winked, nodded toward the two women. "Spotted this pair about to hotfoot downriver. Never hurts having some help running ponies into camp."

"Good! I'm putting you in charge of the captives, Romero."

"You don't say?" He eyed one of the squaws.

"I'm doing this because you speak their language, know their culture," Custer continued. "Moylan will assign you a squad of men. See they have every woman and child rounded up and brought to the center of camp."

"'Bout time I get a job to my liking." Romero looked at one of the young squaws. She smiled, turning away.

"Be off with you, then," Custer said.

"Hep-hah!" The scout nudged his squaws and ponies into camp.

CHAPTER 9

B Y now the Osages had herded most of the shivering captives into the center of camp, using switches to whip slow-moving Cheyenne women and children toward the holding area. The trackers used this ages-old form of humiliation in order to show their prisoners no better treatment than they would give a camp dog.

Seeing the cruelty etched on the Osage trackers' faces, the women wailed quiet, discordant death songs. Their fear set the captive children screaming for their own lives. A chilling chorus slashed through the devastated camp.

Custer rode up. Romero figured the commander's curiosity had been aroused with the noisy keening of the women and children. The Mexican felt Custer's eyes on him as Romero moved among the captives, interrogating them. From time to time, he glanced over his shoulder at Custer. The soldier chief appeared to savor his triumph. Every trooper who approached saluted him. Even the blood-eyed Osage scouts had shown great respect for the soldier chief. Romero watched the prisoners' dark eyes.

None of this royal treatment of the soldier chief was lost on the captives.

"Romero!" Custer called out.

The stocky scout trotted up to the buckskin-clad soldier chief astride his dark horse, leaving behind the gray-haired woman he had been questioning.

As the younger sister of Black Kettle, Mahwissa had been one of the first to recognize how the soldiers and Osages alike treated this soldier chief who had devastated her sleeping village. Mahwissa whispered woman-talk to the young woman next to her.

"General?" Romero stared up into that light of new day behind Custer's curl-draped collar.

"I want you to tell me who that young woman is."

Romero scanned the prisoners. "Which one, General?" There was no mistaking that gleam in Custer's eyes.

"The young one, there with the red blanket. A smudge on her cheek."

"The real pretty one, eh? Not at all like them older, fatter ones, is she?"

"Just find out who she is for me."

"Aye, General."

Romero obediently approached the young girl. The other women near her fell back. Only Mahwissa stood her ground beside the girl.

"What is your name, little one?" the scout asked politely. She didn't reply. Then his tone grew cruel and insistent. "I asked your name!"

From the earliest days of his captivity among the Cheyenne, Romero had learned that a woman must not refuse to answer a man. Yet this haughty young one wouldn't speak.

Angered by her insolence, Romero grabbed the girl's

chin, lifting her face to look directly into his fiery eyes. She jerked her face from his hand. The scout brought his arm back to strike.

Mahwissa lunged to grab the scout's arm as Custer's voice split the air. *"Romero!"*

The interpreter turned slowly, his squinted eyes flashing contempt.

"Only her name," Custer said.

"Monaseetah."

Custer and Romero both turned jerked in surprise. Mahwissa's old voice had cracked the brittle tension between the two men.

The scout turned back to Custer. "Says the girl's name is Monaseetah."

Custer slid from Dandy's back. His eyes never left the girl. "What does that mean in Cheyenne?"

Romero chewed on that a moment the way he might chew on some gristle. "Close as I can figure, means 'The Young Grass That Shoots Up in Spring.'"

"A mouthful. I like Monaseetah better. And the old woman?"

Romero inquired. The old woman responded happily this time. She had read the pony chief like spring clouds.

"Her name is Mahwissa," Romero called back. "Claims to be a sister to old Black Kettle. She says he was killed in the fight."

"Sorry to hear that. I was hoping to have a chance to meet him. Bargain for captives, perhaps. Unfortunate."

"She says he died down at the river crossing. Trying to make a run for it."

"Live to fight another day, eh? So, with all that talk she's made, what else she tell you about herself?"

"She wasn't jabbering about herself. Busy telling me about the young one."

"Yes?"

"She's the daughter of Little Rock, who was second in power only to Black Kettle. Seems we rubbed 'em both out this morning."

"A chief's daughter, you say?"

The interpreter spoke again to Mahwissa.

"Girl's seventeen summers now," Romero reported to his commander. "The old gal says Monaseetah is married."

"Her husband run off with the rest?"

"Lucky one to get his tail over the hills when we rode down on this camp. But, there's something more." Romero shook his head.

"How's that?"

"Old woman says the young gal's father had to buy her back. Eleven ponies. And the usual plunder: blankets, robes, a kettle or two, maybe a gun . . . such truck as that. Seems she brought such a fancy price since she was a chief's daughter."

"Not married now, you say?"

Romero glanced at the young woman, seeing how she flicked her black-cherry eyes at Custer. Eyes showing no fear. Instead, Romero saw a welcome for the soldier chief written there. In Custer's eyes gleamed a great interest.

"By Cheyenne custom, Little Rock had no choice when Monaseetah's husband gave her back."

"Her mother here in the group?"

Romero shook his head. "Killed by Chivington's dirty work at Sand Creek. You like the gal, eh, General?"

Custer blinked. But his eyes hardened once more.

"Interested only in her sad story. The girl without any family. She just might be of some service to us yet."

"No good to a man except in the robes—"

"A guide! She knows this territory. I'll use her to translate."

"You're not serious, are you, General?" Romero didn't wait for an answer. "Shit—I forgot more about this country than she'll ever know. And you go try to make a translator out of her? She can't speak a word of English!"

"Perhaps she's bright. And can learn enough to act as an interpreter."

"General, all due respect—"

Soldiers' shouts and women's screaming whirled Custer about. One of the bloodied captives wrenched past a young private, rushing for the soldier chief. Romero grabbed her before she reached Custer.

"What the devil's this one babbling about, Romero?"

"This one . . . isn't Cheyenne!"

Custer studied the woman. "What, pray tell, is she?"

"She's Arapaho."

"What in God's name is she doing in a Cheyenne camp?"

"Been visiting relatives in Black Kettle's camp. But she didn't come from a long way off."

That stopped Custer cold. "Not far off?"

"A short ways down the river, better than nine hundred lodges all fixing to ride down on your soldiers here."

"Utter nonsense! It simply can't be. Those pony tracks led us right here. Question that other one, Romero . . . Black Kettle's sister. See if she has anything useful to tell. When you're done with her, I want one of the captured ponies selected for each of our prisoners. Woman and child. They'll ride back to Camp Supply."

"Few of 'em aren't able to sit the back of a horse, General. Figure we could pack 'em in the wagons?"

"Splendid idea. Put the little ones . . . and the wounded in some of Lieutenant Bell's wagons for the trip—"

"General!"

Custer turned as Captain Thompson lumbered up, two troopers behind him. Each soldier had a small white child clamped fiercely to his back.

"General," Thompson wheezed, "we found these two young'uns hiding in a lodge down a ways. Must be white captives. What we do with 'em, sir?"

"Why . . . find them some clean clothing. Then feed them a decent meal. We'll take them back to Camp Supply, then forward them to Fort Dodge on the Kansas frontier. Likely someone will soon be around to claim them."

"General Custer!" Romero shouted. "C'mon over here. The old woman . . . she wants to see you. Something to do with the young one in the red blanket."

"By all means—let's see what this squaw has to say."

Mahwissa trudged up to Custer, stopping toe to toe with the soldier chief as she began jabbering.

"Says the Cheyenne call you *Hiestzi* now, General."

"Which means?"

"*Yellow Hair.* Color of winter grass out here on the plains."

"What's this to do with the young one there?"

"Seems the girl's got no mother or father now—"

Custer shook his head. "Hurry with this. I've got pressing matters to attend to."

Mahwissa had watched confusion slowly cloud the soldier chief's face. Pushing Romero aside, the old woman laid Monaseetah's hand in Custer's buckskin glove, holding both hands out before her. When Custer tried to yank his hand away, Mahwissa refused to let go, raising her mystical chant to the heavens, eyes closed in prayer.

Intrigued, Custer stopped pulling to free his hand, gazing down into the young girl's deeply beautiful face. Her eyes never rose to his, but closed in prayerful reverence.

With each passing chorus of Mahwissa's singsong chant, Romero's smile widened.

Suspicions pricked, Custer demanded, "What's this all about?"

Mahwissa released the couple's hands.

"Prayer to the Everywhere Spirit, for his blessing."

"Blessing!"

"Mahwissa's married you to this young gal."

"By the gods, Romero! You bloody well know I'm married already!"

"I know. But the Cheyenne don't."

Custer seethed with rage. "You tell them I'm already married. I won't be made the butt of their pagan hoax!"

"Not a joke, General."

"Tell them I already have a—"

"No difference to them Cheyenne. Monaseetah won't fret being your left-hand wife."

"Left-hand?"

"You already got a white woman for your right hand."

Custer calmed a little. "A ceremonial thing, is it?" He drew himself up, puffing his chest. "Given the formality of this woman as a conquering hero."

"Not just a ceremony to the Cheyenne, General. A real wedding. The young one's your wife."

"My *wife!*"

Romero listened to the nearby troopers snicker at the shriek in Custer's voice.

"You're her husband, General—till you send her packing someday . . . back to the Cheyenne."

"I see. When we've completed this campaign, hmmm? A long, long winter gone from now."

"Hey, General!" Clark intruded, hurrying over. "Take a look yonder." He waited for Custer's attention to be ripped from Romero and the young captive. "Look up on the ridge . . . over there."

Custer followed the scout's arm. Half-naked bodies bristled atop the hills to the south, southeast. Warriors on horseback, gathered in small, angry knots glaring down at the plundered Cheyenne village.

"Some of the defeated warriors, Clark. The few fortunate enough to escape my net."

"You're wrong, Custer."

"Care to tell me who those warriors are?"

"They're not Cheyenne. More like Arapaho. Some Kiowa. I figure for the next few miles downriver lay more camps than any of us ever counted on stumbling into. More warriors than we could fight in one day."

"By Judas's judgment!" Custer laughed. "That bunch is up there to keep us from finishing our job."

"What job, General?"

"Destroying the plunder . . . these lodges. And we'll have to take care of the ponies."

"Dammit!" Clark's eyes flashed. "Best you listen to your scouts, General."

"You boys are becoming nervous old women!" Custer chuckled as he turned away. His laughter drew cackling from the soldiers assigned to guard the captives.

"General, you've gone and poked a huge nest of wasps here." Clark glared at Custer's broad back. "You hear me?"

The general leapt aboard Dandy without another word.

"General! Dammit! One day you're bound to have to listen to your scouts! One day real soon!"

Suddenly a detail of blue-tunics whipped their frenzied mounts down the north bank of the Washita and into the icy river without slowing. A handful of soldiers on foot momentarily turned on the bank to return fire into the timber before plunging into the water, terror written on every face.

As the dozen scrambled up on the bank, Moylan whirled up, arriving on the scene beside Custer, both men's horses sending sprays of muddy snow cascading over some of the drenched troopers.

"Sergeant Johnson!" Custer called to the lead man.

"Yessir, General!"

"What in blazes goes here?" Custer demanded.

"Had to abandon the coats and packs, sir."

"Abandon them?"

"We was overrun! They rode down on us—"

"Overrun by who?"

"Warriors, sir! Found out where you left us off to guard the packs and coats—"

"Precisely, Sergeant. Your detail was to guard that army property. Those of you who deserted your assigned posts could be subject to courts-martial for the loss of that government property . . . in addition to abandoning your posts."

A good portion of Sergeant Niles Johnson's untried recruits murmured between themselves, angry and fearful. Johnson alone understood that George Armstrong Custer had never once retreated in his entire career.

"I done it to save the men, sir. We was about to be overrun and I didn't want to sacrifice my command. I knowed reinforcements was here to help us—"

"Save the men? That's not your department to decide, Sergeant."

"Sir. Respectfully . . . it weren't coward—"

"Begging your pardon, General," Clark interrupted.

"What is it, Clark? More valuable advice?"

"Dammit, General! They ain't all Cheyenne breathing down our necks! This little camp ain't the only village in this valley. I savvy the sergeant's men were chased off by the same bunch of Arapaho that came boiling after Godfrey's blood. Maybe the same bunch jumped Major Elliott and his boys."

Custer stared into the trees across the Washita, then suddenly wheeled on his adjutant. "Moylan, have Benteen's men go with Hard Rope to bring the pony herd across the river."

Clark shook his head. "What in devil's dust do you want with them ponies?"

"Their destruction, Mr.—"

The unexpected roar of more carbine fire rumbled over the frightened shouts of panicked men from the north side of the river. The winter air split with Indian screeches and the sharp cracks of their rifles, just as Lieutenant James M. Bell bounced up from the riverbank on the hard seat of his army freight wagon.

Wide-eyed, Bell hunched over like a bent old woman, whipping his team straight down the sharp incline into the crossing, splashing headlong into the river. On his heels rattled the rest of the noisy freighters, each one driven by grim-lipped, bug-eyed soldiers, every teamster jockeying to be the next wagon into the ford. With the clattering wagons galloped a double fistful of the regiment's pack mules, b llering hell bent for election through the ranks with brass-lunged *scree-haws* and spraying rooster tails of icy water. One wagon lumbered over on its side to avoid a collision. It bounced a few yards across the rocky riverbottom on two wheels, then clattered back down on all four, the driver no longer clutching the reins but clinging to the seat instead.

First up the slope into the village, Bell wheeled his wagon hard as he brought his wild-eyed animals under control and leaned all his weight back into the brake. The iron-rimmed wheel protested as loud as any of the screeching warriors at that moment making their colorful appearance on the north bank.

"Lieutenant Bell!" Custer called.

"Reporting, sir!" The older officer trotted up to the general, sloughing red mud over his boots.

"Let's have your report," Custer yelled above the bursts of carbines fired at the screeching Indians on the north bank.

"A while back I heard some rifle fire coming from the direction where we left Johnson with the packs and coats, sir!" He was breathless. "Took my drivers to assist the sergeant's men."

"Go on."

"Figured we could help drive off the warriors. But there were more damned redskins around those packs and coats than I ever hope to see again in all my days!"

"Tell me all of it."

"Headed the wagons 'round the hills and raced down to the crossing near the horse herd."

"The horse herd?" Custer's voice rose an octave.

"Yessir."

Custer waved his arms wildly. "By God's back teeth, those red buggers won't get their bloody hands on their horses!" Custer turned back to Bell. "Lieutenant, you're to be commended for your quick and decisive action in the face of the enemy. I'll see to it you receive a regimental commendation when we return to Fort Hays. Didn't lose any men in the run?"

"No, sir. All present and accounted for."

"Splendid! Have one of your men find Captain Thompson. I'll have Thompson take a detachment back to find our property."

"Yessir!"

"Very good, soldier." Custer clapped his gloved hands together. "I've captured their village. Now it's time for me to crush the spirit of those who escaped my noose."

CHAPTER 10

WORK continued in earnest pulling Cheyenne property from the lodges. A count to record captured goods had started when shouts cracked the still air, floating across the river. Hard Rope and Romero led the first of the Cheyenne ponies into the Washita. The Seventh Cavalry had the Cheyenne herd.

Benteen's troops had driven off the warriors and recaptured the ponies. In a brief running fight, his two squads lost a few of the animals but took no casualties. Like milkweed down before a wind, the hostiles had scattered and fled. Then Hard Rope and Romero had showed Benteen's men how to get that herd moving south onto the river trail.

More than nine hundred prized Cheyenne stock splashed out of the Washita, up the south bank. The ponies burst into the captured village, nostrils flaring, tails held high, fresh dung dropped fragrant on the muddy snow.

"Drive them into the meadow southeast of camp!"

Custer shouted as Hard Rope cleared the top of the bank, riding among the herd leaders.

"Some good-looking stock there, General." Lieutenant Godfrey dismounted beside his commander.

"I'm going to let each troop commander select a pony of his own. Then we'll cut out a few to replace the mules we've lost. After that, Romero will see that the captives ride a pony back to Camp Supply."

"And the rest of 'em, General?"

Custer turned to Godfrey. "The rest are yours."

"Mine?"

"The herd is yours to destroy, Lieutenant."

A quarter-hour later the ponies grazed in the open meadow southeast of the Cheyenne camp. Custer called in the captain and lieutenant of each troop to make a selection after he gave his brother Tom first choice. When all officers had finished cutting out their chosen ponies, Custer signaled to his Cheyenne interpreter.

"Romero, Lieutenant Godfrey's men will assist you capturing mounts for the captives. When you have enough ponies for the women and children, take them back to camp. Tether them near Bell's wagons."

It didn't take long for the prisoners to show up at the edge of the herd, each woman carrying one or more rawhide or buffalo-hide hackamores rescued from the loot taken from the lodges for counting. What animals would be spared the coming slaughter were soon picketed near Lieutenant Bell's wagons.

"How do I handle this destruction for you, sir?" Godfrey's mouth had gone dry. He watched Custer climb into the saddle.

"Don't waste a lot of our limited ammunition, Lieutenant but your four companies will have to shoot each one."

Godfrey nodded, turning to set his men to their grisly task.

It wasn't long before the soldiers discovered that Indian ponies didn't take to the smell of white men. Again and again they darted away from the confining ring of soldiers, making it tough keeping the animals corralled when the firing began in earnest. Custer's slaughter was under way.

Overhead, the winter sun reached midsky, softening the snow into slush, turning the ground into red gumbo beneath the churning of so many hooves and boots. Some frustrated, cold troopers slipped and fell among the frightened, wild-eyed ponies, grumbling curses.

With every boom of a Springfield in that muddy meadow, another Cheyenne pony dropped, its blood seeping into the Washita snows. The whole process took three entire companies more than an hour and a half.

By the time the last frightened, snorting pony dropped to the slime of bloody snow, better than 875 animals lay dead. The earthy odor of their fresh dung was like a heady perfume on a cruel wind. Puffs of steam hissed from each bullet wound. The stench of blood and dung and death hung like an ache over the camp.

With an unbridled fury the milling warriors watched the soldiers loot the village.

Worse still, they could only watch as the slaughter of the prized Cheyenne herd took place. Ponies shot like so many white men's cattle in a butcher pen. The warriors were helpless to stop the destruction. Deep in each red breast beat an agony at so great a loss of the plains warrior's greatest possession.

Black Kettle's band was no more. The survivors would never recover from the loss of those hundreds of ponies that enabled them to continue their nomadic way of life. In less than one journey of the sun, this band of people had been rubbed from the breast of the Mother of All Things.

"We must go on making war against the pony soldiers—fighting for those who cannot!" Arapaho chief Left Hand cried out in fury and dismay atop a tree-lined hill.

"No!" shouted Skin-Head, another war chief, his shoulders slumping in defeat. "These soldiers have dealt us a vicious blow—we must learn from it. This is surely what happens when the pony soldiers hunt down the warriors who raid their white settlements. These pony soldiers slaughter old men, and call it battle. They capture women and children . . . if those helpless ones do not already lie dead in the snow beside the young men."

"Cowards speak of giving up! Are you a fool? Is your mind so small not to remember our fight in the snowy meadow this morning?" Left Hand asked. "Those pony soldiers fought with courage. They died like men. Not like these butchers!"

Skin-Head agreed. "Look what crimes the white man commits now. Not only has he killed our people, he hungers to destroy our way of life!"

"*Keeyiii!* Black Kettle could not fight an enemy who attacks and kills old people, who murders children and butchers ponies!"

"Next they will burn Cheyenne homes."

Soldiers stacked most of the captured Indian goods in huge piles or displayed the items on blankets and robes between the lodges.

Tom Custer stopped beside his brother and Lieutenant Moylan. Nearby, stood some of the civilian scouts and a handful of the Osage trackers.

"Look at that plunder, Autie. I'm taking some of these weapons back with me."

"Help yourself, brother. Just make it quick."

"What're you gonna do with the rest of it?"

"Not going to leave it behind, Tom. Better grab what you want. Moylan, fetch me Captain Myers."

Myers rode up minutes later, saluted. "General?"

"You'll be in charge of the destruction of the camp. Tear down the lodges, Captain . . . put them to the torch— poles and all."

"All the lodges. Yes, General. Any further instructions?"

"Myers, on second thought—"

"Yes, sir?"

"All the tepees . . . but that one." He pointed to a lodge but a few months old, sewn from cowhides taken in a late-summer hunt. "I want that one taken down and the cover folded for travel. Strap every lodge pole to one of Bell's wagons. Have Romero's squaws help your men dismantle and pack it for transport."

"A souvenir, sir?"

"You might say that."

"Want to save some robes, maybe some blankets to use in the lodge?"

"No. We'll burn everything here. Gad, the lice and vermin must be thick on it all."

Myers left to pass along instructions. Within minutes, the first of the Cheyenne lodges came down. Soldiers moved in and out of the tepees.

Captain George Yates approached the commander, shaking a long sheet of foolscap on which he had been scribbling his tallies with the nub of a pencil he moistened on the end of his tongue. The handsome blond hometown Monroe officer cleared his throat nervously before beginning his report, his breath steaming like a halo round his bearded face. "We count two thousand one hundred and eighty-five blankets, five hundred seventy-three buffalo robes, and another three hundred sixty untanned hides. In addition, we captured two hundred forty-one saddles along with numerous lariats, bridles, and other tack used by the hostiles."

"What of the Cheyenne weapons?" Tom Custer asked.

"Better than a hundred hatchets of various sizes. Along with thirty-five revolvers and forty-seven rifles. As near as we can estimate, we also captured two hundred fifty pounds of lead and better than five hundred thirty-five pounds of gunpowder. Some ninety bullet molds, along with over four thousand arrows and arrowheads, seventy-five spears, thirty-five bows and quivers, plus a dozen rawhide shields."

The commander turned to his scouts. His bright blue eyes found the Mexican. "This camp could have taken care of itself had we failed to surprise them—wouldn't you say, Romero?"

"I suppose if you gave 'em the chance . . . might've been a different story to tell by the end of the day."

"Go on, George. What else?" Custer prompted.

"Better than three hundred pounds of Indian tobacco was seized, sir. Along with that, we didn't even try counting what must be thousands of pounds of dried buffalo meat they put up for the winter."

"No need to weigh it."

"Yes, sir," Yates replied, eyes dropping to his list once

more as it fluttered in a gusty breeze pungent with the acrid odors of smoke and burnt powder, heady with horse dung and aromatic red clay turning to muddy slop under a winter sun. "The next discovery is interesting, General. We captured some meal flour and other bags of provisions, all in burlap stamped 'Department of the Interior.'"

"So this tribe was at the Medicine Lodge treaty conference last year."

"I'd bet on it," Romero replied.

Yates continued. "Nearly all the Cheyenne's clothing is in our possession. Those who escaped have only what they carried on their backs."

"That's the way I planned it. Dawn's the time to catch 'em napping, don't you see? Does that conclude your report?"

"Yes, General."

"Very good. Then go to Myers with my suggestion that he put all this captured matériel on those piles he's making of the lodges. I suggest he pour some of the Cheyenne gunpowder over the lot of it. Have him see me when he's ready to set it afire."

The tall, husky Yates saluted and was gone.

In less than half an hour Custer's chosen lodge was secured in a wagon for the return trip. Meanwhile, the remaining tepees had been gathered in mountains of buffalo robes and tanned hides, blankets and weapons, clothing and food. Everything was to be destroyed, save for those few ponies the prisoners would ride while leaving behind their winter home along the Washita.

"Yates told me you wanted to see me," Myers said when he arrived.

Custer saluted the captain. "Torch it all!"

Myers signaled his men. They tossed their flaming brands on each mountain of captured goods. The powder caught and flared. Some exploded, spraying showers of brilliant sparks over the scattering troopers. With the goading of a freshening breeze, the mountains burned like bright funeral pyres. The shivering troopers inched as close as they dared to warm their fronts while their backsides froze in a brutal wind. The troopers turned around and around, reveling in the warmth of the dancing flames. Over the trees and up the slopes of snow-whitened hills climbed a black, oily haze. Dark clouds reeking of destruction and death sent the warriors on the surrounding hillsides to keening in grief or angry fury.

Tom turned to see his brother staring at the hilltops bristling with enemy warriors. Custer's azure eyes were as merry as ever.

"You know those red bastards are vowing revenge on your Seventh Cavalry, don't you, Autie?"

"Yes, Tom. Promising someday to reverse the fortunes of war. Cursing us—that come a day they'll destroy the pony soldiers the way we've destroyed Black Kettle's band."

"Don't laugh too hard, General." Ben Clark stepped up to the Custer brothers. "You ain't begun to wipe out the Cheyenne nation. Curse the man who can't see there's a lot of fight left in those warriors. Pity the man who thinks he's got 'em whipped."

A winter sun raced into the western hills faster than a mule with the smell of a home stall strong in its nostrils. Securing the village had burned more time than Custer had planned. His count and destruction of the captured goods had taken far too long. Tom watched his brother grow angrier as winter's light drained from the day.

"Look around you, Tom. Not one of these men realizes the danger in our march back to Camp Supply. We're hampered now not only by our own wounded, but we're dragging along better than fifty prisoners."

"We'll get out of this valley without getting jumped. You've done it before, Autie. Just have to make a night march of it."

"Even doing that, I'm troubled we'll draw attention to our supply train near the Antelope Hills. If we march in that direction, the hostiles might figure where we're headed. And that could spell a sentence of death for the men guarding the train. The warriors could reach them on fresh ponies faster than we'll be able to march."

"Or set up an ambush for the rest of us along the way," Tom said. "Tough choice. I know how it's eating at you, Autie. You grip this victory in your hand—something to redeem you before your superiors, to show them the injustice of that court-martial. But that year away from the regiment was really nothing more than an annoyance diverting you from your goal—"

"That's it, Tom! A stroke of genius!"

"What'd I say?"

"We'll do the same with the hostiles! And at night, as you suggested. We'll draw them away from our supply caravan. The way a sage hen draws the weasel from her nest."

"It can work, Autie!"

"Tom, it's got to work." He whirled. "Lieutenant Moylan! Prepare the men to move out in columns of two. I

want the regimental band in front, right behind our scouts.
Post all guidons. Have them snapping, Lieutenant."

"A march . . . now, sir?" the adjutant inquired, glancing at the sun sinking behind the hills.

"Why, Mr. Moylan, we're going to march on down the
Washita and chase the rest of these beggars right out of the
country!"

Within a matter of minutes, the Seventh Cavalry had
mounted, strapped in, and tuned up. Long after Custer's
"Forward, ho!" had echoed back from the hills, troopers
shivered with the falling temperature. Nauseous from the
hard, icy knots in their shrunken bellies, some grumbled.

"Hey, Sarge! What the divil is Ol' Iron Pants trying to
do?"

"What'r you griping 'bout, Dooley?"

"Thought we was marching back to Camp Supply. But
me got the feeling we're nosing round for more Injuns!"

"Just shuddup and keep that nose of yours in the wind,
soldier!"

"Will you listen to that, Dooley?" Private Miller said.
"Custer's band is playing your song! 'Ain't I Glad To Get
Out Of The Wilderness'!"

"Didn't you hear the sarge up there?" Dooley snarled.
"Shuddup!"

Miller shut his mouth. But that didn't stop him from
wondering why Custer wanted the regiment to make such
a grand and noisy spectacle of their march. *Don't seem like
smart soldiering,* he brooded, *warning the Injins before we can
sneak up on 'em.*

But veterans like Sergeant Mathey knew exactly what
Custer had up his sleeve.

★   ★   ★

"They cross the river!" Sees Red shouted as he skidded to a stop before his Kiowa chief.

"Coming our way?" Satanta asked.

"They blow their horns in the falling light."

"The soldiers come to destroy our villages now," Lone Wolf added sadly.

"It is good the women and old ones have already started on the trail to Hazen's post, my friend," Satanta replied.

"Soldiers come. Attack all the villages. I will see that all our people are gone, our campsites bare." Sees Red wheeled about and was gone.

"This soldier chief attacks at night," Satanta murmured. "Is he a man? Perhaps this soldier chief has no soul."

No mistake about it; the warriors watched the pony soldiers cross the river, plunging into the same hills where Godfrey had been turned back by the Arapaho.

"He is coming! The pony soldiers intend to attack all our villages!"

The once bristling hilltops shed themselves of all but a handful of feathered warriors, the rest already gone to warn their villages of the army's approach. Warriors prepared to fight, protecting their women and children and old ones while the lodges came down and the camps retreated into the wilderness.

As the smoked buffalo hides fell, leaving naked lodge poles behind, the frantic women herded travois ponies, children, and dogs after the old people scurrying into the fading winter twilight.

Pony soldiers in blue and buffalo fur come! Already they have laid waste the Cheyenne camp of Black Kettle!

Aieeee!

It seems the soldier chief is a madman, leading white soldiers who won't even halt for the coming night when a man's soul is in such horrible danger should he be killed after dark!

"Are these soldiers devils?" Skin-Head asked of Left Hand.

"Truly, the soldier chief himself has no soul."

CHAPTER 11

Near midafternoon on the thirtieth, Moses Milner spotted a band of horsemen emerging from the gray oak timber a mile below. Barely two days ago, Custer had dispatched Milner and Jack Corbin to ride north to Camp Supply with word on their victory for General Sheridan. Now, on their way back to rejoin Custer's column, it appeared their return might be in doubt.

"We got company, boy," Milner barked.

"I see 'em," Corbin replied. "And lookee yonder."

"Brownskins. Damn!"

A handful of feathered warriors burst from the timber a mile to their left.

"More visitors over 'long the creek." Corbin pointed to the right.

"Hostiles?" asked Ed Guerrier, a courier sent by Sheridan to ride back to Custer's Seventh Cavalry with Milner and Corbin.

"Time we made ourselves scarce, fellas," Joe said.

"Don't have to tell me twice!" Guerrier replied.

Corbin was first into the trees. He reined up and slid from his horse before it completely stopped. "We almost made it, California Joe."

Milner spit mud into the snow. "Them red niggers'll pay dear to raise this ol' scalp, they will."

Guerrier joined the pair after tying their horses back in the darkened timber. "I count three bands of 'em."

"They're tracking somebody," Corbin said.

"Can't figure why we ain't run onto the general and his troops by now," Milner hissed. "It don't fit that we run across this war party first."

"Lookit that, Joe," Guerrier said.

"Well, I'll be a mother's son," Milner whispered.

Down below in the meadow the central party of horsemen had reined up. One of the figures held something to his face for some time. Meanwhile, the handful of Indian horsemen rode in from the left flank. A moment later riders came loping in from the right.

"If that don't beat all!" Milner said, scrambling to his feet. "It's Custer his own self. C'mon, Ed. We'll introduce you to the boy."

Back in the saddle, the trio cleared the timber. Once free of the trees, Milner spurred Maude to a gallop, tearing his old sombrero from his shaggy head. Back and forth he waved it at the end of his outstretched arm. "Whooooop! Hep-hawwww, ol' gal," he shouted to the mule.

Custer bounded ahead of his columns alone, his arm held high above his buffalo cap. He reined up and waited once he recognized Milner's wild cheers. All three scouts rode up abreast, bringing their army mounts to a snow-spray halt a few feet in front of Custer.

"Afternoon, General!" Corbin sang out every bit like a boy just returned from a romp in the hills.

"General!" Milner saluted in his own lazy way, then spit a brown stream of tobacco juice to the snow. "Mighty glad to see it's you and your soldier boys."

"Sorry to disappoint you, Joe—you think we're a war party out to relieve you of your sizable scalp?"

"I counted on you being soldiers when I first got my eyes fixed on you until I saw two Injuns in your squad. Forgot about all them Osages come along. Damn—General! I'm powerful glad to see your face again!"

Custer turned to Guerrier. "I suppose you riding in with these filthy renegades bodes good news, eh?"

"Can't keep a thing from you, can we, General Custer?"

"I take it you fellas got to Camp Supply and General Sheridan with my report?" Custer inquired.

"In the flesh!" Milner grinned.

"You were right again, Joe. I wanted to send a whole squad with you boys." Custer smiled.

"A fancy notion that'd been, General. Always a heap better to have just two for the journey. More can be done by a lot of dodging and running than we can do by fighting."

"Two sprightly men can do far better than twenty, Mr. Milner. I congratulate you both!"

Milner beamed proud as a boy given a shiny penny. "Why, I was some happy to see Little Phil my own self! He was monstrous glad to see me back so soon too. Say, did I ever tell you I used to know the general when he was a second—or was it a third?—lieutenant? Post quartermaster back to Yakima country in Oregon years ago?"

"Sheridan a lieutenant? That was before my time! Well, Jack—what's word from the general?"

"He turned us near right around, riding south with a packet of orders, dispatches, and letters for the men. Sheridan was damned happy to hear your fight was a success. Spent near four hours stomping up and down, in and out of his tent. Reading your report over again. Asking us questions about the Indians."

Milner jabbed a hand half-covered with a threadbare mitten inside the flap of his greasy mackinaw coat to bring forth a leather pouch. From it he pulled a piece of foolscap folded and sealed with a dollop of blue wax. Nudging his old mule forward two steps, Milner handed it over to Custer.

The soldier ripped open the notice, his eyes flying over the familiar Sheridan scrawl. The general's words to his field commander were brief and to the point, the way Sheridan was in person.

"Splendid!" Custer cheered. "Lieutenant Moylan, have the officers form the troops for review in that meadow ahead."

"Yes, sir!"

Custer watched his adjutant gallop away, heading back along the columns. Not until the companies began marching into the wide meadow did he turn once more to the three scouts.

"How far are we from Camp Supply?"

"You'll be there by this time tomorrow," Corbin answered.

Custer slapped his right thigh. "By glory, back home with our victory, gentlemen! What say we share this good news with the regiment?"

Custer nudged Dandy into a showy hand gallop as he tore into the meadow where the troops had gathered for review. With Milner, Corbin, and Guerrier at his side, wagons behind him facing rows of weary soldiers, and the Osage trackers scattered around the captives, Custer began his speech.

"I have most welcome news for the gallant and courageous men of the Seventh Cavalry: the finest cavalry the world has ever known!"

He waited a moment as the cheers and shouts died among the ranks. A hard knot of sentiment clotted in his throat.

"Moments ago we received word from General Philip H. Sheridan, who most eagerly awaits our arrival at Camp Supply. Almost as much as you look forward to getting there yourselves!"

Another spontaneous cheer mingled with hearty laughter. The tension of a cold march and bloody campaign drained at last from weary shoulders.

"In this dispatch handed me moments ago"—he waved the sheet high in the breeze—"General Sheridan sends his highest compliments and praise to the officers and men who comprise the finest horse soldiers on the face of this—or any other—continent!

"The General says:

> "'The Battle of the Washita River is the most complete and successful of all our private battles, and was fought in such unfavorable weather and circumstances as to reflect the highest credit on yourself and regiment.
>
> "'The energy and rapidity shown during one of the heaviest snowstorms that has visited this section of the country, with the temperature below the freezing point, and the gallantry and bravery displayed, resulting in such signal success, reflect the highest credit upon both the officers and men of the Seventh Cavalry; and Major-General command-

ing, while regretting the loss of such gallant officers as Major Elliott and Captain Hamilton, who fell while gallantly leading their men, desires to express his thanks to the officers and men engaged in the Battle of the Washita, and his special congratulations are tendered to their distinguished commander, Brevet Major-General George A. Custer, for the efficient and gallant services rendered, which have characterized the opening of the campaign against hostile Indians south of the Arkansas.' "

Upon hearing the congratulations of the highest-ranking officer in the whole of the department, lusty cheers rang through the winter-cloaked meadow.

"He goes on!" Custer shouted above the clamor.

" 'For your bravery in the face of hostile fire, for your steadfastness in the face of bitter cold and conditions that deprived you of warmth and food for much of your campaign, I express my eternal gratitude to you, your officers, and your men. What is more, my dear friend Custer, you will have the eternal and benevolent gratitude of those very citizens of the frontier who are bringing the blessings of civilization to this wilderness, order out of chaos. In summary, be assured my superiors, both Generals Grant and Sherman, have been apprised of the efficient and gallant services rendered by the Seventh Cavalry, U.S. Army, under the capable command of the late brevet Major-General of the Army of the Potomac, your most able Lt. Col. George A. Custer.

By command of LIEUTENANT-GENERAL
PHILIP H. SHERIDAN'

"Scouts Milner and Corbin have rejoined our command. Besides some long-overdue letters from Fort Hays, they have some exciting news, gentlemen! They tell me this will be the last night you sleep on the trail. Tomorrow night . . . we'll be quartered at Camp Supply!"

That singular bit of news caused cheering that drove masses of blackbirds flapping from off their roosts in the skeletal trees. At the height of the clamor, Custer signaled Moylan and his standard bearer to follow as he whirled his dark stallion about, leading his columns from the snowy meadow.

Mahwissa beamed maternally at Monaseetah. The young Cheyenne princess fluttered her eyes, embarrassed that she had been caught gazing hypnotically at the soldier chief.

"*Hiestzi* is brave. A leader of strong men. One who can exhort and inspire." All this Mahwissa said to the young woman beside her.

"And he will make a fine husband for you. Many fine warrior sons will spring from the fire in his loins, Monaseetah."

Romero rode behind them, herding the captives like cattle, prodding and swearing at the prisoners in their own Cheyenne tongue, whipping the rumps of the Indian ponies that failed to move quickly enough to suit him.

"My first child comes soon," Monaseetah whispered. "From that dog of a husband I was made to marry in the shortgrass time." Monaseetah pouted, her head hung in shame.

"You are heavy with child?" Mahwissa asked, surprised.

"It comes soon."

"I did not know this when I married you to the soldier chief."

"I kept it a secret after my father ransomed me back from the bad husband."

"But you do not show!" The old woman's eyes narrowed on Monaseetah's belly, well hidden beneath the folds of her red blanket.

"A curse of the young, Mahwissa."

"Your young body won't put on much fat in the way the cow buffalo readies for her calf."

"For three months now the land sleeps beneath the cold mantle of winter. I hide myself beneath warm robes and blankets."

"I see, young one." Mahwissa gazed into the distance.

"He will not be ashamed of me?" Monaseetah pleaded in a little-girl voice ringing with fear and loss. "Will *Hiestzi* throw me away when he finds I carry another man's child?"

Mahwissa studied the course of Wolf Creek. "I do not think he will throw you away, little one. However, the white man is a strange animal for me to sort out. It will take many winters perhaps for you to learn about him. But I have seen how this soldier chief studies you with his eyes of blue fire. The yellow-haired one cannot hide his heat for you."

"I think I want him to want me. Never before have I needed a man."

"Little one, for two summers now you live in the body of a woman—a body that drives the young men wild with burning for you. Yet until this very moment you were but a little girl. Perhaps you now become a woman in full."

"Why then does my heart give me such pain in missing him, or when I want him to look at me with those egg-blue eyes that tell me he wants me too? Why is there so much pain if being a woman is to bring me so much pleasure?"

"Ah, young one! Yes, there is real pain, much hurt and anguish to be suffered. I am afraid you will suffer that anguish all too soon in your young life." She looked away, letting her moist eyes clear.

"There are men you might fall in love with," Mahwissa continued, "men who will bring you so much more pleasure and happiness than sadness. I pray the soldier chief you give your heart to is not one who will leave a scar upon it."

"A scar?"

"Yes, little one. On your heart a scar borne of sadness and despair, an empty ache that can never be filled. The more you feed that kind of love, little one . . . the more empty you become."

By late that afternoon of the last day of November, breezes from the south blew a warm, welcoming breath at the column's back. That night the troopers slept in their creekside camp, relishing an end to weeks of flesh-numbing cold.

Little snow remained to chill the wild land with the coming of the next morning's sun, and what few drifts had escaped the chinooks warm breezes hid themselves in the shadows and shade of gullies and draws. Throughout the day Custer's troops enjoyed welcome winter sun caressing their backs with warm promise. Spirits climbed; the men knew they drew close to Camp Supply. Yet amid the joy of a triumphant return was found a hardened, joyless handful who remained angry at the fate of Elliott's men, abandoned in the valley of the Washita by their regimental commander. For now, the grumbling remained subdued. For now . . .

No man could be as exuberant with this triumph as the commander of the Seventh Cavalry himself. Again and again he considered the approach of his twenty-ninth birthday, barely four days away. What a glorious gift this campaign had proven to be—once and for all healing every last caustic wound done him at the hands of both detractors and superiors alike who had doubted his abilities, both as a commander of men and as an Indian fighter.

How he yearned for Libbie to be with him on his birthday. . . .

Inside—deep and unsettling—reeled something foreign. It caused him to twist in his saddle and gaze behind him at that long line of bundled troopers snaking around the brow of a hill. Back there, somewhere near the end of the procession, marched the prisoners. He squinted his eyes, unable to catch even a brief glimpse of the captives.

Why in God's name am I doing this to myself? Something's overwhelming me.

Once only had he lost control. "That awful, drunken scene played out in front of Judge Bacon's house in Monroe many years ago," he whispered to himself. "No, perhaps I allowed myself too many liberties with that Lyon woman down in Texas just after the war while Libbie visited Monroe—Mrs. Farnham Lyon. And the next year, that young wife of a fellow officer on Sheridan's staff, during that stopover in St. Louis, while Libbie and I made our way to the regiment's first home at Fort Riley. Twice already . . . would that there be no more."

Over and over Custer reran through his mind those lines he had penned in his journal a short day and a half after the battle, scratching out words of passion, unable still to escape a haunting vision of those black-cherry eyes and wind-rouged cheeks burnished rose beneath a winter sun as she flicked her quick, inviting smile up at him.

> Monaseetah is exceedingly comely . . . her well-shaped head was crowned with a luxuriant growth of the most beautiful silken tresses, rivaling in color the blackness of the raven and extending when allowed to fall loosely over her shoulders, to below her waist.

Custer reveled in the warm breeze at his neck. "I must keep that journal safe from prying eyes that might by accident or design seek to read between those lines. Surely any man reading my thoughts would discover I care all too much already. Pray, how could I ever claim innocence?"

Custer was startled by a voice.

"General?"

The commander turned, finding Moylan at his side.

"For a moment there I figured you nodded off with your eyes open . . . as you often do. Seems you were gone somewhere in a dream perhaps."

"What is it, Lieutenant?"

"Corbin's riding in."

Custer glanced at the bone-yellow sun nailed against a pale, winter-blue sky. Late morning.

"Maybe he's spotted camp, Lieutenant."

Custer kept his men at a march as the scout charged up at a full gallop. Wheeling his mount in a knee-sliding circle, Corbin brought the snorting, sidestepping animal alongside the Seventh's commander.

"Quite a show, Jack."

"I been on into camp. They're waiting for you."

"Much farther?"

"Ain't but a stone's throw now. Less than two miles. They got every man-jack called out—seems Sheridan fixes to welcome you home in real style."

"He does, eh? Then I suppose there isn't a better spot than here and no better time than the present to shape up our columns. Moylan, pass the word that we'll halt on that bench up ahead. I want the men prepared for review before General Sheridan!"

"Hurry, goddammit, Perkins! You're gonna miss the best show of your miserable life!"

"I'm coming, Hinkle. Damned boots rubbed a blister on the back of my heel. Governor Crawford showed no mercy on us Kansas boys."

"Lucky any of us survived that snowstorm. C'mon! I hear this General Custer puts on a show no man can forget! Pick up your feet. I don't wanna miss a minute of his ride-through. Custer's the man who not only whipped J.E.B. Stuart's 'Invincibles' and turned the tide at Gettysburg—but he's the one who forced ol' Robert E. Lee himself to throw in the towel at Appomattox!"

Beneath a glorious winter sun warming this first day of December, the air more vibrant than it had been for weeks, General Philip H. Sheridan formed the men to review Custer's regiment. Flanked by his officer staff and joined by every infantryman not otherwise on duty in camp, along with the Nineteenth Kansas Volunteers who had failed to march through the snows of Indian Territory in time to join with the Seventh Cavalry before the attack on Black Kettle's camp, Sheridan awaited his dashing young protégé.

"Custer won't dare disappoint any audience, Perkins," Hinkle said. "Someday you'll tell all your grandchildren about this day—seeing the Boy General hisself marching home in victory after his Seventh Cavalry crushed the Cheyenne nation!"

First into view rode the Osage trackers, led by Little Beaver, the aging, stoic warrior who had painted himself for this grand march. Right behind him pranced Hard Rope and the younger trackers, each singing his personal war chant—songs of victory and glory, accompanied by frequent whoops of joy punctuated by firing their army-issued rifles into the air.

Up and down the column galloped a young warrior named Trotter who brandished aloft the long scalp of a Cheyenne he flaunted for all to see—a scalp he bragged belonged to none other than Chief Black Kettle himself. Other Osage trackers waved captured lances they had decorated with dangling, blood-encrusted Cheyenne scalps. Some beat on small hand drums while others shook their bows and rawhide shields, all astride their prancing mounts, every mane and tail resplendent with red and blue, green and white strips cut from captured Cheyenne blankets.

Directly behind these joyful warriors who had just secured a victory over a longtime enemy rode Lieutenant Silas Pepoon's civilian scouts. Ben Clark and Jack Corbin rode in tandem, Moses Milner and courier Ed Guerrier on their heels. Only Milner had refused to clean up for Custer's show. His well-matted beard still bore bits of fluff and lint, scraps of many a meal. On his head the long-tangled hair was in much the same disheveled condition, and everything about him remained coated with a well-cured patina of red dirt and mud.

Right behind the scouts marched the regimental band,

piping that airy, raucous theme song of the Seventh Cavalry, "GarryOwen":

> Let Bacchus's sons be not dismayed,
> But join with me each jovial blade;
> Come booze and sing, and lend your aid
> To help me with the Chorus.

> In place of Spa we'll drink brown ale,
> And pay no reckoning on the nail,
> No man for debt shall go to jail
> From GarryOwen in glory!
> No man for debt shall go to jail
> From GarryOwen in glory!

> We are the boys that take delight in
> Smashing the Limerick lights when lighting,
> Through the streets like sporters fighting,
> And tearing all before us.

Let no man mistake that jaunty Irish quickstep now firmly identified with the gallant Seventh Cavalry and its dashing young commander. A hundred years before, this regimental march was named for "Garry Owen," Gaelic for Owen's Garden, a suburb of Limerick, Ireland, which throughout the eighteenth century was noted for its rowdy melees of drunken soldiers. While the merry tune had been associated with such groups as the Queen's Fifth Royal Lancers, it was later adopted by some units of the Union Army of the Potomac during the Civil War.

But by 1868 this rousing, heart-pounding Irish melody

firmly belonged to one regiment and one regiment only—the Seventh Cavalry.

To the stirring call of trumpets, Custer pranced into view astride Dandy, curried and gleaming for the triumphant entry. Custer's buckskin leggings had been brushed clean for the occasion, their long fringe fluttering on the breeze, topped by a hip-length sack coat trimmed with fur collar and cuffs. He had combed his red-blond beard, letting his shoulder-length curls stream over his collar. Atop his head sat a pillbox otter cap.

"What a figure he cuts, Hinkle!"

"I'd say! See how firmly he's in control of that sidestepping stallion, waving to spectators like they was paying him court!"

"That they are, Hinkle!"

Directly behind Custer plodded the captives. He had expressly wanted the Cheyenne to witness the grand spectacle first-hand, to experience how the soldiers revered their Boy General. Scores of widows and orphans trudged past Sheridan, their dark eyes averted, many hiding their faces. They feared torture and death now that they had come to the pony soldier camp. Some older women keened their death songs.

The enlisted men of the Seventh Cavalry followed the prisoners, while behind them rumbled the wagons of Lieutenant Bell's quartermaster corps. In some of the slat-beds rode the wide-eyed and fearful wounded captives. In another lay Custer's resplendent Cheyenne lodge. As the last wagons rattled into view, Custer pranced around in a tight circle, then nudged Dandy forward with his golden spurs.

"General Sheridan!" Custer called out, saluting.

"Custer, my friend!" Sheridan saluted, then presented a bare hand to the young officer. "How glad I am to see you."

"No more happy than I!"

"You've done it, by damn! Showed 'em all, haven't you?"

"I hope now to get on with my career—what needs doing here on the plains."

"There's not a goddamned thing to stop us now, Custer. You've seen to that with this stunning victory. Like the Shenandoah, you haven't let me down!"

"Thank you, sir."

"Come, Armstrong. We'll have some refreshments at my headquarters. You can tell me all there is to tell of routing these bloodthirsty savages!"

"It'd be my honor. I'll return in a moment after I've passed the orders for encampment."

"Dismissed!" Sheridan saluted again, that Irish smile bright within his dark beard.

Custer answered the salute, then brought Dandy around smartly with the gold spurs.

"I won't dare miss our victory celebration, sir!"

BOOK II

SWEETWATER

CHAPTER 12

"CLARK! Glad I found you!"

Ben Clark turned to see Captain Frederick W. Benteen headed his way. "Benteen, isn't it?"

"Right!" The young, bearded officer presented his hand. "Didn't know you'd remember me from the Washita."

"Yeah, I remember," he replied, suspicions aroused. He went back to sharpening the knife on a whetstone. "What can I do for you?"

Benteen settled on a stump near the scout. "I figured you'd be the man for what I had in mind. Got a good head on your shoulders—a memory as sharp as that blade you're honing."

"Sounds like I'm the family turkey getting fattened for the holiday feast, Captain. You said you'd found me a'purpose for something. Care to spit it out and stop knocking 'round in the brush so much?"

"I've something of great import to ask of you, Ben," the young captain began with a rush. His eyes slid this way, then that. "I really think it best we talk somewhere a little more private. This spot's a bit too public."

Clark measured the man. "So tell me, why something private?"

"Too many ears in an army camp. How quickly I learned that during the Rebellion down south."

"You were regular army?"

"Breveted a lieutenant colonel. Proud of every battle and the action of those men assigned to me." Benteen hunched forward to whisper. "That's precisely the reason I find myself talking with you."

"I was a Jayhawker myself. Odd to think a Missouri boy like you'd go over to the Union cause. Me, I had a Cheyenne wife at the time. Did what I could for the Union army, what was a decent employer—but I get the feeling none of that's what you've come to hear."

Benteen warily cast his eyes around. "I've watched you and have come to believe you're a man to trust. I want you to keep what we say here in confidence. Can I trust you, Ben?"

For the first time Clark really studied Benteen. "I suppose if it's all that serious, Captain—" he spit a brown stream from the side of his cheek, "then it's something worth the telling, ain't it?"

"More of a question, Ben." Benteen slid a little closer. "What do you know about Major Joel Elliott's men in Black Kettle's camp on the morning of the battle? Where they were, what they were doing, any of it."

"Suppose I'd know about as much as the next man." Clark knit his brow, scowling at Benteen.

"Did you know of Custer's refusal to send Elliott any aid when he first learned of the major's predicament?"

"Whoa! Hold on a goddamned minute! Just what the Katy hell are you after here, Captain?"

"Looking for corroboration for the many reports concerning Custer's refusal to offer Elliott assistance. Not only that, but Custer failed to determine what became of Elliott's squad later in the day." He began counting off on his rough, callused fingers. "Before it got too dark. Before leaving the battlefield. Before leaving the damned Washita Valley itself. Who in hell's creation knows right now what happened to Elliott's men except—"

"All wiped out," Clark said calmly. "Down to the last man."

"How can you be so—"

"If they wasn't dead when the general pulled out of that valley, they sure as hell are now."

Benteen straightened. "Precisely the information I want to hear from someone who'd know—"

"Why the hell you want me to tell you anything? What good's it going to do you? Or the general himself? Most of all, I can't help but wonder what the hell good's it going to do Elliott and his soldiers."

"Precisely, Clark! If we see that something's done about Custer, we can prevent this sort of sad affair from repeating itself. We want to be sure Custer never orders another field officer into battle, then abandons the man."

Clark eyed Benteen for a long moment, sizing the captain up as a cranky man who carried around every bit as big an ego as Custer. "So, tell me what you plan on doing to make things any different for the boys in blue."

"If the requisite testimony's there, we can bring Custer up on charges on this Elliott matter. Beginning with the abandonment of his men under fire, all the way to his failure to properly search the area for survivors."

"You want to file charges against the general?"

"Yes. If the investigation leads to charges. We'll need affidavits from witnesses like you."

"Me! Who else you got to testify?"

"Right now we have a few soldiers from Godfrey's company who heard some of the scattered rifle fire from across the river and were present when Godfrey told Custer about—"

"All right. You got Godfrey. Who else?"

"Uh . . . no, Ben. You got the wrong impression there. I can't convince Godfrey to testify against Custer, nor prefer any charges."

"Who else? You've got some other officers."

Benteen swallowed hard. He felt his one chance slipping through his fingers, fluttering just out of reach. Hoping Clark would help him cement together a case. "Since we can't get an officer to prefer charges against Custer, we were hoping to find one of you civilian scouts—"

"Can't find an officer to prefer charges!" Clark squeaked. "Captain, it sure sounds like you've got yourself a real bitch of a problem here—and Ben Clark ain't the man to help you out of it."

"But Custer could've ordered—"

"My God, Benteen! Haven't you realized this Injun fighting ain't at all like chasing Rebs? Rebs fought you like white men. They didn't butcher and maim—hack off your head and arms, legs, even worse. The sun was going down on your regiment. Custer sat in the middle of a thousand warriors, all madder'n a bunch of riled-up hornets with what they saw done to Black Kettle's camp—not to mention the pony herd. Ain't a damned thing more that man could've done one way or another would've changed things for Elliott's men."

The young captain sighed deeply, then swiped at his dripping nose, reddened with the cold of twilight. "I take it you won't reconsider."

"Not a thing I got to say is going to help those men now."

"Really figure they're dead, don't you?"

Clark glared flints at Benteen for a long moment. "I said it before. Doesn't matter much anymore. Not even to Elliott and his men. If they weren't dead before we pulled outta the Washita . . ."

Benteen filled in the scout's pause. "They are now."

"Nothing I can do help 'em now."

"What about all the Major Elliotts or the brave troopers to come who'll serve under Custer in the years ahead? What about them?"

Clark shook his head. "The future, Captain? Seems like that always takes care of itself—or it'll take care of George Armstrong Custer."

Clark dropped to his knees and threw some chunks of kindling on the fire. "I damn well won't be around, if you want to know what I think. You boys play soldier long enough, hard enough, maybe you won't be around long either."

Clark plopped back down on his stump. "Truth is, I don't like Custer any better'n you. But the way I figure it, I've got a job scouting for the man. If Custer doesn't choose to listen to me, that's his business. But I know damned well someday it'll be his neck, providing he doesn't start paying heed to his scouts."

Benteen creaked to his feet, realizing the scout wasn't about to change his mind.

"That's just the difference between me and your soldiers, Captain. I got enough good sense to know when I should disappear over the next hill. I know Injuns. I know the country. That's why I'm a scout—and a civilian. And I'm learning a lot about army officers, too, this goddamned winter."

The man in buckskins rose, squarely facing the captain. "I keep my hair 'cause I've learned what goes on inside you brass-buttoned, paper-collar officers."

"Regrettable you can't see things my way, Ben." The captain resigned himself to defeat. "You could've been a big help to a lot of young soldiers."

"Let's just say I'll keep my own fat out of the fire."

"Read you loud and clear, mister."

"Your soldier boys could help themselves the same way if they'd a mind to."

"That's where you're wrong, Mr. Clark. The army shoots deserters. Being a soldier means following the orders your superior officer gives you."

"Even if that order will kill you?"

Benteen swallowed hard. "I suppose that's in the nature of military life, Mr. Clark."

"Then I ain't in so bad a shape, am I, Captain? I've got no one but me to follow. While you and your soldiers . . . you have General Custer. Clark slipped his knife into its sheath, then high-stepped the log he had been sitting upon. He disappeared down a row of company tents without another word.

Benteen watched the scout fade into the twilight. "Make

no mistake about it, Mr. Clark. You surely do have the better end of the deal."

Twilight fell by the time Mahwissa and Monaseetah raised Custer's captured Cheyenne lodge beside his Sibley tent. A hundred yards away the triumphant Osage trackers celebrated around a huge bonfire down on the banks of the Beaver River. Roasts and ribs broiled on stakes jammed into the softening ground near the edge of the flames. At last the Osages would count coup over their old enemies. For too long they had hungered to dance with the blood-encrusted Cheyenne scalps. Out would come the drums and some of the pony soldiers' whiskey. On through the frosty night the trackers would dance to celebrate the army's winter victory on the Washita.

"General?"

Custer had been watching the two Cheyenne women struggle with the lodgeskin lashed to the lifting pole. At Lieutenant Moylan's voice he turned, as the women pulled the heavy, painted buffalo hide in both directions from the rear of the lodge, circling to the front to lash the lodgeskin together above the tiny doorway using long willow pins.

"Yes?"

Moylan was not alone. "Sir, may I introduce Daniel Brewster?"

Custer yanked a buffalo mitten from his right hand. "A new recruit, Moylan?"

"Not exactly, sir."

Custer studied the young man. "Mr. Brewster, is it?"

"Y-yes, sir," and he bowed his head, shuffling his big feet for an awkward moment after he dropped Custer's hand.

"Lieutenant, care to explain why Mr. Brewster's here, if not a recruit for the Seventh Cavalry?"

"Sir, Daniel here—" Moylan cleared his throat nervously, "he's been waiting down here at Camp Supply for a while already . . . waiting for our return from the Washita.

"Not exactly to join up," Moylan continued. "But he did come to ride with the Seventh, sir."

Brewster stepped up, crushing the soft brim of his worn slouch hat in his huge, scarred hands. "I tried to get to Fort Dodge, General. Before you pulled out."

Custer appraised the young man all the while. He'd make a fine recruit—strapping, hale fellow that he was. Brewster stood just above six feet. Just as surely he carried close to two hundred pounds across his broad frame. It wasn't likely a man would find an ounce of fat on the boy—young men of his breeding and background had sweated off every bit of tallow every day of their hard, simple lives.

Daniel Brewster's face, well tanned beneath a hat's brim line scarred across his forehead, told the rest of the story. That, and the huge ham hocks of work-worn hands that hung at the end of arms the size of an elk's foreleg. Especially those hands—roughened, cracked, callused, and perpetually scabbed. The sort of hands owned by a man who could wrench more pleasure out of the simple things of each day's existence than Custer knew he ever would. For that alone, he instantly admired this young man. More than that, he found himself genuinely liking the open, sun-baked face and deep-seared eyes that held hidden some sad story of long-earned pain.

"Lieutenant, why don't you fetch some coffee. What say

to that, Mr. Brewster? Then we'll talk over what made you trail the Seventh Cavalry into Indian Territory."

"I . . . I'd like that very much, General, sir." He crimped the soft slouch hat, then nervously tugged at his heavy mackinaw coat. Both had long ago seen their better days. Each sleeve bore a crude leather patch at the elbow. Custer could see the stitches on the patching were not those of a man's thick, clumsy fingers. Not a plowman's handiwork. Instead, the hands which had sewn Daniel Brewster's patches had been feminine, precise—and loving.

"Let's have a seat over there." Custer pointed to some cottonwood logs rolled up to his cheery fire. He found himself glancing over as the women finished pinning the hide together from the doorway up to the smoke flaps, then drove long pegs through the edge of the hide into the cold earth with hand-sized stones used as mallets.

"When I missed catching your army back to Fort Dodge, had no choice but to ride down here on my own. Got pinned down in the middle of that Cimarron River country for a few days while a blizzard blew over. By the time I rode in, you had already pulled out on me again."

Moylan brought two cups of coffee, then stepped away.

"Sounds like you've had a straight run at some bad luck trying to catch up with us. Why don't you tell me what you're doing here."

Brewster watched Custer sip his coffee. "Making decisions still pretty new to me, sir. Ever since my pa and brother got killed, I've been the one to take care of my mother and sister."

"How was it your father and brother died?"

"The war, sir." Brewster looked away self-consciously.

"What engagement?"

"Gettysburg."

"Meade lost too many good men those three days at Gettysburg. Every inch of ground bloody expensive for both armies." He gazed into the firelight, remembering the horrible sacrifice in young life that had littered the hills and meadows as wave after wave of Pickett's infantry and charge after charge of Jeb Stuart's cavalry had hurtled themselves suicidally against Union positions. "Left to care for your mother and sister?"

"Mama passed on soon after." Brewster turned away, pulling hard at his hot coffee, scalding his lips and tongue.

"You've had much more than your share of grief in five short years. How'd your mother die?"

"Lost her mind from grief, sir. Too much for her to bear—both a son and husband taken at once."

"Yes . . . I can understand." In his mind appeared the vision of that heartrending scene replayed every time he himself had to bid farewell to his own mother following a visit back home. "How'd you find yourself out in Kansas, Mr. Brewster?"

"Thought it best for me and my sister to get a fresh start out this way."

"Yes. A fresh start in a new land . . ."

"I happened across a nice parcel up on the Solomon River, about a two-day ride from the Smoky Hill. Then I sent for Anna Belle—my sister, General."

"Ah, it was your sister, after all."

"Sir?"

"The patches," he explained, pointing at Brewster's elbows.

"Oh, them." Daniel grinned. "Sewed by my sister just before she got married back in June. Man named John

Morgan—nice fella—lived up the river from us. Carpenter by trade. From the east too. Trying his hand at working the land. A kind, good man for Anna Belle."

His voiced trailed off as he stifled a sob, head falling onto arms he crossed atop his knees. His whole body shook with a long-pent sorrow. "They . . . they come and shot my sister's husband! Been married but a month . . . shot him as he ran back to his cabin . . . cut down not far from his own door. Running for his rifle."

"Who shot him?"

Brewster raised his head, wiping the back of a hand across his face, wrenching tears and sniffles away on a wool sleeve. "Indians shot him right in front of my little sister."

"Your sister tell you the story?"

"No! The same damned red niggers drug Anna Belle off with 'em after burning the place! John was hurt something fearful. But he lived. Wanted to come find Anna Belle with me, but he's still bedrid and weak."

"You don't figure on joining the Seventh to even the score . . . do you, Mr. Brewster?"

"General, I only want to find my sister. That's why I'm here to beg of you, sir—" he grabbed hold of Custer's tunic in his huge, trembling hands, "Let me go with you when you head back after the rest of them murderers. I'm gonna find my sister."

Custer rose slowly. "It's not as simple as all that. Let me put this in the kindest possible way, Mr. Brewster. My orders are to put an end to the Indian depredations—their marauding, murdering, stealing, and kidnapping white prisoners."

"Like my sister—"

"I feel for your plight—really I do. After all, it's due to

sad, sorrowful cases such as yours that I've brought my Seventh Cavalry in the middle of this winter to the heart of Indian Territories. I'll find and punish the guilty Indians. Still, I cannot allow any civilian who feels it his right to use the Seventh Cavalry and the U.S. Army to exact his private revenge."

"I ain't asking you for no special treatment!" Brewster blared, leaping to his feet. "Said I'd work for my keep, even if you can't pay me no wages while we're on the march. I ain't out after none of them savages. Just want my sister back."

"It's quite out of the question, taking you along with this fighting force. While we hope to free any and all white captives . . . that's by no means the priority of my orders. I'm concerned with the punishment of those Indians responsible for crimes the likes of which your sister—"

"Afraid you didn't understand. It ain't just that she's all I got, sir . . . I'm all Anna Belle's got in this whole world. Lord God in heaven knows she's counting on me in her every prayer. Being all my sister has, I can't stop trying to rescue her."

"Afraid my mind's made up, Mr. Brewster." Custer sipped at his coffee, finding it had grown cold on him. He sloshed it toward the fire ring. "In any event, you're free to remain here at Camp Supply until our return. If we locate any camps holding white prisoners, we'll promptly return those captives here. It'd be my fervent prayer that we'd find Anna Belle safe and as sound as could be."

"Thank you anyway, General." Brewster dug out a pair of threadbare wool mittens from the deep patch pockets of his mackinaw. "Gotta go ahead on my own. Already decided if you didn't see fit to take me with you, I wasn't about to wait no longer. Been almost a half-year now. Gotta do something. She's counting on me."

He surprised Custer by taking two long steps around the fire so he stood nose to nose with the Seventh's commander. Something wounded and pinched had come over his face.

"Maybe no one ever counted on you, General. So you don't rightly know how it feels for me to be all she's got left in this whole dang world. I know the Lord God's gonna help me. Well, I spoke my piece. All I come to say. Thank you for your time, sir."

Awash in thought, Custer watched Brewster go, studying the strong, wide back, the thick arms stuffed like sausage into his bulky wool coat, and those cracked, flop-eared boots crusted with red clay.

"Brewster!" Custer was still not sure why he hollered out.

"To hell with you, General!" Brewster stopped, whirled about.

"Come here, Mr. Brewster. If I have to, I'll call the guard."

He lunged forward, glaring at Custer. Jaws clenched, both big hands tensing at his sides. "That's what you figure to do, huh? Throw me in irons so I can't go after Anna Belle on my own? Damn your cowardly hide. If you don't have the backbone it takes to go after them murdering red savages, there's men who will."

"Done, Mr. Brewster?"

"Go 'head. Fetch the guard on me!"

"You're on army land, within a federal territory ceded to the Indians. Calm yourself—"

"Calm myself? My sister's out there!" He pointed into the darkness.

"As a civilian employee of the Seventh Cavalry, Mr. Brewster, you'd better cease your noisy tantrum this instant—or I most certainly will be forced to clamp you in irons."

Brewster's mouth gaped. "A *civilian* employee of the Seventh Cavalry?"

"I used those exact words."

"You mean, work for the army?"

"Unless you figured this was to be a free ride."

"Why . . . no, sir. It's just that—"

"I'm assigning you as a substitute teamster."

"Thank you, General!" He scooped up Custer's hand, pumping the whole arm enthusiastically.

"You thought you had me figured out, didn't you, Mr. Brewster? That's your first serious mistake. Learn from it."

"Why'd you change your mind?"

"That's something I can't begin to answer." Custer stared into the firelight thoughtfully.

"Where're the teamsters camped, sir?"

"We'll get you there straightaway. Moylan!"

"Yessir!"

Custer watched his young adjutant trot into the light. "Take Mr. Brewster with you. Introduce him to Bell. Give the lieutenant my compliments and have him get Mr. Brewster outfitted."

"You've hired him on, sir?" Moylan's voice rose with excitement.

"As substitute teamster. He'll earn his keep while we attempt to free his sister. Isn't that right, Mr. Brewster?"

"Yes. Absolutely, sir!"

"C'mon, Dan." Moylan slapped the young farmer on the shoulder. "Let's go find you a warm blanket to roll up in tonight. You're in the army now!"

"Not just the army, Myles!" Brewster cried. "By damned—I'm part of the Seventh Cavalry now!"

CHAPTER 13

C USTER wasn't all that sure why he found himself standing here in the dark belly of the captured buffalo-hide lodge, his eyes growing accustomed to the tar-black night.

It had seemed like such a grand idea at first. Tingling in anticipation of coming here to the lodge, to her, he had tried and failed to sleep. He listened to the rhythm of her quiet breathing, trying to convince himself he had come only to assure himself she was safe here in her blankets.

Earlier that evening he had fed the two women at his private table. Eating as though they hadn't been fed for days, both had devoured every scrap of turkey and venison set before them. Afterward they had sipped steaming coffee while distant chants of the Osage scouts drifted up from the riverside victory dance.

Using a candle lantern, Custer had led the women back to the compound where the captives were kept under guard. Mahwissa disappeared toward the closest of those little fires surrounded day and night by women and children. Instead of following, Monaseetah had turned, gazing fully into the very pit of him. She signed to him that she wanted to sleep in the lodge he had brought from the camp of Black Kettle. He asked her why she would prefer to sleep alone in that cold lodge when she could stay here to sleep warm among her people. Monaseetah let him know she couldn't be warm in those tents of the white man. No fire pit. Better to sleep in the lodge, where she could build a fire that would warm the frost from the robes before she slipped between them to sleep.

"I have no blankets or robes in the lodge," he signed.

Monaseetah had gone off toward the prisoner tents. In a few minutes she trudged back, dragging behind her a bulky pair of buffalo robes encircling four army blankets. These, she signed, along with the red wool blanket she had worn from the battlefield—they would keep her warm on the coldest winter night.

Dragging firewood to the lodge, Custer realized he felt about as nervous as he had that first day at Bull Run seven long years ago. Green—right out of the Academy. In that awkward silence, she intimidated him from across the first dancing flames with those sinful black-cherry eyes of hers.

He had struggled to his feet and hobbled stiff-legged to the doorway. She caught him before he could duck out.

For the first time she reached out to touch the back of his hand. A shudder coursed through him like a bolt of spring lightning flaring across the prairie. She slipped her fingers into his palm, nestling his hand gently between the two of hers, then brought it to her cheek. Monaseetah closed her eyes, kissing the soldier's freckled, callused hand. Repeatedly she murmured the word in Cheyenne before realizing he didn't understand her tongue.

She made the sign: "Husband."

Custer gulped. He listened to dry limbs crackling in the fire pit. Above it all, he heard the labored racing of his eager heart pounding in his ears.

At last he signed that he could not be her husband. "I have a wife. Among the white men, one wife is all a man must have."

"Why is your wife not here? Among the Cheyenne, a woman journeys with her husband."

"When I fight, my wife does not travel at my side." He refused to look into those dangerous eyes of hers again.

"Yellow Hair, I am your wife for here . . . for now."

It was all he could do to shut his eyes and grope his way blindly out the door into the numbing, forgiving darkness. He had cursed himself—because George Armstrong Custer had never retreated.

Never had he confronted an enemy so powerful. An enemy who wielded such a magnetic hold on him. Except Libbie.

Sweet Libbie . . .

Lord! Why am I standing here again, staring at the dying red coals in her fire pit . . . their crimson carcasses writhing like coupling lovers in this warm, musky darkness. Why did I return?

Sweet love of heaven, how he had tossed in his blankets! the delicious, exquisite temptation of Monaseetah's taunting him. Its fire smoldered along his limbs. He struggled to put her out of his mind, to escape into the numbing anesthesia of sleep.

But Custer had been unable to forget her. His mind conjured a vision of her with the gentle kiss of slumber caressing her copper face. So he arose and went to her lodge again.

In the aching silence of the lodge, he heard her rustle in her sleeping robes at the back of the lodge. Custer realized he wasn't dreaming anymore.

Her coppery, fire-lit skin slid free of the black-brown fur. Custer's nostrils flared involuntarily. He smelled her presence even before he saw the woman slipping toward him.

Now Monaseetah came into him, naked. Stripped of everything but her newfound desire for the soldier chief.

She tugged aside the flaps of his buffalo coat, slipping inside its warmth with him, snaking her arms around his waist. She buried her cheek against the warm, itchy wool of his blue tunic and sighed.

Custer shuddered involuntarily, more frightened than he had ever been—*scared of a seventeen-year-old captive Cheyenne girl!*

Custer found his hands at her shoulders, his fingers moving along her soft, fragrant flesh burnished bright copper in the firelight. He pulled her to him hungrily. Monaseetah's firmness met him, startling him, her breasts exciting him all the more.

Placing his hands on either side of her hips, Custer caressed their round, sensual fullness. With the appetite of an animal caged too long, Custer drank in the scent of her hair. His fingers traced the firm roundness of her belly.

Monaseetah moaned, whimpering with a primitive animal cry captive within her.

Suddenly, as if shot, Custer jerked back.

She . . . she's with child! He pushed her back and whirled away. *What the devil am I doing? Thank God I was able to stop myself in time. . . .* Before he had succumbed to the crazed animal he knew all too well prowled the nether regions of his soul. He could yet sense the creature howling in the pit of his being, growing hungrier still.

She drew away, to her bed at the back of the lodge. Monaseetah drew the favored red blanket about her shoulders, covering her slim body.

She called his name. *"Hiestzi?"*

He could not face her.

"Hiestzi?"

He took a step toward her and gazed down at her copper face. "I don't know Cheyenne," he replied helplessly. Then remembered to form the words in sign.

She chose her words carefully, hands dancing before her, symbols coming together that allowed her to talk with the man who had captured her heart.

"Hiestzi is your Cheyenne name—Yellow Hair. I had hoped you came here tonight to become my husband in the way of the Cheyenne."

"No!" he shouted, then used his hands. "I am not your husband. I have a wife waiting for me many miles away."

"But you came here to sleep in my robes tonight—"

Custer shook his head, turned away. To look upon her was to cause madness, to invite a consuming passion that knew no satisfaction. He shuddered with the lie of it in his soul even as the words formed in his hands.

"I do not want another man's wife. You carry another man's child."

Tears gathered in her eyes, tumbling uncontrollably, cascading down her cheeks.

"I have no husband, Soldier Chief. This one who forced his bitter seed into my belly—a cruel man."

"Monaseetah, I told you—I have a wife."

"This wife of yours, does she lie with you?" She pressed

her warmth against him. "Does she give you pleasure and happiness?"

The musk of her invaded every blood vessel within him. Custer turned away, staring at that black hole of the doorway. Then he looked again at the girl.

She sat up and the robe fell away from her dusky breasts. Her eyes as warm as coals, she signed to him. "I am a part of you now, *Hiestzi*. I am that wilderness you carry inside you now."

As suddenly as she had signed her words, he was gone.

Custer ducked his head, savagely tearing aside the door flap, exploding from the lodge. He was several steps away from that dark cone punching a coal-black hole in the starry sky before he drew another frosty breath.

"Damn her!" he rasped.

Stomping off toward his Sibley tent, Custer paused a moment by that fire the headquarters guard fed through the night. The warmth worked at that icy knot clabbering in his belly.

"General." The orderly snapped a salute as he slapped his Springfield carbine alongside his leg.

"Goodnight, Corporal." Custer tore through his own tent flaps.

He lay upon his cot. No one to see the tears of shame on his face.

There's something to the Indian girl I don't yet understand. Hers is not the trick of some painted-wagon, side-show, snake-oil drummer. Something more to her than even that mystical cloak the Cheyenne use to explain everything unexplained—medicine.

That's exactly what he needed, all right. Medicine. Something to quench the burning, put out this smoldering fire threatening to flare.

Custer nestled a warm place for his cheek, praying for sleep to overtake him quickly. Blessed, peaceful sleep. Just a little sleep—that would be medicine enough right now.

Since the Seventh's return to Camp Supply four days ago, Sheridan had grown increasingly disappointed by the progress of his winter campaign. Where he had hoped to attack large concentrations of guilty hostiles, Custer had instead defeated a small village of Black Kettle's Cheyennes. Instead of that blow putting an end to the nagging Indian problems on the southern plains, reality showed him Custer had dealt nothing more than the first blow in what could become a long, drawn-out, and very bloody conflict.

Winter wrapped the prairie in white and cold. If Sheridan were to deal with the tribes still at large, he would have to do it soon. In the space of a few weeks spring would begin its relentless creep out of the south. By then the tribes and their grass-fattened ponies would again have the strength to move about quickly. By then the warriors would be out and raiding once more.

If he was to continue his fight, Sheridan understood, it must be now, deep in the heart of winter. And he must continue the fight—whirling, whirling as he had done in the Shenandoah valley, using Custer as his firebrand—until the hostiles cry "surrender" and turn back to their reservations.

"General?"

Sheridan turned on his camp stool, finding the young lieutenant colonel at the open door of his Sibley.

"Custer! Please, come in! Here—sit there on the bed. Best seat in the house."

Custer settled as Sheridan stuffed more wood into the sheet-iron stove at the rear of his personal quarters.

"Do you know what day this is, Custer?"

"Why, it's Saturday."

Sheridan's dark, brooding, Irish eyes lit up as he smiled. "I know that, Armstrong. What's the date?"

"December fifth."

"Damned straight, it is!" he roared as he slapped a knee. "It's your birthday, for God's sake! So I have a birthday present for you."

"I didn't know you knew . . . remembered my birthday."

"Damn it, Armstrong, I've always known when your birthday is—and this time, I have something very special to give you."

"Yessir?"

"While there's nothing to wrap and place in your hand, my gift to you is something nonetheless very tangible."

"I don't follow you . . ."

"And I hadn't expected you to understand me." Sheridan turned fully around to face his friend with a smile. "Simple. We're going after the rest of the hostiles. Happy birthday, Custer!"

"Thank you," Custer replied, a little hollowly. "When are *we* leaving?"

"Monday, day after tomorrow." Sheridan shuffled through some papers and maps on his field desk. "Your Lieutenant Bell, his quartermaster corps, and teamsters are about done preparing the wagons and supplies. I've planned to be out thirty days. That should be enough time to locate and crush the hostiles."

"Thirty days?"

"That's right," Sheridan replied, searching Custer's eyes carefully. "What's on your mind?"

"Just the weather, sir. Dead of winter. The certainty of much more snow. What may seem like it could take only thirty days . . . well, might last more than sixty."

"I see," Sheridan replied quietly, a little steam slowly whistling out of his enthusiasm.

Scratching at his beard, the bantam Irishman rose stiffly and paced to the tent flaps, peering out at the bustling camp.

"Grant and Sherman want me back behind that god-damned desk again. So, like other battles we've fought together, we'll just have to see what we can accomplish in those thirty days."

Sheridan turned, seeing concern cross Custer's face.

"You let me go, I'll get the job done for you with—"

"I covered your ass in the Shenandoah with Merritt and others, Armstrong," Sheridan confided, leaning forward. "And I did it again last month with Sully before you marched on the Washita. We make a good team, so don't fight the bit on me now."

Custer flinched at the scolding. He nodded. "What instructions do you have for me, General?"

"Come back tonight, and we'll discuss how we'll mop this up."

"General?"

"Yes, Armstrong?"

"What would you have done—personally—following the Washita engagement?"

Sheridan glanced into those ice blue eyes and found he could not hold Custer's hard gaze for long at all. "I suppose most would have done exactly as you did. Protect your victory, protect your men. Give priority to your wounded and the captives. You did the best you could under the circumstances."

"Thank you, sir." That helped a little.

"It's not my place to second guess you. You did only what you believed was right at the time."

After a full evening of final planning with Sheridan, Custer hurried back to the warmth of his Sibley late Sunday. At dawn his troops would be miles south, marching on the Washita Valley once more. He banked the fire in his stove for the night, trying to push Monaseetah from his mind. Try as he might, still she troubled someplace deep in the core of him.

Custer stood by the sheet-iron stove unbuttoning his tunic, letting it hang open a moment while he plopped down on his bed to struggle with his cold, wet boots. When the boots relented, he slipped his feet inside a pair of buffalo-hide moccasins she had made for him.

A quiet, unsure rattle at his front flap startled him. Custer flared, angry that he had not tied the flaps earlier so he could tell the soldier to go on his way, at this late hour.

Custer angrily stomped to the door. Ready to tear some soldier's head off, he flung wide the two flaps.

"Monaseetah."

Her name was all he could say. In a whispered rush of wild surprise caught high in his throat.

Her eyes touched him gently with their promise. Ribbons of heat stung their way across his cheeks. Like being squeezed in a vice . . . tightening. Her eyes held him for an instant before she slipped past him into the tent.

Determined, she had decided she would go to him, to claim the soldier chief as her own. *Hiestzi* was her husband.

Tonight she would become his woman.

With one hand Monaseetah flung her red blanket to his bed, where that it lay atop a dark buffalo robe. Only then did her eyes reach out to capture his.

"You cannot stay here," he pleaded in a small voice. He took two steps toward her, not daring to draw any closer. What sweet poison she had become.

She came to him as Custer swept toward her, enclosing her tiny shoulders. She sobbed—*Hiestzi* embraced her at last.

The smell of her readiness swept into his nostrils. Filling them. Tingling his every nerve ending with its fire.

The last moments before every battle had always aroused the same feelings in him, exciting the same sensations: anticipation, with a generous measure of apprehension. Drawn, knowing he would succumb—yet he was suddenly positive that he stood on the brink of something he would always regret . . . for the rest of his life. Still, despite that lifelong remorse and possible damnation, he must have her.

She was his mate.

Custer realized he had known of its certainty from that first night at Camp Supply when she had pressed herself to him by the fire's glow in her lodge.

As his anxious fingers raked into the long, silken hair at the back of her neck, pulling her face up toward his, Custer felt her nipples grow rigid beneath the doeskin dress clinging to her firm breasts, demanding his touch.

As his dry lips crushed hers in Monaseetah's first kiss, Custer realized his own readiness. It strained at his trousers, yearning for escape, surging for relief within her deepest regions. With his tongue, Custer gently forced her lips apart, then her teeth, drinking in the animal taste of her.

She shuddered beneath the savagery of his desire for her. Frightened at first, remembering a brutal husband, she quickly realized Yellow Hair had become all she had ever wanted him to be. Certain now that the animal surging for release in *Hiestzi* would free the animal in her own being. There came a heated moistening between her legs where before she had experienced only revulsion and pain. For the first time in her young life she sensed her own readiness for a man.

Monaseetah gasped, drawing away from Custer's mouth to reach for the buckle on his belt. His lips lay panting against her ear, his breath raspy, labored. To stand here now with her, after all the years looking for the woman who could stir within him exactly this fire she had put a sulphur-head match to.

His breath caught high in his throat as she pulled open the fly to his trousers and long-handles, reaching inside for his rigid, ready flesh. Custer was certain he'd never breathe again as she hungrily kneaded his burning, swollen flesh—sending him toward a passioned, woman-hungry fury like nothing he'd ever known.

Monaseetah stopped, moved toward his bed, glancing over her shoulder at him. He stared—hypnotized and immobile—while she slowly inched up the fringed, calf-length hem of her soft doeskin dress.

She dropped the dress at her feet, then climbed atop his low prairie bed. On her hands and knees, she gazed back over her shoulder at him with a toss of her long, raven-black hair. Taunting him with all that she had to offer, taunting him to come to her the way the ponies mate.

Custer understood immediately.

He tugged at his trousers, slipping suspenders off his shoulders, hopping across the warm buffalo robe that served as a tent rug. He yanked the blue wool tunic off his shoulders, tossing it all in a tangled pile at the edge of his bed.

His mind raced. Ever so slowly his fingers crept across the silky skin of her buttocks. Then crawled over the firm roundness of her hips. After exploring her back and shoulders, Custer cupped the full, firm melons of her young breasts.

Monaseetah threw her head back at the fire of his touch. Never before had anyone put his hands on her swollen, milky breasts. It was as if *Hiestzi* had branded her as his woman. Heated, eager for mating, she ground her buttocks back into him. Yearning for his flesh to mingle with hers. Still he continued to fondle her hanging breasts, torturing her deliciously.

The woman reached between her legs, taking hold of his rigid flesh, guiding it as quickly as a warrior's lance toward her waiting passion. Animals, they moaned in unison as she ground her buttocks back against his belly. Firmly planting him inside the heat of her.

They coupled, mated, loved. At the moment of release Custer collapsed atop her. Monaseetah's own quivering legs were no longer able to hold her. They tumbled together, the man clinging to his woman as if he would never let go.

Custer cupped her silky chin in his rough hand, turning her head to look at her face. Wiping a few hot tears from Monaseetah's cheek, he let his own eyes say what his trembling tongue could not.

"Love," was all she breathed—her very first English word.

Moments later she heard him snore softly against the back of her neck, his rhythmic breathing tickling the long, damp hair pasted against her flesh. He had collapsed into a deep, peaceful sleep with his arms locked about her.

Outside a hard, icy snow flung itself against the stiff, oiled canvas. A harsh rattle of the wind reminded her of horses' hooves racing along the crust of ice at the edge of a winter river. She sensed the night as if it were stampeding over her, trampling her beneath its thousand sharp, slashing hooves.

The sob in her heart echoed the eerie howl of a solitary wolf, crying out in loneliness for its mate, lost in the winter-wilderness storm.

Blinded and cold and alone.

Clear, sharp notes signaled reveille through Camp Supply, Indian Territory, before dawn. Yet it wasn't until ten that the call for "Boots and Saddles" sounded through the river camp, ordering each trooper to ready his horse for the coming march.

On this trip into the heart of the Indian wilderness, ten companies of the Nineteenth Kansas Volunteers would bolster Custer's regiment, men recruited and organized solely to punish the hostiles responsible for kidnapping and murdering their way across the Kansas frontier during the previous summer and autumn raiding seasons. In addition, Custer welcomed journalist De Benneville Randolph Keim along. The twenty-seven-year-old reporter for the New York *Herald* joined Custer's headquarters command to record for posterity this Custer campaign to "polish off Sheridan's red menace" terrorizing the southern plains.

Just past midmorning the long-awaited order for the advance blared through the valley, echoing down the columns of two. A dark snake of cavalry bundled in buffalo coats and mittens uncoiled itself, stretching across the dazzling snow, slowly worming its way southward once more. In two hundred wagons cloaked in winter's frost creaking atop cold hubs, the army freighted its forage for the horses and mules, in addition to rations sufficient to last Custer's troopers a full thirty days.

Just ahead of the eleven companies of Custer's pride rode Lieutenant Silas Pepoon's civilian scouts, including some fifteen Osage and Kaw trackers who had proven themselves during the recent Washita campaign. The Osages had led Custer to the winter village of their old enemy, the Southern Cheyenne of Black Kettle, nestled like a sow bug in the valley of the Washita River. Now the trackers hungered for more Cheyenne scalps.

Behind Custer rode better than seventeen hundred men thrusting once again into the heart of Indian Territory on this bloody mission.

His dark bay kicking up sprays of new snow, Custer tore back to the head of the columns to join his commander, Lieutenant General Philip H. Sheridan, new Commander of the Department of the Missouri, who brought along his entire staff for this winter foray south into hostile country.

"General!" Custer saluted smartly. "If you'd have a look behind you, I think you'll find the most glorious sight to greet an old warrior's eyes!"

Twisting in his cold saddle, Sheridan gazed back at the long lines of mounted cavalry and quartermaster wagons, scouts, trackers, and interpreters. As grand a sight as the hero of the Shenandoah campaign had ever laid his eyes on, stretched out as they were across the snow beneath this low-bellied sky gathering cold and angry overhead. He couldn't help but smile. "Does an old horse soldier's heart good."

"I know just how you feel, sir. Once a man's ridden at the head of a cavalry column, it's not an easy task for him to slide from his saddle—forced to ride nothing more than an overstuffed horsehair chair stuck behind some desk."

"Goddamn right!" Sheridan growled. "I'll see to things personally now. Why, if we can get in one or two more good licks, we'll put an end to the Indian troubles in my department!"

"I'd stake my commission on it, sir. What's more, you'll be in on those very strikes yourself. You can watch my Seventh humble the pride of the southern tribes, bringing peace to this wilderness."

The dark little Irishman flashed a smile. "Glad we see things my way, Custer."

Not knowing why, Custer turned, looking for her back in the long, winding columns behind him. Circled by Pepoon's scouts, she rode beside her two older companions, Mahwissa, the old sister of Cheyenne chief Black Kettle, and Mahwissa's favorite friend, the ancient Sioux Stingy Woman.

Drawing her bright red blanket across her cold cheeks, Monaseetah's beautiful eyes were all there was left for him to see. All he needed to see to feel touched once more by her animal warmth.

Custer kicked Dandy into a lope, speeding to the head of the columns. Headed into history.

CHAPTER 14

NEVER before had De Benneville Keim laid eyes on such a wild and desolate sight as the winter valley of the Washita into which Custer's troops had descended yesterday afternoon. Pale, milky light slanted eastward, nudging skeletons of winter-robed hackberry and blackjack oaks in an area known as "the shinnery." It was as if all the bare and lifeless vegetation foreshadowed this as a valley of death, beckoning and luring the soldiers down the trail. Keim shuddered, trying to convince himself a corpse couldn't be any colder six feet under the icy crust of the wind-scoured snow. At twilight Moylan's thermometer stood at eighteen degrees below zero.

The fires had helped little this morning as the shivering troops rolled out of their tents and robes into the bitter winter dawn. To defrost his limbs and working parts, a soldier was forced to broil one side while freezing the other. Most gathered hunchbacked around the roaring fires, slowly turning themselves as if they were themselves dripping hump roasts browning before the dancing yellow-blue flames.

As the sun broke a frosty saffron over the hills to the east, brass trumpets sounded "The General," a call requiring the grumbling soldiers to break from their warm fires and strike their tents. When the wagons were loaded, Custer lost no time in ordering "Boots and Saddles" sounded. Kicking snow and pouring the remains of coffee from the battered pots over the coals, the last details clambered aboard their wagons.

"Advance! Column of twos!"

Lieutenant Myles Moylan, Custer's adjutant, passed the command down the columns, his shouts startling flock after flock of black-feathered scavengers from their communal roosts in the bare-boned trees. Across the snow those last few miles due east to the site of what once had been the winter camp of Black Kettle's Cheyenne, last November's trail lay plain enough for any shavetail recruit to read.

Wide and deep—like a saber slashing into the still beating heart of Indian Territory.

South across the icy river Custer led Sheridan and his staff into the devastated village, followed by the scouts, Osage and civilian alike, before the troops themselves were allowed to cross the Washita. All around them erupted the ear-splitting clatter of a thousand crows and wrinkled-neck buzzards taking to the wing, scavengers protesting this disturbance of their free meals. Some of the birds were so gorged with flesh they had difficulty taking flight to escape the men and horses.

Within the ruins of the village, snarling, howling, barking wolves and coyotes confronted the soldiers, four-legged predators drawn to this place by the potent stench of death.

Some of the men pulled bandannas over their noses or hid their faces behind tall coat collars. A handful grew sick enough to throw up what remained of the hardtack and salt pork they had wolfed down hours ago.

The charred lodge poles Custer's men had burned the day of the battle lay like black monuments poking from the new snow.

As far as the eye could see, the ground was littered with grotesque, frozen corpses. But as plain as the cold nipping any soldier's cheeks, a man could see moccasined feet had visited the village after Custer had pulled out. While some of the bloodied bodies had been wrapped in blankets and bound up with rawhide cords by now, very few had actually been hoisted into the forks of the skeletal trees, as was the Indians' custom. Plainly, Black Kettle's village had not camped alone along the Washita this winter.

Once man had abandoned the valley, gangs of buzzards, crows, wolves, and coyotes had begun their grisly work. Every corpse was partially eaten.

"General—" Custer turned to address Sheridan, "if you'd come with me, I'll show you a vantage point where you can see the entire battlefield. From there I can describe the process of our fight for you, Lieutenant Colonel Crosby, and your staff."

"Very good, Custer." Sheridan coughed, gagging on the stench. "Lead on."

"You'll come with us, Mr. Keim?" Custer asked.

Keim nodded eagerly. "Wouldn't miss it, General Custer." During the war, Keim had become a favorite of U. S. Grant, extolling Union victories as a field correspondent. Sherman had grown to hate reporters during the war, and they returned his hatred in kind. Sheridan stood somewhere in the middle, wary of the press, yet recognizing their political importance.

Custer led Sheridan to the knoll just south of the village where he had watched most of the battle action that morning his Seventh Cavalry crossed the Washita. On their climb they passed more dead Cheyenne stuffed back in the thick brush to conceal them from predators until a more proper burial could be arranged.

"Moylan," Custer said, "have Lieutenant Custer and Captain Keogh each take a squad to search south and east of here. Scour the area for any sign of Major Elliott's command. I suggest they begin at a two-mile radius, where we had to leave off the day of the battle. Work out to a three-mile radius in a sweeping arc. If nothing's found, proceed five miles out from camp, but no farther. I don't want my men strung out from our support should the need arise."

Moylan saluted, wheeling downhill toward the rest of the command.

"You have reason to fear the hostiles might still be in the area?" Sheridan asked.

"I'd be afraid to gamble. It's certain the Indians have returned to care for their dead."

"That'd be another stroke of Custer's Luck, wouldn't it?"

"I can't imagine being lucky enough to catch another village napping."

The wind shifted, carrying to the hilltop a heavy stench from southeast of camp. Sheridan requested his field glasses. With them he pinpointed the odor. Some two hundred yards beyond the camp perimenter lay the bloated, stiffened carcasses—better than eight hundred

Indian ponies Lieutenant Godfrey's troopers had slaughtered. Among the remains of what had once been the pride of the Cheyenne now roamed a pack of fat, sated wolves and their coyote cousins, joined by some Indian dogs.

Each animal bristled, snarling its anger as Lieutenant Thomas W. Custer's search detail skirted the deathly meadow, pushing a little south of east from the Indian camp.

Following a trail not difficult to read, the lieutenant's men climbed a low wooded ridge, then descended toward a dry tributary of the Washita. Several yards west of that ravine, Tom Custer signaled a halt. On the ground ahead huddled a mass of crows, ravens, and turkey buzzards, all busy over something . . . or someone.

A foul, sweetish odor intensified as the soldiers warily approached on foot, leading their mounts. The solitary body had been left for the birds of prey to work over. Enough flesh still clung on the torso to show bullets fired into the carcass after the soldier had been killed.

"Turn him over," Tom Custer ordered. "I wanna see who this was."

One green recruit scuffed through the snow, holding a bandanna over his mouth and nose. His stomach revolted and the boy coughed away the sting of bile in his mouth.

"Grimes," Tom Custer growled at his veteran sergeant. "Help the boy."

Grimes yanked his collar up to his nose, scowling and mumbling a curse. Everyone understood, including Custer. There wasn't a single man among them who relished getting any closer to the half-eaten corpse than he absolutely had to.

A few of the men gasped as Grimes rolled the mutilated

body onto its back. The soldier's entire skull was black with old blood from the eyebrows clear back to the nape of the neck—completely scalped. No quick job here. Though his features had become distorted in mutilation and weeks of severe cold, no man could mistake the long, dark dundrearies bristling along the dead man's cheeks—sideburns allowed to stretch down along the jawline, all the fashion rage in the East at the time.

"Sergeant Major Kennedy," Tom Custer snarled. "Attached to Elliott, wasn't he?"

The lieutenant knew the answer to his own question. Kennedy had been a seasoned veteran of the Civil War, riding with Major Joel Elliott's company.

"Yes, he was," answered Corporal Harper. "But why'd he be out here . . . alone, sir? You figure it?"

"Only a guess, Harper. Man like Kennedy had a real good reason to let himself get caught alone by the Indians way he was. This far from the village."

"Bloody butchers! Wasn't a damned thing Kennedy was afraid of, Lieutenant," Grimes cursed.

At last Tom Custer's eyes rose from the naked corpse to peer into those snowy meadows rolling away to the east in gentle swells. "Boys, I don't like to think about what I figure we're gonna find up ahead, across this wash here. Seems, though, we got the lieutenant colonel's orders." He stuffed a boot in his stirrup. "Let's find out what happened to the rest of Elliott's men."

"Lieutenant?"

"You got something to say, Grimes?"

"I'd like have this stream named Sergeant Major Creek." He wiped a mitten on the end of his dripping nose.

Custer slewed his eyes around the men. "Sergeant, don't

think there's a man here gonna kick about naming it in
honor of Kennedy. Well done, Grimes. Let's go find the
rest of 'em."

There was hardly a man following Tom Custer up the
other side of that dry ravine into the snowy meadows who
wouldn't remember the bloody, precision handiwork someone had practiced on Sergeant Major Kennedy.

"Eyes front!" Tom Custer barked his sudden, raspy
interruption.

They watched the great flocks of ravens and crows
blacken the skies as the birds clattered into flight. That
noise of their flapping wings rushed over the soldiers like a
thunderous tide upon the sands, echoed in its ebbing by
snarling wolves and coyotes scattering before the approaching horsemen.

Barely two hundred yards east of the dry tributary lay
sixteen bodies, each frozen in death as solid as timberline
granite. The chalk-white corpses lay in a ragged circle, face
down, feet toward the center. Each man defending his
piece of the perimeter.

Skirmish formation?

Hardly, Tom Custer thought. *Perhaps they did the best they
could, caught where they were.*

He had fought enough during the final months of the war
to know of its horrors. As the Union armies tightened their
noose around Lee's Army of Northern Virginia, Tom Custer
himself had won first one, then a second Medal of Honor,
dashing single-handedly against Confederate artillery,
snatching the Rebel colors from a flag bearer before returning to the Union line. So it didn't take a vivid imagination
for the lieutenant to gaze across the meadow, watching the
horror of it happening right before his eyes—Major Joel H.

Elliott wheeling that snorting, frightened mount of his. Finding his war-seasoned sergeant major. Orders given for a desperate ride . . . a plea for reinforcements . . .

Tom Custer spit dryly into the old snow near his feet. Kennedy never made it.

Knowing Kennedy, Tom Custer brooded, *he must have taken some of the red bastards with him on his howling journey into death. No doubt he sold his life at a dear cost to his killers. Those goddamned Cheyenne can take pride in killing a mighty enemy.*

What no man in the Seventh Cavalry had known back on that cold November day of the battle, what Elliott himself could not have known until it was too late, was simply that there were hundreds upon hundreds of warriors boiling out of other winter camps farther east down the Washita, as if someone had overturned a dried buffalo chip on the prairie to watch the grub beetles scurry this way and that.

By now the soldiers had some idea there had been other camps strung out along the icy river. Many warriors. Just how many, no soldier could have known for certain on that day Black Kettle sang his death song. Custer and his troops had simply been too eager to attack the solitary Cheyenne camp the Osage scouts had found for them, so eager that no one really saw need for further intelligence. No man realized some five thousand Indians lay sleeping in those other Cheyenne, Arapaho, Kiowa, and Comanche villages downriver. Combined, they were one huge, snaking village spread some twelve to fifteen miles along the meandering Washita. On the morning of the battle those other camps had awakened to the endless rifle fire long before any of Black Kettle's escapees had straggled to their villages carrying the shocking news. Unbelievable, frightening news: Pony soldiers!

Elliott's men pursued some of those very same Cheyenne fleeing from the slaughter of Black Kettle's camp right after the old chief and his woman had been cut down by Lieutenant Cooke's sharpshooters stationed in the trees across the river.

When the small band of Cheyenne escapees split into two groups, each heading in a different direction, Elliott divided his men. The old and very young Indians, sick or already wounded, all darted to the left, scurrying among the thick brush. Quickly surrounded, the soldiers herded this group back to the village.

At the same time, Elliott's squad of some eighteen blue-coats mounted on gray horses continued after the warriors and young women dashing to the right, those stout of leg and able to lead the pony soldiers on a chase among the oak and cottonwood, through the hackberry brush.

It was but moments before the horsemen overtook the slowest warrior and brought him down. Then a second was left bleeding a slow death farther on. The rest sprinted ahead, scattering like jackrabbits before their pursuers. A third, then a fourth Indian fell beneath slashing army hooves.

Too late Elliott had his attention drawn to the timber looming before them. Only then did his men notice the trees to their left. And right. Of a sudden it seemed as if the trees belched warriors—each one brandishing a bow or rifle, lance or war ax.

Frantic, the pony soldiers reined up, savagely haunch-sliding their lathered mounts into a snow-blinding halt. They wheeled, clattering, bumping against each other, their horses rearing in fright. The noise of warrior screams, the high-pitched death song of eagle-wingbone whistles drowned all sound. The tide of this nasty little battle had suddenly swung out of reach for Elliott's desperate band of blue-coats.

The narrow gap through which they had just confidently galloped suddenly closed like a puckered strip of sun-dried rawhide. No way out now; they found themselves surrounded by angry, blood-eyed Arapahos led by Powder Face and that battle-famous war chief, Left Hand.

For most of the eighteen, it would be their first, and last, experience of bowel-puckering terror as hundreds of warriors rode in, surrounding them, tightening their deadly gauntlet like a feathered noose . . . no escape. A screeching horde swept around the frantic, wild-eyed army mounts. Everywhere! Firing their iron-tipped arrows into the horses, aiming their old rifles at the soldiers. Biting. Stinging. Whistling like a thousand wasps.

"Kennedy!" Elliott barked, releasing the reins as his horse dropped, thrashing. "Ride, goddammit! We're not far from the Cheyenne camp!"

"Yessir!" Kennedy flew into a saddle with one fluid motion, laying low along the horse's neck as he held his hand down to Elliott. "Good luck, sir!"

"We'll hold out till you get back!" Elliott gripped Kennedy's bare hand, shoving a second pistol into it as he stepped back, watching the veteran savagely kick the mount into motion.

"Godspeed, Sergeant," Elliott whispered the instant before the iron arrow point pierced his chest. He sank to his knees like a sack of wet oats, gasping. "God help us all."

A proven battlefield veteran during the war, Elliott fought the pain and ordered his men to dismount, to prepare for a skirmish. All of them were on the ground by then. Not a man could he spare to hold the frightened, rearing horses. He ordered the horses released. Hell, they weren't of use to them now. No chance for escape on horseback anyway. Their only hope lay in the thought *that Kennedy would make it through, back to the village, bringing reinforcements.*

With the screeching and blanket-waving of the Indians, the horses clattered off. Now the soldiers were alone. With not one chance in a thousand of pulling themselves from the dripping jaws of this ambush.

"Down on your bellies, goddammit! Circle up!" Elliott yelled, snapping the arrow shaft off close to his bloody coat.

With their feet toward the center, they each could cover another man's backside.

They made a hot time of it for the screeching warriors while it lasted. Each one still carried close to a hundred cartridges for his carbine. Again and again, Elliott reminded them of their duty through those final minutes.

"Sell your lives dearly, boys! A hundred of 'em for every one of us!"

They did indeed sell their lives dearly. One by one, for dying is a one-man job at best. From the start the fight could not have lasted very long at all. Ridges to the south and east afforded good positions where the Indians fired down into Elliott's grim circle. A desperate scrap lasting less time than it takes for the winter sun to travel from one lodge pole to the next. Less than fifteen white man minutes.

Perhaps long enough for a man to shave with a straight razor. Surely the fight lasted no longer than it took for the victorious warriors to perform their bloody work on the soldiers' bodies afterward, before they pulled out to chase after those troopers Custer had left behind earlier that morning with the regiment's coats and haversacks.

That many warriors simply didn't need much time to complete their butchery of Elliott's lost command.

★   ★   ★

As his men drew closer, Tom Custer saw that more than frozen stalks of winter grass rose tall in the hallowed air around each corpse. The back of every soldier bristled with a score or more arrows.

The search detail slid from their horses in grim, tight-lipped shock at what greeted their eyes. An unmasked revulsion was written plain as paint around every soldier's eyes, in the set of every trooper's jaw, as each man stumbled through the tangle of mutilated bodies, trying vainly to recognize a familiar face.

Hoping he would not.

Major Joel H. Elliott and his fifteen men had all been butchered in the most gruesome manner possible. Every torso bullet-riddled. Pinned with arrows. Backs, buttocks, and legs gashed. The hostiles had slashed most every throat, and at least four heads lay beside their frozen bodies.

"There were eighteen men still unaccounted for when we left the Washita, boys." The younger Custer swallowed deep against the gall rising in his throat. "With Sergeant Major Kennedy, Elliott, and his fifteen men here, that still leaves one man unaccounted for on the day of the battle. One soldier to find."

"Never gonna find that boy, sir," Grimes growled.

"My detail ain't leaving until we find a body, Grimes."

"Better yet, Lieutenant—I say we find the Injuns did this to our boys!" said one of the sour-faced troopers.

"Time enough for that!" Tom Custer snapped. "Time now to see these men get a fitting burial."

He turned, searching the whitened, bitter faces for a man to count on. "Schmidt?"

"Yessir?"

"Head back to General Custer," he ordered. "Tell him what we found. Request a wagon—no, make that two. Bring the wagons here to recover the bodies of these poor soldiers."

"Understood, sir." Schmidt leapt to the saddle, wheeled his prancing horse in a circle, galloped off toward the destroyed camp of Black Kettle's Cheyenne.

"Damn them all!" Tom Custer drove one gloved fist down into the open palm of his other hand.

"There'll come a time when Autie and I will make these goddamned bastards pay for what they've done here!"

CHAPTER 15

L IKE any morsel of gossip, the discovery of Elliott's command spread through the regiment like wildfire. Barely controlling his own rage, Custer ordered three of Bell's wagons emptied and dispatched with another squad to follow Sergeant Nels Schmidt, with orders to bring in the bodies of Elliott's men. At the same time, Sheridan and Custer determined to take two companies of troops with them as they marched downstream toward the nearby camps deserted following Black Kettle's defeat.

"From the lay of the land, Custer, I get an idea why you didn't learn of the other villages until it was almost too late."

"Not just the rolling countryside, sir. Bloody poor scouting on our part. Should've known more of what I was going into before I attacked that Cheyenne village."

"You feel lucky you rode out of this valley with your hair?"

"It'd never come to that, General! Not like poor Elliott!"

"Perhaps it was fortuitous that you retreated from the

Washita when you did. Appears you would've had your hands full finding time to scratch your ass with thousands of hostiles breathing down your neck."

"I've learned *my* lesson. Too late for Major Elliott to learn his. Have to rely more on my scouts. Pay a bit more attention to their advice."

"Haven't learned it all yet, eh, Custer?"

Custer flashed a nervous slash of a grin at Sheridan. "No. Seems life has a way of dealing me a surprising card every now and then."

Both chuckled at Custer's easy joke on himself, until a small group of civilian and Osage scouts, clustered in a loose knot up the trail, drew their attention. The guides sat sullen and silent atop their horses, waiting for Custer to ride up.

Corbin spoke first. "Joe's downstream, searching a village. This'un here appears to be where the Arapaho pitched camp."

"Very well. Lead on, Jack. Show me what you've learned."

By late afternoon, Custer had scoured every camp. The best estimates by trackers and scouts alike put the number of Indians who had been camped in the valley of the Washita the morning the Seventh Cavalry thundered into Black Kettle's camp as somewhere between five thousand and sixty-five hundred. What could quickly raise the hackles on the back of any trooper's neck was that of this number, at least a third could be counted as warriors of fighting age, each one of them carrying government-issue weapons, each warrior spoiling for a good scrap with the U.S. Cavalry.

The Osages informed Custer they believed the small

camp had been Arapaho under Little Raven; the largest, Cheyennes under Medicine Arrow; and in addition, two bands of Kiowas under Satanta and Lone Wolf. They had found enough signs in the abandoned camps to know the Washita had been visited at the time of the battle by some small bands of Apache and Comanche.

"When I said you'd struck a nest of yellow jackets, General"—Moses Milner paused to spit a stream of brown juice into the trampled snow, "was I far wrong?"

"No, you weren't, Joe," Custer admitted. "Appears there was plenty enough of 'em to fight that day."

"Them Cheyenne can give a fella all the fight you want—if'n you plan on running onto 'em again sometime down the line."

"Soon, Joe," Custer growled. "I want to find out what these Kiowa and Cheyenne are made of."

In every camp lay signs of a hasty retreat. Stuffed in the forks of the winter-bare trees stood hundreds of peeled lodge poles the tribes planned to use as replacements come spring and breakup of the Washita camps. As the cavalry officers rode into the last abandoned village, identified by the Osages as a Kiowa camp, they noticed hundreds of buffalo robes and old, vermin-infested blankets scattered across the grounds. Kettles and other cast-iron cooking utensils had been abandoned in a hurried and disorderly flight, along with adzes, knives, even an ancient coffee mill.

"Near as the scouts can determine it, General," Custer said to Sheridan, "this was Satanta's crowd—camped right here."

"General Custer!"

They wheeled at the sound of the familiar voice. Ben Clark jogged up to the cluster of officers.

"Begging pardon, General Sheridan. Should be calling the lieutenant colonel by his proper rank."

"That's quite all right, son." Sheridan smiled genuinely.

"You act as if you've got the jitters bad, Ben. Seen a ghost?" Custer inquired.

"Kiowas—the ones raiding Kansas, sir."

"How're you so sure of that?" Sheridan demanded.

"We finally have some evidence, General. No mistaking it now."

"Show me!" Sheridan flagged his arm impatiently.

Clark led the officers past snowy circles clearly showing where the lodges had been pinned to the earth, each complete with a blackened, rock ring signifying a fire pit. Milner, Corbin, and a handful of Pepoon's army scouts waited with Hard Rope and other Osage scouts in a mute circle.

As Custer and the others approached, the scouts shuffled out of the way. On the ground lay two stiffened, snow-dusted bodies. They were not Indians.

The smaller of the two was a boy about two years of age. While he appeared malnourished, with sunken cheeks and ribby flanks, along with several bruises coloring his death-pale face, no man was certain just how the boy had died.

Beside the youngster lay a larger corpse, more pitiful to look at. Despite the blood, decay, and predators, any man could tell she had been a beauty—blond, in her early twenties. Her skull crushed. Two bullets fired point-blank into her forehead from such close range that powder burns smudged the edges of the tiny, puckered holes.

"They ain't been captive here long, General," Milner said, breaking the tense silence.

"Why do you say that?" Custer inquired.

"She's still got her civilian clothes on. That dress, them gaiters on her legs to hold up them torn stockings, all of it. She been here very long at all, them clothes'd be worn out. Be wearing Injun dresses an' leggings."

"I see . . ." Custer's voice trailed off.

"You might want to see this too, General." Jack Corbin stepped up, opening his hand. In it lay a small piece of cornmeal cake.

"What's that, pray tell?" Sheridan demanded.

"Food for the road, sir," Corbin answered sourly.

"Found it when we turned the body over. Gal had it stuffed down between her breasts. Near as we can figure, she was fixing to light out," Milner said, his teeth tearing at a new hunk of black tobacco.

His eyes slewed around the group of high-ranking officers for a few breathless moments more before he continued. "When Custer's soldiers rode down on Black Kettle's camp, the news traveled downriver damned quick. Wasn't long before news hit this village and all hell broke loose, most like. Warriors hustling out for the fight, getting weapons and ponies ready to ride out to do battle. Women and kids screeching to beat the band, tearing down lodges so the camp'd hit the trail running."

"Goddammit! What of the woman?" Sheridan griped, perturbed at the long-winded way of scout Milner.

"General—" Milner spat a stream of tobacco juice, letting Sheridan suffer a bit more of a wait, "we figure this poor woman got wind of what was going on in all the excitement. Somehow she figured out the army was attacking the villages and she sure didn't want to be dragged along by the squaws when they broke camp. Seems she figured to tear off and make good her escape, get downstream someways to soldiers. But that's probably when she was found out."

"And murdered!" Sheridan roared into the silence around him.

"Two bullets in the head, close range. That's murder in my tally," Milner said.

Custer knitted his bushy blond eyebrows to tell Milner he disapproved of openly baiting his superior. "Before or after her skull was crushed?"

"She's shot after. Dead a'ready."

"My Lord!" Sheridan whispered angrily.

"First time a man sees such savagery, General, it leaves its scar," Custer said.

"Granted, I witnessed my share during the recent rebellion—yet I saw nothing as inhumane as this."

"I wouldn't call an Indian *human* by any stretch of the imagination, General," said Schuyler Crosby, Sheridan's aide-de-camp.

"Spoken like a truly ignorant soldier boy!" Milner spat at the well-scrubbed officer.

Crosby puffed like a challenged prairie rooster. "Why, I'll not be lectured by some half-savage, unkempt wild man smelling no better than an Indian of bear grease."

"Ain't no different than any stupid pencil-pushing desk soldier smelling of lilac water yourself!" Milner barked back into the trembling officer's crimson face.

"Gentlemen! Please!" Custer barked.

For the moment it appeared the young Lieutenant Colonel Schuyler Crosby would draw his pistol on Milner.

Custer was certain that should Crosby break leather with that revolver of his, Crosby would be the dead man.

Custer clamped Crosby's wrist. "I recommend you think twice about it, Colonel, then take your hand from your belt and scratch your nose with it."

Crosby stared into the cold, icy blue of Custer's eyes. Instead of scratching his nose, Sheridan's aide jerked his arm free as he wheeled about and stomped off.

"You were a bit hard on him, Joe," Custer chided.

"Nowhere near as hard as I'd been had the dumb bastard cleared leather with that popgun of his." Milner brought his left hand out from under his coat where he gripped his own Walker Colt. "Never got the goat of a man so quick before."

"You egged the man on!" Sheridan moved closer, his eyes flaring with accusation.

"Begging pardon, sir!" Custer stuck an arm out, stopping Milner from starting a ruckus with Sheridan. "I think Crosby there was provoked by nothing more than his own impetuous nature. Besides, I agree with Joe."

"Agree?" Sheridan snapped.

"We really aren't all that different from the savages we're chasing, General."

"Explain yourself, Custer."

"Simple, General. Only difference between us and the Indians is that these hostiles live more closely to nature and the wilderness than white men do. We have in all of us that selfsame capacity for brutality. Since the red man's that much closer to the wild side of a man's soul, it doesn't take all that long for him to get from peaceful happiness to the savage murder of a woman when she's seen as nothing more than an enemy who's trying to escape."

Sheridan fumed. "Explain why—"

"Ironic thing about it was that Crosby was just about to prove the very point Joe was making."

Sheridan huffed at last. "I suppose you do have a point there."

"I'll send Moylan with some men back to remove the bodies to our camp for the night. Given a decent burial."

"Very well," Sheridan growled, still shaken by the fiery exchange that had nearly ended in bloodshed.

A winter sun had begun to settle among the western hills when Sheridan jabbed a finger into Custer's chest. "Custer, we must stop them now. There's no other course." The iron was in Sheridan's voice.

"Believe me—we'll stop them. If the General pleases, a moment in private?" Custer turned away from the cluster of officers with Sheridan at his side and stepped off a few yards.

"General, we can't afford to get bogged down here on the southern plains. We must remember not to put a match to the situation here . . . or we won't be free to see to problems north of here."

"You concentrate on this damned department," Sheridan growled. "It's your job—and your career. If *you* don't stop these wild savages from murdering and stealing and Lord knows what right here and now, by God, you never will make command!"

Custer held his pride in check. "Your plans for this operation show we can stop them here, this winter."

Sheridan bit off the end of a stogie. "Better you decide what you're gonna do with your career, Custer. Lines are being drawn, not only out here but in Washington City. Can't you see there's a great imbalance in justice here on the frontier."

"Justice?"

"If a man in these parts commits murder, what do we do to him?"

"We hang him."

"Precisely!" Sheridan's face grew more animated. "If a man steals a horse, what do we do?"

"Imprison him."

"Right again."

"I don't get your point, General. What's all this have to do with the hostiles?"

"When the goddamned redskins commit these same crimes, we give the bastards better annuities! More blankets, flour, sugar—and guns. Always the guns! Under this present confusing government policy the civilization of the wild man will progress very slowly. If at all."

"I agree. If the government only kept the weapons from the young warriors. The officials back east who're awarding these annuities to the hostile tribes are the same officials bawling for the army's help in stomping out the raids and killings. If they'd keep the guns away from the agencies, the history of these plains would be written with far fewer bloody chapters."

"My young friend," Sheridan said, "you're beginning to understand the bitter truth about the soldier's life. History's not written by soldiers like us. History's written by the politicians. They're the ones who hold the real power. We poor soldiers do nothing more than live or die in those scenarios written for us by the men who wield the true power. With all our might of men and arms—we old soldiers are nothing more than paper tigers."

"I'm surprised to hear you say that, sir. I can't believe

we're unable to change the outcome of things here in the western lands."

"If you don't believe me now, young friend, I'll give you a few years. Then you should see things in a truer light. You'll realize we have no real control over the destiny of this frontier."

"A few years?" Custer swallowed. "I don't have that long to wait, General. With the way things are going now, it'll be eight to ten years before I can expect to make colonel. Too damned many officers and too few command slots."

Sheridan whirled on him. "Then if you want to make something of your future, Custer . . . there's one and one way only. You crush these red sonsabitches on the southern plains. Give those starch-collared bastards back east something to sit up and take notice of. You'll make a name for yourself. Hang every goddamned warrior you get your hands on, burn the villages and drive the rest back to their reservations. You do that . . . George Armstrong Custer will never have to worry about his future again!"

A pale winter sun lost itself behind the hills as Sheridan's detail pushed into camp east of Black Kettle's devastated village. Here they'd stay upwind of those rotting pony carcasses.

"Dr. Bailey," Custer said to the surgeon assigned to the Kansas Volunteer Cavalry, "you and Major Jenness will be in charge of identifying the young woman and child. Perhaps someone in your regiment will know the deceased."

"Very good, General," Bailey answered. He and Major George Jenness trudged back to that pair of horses bearing the frozen corpses.

The Kansans spread blankets across the icy snow, then gently lowered both bodies to the ground. Jenness himself carried the grim news to each of the volunteer companies.

An eerie pall of silence descended over the camp of the Nineteenth Kansas. One by one the companies began a sad procession past the grotesque corpses. Two soldiers volunteered to hold torches over the bodies stretched out on the gray of army blankets. Winter's twilight tumbled headlong into the blackness of a tarry, silent night, punctuated only by an occasional cough or sneeze of a soldier standing patiently in line, waiting for his turn to inspect the mortal remains of mother and child.

From those surrounding hills drifted the yips and the howls of four-legged predators, finished gorging themselves for the day. Stiff leather soles scuffed across the crusty, trampled snow as each man shuffled forward in line until his turn came at last, stepping into that spooky corona of torchlight, bending down to stare into the horrifying death masks of mother and son.

Moylan stood beside Custer, shivering involuntarily with the aura of melancholy. *Surely,* Myles thought, *these Kansas men would rather be at home, tending their stock or repairing plow harness.*

He drank long from the tin of coffee one of the Kansas mess cooks kept warm for him. Wondering when he might slip off to find some sow belly. Hardtack, if nothing else—

"Oh, sweet God!"

A soldier's screech yanked Myles out of his hunger. Beneath the fluttering torches the Kansas farm boy's knees went to mush. He fell on hands and knees over the bodies. Confusion broke out as others crushed around him, friends helping the young man to his feet when he sank like a wet sack of oats, sobbing.

"It's her! And the boy, Willie! Oh, goddamn 'em!"

Moylan sloshed the coffee out of his cup, following Custer into the crowd, where together they pushed their way through the volunteers until they confronted Dr. Bailey and the young soldier.

"What's your name, son?"

The soldier studied Custer's face before answering. His dirty cheeks were tracked with tears, his reddened eyes sunken deep in a pinched face matted with the peach fuzz of youth.

"Simms, sir."

"I'm Custer."

"I know, General." His quivering chin dropped against his chest, stifling a sob as it broke past his cracked lips. The soldier's body shook with torment.

"You know the woman, Simms?"

"Yes." More hot tears gushed free. Bailey and another soldier steadied the young private. "She was my cousin's wife!"

"This is her boy?" Custer whispered.

"Willie Blinn."

"That means this is Mrs. Clara Blinn, General," Bailey said, touching Custer with his dark-ringed eyes. "She was with her husband, coming back from a trading venture with several others, when their train was attacked on the old Arkansas River Road, just inside the Colorado line. For three days the savages shot up the group pretty bad, even though the folks used their wagons for cover. Not one mule or horse left standing when the bloodthirsty murderers pulled out."

Custer turned to Simms. "You're that certain this is Clara Blinn and her son Willie?"

The soldier nodded before he spoke, lips trembling, as if he knew should he make a sound it would surely turn into something horrifying of itself. "Yessir. I was there myself. Not many of us come out of that fight."

"You were at the attack on the wagon train?"

Simms nodded.

"Did Blinn himself die in the attack and siege on the train?" Custer inquired.

"No," Bailey replied. "Only seriously wounded. Their kin was hopeful she'd be found alive. Barely twenty-three years of age. Her boy can't be more than two years old now, from what I can tell of his little bone structure."

"General Custer!"

"Over here, Cooke!" Custer shouted into the tar-black of night, responding to the voice thick with the Canadian Scotch accent of Billy Cooke's motherland.

"Ah, General, been searching for you everywhere. Tom—Lieutenant—Custer's detail's bringing in the remains of Elliott's men now." He watched Custer's shoulders sag.

"He was a fine officer. Been with me and the Seventh from the start."

"I remember," Cooke replied. "We joined near the same time, when the new regiment was created."

"They're bringing them soon?"

"Wagons pulling in now."

"What time do you have, Moylan?"

Myles pulled a watch from his tunic pocket, turning it so that he could read the face beneath the dancing torchlight. "Almost nine o'clock."

"Time to go." He took his reins from Moylan and climbed to the saddle. "Dr. Bailey? Please see that Mrs. Blinn and her son are wrapped securely in blankets then bound with rope. Better that we take them north with us. Home to their folk. Can't think of a reason why we should bury them in Indian Territory."

"Not a goddamned reason, General."

Moylan followed Custer as he sawed the horse about, easing his way through that mob of muttering volunteers, who were angry hearing that one of the women captives had been found . . . dead. By the time Custer and Moylan made it back to the Seventh's camp, Regimental Surgeon Henry Lippincott had already ordered a sweeping crescent of bonfires started by the soldiers. In the light of that half-ring lay sixteen bodies. Already a handful of the frozen corpses had been positively identified by friends and bunkies. Custer slid from his cold saddle and Dandy was led away.

"Lippincott."

"General?"

"Thanks for seeing that things got started in my absence."

"You're welcome, General. Regarding disposition of the remains, we'll await your decision."

On his way back to camp earlier, Custer had decided. "We'll bury them here. Where they fell." He looked up from the naked, grotesque corpses. "You seen Benteen?"

"No, General. I haven't—"

"Sir!" An older soldier strode up. "I saw him yonder while ago."

"Thank you, soldier. Run him down. Ask him to see me at once."

"Sure thing, sir!"

Custer turned to the surgeon. "Have you identified Elliott?"

Without a word, Lippincott motioned for Custer to follow. They walked quietly among the soldiers parading past the frozen corpses.

"Several of us think this was Major Elliott."

His eyes narrowed on a corpse brutally beheaded. The scalp of the head they had found had been torn away before the back of the skull was smashed to jelly. Blood and ooze had blackened over the entire head. Lippincott turned the grisly object so the wide, glazed eyes stared up at Custer. Moylan heard Custer draw a deep breath of cold air. The young adjutant swallowed repeatedly to keep his own stomach down.

"That's Major Elliott," Custer agreed, tearing his eyes from the frightening gore. He let another breath out slowly. "As each man is identified, I want it recorded in your medical records. The number and type of wounds, weapons used, if possible—all of it. Wrap each of the remains in a blanket, binding it with rope. Let's make it hard for any predators to get at the men now."

"Very good, sir."

"You've had supper, Lippincott?"

"No. Weren't many of us had an appetite after seeing what was done to these men."

"General? You wanted to see me?"

Custer turned to face the strapping Missourian. "Benteen! Yes. I want your company to prepare a mass grave for these bodies. You need enough room for all the enlisted."

"What of Elliott, sir?"

"We're taking him back with us. He'll not be left here.

As an officer, he deserves the honor of a military funeral. I believe you can understand that?"

"Perfectly."

"We'll lay his men here in the valley of the Washita. Where they fell in duty to their country."

Benteen saluted, his back snapping ramrod rigid. "I'll be at it straightaway. Is there a particular spot you had in mind?"

Custer appraised the officer a moment.

"You're familiar with the country immediately west of the village?"

"I am. We rode in for the attack from that direction."

"There's a hill just west of the village. Dig the grave atop that hill, overlooking the village and the river beyond. From there, a man can see the defeated village and the icy Washita."

Benteen snapped a quick salute and was gone.

"He doesn't like you, General," Moylan said.

Custer turned to Moylan. "He doesn't have to, Lieutenant."

"With your permission, if I was you, I'd picked someone else for grave detail, sir."

Blue eyes flashed in the torchlight. "Mr. Moylan, you aren't me. Besides—" Custer gazed after the tall Virginia-born officer disappearing into the gloom of night, "Benteen's a good soldier. He may hate my insides, and I his—but Benteen is a soldier above all. And he'll always do exactly as ordered."

CHAPTER 16

By midnight Benteen sent a young corporal with word to Custer that his men had finished the mass grave.

As officers and enlisted climbed the knoll behind the three creaking wagons burdened with blanket-wrapped corpses, an eerie pall descended over them all. Torches flickered in the mournful wind that sighed through the bare hackberry and blackjack. Even the moon hid its pale face behind a death shroud of clouds. An uneasy cloak of dread fell upon those men crowding the trench where the bodies lay side by side by side.

Benteen sensed the hair rise on the back of his neck as a wolf howled from the trees off to the west. He was certain the predator's beastly call signified that something far greater than Custer himself had destined Frederick Benteen to head this detail. He smiled inwardly to himself, but sourly. A small, bitter victory over Custer.

Benteen had been the first to question Custer's decision to abandon the search of the Washita Valley without finding Elliott's men, raising his first objection the moment they

began their march back to Camp Supply. It was Benteen at
the center of those grumbling and secretive complainers
who called Custer to task ever since that retreat from this
bloody valley. Only right that Benteen now had a hand in
laying these men to rest.

"What a bitter sacrifice," Benteen whispered to Lieutenant Edward Godfrey beside him at the lip of the dark
trench.

Although he was a junior officer, Godfrey had made it
clear to Benteen that he had disagreed with Custer that
morning of the battle. The young lieutenant had with his
own ears heard Elliott's men having a hot time of it. He was
amazed that Custer had refused to ride to the major's aid.

"Many a good soldier sacrificed on the pyre of glowing
ambition," Godfrey whispered.

"Watching good men laid to rest in the ground because
of a bad decision will anger any officer who cares about his
men. There was no reason for this," Benteen said acidly.

"It isn't our lot to understand, is it?"

"Damn him!" Benteen growled under his breath.
"Custer was more interested in counting the captured
goods—not to mention his interest in the condition of a
certain Cheyenne prisoner—than he was interested in the
lives of these men butchered by Cheyenne warriors."

As Benteen's men lowered the last body into the long
trench, Custer himself stepped forward, pulling the buffalo
cap from his head.

"Men." He coughed. "I don't have to tell you what it
means to lose good soldiers like this." Custer ground the
buffalo cap between his two wind-raw hands, staring into
the trench before his eyes raked the somber, torch-lit
assembly.

"When a man becomes a soldier, he doesn't expect a life of ease. Even the chance at a long life. A soldier asks only to be given the chance to serve the Republic."

Custer paused as some of the mourners finished muttering quiet comments, others adding "amens."

"These men offered the ultimate sacrifice. A sacrifice not only of blood . . . but of love. Love of country. Love of soldiering. Each one was a soldier. I pray each of us will remember these men as that: *soldiers*. Not as dead men, for they are not. These gallant souls have gone on to a better reward. These empty shells we bury here serve only to remind us that once they were our fellows, our companions, our friends. Let us remember them as they breathed, and as they fought."

Custer stepped back. "We commend their spirits to God. Amen."

He turned, jammed the cap on his head. Blue eyes scanned the crowd until he found Myers and Thompson.

"Gentlemen," he sighed, "you both will see that some of your men remain behind to assist Benteen in covering the remains."

Myers glanced at Thompson. "Yes, sir."

"Carry on, gentlemen. I'll be in camp if you need me. Yates will be in charge of securing our perimeter for the night."

They watched Custer wheel and plod downhill. Myers said, "Times I don't understand the man."

Thompson shuddered. "It gives me the creeps. Seeing the general not acting in his right mind—what with these men buried here—the wind and wolves all a'howling at us. Damn!"

Myers chuckled with a hollow sound. "Even the trees

around us look like some kind of hoodoos with wild arms scratching against the sky."

"Like they'd grab right ahold of a man."

"Let's be about our assignment, Mr. Thompson."

"Yessir."

"I suggest your detail scour the hillside for deadfall. Use it to cover the grave so that no goddamn wolves dig up the bodies after Custer's gone to so much trouble to get them buried. And buried quick."

"He's washed his hands of it all now, hasn't he?" Thompson whispered.

"For the time being. Time comes, that him leaving Elliott behind to die will come back to haunt Custer. My sainted mother was one to say the raven always comes back to roost. They always do. Custer might've washed his hands of the whole grisly matter. But as much as he'll scrub, Custer'll know his hands will never come completely clean. Someday this'll come back to haunt him."

"Think he'll *ever* be shet of it?" Thompson asked.

"No," Myers answered. "Custer'll carry the blood of young soldiers on his hands till his dying day."

By first light that following morning the entire command of the Seventh Cavalry and Nineteenth Kansas Volunteers marched southeast down the Washita.

By midmorning, Custer's scouts discovered that the Indian trail split into two directions. Moses Milner and the others sat atop their winded animals among the milling Osage and Kaw trackers, waiting for Ben Clark to bring Custer up.

"Sure wish you'd think about getting yourself a regulation mount, Joe." Custer smiled.

Milner eyed him suspiciously, then spit a brown track to the snow. "You got something again' mules?"

"Just figure a horse would outshine that cantankerous, wheezing bag of bones you ride."

"General, you ain't ever been held up on my account, have you?"

"Can't say as I have, Joe."

"Anytime you'd care to wager, I'll give you handicap with you on your finest charger and me on the old gal here: I'll beat you into camp before light falls from the sky, any day you choose."

"What handicap would you be foolish enough to offer?" Custer appraised Milner's mule more carefully.

"Why, General, I'll give you a couple mile on me. Maybe even three—you think you'd need them?"

"Now, why would I need such a handicap, Joe?"

"Damn, General—but I'd give you more credit than you deserved, I suppose. You got yourself a handicap a'ready, if for no other reason than you're mounted on a army horse!"

Milner spit into the snow as all the scouts laughed at his joke on Custer. Jack Corbin rode into view, whipping his winded pony into that circle of civilians surrounding Custer. He gallantly ripped off his greasy hat and swept it low in salute.

"Morning, General."

"Mr. Corbin."

"You was right, Joe," Corbin declared.

"Ain't many times I been found wrong, Corbin." Milner's tone slid out a bit on the caustic side. He removed the stubby pipe from his lips. "Why you so all-fired anxious to prove me wrong, anyhow?"

"You boys care to let me in on this?" Custer asked impatiently.

"Joe figured them villages would break up," Corbin announced. "Sure enough, they did."

"Why'd you figure them to split up, Joe?" Custer asked.

"Simple. First, there ain't a good chance for the bands to find much game in winter. Easier hunting if they split up. Next, there's always some Injuns wanna go off one way, and others wanna go off on another. Still more up and decide to try someplace new entirely. Last reason, General, Injuns is just Injuns."

"What in thunder do you mean by that?"

"Simply 'cause Injuns choose to split up every time they got the army on their back trail."

"I see." Custer stared off to the southeast. "You able to say what the hostiles might do?"

"Couple camps moseyed down the Washita this direction," Corbin answered. "The bigger passel of 'em headed due south."

"Heading for the Red River, General," Milner declared.

"You figure we could find a couple of villages marching down the Washita?" Custer said.

Corbin nodded. "That's right. Imagine they'll be heading straight for—"

"Fort Cobb," Custer finished Corbin's sentence. "General Hazen and Fort Cobb, Indian Territory!" He slapped his thigh.

"You figure to run 'em down, General?" Milner smiled with the pipe between his yellowed teeth.

Custer said, "We'll follow the hostiles straight to Fort Cobb. I'll be busted before I'll let those murderers hide behind Hazen like a bunch of schoolboy brats behind their mama's skirts."

Corbin cleared his throat. "They've got a few days' start on us already."

Milner threw his head back, laughing. "Shit, young'un—ain't I taught you any better? Village packed with women and kids and old folks ain't able to move anywhere as quick as mounted cavalry." He turned to Custer, finally removing the stub of his pipe from his mouth. "General, you follow me and Jack—we'll get your command downriver to Fort Cobb as fast as your cavalry can march!"

"To Fort Cobb, sir." Jack Corbin pulled his gray charger round, signaling the nearby Osages to follow him.

Custer turned to Milner. "It'll be easy enough to bottle up one band of hostiles there at Fort Cobb. Then all I have to do is countermarch southwest to pick up the other trail you say the big bands are taking."

"Pretty tidy, you ask me, General. You play this hand right, you can whup 'em all afore spring."

The azure eyes twinkled. "Not just this one hand, Joe. I'm dealing the cards now. And these bands are about to lose the last call of the night!"

"You are Medicine Arrow?" Satanta asked of the large, gray-headed Cheyenne warrior seated across the fire from him.

"I am Medicine Arrow." The deep voice filled Satanta's lodge. "You are the one they call the White Bear?"

"Yes, I am Satanta. This is Lone Wolf," he replied, indicating the older warrior beside him. "He is chief of a small band of Kiowa who follow the seasons with my people."

"We know of Lone Wolf," the Cheyenne leader stated. "My chiefs and warriors want to know if the Kiowa will join us in wiping out the soldiers of Yellow Hair before he can destroy any more sleeping villages."

Satanta and Lone Wolf studied one another across the time of three breaths.

The younger Kiowa shook his head. "We have decided not to join you in making war on this Yellow Hair. We came here to the foot of these mountains to escape his soldiers. If your warriors want war with Yellow Hair, the Kiowa will leave this place for Hazen's fort, the one the white men call Cobb. With Hazen we won't have to worry about pony soldiers in the night."

Medicine Arrow laughed so loudly it shook the lodge poles. When he finished, his granite eyes narrowed on his Kiowa hosts.

"I was a fool to ask Satanta and Lone Wolf to meet me here on the north fork of the Red River, here in the shadow of the Wichita mountains, after Black Kettle was killed and his village wiped from the face of the land."

The words poured like poison from sneering lips. His cruel mouth was little more than a scar slashed across his dark face. Satanta sensed the coming sting of the Cheyenne's rebuke.

"A fool I was to ask White Bear and Lone Wolf to join the Cheyenne, for now I see the Kiowa nation lay down and show its belly for the white dogs," Medicine Arrow spat. "Like the runt of the litter, you cower before Yellow Hair even though he does not threaten your villages."

"Our eyes saw the destruction brought by the Yellow Hair's soldiers—"

"*Silence!*" the Cheyenne roared.

The lodge packed with Kiowa and Cheyenne warriors stirred nervously. This was a bad thing, friends saying evil of friends. Perhaps, this trouble came by the white man's evil.

"You Kiowa dogs cannot call yourselves warriors! Cheyenne Dog Soldiers will protect you as we protect our women. Or we can watch you destroyed, withering as the grass before the winter winds."

Amid the silence of the lodge, Medicine Arrow held his bare palm over the flames, his eyes narrowing on Satanta and Lone Wolf, watching their reaction as he burned his own flesh. His wolfish grin grew bigger, until he removed his hand from the flame, showing the Kiowa his charred totem of bravery.

"There, my sacred little brothers! If I would burn my own hand, would I not destroy your camps and all therein if they offend me?"

The Cheyenne chief leapt to his feet, accompanied by the Dog Soldiers who joined him in this grand council of tribes.

"Run, Kiowa! Run! Hide behind your soldier chief who will protect you from Yellow Hair. Know that the mighty Cheyenne are not running. Nor will we hide from Yellow Hair. We stay the winter as we have for winters beyond count. When spring brings forth the buffalo for our hunters, we journey to the Llano Estacado in the south."

Medicine Arrow glared down at the warriors clustered about Satanta and Lone Wolf. "Once a powerful nation, the Kiowa. Once our brothers in war, vowing to wipe the white man from the face of the land. Now a race of dogs tucking tails between their legs when the name of Yellow Hair is whispered."

He kicked the fire pit, sending embers and burning wood scattering before the Kiowa's feet. Sparks shot into the smoke hole overhead like summer's fireflies.

"Do not worry for me, Kiowa brothers. Yellow Hair dares not attack Dog Soldiers. Worry only for yourselves. Proof of that lies rotting along the banks of the Washita. You have seen that the soldiers of Yellow Hair kill women." He laughed, like the metallic scraping of knife blade on stone. "Shake, gutless Kiowa! For you are no better than squaws!"

Medicine Arrow swept from the lodge like a spring thunderstorm, followed by his tense warriors. Outside, the noise and bluster of their passing from camp faded, until the Kiowa sat in silence once more.

Satanta studied his old friends, the chiefs of the Kiowa bands. Brooding on what to say the way a toothless one chewed on boiled meat. His own son stood.

"Tsalante wishes to be heard?" Satanta said.

"Yes, Father. In my twenty summers the Kiowa have never been pressed between two forces as we are this winter." He held up one hand. "We fear the pony soldiers of Yellow Hair, for they have wiped Black Kettle off the earth." Tsalante listened to the murmurs of the old men as he brought up his other hand. "Over here we have the mighty Cheyenne, who would have us join their war on the soldiers. Like Yellow Hair, Medicine Arrow has the might to destroy our Kiowa villages."

"Your son speaks with the wisdom of many winters," Lone Wolf admitted sadly. "We are caught in between. With no place to go."

"I cannot accept defeat," Satanta said, wagging his head.

"It is true!" Lone Wolf argued. "Either we flee the jackal by running into the wolf's mouth, or we flee the wolf and find ourselves caught in the jackal's mouth. We have no choice!"

For a long time, Satanta stared at the flames dying near his feet. He finally sighed, straightened.

"Satanta has decided. As chief I must do what is best for my people. Not only what our warriors clamor for. Satanta does what is best for the women and children. The old ones. The sick ones who will not last the winter."

"You are chief," Lone Wolf replied. "Your word will stand."

Satanta went on, "I tell you this, brothers. If Kiowa join with Cheyenne against Yellow Hair now, we would have the pony soldiers to fear."

"This is true," Lone Wolf answered while others muttered their agreement.

"But if we go to Fort Cobb and live in peace as the Yellow Hair wants, we have only to fear the wrath of this evil one called Medicine Arrow."

"His Dog Soldiers are many!" Lone Wolf cried.

"They are few, while the pony soldiers who would crush us are like the stars overhead," Satanta answered sadly. "Better to have the pony soldiers to protect us against the war-crazy Cheyenne—better that than live in fear of pony soldiers wiping our villages from the face of the earth."

A day after the expedition left the battlefield, a harsh storm battered Custer's command, dumping two more feet of fresh snow on the surrounding countryside. Hacking a path through the wilderness became an ordeal. Civilian teamsters struggled in the predawn darkness, chipping harness and tack out of the ice as they readied their wagons for the day's march.

Brutal winds slashed at the men for two days. Civilian and soldier alike used axes, picks, and shovels to cut through frozen drifts blocking the trail or to chop ice from slippery creek banks.

On the fourth day the skies cleared as welcome, southerly winds breathed warmth across the land. At first the troopers hailed the warmer weather, until they found the red clay and snow turned to red sticky gumbo. Harder work than before. Custer employed more than two hundred troopers in clearing the narrow trail made by the fleeing Kiowa, hauling his heavy wagons through boggy meadows and windswept lowlands. Hour after hour the men hacked at the impenetrable undergrowth; the columns slogged through a quagmire sucking greedily at every wagon wheel, hoof, and boot.

While the command struggled crossing a sharp ravine on the morning of the seventeenth of December, the air rang with excited whoops. Corbin and Clark galloped into view, tearing through the scattered work details.

"You found something?" Custer piped eagerly, standing in his stirrups as the two scouts slid their horses to a halt.

"Found your Indians, General," Ben Clark announced. "The bunch skedaddling to Fort Cobb."

"What're they up to now? Haven't made it to Hazen, have they?" Custer rapid-fired his questions.

"Party of warriors on the trail ahead, waiting for us. I figure the Kiowa been watching us for some time."

"By the gods of Abraham! Tell me something I don't already know!"

"Sir . . . Injuns waiting under a flag of truce."

Custer was speechless. He opened his mouth three times before any words broke free. "By God's blood! Like

Lee himself at Appomattox Wood! Gentlemen—let's parley with these Kiowa."

Less than a mile ahead Custer ran across some of his Osage and Kaw trackers who normally scouted the flanks. For the moment they sat staring across an open meadow stretching away to the east. Some eighty yards off waited a half-dozen mounted warriors, most with the butt of a rifle resting atop a thigh. In the middle sat an unarmed comrade who carried only a white scrap of cloth tied at the end of a long willow branch.

"By all that's holy! We got 'em on the run now, boys!" Custer's teeth flashed like high-country snow beneath a winter sun.

"Don't trust them Kiowa," Milner growled.

"Joe, you, Ben, and Jack come with me," Custer ordered. "We'll see what these red fellows have on their minds."

Custer kicked his mount into an easy lope. Halfway across the meadow, he threw up his arm, halting his scouts. He circled his horse twice, a signal he wanted to parley. The Indian bearing the white flag broke from the rest, galloping toward the white men.

"Any of you know Kiowa?" Custer asked.

"I might know enough to get us by today," Clark answered.

Custer appraised the messenger reining to a halt before them, his ribby pony nose to nose with Custer's stallion. Dark, hooded eyes flicked over the three scouts, not missing a weapon carried by any of the white men. The black-cherry eyes came to a rest on the soldier chief. Custer's buffalo coat hid much of his uniform. But from the way the messenger studied him, Custer sensed the man knew who sat before him.

"Go ahead, Ben. Let's find out what this fella wants."

Clark tried out some of his rusty Kiowa. What he got for his trouble was an amused look in return.

"I'm no Kiowa," the messenger spoke in English, smiling.

"Not a Kiowa?" Custer demanded.

"Goddamn! Why, we had it banked you was Kiowa," Milner put in now. "Satanta's, or Black Eagle's bunch."

The messenger lowered his white flag across his left arm, throwing a thumb over his shoulder. "They are."

"They are . . . I don't understand." Custer shook his head.

"Like I said, I'm no Kiowa."

Clark couldn't figure it. The messenger looked as Indian as the next warrior he'd run across on the plains. Those eyes and that nose . . . this stranger was born in buffalo-hide lodge. No doubt of that.

"My mother was Comanche. My father Texican. I'm in the same line of work you three fellas are. Scout for the army. Work for Hazen down to Fort Cobb. Name's Cheyenne Jack."

"You rode up on our advance with those warriors," Custer said.

"Fort Cobb ain't but twenty-five miles off." He studied Custer a moment more. "Who I got the pleasure of addressing?"

"This is General Custer, boy," Milner spouted proudly.

Clark watched the half-breed's eyebrows climb a notch.

"You're the outfit destroyed old Black Kettle's village, eh? We heard you was out and about in the country for the winter. Well, I'll go to hell in a hand cart if General Hazen didn't have that one ciphered right."

"Hazen ciphered what?" Custer put an edge to his voice.

"We've known all about what you did to that village for some time now. Didn't take long for word of that fight to come downriver. Week later, some Kiowa showed up on Hazen's doorstep and we got a better look—"

"Are the Kiowas with Hazen now?" Custer demanded. "That why a civilian employee of the army is riding the wilderness with those hostile Kiowa warriors?"

"General," the half-breed began as he untied his white rag from the willow branch, "I'm a scout for the same army you work for. We're the same, just work for different commanders is all." He tossed aside the branch, stuffing the cloth in his blanket coat. The breezes dallied with his long braids wrapped in red trade wool. A pair of eyes glinting like obsidian never left Custer's.

"So, General George Armstrong Custer, best you savvy these Indians knowed of your coming our way for some time. You've got yourself a slow and noisy bunch of soldiers."

"Get to the point of it!" Custer slapped his thigh in angry exasperation.

"I got a message here Hazen wanted me to deliver to you personal."

"Well? Out with it, man."

"I would. But I never learned to read, sir. Besides, every good army scout knows he can't read official army papers."

The half-breed fished out a folded parchment, sealed with a small dollop of wax deeply carved with the impression of an *H*. He held the parchment out. With a flourish

Custer scooped the folded document from the messenger's hand.

Ripping it open, he immediately read to himself:

Commander in the field, U.S. Army—

Indians have just brought in word that our troops to-day reached the Washita some 20 miles above here. I send this to say that all camps this side of the point reported to have been reached are friendly, and have not been on the war-path this season. If this reaches you, it would be well to communicate at once with Satanta or Black Eagle, chiefs of the Kiowas, near where you are now, who will readily inform you of the position of the Cheyennes and Arapahoes, also of our camp.

Custer's eyes climbed from the letter, flecked with cold fire. "Does Hazen know who he's addressing?"

"He ain't got idea one, General Custer."

"With me rides the commander of the Department of the Missouri, Philip H. Sheridan himself! Hazen would be interested to know that fact."

"I'm sure he would."

Shaking the brittle parchment like an autumn-dried leaf in a tremble of rage, Custer said, "Hazen's protecting the Kiowa?"

"He doesn't figure they need protecting, General," Cheyenne Jack replied. "He just wants to make sure Kiowa camps aren't butchered like Black Kettle's."

"Black Kettle's! We followed a trail of a hundred war ponies straight to the heart of his village!"

"A hundred warriors in Black Kettle's village? If that don't smell of horseshit! Black Kettle's band hasn't counted a hundred warriors since Sand Creek almost wiped his little band out for good."

Custer slapped a gloved fist into a palm. "Suppose you tell me what's going on with Hazen and his Kiowa!"

"Love to, General. But, I don't know any more than what I see with my own eyes."

"And that is?"

"Kiowa rode in some time back, telling what happened upriver to Black Kettle's camp. Last fall Hazen hoped the tribes would come to Fort Cobb for safety. But you caught the Cheyenne hunkered for the winter."

Clark watched Custer's eyes narrow.

"Hazen protecting his wards, eh?" Custer snapped.

"Looks that way."

"And now he's got the Kiowa under his wing? After they sent warriors north to rape and pillage and burn and kill? Right?"

"Hazen doesn't figure the Kiowa had a thing to do with that."

"I'm sure Hazen doesn't!" Custer scowled, once again scanning the message from the commander of Fort Cobb. "What's he mean the Kiowa will tell me where the Cheyenne and Arapaho are?"

"Cheyenne and Arapaho are assigned to Fort Cobb by treaty, General."

"By treaty, you say? Seems that Hazen's wards didn't stay at home this past summer, did they?"

"If you mean that Hazen's to keep the tribes under his thumb at all times, watching every move they make across the seasons—you're poking into a blind hole there. Hazen isn't here to wet-nurse a single band of these Indians. It's his job to prevent the trouble that you enjoy stirring up."

"How dare you lecture me on army policy!" Custer sputtered.

Cheyenne Jack straightened. "I ain't lecturing, General. You asked the questions. I answered 'em. Now, I'm all talked out."

The messenger tugged on the reins, backing his Indian pony from the crescent cluster of scouts.

"Wait! You just hold on there!" Custer shouted, nudging his horse forward until he sat opposite the half-breed. "These Kiowa know where the escaping Cheyenne and Arapho are?"

"That's what Hazen told you, ain't it?"

"I take it they aren't nearby?"

"General, you hit the mark on that one."

Custer flicked his eyes to his scouts. "You hit the nail on the head this time around, boys."

The half-breed perked up, curious. "How's that?"

"We already learned the tribes had split up, didn't we, fellas?" Custer said. "So all we had to do was find out which band of murderers went where. My scouts told me the Kiowa headed down here to Fort Cobb. We just needed you to confirm where the Cheyenne are headed."

Cheyenne Jack's dark eyes slewed over Custer's scouts. "Sounds like you know it all but the shouting."   .

"You're riding back to Fort Cobb now?" Custer asked, his eyes accusing.

"Shortly."

"You'll report to General Hazen?"

"Like I said."

"Be sure you get it right, then. That's Philip H. Sheridan, Commander, Department of the Missouri. And George Armstrong—"

"*Custer*, of the Seventh Cavalry." Cheyenne Jack smiled, a lick of humor crossing his face. "I won't forget you, General."

With that the half-breed wheeled his horse. He turned in the saddle to holler over his shoulder, "Won't anyone ever forget George Armstrong Custer and his Seventh U.S. Cavalry."

CHAPTER 17

B Y the time the soldiers had camped that afternoon of the seventeenth, the Osage trackers had located the Kiowa camps. From their brown lodges oily smoke raked across the sky a few miles north of Fort Cobb along the icy Washita. Custer figured it was time to let Sheridan in on how Hazen had been protecting the very tribes he had been sent to punish.

Sheridan fumed when Custer told him the commander of Fort Cobb had made government wards of the guilty Kiowa.

"Seems he promised the chiefs that if they camped near Fort Cobb they'd be safe!"

Sheridan's Irish temper boiled furiously. "Damn is hide! That bastard's got my hands tied, Custer!"

"Got your hands tied?"

"When you brought me news upon your return to Camp Supply—that you'd found evidence in Black Kettle's village that his band had received annuities—I passed word on to division H.Q. I wanted Sherman to know you found them in a hostile village."

"What's this got to do with Hazen and the Kiowa?"

"Goddammit, Custer! Can't you see? I'm made to punish the Indians Hazen is instructed to feed!"

"Sherman?"

"Sherman would have no part of such idiocy! Goddamned Indian Bureau. Time you realized this, Custer. They wear the pants these days over at the War Department. And when they run the War Department, they run Sherman." Sheridan slammed a fist down on his field desk, scattering papers and maps. "Something must be done to end this insanity."

"You're saying on one hand the government's told to feed and present gifts to those murderers, while the other hand is ordered to hunt them down and shoot them all."

Again, the hero of the Shenandoah drove a fist onto his field desk. "I'm ordered to fight these goddamned savages while Hazen feeds the beggars. Even shelters them in the shadows of his post! We'll just have to find a way around Hazen."

"A way around Hazen?"

"Bastard's got me trapped. I can't burn him, Custer," Sheridan moaned. "As an officer, I'm obligated by Sherman to honor Hazen's command here in the Territories."

"But you're his superior!"

"Best you start to realize the army has two fathers when it marches into Indian Territory: Sherman and Grant on the one hand," Sheridan said, gazing at his boots, "and the Indian Bureau on the other."

"Hazen takes his orders from civilians?"

"Most of the time."

"I must protest! To bring my command all this way, and now you tell me I'm forced to fight with one hand tied behind my back? I've got the Kiowa right where we want them. I can punish them now. Attack! The Nineteenth Kansas is itching for a good scrap. They feel cheated, you understand."

"Cheated?"

"They weren't in on the Washita battle."

Sheridan knitted his dark brows. He grappled with the problem a moment longer before speaking. "I must give the Kiowa a chance—"

"A chance, sir? Why not give the Nineteenth Kansas a chance for glory?"

"Goddamn your hide, Armstrong!" Sheridan's black eyes were full of sudden fire. "You're the impetuous one. Can't you see for once that this is something even bigger than you? Hell, even your friend Phil Sheridan couldn't protect you if you galloped off into that Kiowa camp and wiped them out.

"Who the hell do you think saved you from reassignment to some dead-end, no-account, chair-jockey job when your year of court-martial was up?"

"I had no idea—"

"You don't enjoy much favor back in the War Department, Custer. Mind you that! Grant himself wonders why he had to spend so much time explaining his fair-haired Boy General who shoots deserters without trial. When Grant and old Bill Sherman start peering over your shoulder, you'd best watch your backside."

"But one swift blow here!"

"Oh, shut up, Custer. This isn't the Shenandoah. Don't

you realize the hour has come and gone when you and I can move freely, without shackles in this army?"

"I thought we were to punish the tribes."

"Time you learned about the world. You listen to me and listen good, because I'll say it once. This whole winter campaign's got nothing to do with these blessed Indians. If they all starved to death, I wouldn't give a goddamn. What it's about is you. I designed this campaign for George Armstrong Custer. You're here this winter on probation. Oh, the little bastards with all their braid back in Washington didn't want you to know that, but there it is. I talked and talked and finally convinced them that this winter campaign needed someone with your abilities. We don't want you to think. You're paid to follow orders. Not go charging off. I did my best for you as a friend. But you'd better understand—you've been handed your last chance to make something of your military career."

Sheridan let that sink in a moment while he drew the withered stub of a cigar to his lips. "That shit about you chasing back after Libbie without permission the way you did—and shooting deserters! You almost bungled yourself right into some dead-end command. With no chance to crawl out of the hole you'd buried yourself in."

Custer remained silent, staring at his boots. For the first time in their long relationship, he couldn't look Sheridan in the eye. "What is it you'd have me do, General?" His voice had that clear, controlled ring to it.

"From this day forward, you'll never question a command given you, nor waver from it. Is that understood?"

"Understood, General."

"Armstrong, can't you see I need you to keep your nose

clean? If you botch things now, they'll reassign you. I need you here with me."

"Yessir."

"There's this matter of the Kiowa now, Custer." Sheridan turned to his field desk, where he glanced at a slip of foolscap on which he had been scribbling some plans of operation. "We'll talk with these Kiowa first."

"Talk them into returning their prisoners?"

"If there are any left alive," Sheridan growled. "I'd love to hang a few of those bastards for what they did to Mrs. Blinn and her boy."

"From what you've told me, that would only get us in more trouble back east."

"You're learning, aren't you?" Sheridan slapped a paternal hand on Custer's shoulder. "For the time being, we'll try talking with them. Surround the villages in the event our parley fails. You must exhaust all diplomatic means before using any firepower."

"Diplomacy with murderers, sir?"

"That's what Washington asks of us, Custer. You're a soldier, and a soldier—"

"Follows orders."

"I know to some it might seem futile," Sheridan said. "But you concentrate on one thing and one thing only until this campaign's over."

"What's that, sir?"

"The white captives these red bastards kidnapped. You remember them. When you eat and when you sleep. You think about those poor women and what they're going through at the hands of the savages. And remember that it rests in your hands to free them. Destroying one village after another won't win you favor back in Washington. Freeing those captives will."

"And Washington is the key to my promotion."

Sheridan smiled that Irish smile of his. "Now you understand how the game's played."

"Got a good teacher in Philip H. Sheridan."

"Before this winter campaign's over, Custer—we'll wrangle that promotion out of those bastards back east. We'll make you colonel and get you your own regiment if we have to hog-tie President Grant himself."

When Custer came face to face with the great Kiowa war chief Satanta, both men led armies itching for battle.

After deciding not to join Medicine Arrow, Satanta fumed at the arrogance of the Yellow Hair in following the Kiowa like a hunting dog trailing wounded, bleeding quarry, knowing full well those pony soldiers on his back trail were capable of destroying his villages at will.

On the other hand, Custer remained bitter, licking his own wounds. More than anything, he had wanted to capitalize on the Washita victory, taking the war into the Kiowa strongholds. No matter what any man might say about him, Custer had learned exactly what the Indian warrior understood best. Sheer might. War itself.

Blood was a common language understood by all peoples.

Custer's horse pawed at the crusty ground.

"Joe—" His eyes found Milner. "Take Corbin, Clark, and Romero. Maybe the Mexican can help Clark interpret Kiowa for me."

"What you got in mind, General?" Romero asked.

"Ride to the middle of the clearing and wait there.

Appears they brought their head men with them this morning. Go find out when I can parley with Satanta and the others."

"Lookee there, will you?"

Custer whirled. From the far side of the clearing two warriors left the main body, heading down a short, gentle slope heading from the trees into the bottom of the bowl.

"Time to earn your pay, Joe."

Milner grinned within his greasy beard. "Looks like the curtain's going up on this road show at last, General. 'Bout damned time."

Custer gazed at the two crossing the windswept meadow. "Couldn't agree more."

"I think it best you send just two of us out to meet them fellas," Milner advised sullenly.

"Because they've sent two?"

"Right." Milner nodded. "Make a good show of the soldier chief's intentions."

"All right." Custer sighed. "Joe, looks like you and Romero will be the ones. Go find out when I can meet with the chiefs."

"They'll keep us as far away from their village as they can, General," Romero said. "Won't be anxious to talk to you with their women and kids around."

"That's fine with me." Custer glanced over his shoulder to check on his troops snaking their way down the river some distance behind his advance party. "We won't push any farther till our command can support us."

Better than a mile back, those long, dark columns of Seventh Cavalry and Nineteenth Kansas Volunteers had begun to reach the high ground north of the river. They made an impressive show of it snaking against the white tableland. Every bit as impressive, however, were the warriors backing the two delegates descending into the frosty meadow.

"Better than five hundred warriors, by my count, General," Clark said.

Back and forth across the hills loped the Kiowa decked out in full war regalia. Their songs of war and profane challenge crackled through the air, which was heavy with the excitement of impending battle. Waving aloft their rifles and lances, bows and shields, even a blind man could tell the young warriors weren't the least bit interested in suing for peace.

What really concerned Custer were those warriors hanging back among the trees ringing the meadow. With him now were enough men to make a good stand of it should the need suddenly arise: Lieutenant Pepoon's fifty-man squad of civilians, Osage, and Kaw scouts, every man-jack of them armed and expecting a surprise if not outright treachery from the Kiowa. Captains Myers and Yates waited with Lieutenant Tom Custer. And beside the younger Custer sat reporter DeBenneville Randolph Keim, never straying far from center stage on Custer's winter campaign.

Custer settled on his McClellan saddle as his scouts reined up before the two warriors. All four moved their arms and hands, conversing in prairie sign.

In less than a minute, the scouts headed back toward Custer's group at a lope.

"I don't like the looks of that, General," Clark said.

"What's gone wrong, Ben?"

"Maybe nothing at all, General. Just figure they should've talked longer."

"By Jupiter!" Custer growled. "The truce break down?

Is that why they're coming back here at a gallop?" Custer wheeled, feeling the hairs prick along the back of his neck. "Cover 'em, men! Watch the bloody trees. I don't like the smell of this."

Behind him rose the familiar clatter of men checking the loads in their weapons, unsnapping the mule-eared holsters, resettling their cold rumps on their colder saddles. Itchy. Itchier still as the two scouts came skidding back beside Custer.

"You won't believe this, General!" Milner yelled, yanking his mule up in a snowy cascade.

"Don't try me, Milner! I'm in no mood for your humor."

"Those two back there seem upset with you," Romero explained. "They weren't about to talk with us. Want to see the pony soldier chief himself."

"Smells like a trap, Autie," Tom Custer said, inching closer. "Look at 'em. Just laying for you, waiting to get you in their claws."

Custer glanced at his younger brother. "Does have the foul smell of a trap, doesn't it, Tom?" Then he looked at Milner and Romero. "Why're you two grinning like coon hounds on the scent?"

"Them red niggers ain't planning no ambush, General," Milner answered.

"With my own eyes I can see two warriors sitting there as bait for me—"

"Them two ain't no everyday warriors, General," Milner interrupted. That's the head boys of the Kiowa nation sitting out there, waiting to talk with you personal. That's ol' Satanta and Lone Wolf themselves!"

All eyes in Custer's group focused on the two horsemen in the center of the snowy bowl. One of the Indian ponies pawed at the frozen ground anxiously. Its rider brought the pony under control.

"Lieutenant Colonel Crosby?"

"Yes?" The older officer, dressed in blue and a buffalo-hide greatcoat, nudged his horse forward beside Custer. Sheridan's aide-de-camp was, as always, impeccably attired. Regulation army.

"It would please me if you came along with me to meet these warrior chiefs as General Sheridan's personal emissary."

J. Schuyler Crosby studied the pair of Indians. "Colonel Custer, believe me—it'd be an honor, sir."

"Very good. Mr. Keim? Care to go along? Recording first-hand what occurs for your readers back east?"

Bobbing his head eagerly, the young newspaperman tapped heels to his mount, joining Romero. "You'll never have to ask a question like that twice, General Custer!"

"Fine." Custer let his eyes touch every one of those who would accompany him into the meadow. "Gentlemen, be aware that our lives might be at forfeit in but a twinkling of an eye. Check your weapons. Have them ready. Understood?"

Custer set off. Caught by surprise with his dramatic departure, Crosby and Keim dashed behind Custer, while Romero and Milner rode the flanks.

At long last he had come face to face with two of the bloodiest warriors on the southern plains.

"General," Milner whispered as they clattered to a halt, "these boys got a reputation that's smellier than a Comanche's breechclout."

"We'll pay heed, Mr. Milner," Custer replied, blue eyes

searching the faces before him for signs of treachery or
truth.

Satanta bore a hawkish countenance, his eyes shaded by
a heavy, knitted brow, his dark face split by a carved beak
that gave him the appearance of a predator. Beside him sat
Lone Wolf, a little older in years perhaps, but no less
frightening in appearance. Both copper faces were surrounded by straight, raven hair falling well past shoulders
wrapped in blankets. Their dark glinting eyes gazed past
Custer's shabby, trail-worn appearance, attentive to the
small party gathered behind the Seventh's commander.

Satanta flashed a wide smile that showed most of his
teeth as he nudged his pony past Custer, bringing up his
right hand . . . presenting his big bare paw to Sheridan's
uniformed aide. To the Kiowa's way of thinking, one
dressed in this bright blue uniform and wool cloak dripping
with glittering gold braid and festooned with brass buttons
had to be the soldier chief.

The gesture caught Crosby by surprise. Dumbfounded
and unsteady under pressure, Crosby shook his head
violently, refusing to take Satanta's hand. He began to
stammer, trying ineptly to tell the chief that he was not the
soldier chief. A garbled hodgepodge of tongue-tied words
dribbled past his lips.

"I'm not—General Custer—why can't he understand—"

Offended, Satanta angrily jerked his hand back at Crosby's botched refusal. He gazed at his hand as if told he
carried the pox. Then he spit on the ground with a sneer.

Custer realized the danger in embarrassing the Kiowa
chief. From the corner of one eye he watched Lone Wolf
ease his pony to the left, away from possible gunfire. Away

from the impetutous Satanta. In the trees beyond, Kiowa warriors made their first bold forays from the shade, inching closer to their chiefs.

It didn't take a cook to know someone had just thrown some sand in the soup.

"Me Kiowa!" Satanta roared in a tree-ringing growl, banging his chest with a huge ham hock of a fist he had offered Crosby.

"Romero!" Custer called out. "Tell this fellow he picked the wrong man for a chief—and tell him fast!"

"This scared one is not the chief," the Mexican explained.

Again the chief glared at the shaken Crosby. "So you say, Indian-talker. Tell Satanta who is leader of the soldiers who trample across Kiowa land. Who among these poorly dressed hairy-faces claims to be the mighty soldier chief?"

"This one," Romero answered, gesturing. "He who wears a buffalo coat, beside me."

Satanta gave Custer nothing more than a cursory going over before he glowered at Romero.

"Stupid Indian-talker! You take Satanta for a fool, don't you? This is no pony soldier chief. Hear me now! Satanta demands you bring me the pony chief who destroyed Black Kettle's village. He and he only I wish to meet. Not this imposter!"

"I swear you are looking at the pony soldier chief," Romero persisted. Suddenly he remembered something that might convince Satanta. "This one in the buffalo coat is well known on the plains. From the land of the winter winds south to the land of the Summer Maker. He is known to all great warriors."

"Who is this?" Satanta demanded, glaring at Romero.

"Yellow Hair!"

Two sets of dark obsidian eyes studied the soldier chief.

"Yellow Hair truly sits before us?" Lone Wolf broke the silence at last, speaking to Romero.

"He does." Romero nodded.

"The soldier chief who left Black Kettle's village an ash heap?"

Again Romero nodded.

"I would meet this Yellow Hair," Satanta remarked. "His heart must surely be brave to ride into this meadow when my warriors have it surrounded."

Romero turned to Custer. "They understand you're chief of this outfit. Satanta figures your heart must be pretty brave to be here in this meadow when he's got his warriors surrounding it."

Without a word, Custer inched forward, halting his mount nose to nose with Satanta's smaller pony. "Tell the chiefs I do have a brave heart. If they intend to start something, they better do it now while they have the chance to slaughter us."

"General," Romero's voice rose, "you really want me to tell these chiefs you're calling their bluff?"

"No. Just tell them I don't believe they have us surrounded. I have no fear of their treachery, for they'll soon see my cavalry come up behind us."

"Yellow Hair says his heart is strong. He is not afraid, for he does not believe you have him surrounded."

Like quick black birds, four dark eyes darted left and right, finding their warriors circling the meadow.

"Yellow Hair comes from the north, the land your warriors raided. Many soldiers follow Yellow Hair."

Satanta glowered for a moment, studying the soldier

chief. Then surprisingly his countenance completely changed. Flashing a broad smile at Custer, he spoke to Romero. "Does Yellow Hair not enjoy a good joke, Indian-talker?"

"Not when the joke is played on him, Satanta."

The Kiowa chief stuck out his huge hand once again, this time to Custer, as if all were forgiven. "Satanta greets the great Yellow Hair."

Custer glanced down at the offered hand, shaking his head. "Romero, you tell this pompous ass I don't shake hands with any man unless I know him to be a friend."

Satanta's massive jaw clenched. For a second time his handshake had been refused. Long ago he had learned the white man put much ceremonial stock in this hand-shaking business. And Satanta loved ceremony. For two soldiers to refuse his hand could only be a great insult.

"Satanta," Romero translated quickly to fill the electric void, "Yellow Hair would shake your hand only if you are a true friend."

With an ugly sneer the chief looked over at his companion, Lone Wolf. The old one nodded to Satanta in reluctant agreement.

"Remember, White Bear," Lone Wolf whispered, "we have a choice. Will it be jackal, or wolf?"

Satanta nodded. "I choose the wolf."

The young chief directed his eyes back to Custer and his words to Romero. "Why does Yellow Hair come to Kiowa land?"

"Yellow Hair comes to see if the Kiowa's hearts are true."

Satanta considered that a moment behind his hard eyes. "Does Yellow Hair come to slaughter more sleeping villages of women and children and old people?"

"No," Romero answered emphatically. "Yellow Hair is here to talk with the great Kiowa leaders. To learn what's in your hearts. To let them know what is in his heart."

"This is good," Lone Wolf admitted. "What would Yellow Hair say to us?"

"General"—Romero turned to Custer—"what do I tell them you want to talk over with 'em?"

"First, I want the Kiowa to proceed without delay to Fort Cobb. Only there in the shadow of the fort will Sheridan discuss peace with the Kiowa."

Romero brought his dark eyes to bear on the two warriors. "Yellow Hair brings with him a great war chief to talk with the Kiowa chiefs. *Sher-i-dan*. He and Yellow Hair won the war when the white men fought among themselves three robe seasons ago."

The Mexican watched Satanta's eyes light up and flick over to the uniformed Crosby.

"No, Satanta," Romero explained. "This one here is second chief to the great war chief who rides among his soldiers this morning."

Both chiefs nodded, dutifully impressed. Romero smiled to himself. He didn't think a little white lie would hurt getting the Kiowa's attention.

Lone Wolf gestured to Custer. "Yellow Hair and the one who stays back with his warriors must be great war chiefs, to win that long and terrible war between the white men."

"Both chiefs fought side by side," Romero explained. "They come now to bring peace to this land. Or they come to bring war to your camps. The Kiowa must decide."

Satanta glanced at Lone Wolf again, only their eyes talking in cold silence. Finally, the younger one turned to Romero. As he tugged his bright blanket about his shoulders with one hand, Romero saw the other hand held an old cap-and-ball revolver.

"We Kiowa wish peace with the army, Indian-talker," he declared in a clear, strong voice. "Pony soldier chief Hazen knows us to be at peace. He gives us presents and weapons to hunt the buffalo. We live in peace with our neighbors: the Comanche, Apache, Cheyenne, and Arapaho. Yellow Hair and this war chief Sher-i-dan do not know us. When they are our friends, then at last will they know what is truly in the Kiowa heart."

"You will go to Fort Cobb and talk with the pony chiefs?"

"We will talk with these two war chiefs you bring here to Indian land," Satanta replied.

Romero said, "You must go to Fort Cobb *now* to talk with the chiefs in the shadow of Hazen's post."

For a long, stony moment, Satanta glared at Romero. His eyes met Custer's as he answered. "We will go to Fort Cobb. At Hazen's post we will show this Yellow Hair we are at peace with the soldiers."

"Do we have trouble here, Romero?" Custer sounded edgy.

"Not now, General. They're ready to ride on to Cobb with you, to show they're peace Indians and don't want war with Yellow Hair."

"Peace Indians, eh?" He grinned. "Killers of women and children. Well, you just tell these *peace* Indians to fall in and accompany my cavalry to the fort—now. Bloody butchers."

Custer glanced over his shoulder, seeing his troops had deployed themselves near the southern edge of the meadow along the river. Fluttering on the cold breeze were colorful regimental guidons and Custer's own personal standard carried aloft over the band. Sunlight glinted off the shiny brass instruments. It made his war-horse heart swell with pride.

"Satanta and Lone Wolf will go with Yellow Hair to Hazen's post," Romero reminded Satanta.

"This is a good thing, Indian-talker. We will show Yellow Hair what is in our hearts." Satanta turned, raising an arm to signal his warriors on the hillside to the northeast. From the half-thousand crowding the knoll burst some twenty warriors descending the hill at a lope.

"What's going on here?" Custer demanded. "Romero!"

"Who are these who come?" the interpreter barked.

"They are our chiefs, Indian-talker," Lone Wolf explained. "We are first chiefs. There are many head men among the Kiowa. Now Yellow Hair will know what lies in the hearts of all."

"General—" Romero cleared his throat with a disturbing rattle, "old Lone Wolf here says all the chiefs have to sit in on the parley with you—"

"All of these? Why, there's more than twenty of them headed this way!"

Romero chuckled. "Appears you'll have quite a crowd for dinner, General."

Custer relaxed, seeing the Kiowa chiefs smiling. His own famous grin crept across his face at last. "Appears they're about to stretch my hospitality pretty thin, aren't they?"

Custer turned to Lieutenant Colonel Crosby. "Inform General Sheridan that all companies will be on alert for any treachery, Colonel."

"Sounds as if you're expecting some treachery, Custer."

His robin-egg blue eyes studied J. Schuyler Crosby a

moment before he answered. Sheridan's aide had seen little of field service, none of it on the plains with Indians. Crosby was one of those legions in command staffs who had leapt their way up the rungs of the army ladder through a series of prestigious friendships with important officers in the War Department.

"No, Colonel," Custer finally answered. "I'm not actually expecting any treachery from the Kiowa at all."

CHAPTER 18

"I'LL curse their bloody hearts straight into the pits of hell!"

Tom Custer had rarely seen his older brother this angry. More than angry—stomping, raring, spitting-fire mad. No soldier in the valley of the Washita could blame Custer, either. After all, what man wouldn't be driven blind mad when he'd just been lied to, his trust spat on and betrayed.

Yesterday had done it.

Following yesterday's introductions to more than twenty additional chiefs who would accompany Satanta and Lone Wolf to Fort Cobb, Custer had taken his guests back to Lieutenant Bell's commissary wagons, opening the larder for his new friends. All to Sheridan's consternation—and his eventual, begrudging agreement.

"It really isn't much," Custer had argued. "Some hardtack and parched corn, a little of the poor sowbelly we have along. Nothing of value, General. But enough to fill the empty, hard-winter belly of Indian chiefs who always serve their guests a meal before talking over important matters."

When their bellies had been stuffed and the Kiowa custom of complimentary belching satisfied, Custer gave the order to move out once more. By late afternoon the command reached the benchlands near the banks of the Washita. Here Custer's entire command established camp for the coming winter night.

That evening after supper with their copper-skinned guests at officer's mess, Custer and Sheridan began more preliminary discussions with the great gathering of Kiowa, Comanche and Apache chiefs. The army commanders listened to repeated guarantees of peace and friendship for the white man, the army itself, and especially for the war chiefs themselves: Custer and Sheridan.

"Doesn't seem you have much faith in the Kiowa tongue either," Custer whispered to Sheridan.

"Bastards up to their eyeballs in goddamn treachery," Sheridan growled. "The whole scheming bunch followed your columns all day, Custer."

"I feel something in the air, too. And ordered a double guard posted."

Yet there was something more that irritated the young cavalry commander like a tiny thread unraveling from one of his long wool stockings. "The more I listen to the Kiowa's speeches, the more I'm convinced they have no intention of bringing their villages in to Fort Cobb."

"What do you think they have up their sleeves?" Sheridan asked.

"I can only guess—stealing some wagons, running off some stock, harassing our rear guard. Something's afoot, and I can smell it."

By the time he finally closed his eyes near midnight, Custer couldn't escape that hard rock of a feeling lying cold in his belly that he was about to be made the fool. But not by the Kiowa.

The next morning at dawn Custer knew the chiefs had put their foot in it. And what *it* was didn't smell sweet at all.

Awakened by shouting soldiers clamoring around his tent at first light, Custer rolled from his blankets. What he had in his belly wasn't only growling hunger. Suspicion and anger are never a hearty breakfast. Custer burst from his tent to discover the reason for the uproar.

A few yards off stood three of the chiefs. Only three.

A chagrined sergeant of the guard stomped up, saluting. "General . . . Custer, sir," he stammered. "Sometime last night, the rest of the Injuns . . . well—they slipped away through our pickets. Back to their own camps, I guess, General. These three fellas here . . . they hung behind to be the last to go, it seems. And they are setting to fly when we caught 'em."

Custer roared through the troopers surrounding the chiefs like a cat with lightning at its tail. And found Satanta, Lone Wolf, and a Kiowa subchief called Licking Bear huddled together in a ring of army carbines.

"Get me Romero!" Custer bellowed. "He won't sleep in this morning!"

A corporal turned on his heel and darted away.

"I'll watch these blackguards burn in hell before they're shown any mercy from here on out!"

The high-pitched shriek of his voice had done its job. All around him the camp awakened with a start. Within moments Sheridan, Crosby, Moylan, and Tom Custer joined the growing crowd. Dragging in last on the the scene was Romero, groggy and frog-mouthed, wiping last night's sleep from his eyes.

"Tell these buggers I'm holding them for ransom, Romero! Ransom for the rest of their villages—every last nit and prick of them!"

Custer stomped in a small circle as he spoke, sticking his nose into the Kiowa's faces from time to time, roaring, spitting mad.

"They won't play me the fool like this! They've picked the wrong tree to shake this time. You tell them every last word of what I said!"

The coloring of his pale eyes had turned that color of blue at the center of a flame wrapping a sulphur-head match.

"Tell them, Romero. This time they've knocked down a hornet's nest and they're bound to get stung!"

Romero did as he was ordered, and got the response he figured he would. "General, they haven't got an idea what you're mad about."

"They've got to be joking! I'm not blind! The lying swine never had any intention of coming in to Fort Cobb!"

"They say they're your friends, General. Can't figure why the others ran off last night. They say, maybe because they fear you'll harm 'em."

"Blathering fools, Romero! They'll learn not to lie to Yellow Hair. Blackhearted thieves. From what Milner tells me, we'll be at Fort Cobb by nightfall. When we arrive, we'll have these lying brigands slapped in irons!"

"Irons? How are these three Kiowa gonna be any good to you in irons?"

"Don't question me, Romero! Just tell them they're my *honored* guests until their people come in to Fort Cobb. As guaranteed by their own tongues! Their treachery will get them more than they bargained for—their people are to come in immediately or the chiefs will rot in irons!"

Tom Custer watched his brother stomp off to his tent as the interpreter explained their captivity to the three Kiowa. Lone Wolf began singing his mournful death song. Its high, wailing notes cast an eerie pall over the camp as Custer disappeared beyond his tent flaps, his seething anger rolling over him.

"I fought many battles beside your brother, Tom."

The younger Custer found Sheridan at his side.

"Can't remember ever seeing him this angry. Except maybe once."

"When was that, General?"

"In the Shenandoah. Mosby's raiders had hanged some of Custer's soldiers as retaliation against Custer himself. That was the first, and the last time I ever saw him this mad. Until today. Maybe I'd better have a talk with—"

"General, I suggest we all give Autie wide berth for the while. Give him the chance to cool down."

Sheridan scratched his beard. "Anger's a cleansing emotion, Lieutenant. If a man can control it, harness it, there's no telling the power he can exert over others, on events. Your brother carries a weapon he will have to learn to use—before it destroys him."

Tom Custer heard Sheridan move off, leaving him alone near the fire. At this stage in Autie's career, Tom alone knew how deep his brother's anger could run. While the commander's emotions and friendships and passions rarely ran wide, the power of his heart was nonetheless a very deep river.

And Tom Custer realized there were few things which could affect his heart as had the betrayal of the Kiowa this morning. To put his faith in someone or something, only to have it betrayed, was a wound that pricked his marrow.

That evening as darkness slid headlong down the valley of the Washita, Fort Cobb came in sight.

As Custer had promised, he had the three chiefs clamped in leg irons borrowed from the post guardhouse and placed in a heavily guarded Sibley tent pitched beside his own. Through that evening and into the night one or more of the three wailed incessantly, chanting death songs or murmuring prayers to their spirits. Custer didn't sleep, troubled by thoughts as black as the inky sky above.

Winter's chill had long since sucked the sun's light from the heavens when Custer was summoned to Sheridan's tent. Surrounding the Irishman's circular Sibley stood a crude pole fence erected by soldiers. Sheridan waited outside his tent, leaning against the fence. Wearing only his wool tunic, he paid little attention to the plummeting temperature, for it had been one of those warm days filled with sunshine, the type so often found in the Territories during winter.

"Evening, Custer," Sheridan began as the young officer walked up to the tent. "Appears these Kiowa of yours are endeavoring to play us false, eh?"

"How do you read it, General?"

"Seems they want us to listen to their empty, bunghole promises right up to the time the new grass makes their goddamned ponies strong enough to make war."

"You're not confident I can get the tribe to come in? I hold their chiefs!" Custer leaned back against the crude fence opposite Sheridan.

"Don't trust 'em at all. We've given them every opportunity to come in and behave, haven't we? These red buggers are about the worst I've had to deal with. The bastards aren't scared of us—because they know Hazen's gonna protect 'em. Feeding, clothing, coddling the vermin!"

Custer grinned.

"You always liked a good scrap, didn't you, Custer?"

"Pleased to hear you say again how you're fed up with civilians running the army. Things need changing in Washington City, sir. Our Republic sorely needs a new direction entirely, someone strong at the helm across the next critical decade."

"Too goddamned long we've waited for a leader with a military background, someone who appreciates what it is to open up this great country out here. With Grant in the White House, we'll see that change you're wanting." The look on Custer's face stopped him. "What is it, Armstrong?"

"You have a lot more faith in Grant than I do, sir. For one thing, the rumpled bugger took more credit for winning the war than he should have. Sherman and Sheridan handed Lincoln Lee's surrender. Not Grant."

Sheridan smiled. "The way of politics, Armstrong."

"Doesn't change my mind, sir. Grant's not up to the job. Not just any man can do what's needed. Ten years from now, the plains should be pacified."

"The tribes confined to reservations and the land made fruitful, eh?"

"Nothing wrong in that, is there?"

"No wonder you're the hero to so many of these farmers out here, Custer. You share the same dreams they do."

Custer gazed at the twinkling dusting of stars overhead. "Not really, sir. Mine aren't earthly dreams."

Sheridan slapped Custer on the back. "Should've remembered. Long ago recognized that in you. Not about to be held back like mere mortals, are you?"

"You may joke, sir—"

"I'm not joking with you at all, Custer."

"Then believe me when I say I'm destined for far greater things."

"Greater than commanding your own goddamned regiment?"

"As colonel?"

Sheridan studied the sunburned face, bright beneath a torch's glow. "Are you content to climb the ladder one rung at a time?"

Custer grappled with that a moment. "For the time being, sir. I just turned twenty-nine. You're thirty-seven now, and the next lieutenant general, once Grant's sworn in as President on the fourth of March. But look at me!"

Custer wheeled, stomped a few steps away. "It'll be ten years before I become a full colonel and have my own regiment. By then we'll have the plains pacified and there'll be no more battlefields on which to earn my promotions. How the blazes will I ever get those general's stars back on my collar?"

Sheridan scratched at his dark beard, feeling the first of the evening's chill penetrate his wool tunic. "We could help you climb out a bit, Armstrong."

"How?"

The general tapped one finger against his thin lips, as he always did when pondering, considering, plotting. "Yes. It just might work."

"What's that, sir?"

"By God! We'll show up for Grant's inauguration ourselves! Won't that impress the buzzard!"

Custer tingled. "Yes!"

"And we'll get Grant's ear while he's bubbling with his own juices—the new commander-in-chief!"

"Will Sherman go along?"

"Of course! He thinks the world of you, Custer. Despite that business with leaving your command and shooting those deserters in '67—Bill realizes your value as much as I."

"Then you'll both lobby for a promotion for me in March?"

"Is that too soon for you, Custer?"

"No, sir! Not by a long stretch."

Sheridan plopped a muddy boot on a fence rail. "All we'd have to do is have a voice inside the Army Appropriations Committee."

"Senator Chandler?"

Sheridan turned on Custer slowly. "The committee chairman? By God, Custer—you go right to the top, don't you?"

"A man want's to make it to the top, he might as well reach as high as he dreams."

"You sunuvabitch! We'll get you up in army command yet. Between Bill Sherman and Senator Chandler himself, Custer is on his way to his own command! But before we go to Federal City for the inauguration in March, you have a job to do here in the Territories. If you go east with the tribes still out, there's no chance for promotion."

"If the hostiles are punished, I can ride into Washington City assured of promotion."

"You've got to start with these miserable Kiowa. We

don't get their villages in, you don't stand a prayer with Chandler."

"I'm ready, General. They've played me for a fool long enough. These Kiowa have me held prisoner here while I should be out hunting down the other tribes. My patience is exhausted."

"Patience, hell!" Sheridan bawled. "You were ordered down here to the Territories to do a job. You don't have time for patience with these red beggars."

"And if I fail to bring the tribes in?"

"Spring will come, Custer. The grass will green and the bastards' ponies will be strong once more. And you'll be back out chasing and chasing . . . and chasing some more."

"Sir—"

Sheridan cut him off with a wave of his hand. His dark eyes glowed as he spoke, sparking like a wolf that had a hamstrung old bull down, moving in for the kill. "I'm going to see you get that promotion, Custer. See you don't frig this up."

Custer's brow knitted. "What you have in mind?"

"Tomorrow we're going to give those red mongrels an ultimatum." Sheridan tapped a finger between the rows of brass buttons on Custer's tunic. "No more dallying! We'll give them a time limit to perform, or we'll make an example out of one of those goddamn flea-bitten savages."

"How will we—I—make an example of the Kiowa?"

Sheridan whirled on Custer again, half his face dark beneath the torch. "Don't you remember the orders passed down from Grant, to me, to you? The Shenandoah? August 1864? Turn Custer loose on Mosby!"

"You don't mean—not these Kiowa!"

"Why not, goddammit? If those villages don't come in, then string the chiefs up. Hang the bastards!"

"What about the other tribes? If you hang the chiefs—"

"Put the fear of God in 'em. Dammit, Custer—make their assholes pucker when they hear your name!"

"But hanging?" he repeated.

"Better you convince them once and for all that when Custer finds a hostile village, he'll level it like he did Black Kettle's. Take prisoner those who can be captured. And kill everything—everyone else."

"Sir, begging your pardon, but Satanta and the others promised us their villages would come—"

"Bullshit! You'll trust an Indian? Someone told me once that trusting the word of an Indian was like shoveling fleas in a barnyard!"

Custer found himself without a single thing to say. His mind filled with the smoky images of that sleepy Cheyenne village beside the foggy Washita, old men and women and children . . . rolling out of their warm sleeping robes to be greeted with the cold, whistling messengers of death. Young women trying to escape a screeching lead bullet or whispering steel saber. He shuddered.

"No, sir," he answered Sheridan at last. "I'll no longer allow the hostiles to play me false."

Sheridan stepped up to Custer again, more paternal now. "Armstrong, you've been sent here to do a job. If you don't act, the army will simply send someone down here who will."

"I understand."

Sheridan plopped a hand on Custer's shoulder. "Besides, we have plans for you, my boy! So if the army sends someone else down here, the glory and honor and fame would surely go to him."

Custer swallowed hard. "Tomorrow, sir."

Sheridan smiled. "Tomorrow, we'll start back down that road we set out upon when I telegraphed you in Monroe last September. We'll get this campaign back on track. And your promotion in your hip pocket."

"My promotion, sir."

CHAPTER 19

T HAT next morning Sheridan marched over to Custer's tents with his aide at his side. Like Sheridan, Lieutenant Colonel Crosby relished nudging things off dead center.

"Good morning, Custer."

He rose stiffly from his camp stool, shifting the steamy tin of coffee to his left hand when Sheridan waved him back down to his cold perch.

"Good morning, General. Colonel Crosby."

"I've sent for your interpreter," Sheridan began without pleasantries. "Romero—wasn't that his name?"

"That's correct. Mexican. Captured by the Comanche as a child. Traded and retraded from tribe to tribe until he spent most of his childhood among the Cheyenne."

"I suppose he picked up the Kiowa tongue along the way," Sheridan said. "I'm bringing him here because you and I are going to have a little chat with those chiefs. Since we've had no word from the tribe after we released that one old beggar yesterday."

"Good morning," Romero grumbled.

"Sleeping in again, eh?" Custer asked.

"You wanted me for something, General?"

"I did," Sheridan replied. "We're going to have a talk with the Kiowa. I want you to be certain they understand my every word. What I have to say will be very short."

"And *sweet*, General?"

Sheridan's eyes darkened at the grinning Mexican. "Don't you bet on that, Romero. I'm not in any mood to dally with you."

Sheridan turned away, nodding to Crosby. His aide parted the tent flap.

Both chiefs straightened as the soldiers entered, their eyes darting from white man to white man.

"Who is this man?" Sheridan growled when he noticed a young warrior beside Satanta.

"His name's Tsalante, General," Custer explained, gesturing for the young man to rise.

"What the bloody hell is *he* doing here? I gave orders these prisoners aren't to have any visitors."

"Tsalante is Satanta's eldest son, sir."

"That doesn't explain why he's here!"

"Believe me, we had Tsalante completely searched before he was allowed to see his father."

A smile crawled across Sheridan's face. He turned to Custer. "Say, we may just have some use for this Tsalante. Yesterday we sent old Licking Bear back to the village with our message for them to come in to Fort Cobb without delay, but the bastard never returned, and the villages haven't come in as ordered."

Crosby cleared his throat. "The general's quite distressed by that flagrant failure of the Indians to obey his command."

"Colonel Crosby," Custer snapped, "he's not the only one."

Sheridan put a hand up to silence his aide before an argument started. "I want the Kiowa to know that if *we* are expected to speak the truth to them, we should have every right to expect the truth out of them."

"I've never lied to an Indian, sir," Custer replied. "Nor will it ever be said that G. A. Custer lied to a red man."

"What I have in mind is to show these red beggars that I mean to keep *my* oath . . . even if they cannot."

"How can we do that?"

"We're sending a final ultimatum to the Indians this morning. That's where Satanta's son comes in."

"I don't think Tsalante will let you down."

"If the boy fails, Custer, it won't be me he's letting down. He'll be killing his own father."

Custer watched Satanta's hooded eyes searching their faces for some clue. He could tell the Kiowa chief realized this wasn't your everyday parley.

Sheridan signaled the interpreter, patting the buffalo robe beside him. "Romero. Sit so we can talk with the chiefs."

Romero took a deep breath, his eyes briefly touching Custer's. The scout had never liked Sheridan; he'd always been more than a little afraid of the banty Irishman to boot.

"First, I want you to explain who I am."

"General, make no mistake. They know who you are."

Sheridan seemed genuinely surprised. "How's that?"

"General Custer here, he's told 'em you're a great war chief who won the war between the white men back east."

"Sheridan glanced up at Custer. "You told them of me, Custer?"

"Yessir. Explained about the mighty chief who rode with me."

"I see . . ." Sheridan stroked his black beard. "Quite! Well, let's get on with matters at hand. Romero, begin by telling them I'm very angry that Licking Bear didn't return from their villages. I'm even angrier that their people haven't come in to Fort Cobb yet."

While the Kiowa listened to Romero's words, their dark eyes were glued on the general.

When the chiefs had spoken, Romero translated. "They say they're sorry Licking Bear didn't come back. You have them in your leg irons, so they can't go to their villages, can't tell their people to come in. They say if they were with their people now, the villages would be moving to Fort Cobb as you ordered."

"They want me to believe that? Muleshit!"

Crosby laughed nervously. Sheridan waved a hand, shutting Crosby up.

"Tell them that I'm sending Satanta's son with word from them and War Chief Sheridan that if the villages don't come in to Fort Cobb immediately their chiefs will hang."

Romero swallowed hard. The looked carved across his dark features said more than words could, causing a stir among the three Kiowa.

"You want me to tell 'em you're going to *hang* 'em?"

"No, Romero. You tell the young man here that the villages must come in so their chiefs will be spared that hanging."

The Mexican translated. One by one, three pairs of

black eyes widened. Tsalante clutched his father's arm. Satanta reassured the young man calmly.

The younger chief nodded, ready to speak. "We understand we are in the power of the great war chief and Yellow Hair. Maybe you, Indian-talker, can tell these soldier chiefs that we can send my son to our people with our words—but that does not assure that our village will come in to Hazen's post. There must be a council with many men from each village. Together they will decide what to do. The hunting is very poor around Hazen's fort. Already our people are thin from a bad winter of hunting. Our ponies are weak. It would be a hard journey on most of my people. Not just the small and old ones."

Lone Wolf raised his two shackled hands, imploring. "The soldier chiefs must understand we are not the only men to decide matters such as this for our people. We are not like the white man who has a Grandfather making all the rules for his people. With the Kiowa, each man gets one voice in what is decided among our people. That will take time. Tell these soldier chiefs they must give our villages time to decide what they will do. Enough time to tear down the lodges and load our travois. These soldiers do not give our skinny, winter-poor ponies enough time to stumble in here to Hazen's post."

As Romero translated, Sheridan's face hardened.

"No!" he barked. "I didn't come here to bargain. Tell them I've already give their people plenty of time. Explain to this Satanta's son that the Kiowa have until *sunrise* tomorrow to come in. I'll hang the chiefs from that big oak right outside this tent if they don't show by then."

With Sheridan's threat put into Kiowa, Tsalante leapt to his feet, trembling. Crosby immediately jumped in front of

Sheridan, his hand upon his service revolver, Custer's ironlike grip atop Crosby's gun hand in the next heartbeat.

"Leave the pistol in the holster!" Custer commanded.

"Unhand me, Custer! I'll have you on report—"

"Gentlemen!" Sheridan leapt to his feet, struggling to separate the two before matters disintegrated into a brawl. "There's no need of argument. And no need of reports—understood, Crosby?"

Crosby relented. "Yes, sir."

"I'm certain Colonel Custer will apologize for his actions. Am I right . . . Custer?"

"I won't apologize, General. Tsalante's unarmed." He glared at Sheridan's aide. "He poses no threat to any of us, even to someone as nervous as Crosby."

"Damn you! He's a filthy heathen savage!" Crosby roared.

"Colonel Crosby," Sheridan soothed. "Wait outside for me."

Crosby turned to go, then stopped. He glared at Custer before he tore aside the tent flap, stomping into the morning cold.

"General," Custer said, "I think the young man's got something to say."

"He sure as hell does!" Romero was clearly agitated. "Tsalante says you aren't giving him enough time to ride to the villages and get your message spread among his people. They've got to call for a council."

"Dammit! I've heard all that prattle before, Romero!"

"Please listen, General," Custer said. "They may have a point. We must treat them fairly, or what right do we have to ask fairness in their treatment of the white captives?"

"You talk to me of *fairness*, Custer? I saw a goddamned

good example of the Kiowa's fairness back on the Washita. You remember how fairly these butchers treated that pitiful Mrs. Blinn and her little boy?"

"General—"

"Don't assume you know more than me about dealing with these Indians, Custer!" Sheridan steamed. "You deal with the savages in fairness and what the hell does it get you? Lies . . . broken promises . . . one hand taking our food and blankets and handouts—while the other hand burns and kidnaps, murders and scalps!"

"Enough said, Custer. I believe we have spoken about orders. You and I, in private. Haven't we?"

That brought Custer up short, as surely as if someone had kicked him in the groin with a blunt-toed, standard-issue cavalry boot.

"I want your complete backing in this policy," Sheridan continued. "If the Kiowa are serious about doing as we say, if they want their two chiefs alive, they'll be here at Fort Cobb by sunrise tomorrow."

Sheridan turned to the interpreter. "Tell this warrior he's free to go now. Take my message to this people."

"Tsalante, go now," Satanta pleaded, gripping his son's arm. "Take word of this trouble to our people. Quickly, young one!"

"I will get my pony and bring it here before I ride the long trail back to our villages."

Custer watched the youth dart through the tent flaps. Outside he listened to Crosby explain in an arrogant voice that the Indian was allowed to fetch his mount.

Moments later they heard Tsalante galloping up outside. The pony snorted as its rider wrenched to a halt. Quick moccasined feet ran to the tent. As his son burst through the flaps Satanta rose, struggling with the heavy leg irons. He took his son in a warm embrace. They murmured some hurried words between them in that way only a father and son can, before the youth reached out to touch Lone Wolf's hand.

"Hoodle-tay!" the old chief whispered hoarsely, struggling to maintain his stony composure. "Make haste!"

As quickly as he had come, the young warrior whirled about, vaulting to the back of his spotted pony, where he took up the single rein and shot off to the west. Glancing only once over his shoulder at the sun climbing toward a midday peak, Tsalante was off on a race which could mean the lives of two men. Perhaps more.

Crosby held open the tent flap as Sheridan turned to go.

Custer glanced at the two chiefs. "General?" he called out.

Sheridan turned. "What is it, Custer?"

"You haven't left the Kiowa a hand to play."

"Precisely!" Sheridan snapped. "I now hold the last two aces in the deck and I'm playing them. When you play with Indians, you don't play by the rules. Never leave the enemy a hand to play. It's winning that matters in war. Only winning. There are no parades for the losers."

"Don't miss your parade, Custer," Crosby advised acidly. "Shall we go, General?"

Sheridan nodded and left. The flap slid back in place, throwing the tent into darkness. Custer pushed out, greeted by a brilliant winter's day.

Behind him trudged Satanta, dragging along the section of clanking chain that bound his ankles together. Here in the gentle light of early morning the Indian's eyes appeared sunken, dark, and rimmed with gloom. The once-proud Kiowa chief stood hunched and drawn.

Satanta stumbled across the red mud, slinging the heavy chain behind him with every step, clattering past Custer and Romero without a word. When a guard stepped forward to shove the chief back toward the tent with a nudge of his carbine, Custer waved the soldier off.

The Indian stopped, turned, and gazed at the soldier chief for a moment before he settled down on the trunk of a deadfallen oak like a tired old owl. He shuddered, drawing his thin blanket about his shoulders more tightly. Gazing into the blue, cloudless sky, his eyes sought the warmth of the early sun.

As Custer turned toward his own tent, Satanta's mournful voice raised the hackles on the back of his neck. The Indian chief had begun his melancholy death song.

"Romero."

"Yes, General?" The Mexican stepped to Custer's side.

"I want you to find the women."

"Women, sir?"

"The Cheyenne women."

"Yes."

"Bring Monaseetah to my tent."

"Yes."

"I want to see her now."

Custer slipped into the shadows of a huge overhanging oak towering like a monstrous sentinel above his tent.

He needed her.

Waiting for Monaseetah in the frosty stillness of his tent, Custer felt more brittle than he had ever imagined he could be. He stared down at the backs of his pale trembling, freckled hands, sensing something of his own mortality, his own humanness.

Cursing himself for selling his soul for a promotion. Cursing himself, because destiny demanded it of him.

Through that long afternoon Satanta had persisted in his lonely, melancholy vigil. At times he paced back and forth on the west side of Custer's tent. Then he plopped cross-legged in the snow, quietly mumbling his incantations to the earth. At times he shaded his eyes with one hand, peering into the west for salvation, hoping for the approach of his tribesmen. With the falling of the sun and the dying of his hope, the great Kiowa chief scooped pinches of red dirt or cold ashes from the guards' fire.

After chanting a few words of prayer, Satanta put the soil and ashes in his mouth.

Having accepted his death, Satanta said farewell to this land of his ancestors. His mud-smeared, trembling tongue would no more taste the lifeblood of his homeland.

Custer looked at the first tendrils of gray light through the narrow gap in the tent flaps. Dawn wasn't far behind.

He sensed her beside him. The weight of her beneath the blankets. The warmth of her naked body, the firm pressure of her breasts against his side as she lay cupped into him.

He sighed, drinking in the fragrance that belonged to no other woman in the world. Without fail, her scent stirred a wildness in him, something never before touched until she came into his life. Even more, that part of her he carried within had become like a piece of sunshine glinting off frost-glazed tree branches beneath the morning sun. It shared the same place in his being as the heady fragrance that rose to a man's brain as he stood over an open fire at twilight, sparks exploding into the purple sky above, wisps of gray dancing ghostly and haunting on the tickling breezes.

He snuggled against her.

Outside his tent the voices grew louder, tapping like insistent fingertips at the back of his consciousness. They came closer. One of them knifed through the thickness of the oiled canvas.

"Sir—General Sheridan has the prisoners out and he's yelling for you. Says its time to hang the sonsabitches."

"Thank you, Sergeant. Please inform the general that I'll join him shortly."

The boots dashed off; the sound of hard-leather soles pounding across the snow faded from the tent flaps.

Custer was up on one elbow. Then quietly he slipped from bed and pulled his tunic over his arms, buttoning it over his long-handles when her child's voice surprised him.

"Good morn-ning," she spoke in her imitation of his Yankee English.

She was an apt pupil, he had to admit. Custer turned, smiling as he raked a lock of hair from his forehead, combing the curls with his fingers. "Good morning."

He dressed, then pulled his buffalo coat and cap on before he bent over the bed. Monaseetah sat up, raising her lips to his. The blankets slid away, exposing the tops of her breasts.

With stoic resignation, Custer closed his eyes, bent his head, and kissed her.

"Custer!" Sheridan was calling to him from the instant Custer pushed through the flaps. "What's the goddamned

meaning of sending this man out to find the Indians?"
Sheridan stomped up, livid with anger.

"I didn't send him out to find the Indians, General."
Custer turned to Romero. "You have any luck?"

"Coming in at a good clip. Be here anytime."

"Dammit, Custer! What's this man doing out locating
the hostiles?" Sheridan jumped between the two, mad
enough to spit.

"I thought you'd want to know if they were sending a
delegation here to talk with you, the great soldier chief."

*There. That's the quickest way to pull yourself out of the frying
pan without flopping into the fire.*

"Why would they send a delegation to speak with me?"
Sheridan growled.

Crosby stepped up, wearing his smirk. "They aren't to
send a delegation, Custer. The Kiowa are supposed to have
their villages here."

Custer turned from Crosby, paying him no mind. He
sensed he had Sheridan hooked. They hadn't spent all
those years together for him not to know Little Phil as well
as he knew any man. *Still, you best tred lightly, Autie boy. His
dander's up*, Custer reminded himself.

"Why, General—if the Kiowa are sending a delegation to
see you, then you can use them to your advantage. You
want to make an example out of these two chiefs here, don't
you?"

"You damn well know I do!"

"By waiting for the Kiowa delegation to arrive, you can
hang the two chiefs right before their eyes. Seeing their
chiefs kicking at the end of the rope will have a far better
effect than riding in later to see the chiefs hanging limp
from the branch of that tree over there."

Sheridan regarded Custer suspiciously. "Damn, Custer, if I don't get the feeling I'm swimming upstream with my mouth open and heading for your hook."

"I've never steered you wrong, and I won't start now."

"General Sheridan, sir!" The sergeant of the guard trotted up.

"What is it?" Sheridan grumped.

"We got some Indians in custody at the western perimeter, sir," the breathless soldier explained. "Pickets said they rode up at a gallop, but weren't hostile in their actions."

"How many?"

"Twelve."

"They say what they want?"

"'Bout all they grunted was *pony chief*."

Sheridan looked at Custer. His eyes said it all. He knew Custer had him whipped.

"I've got little choice but to bring the Kiowa in."

"By all means, General," Custer replied.

"Sergeant," Sheridan growled, "bring the Indians to me."

As the party of Kiowa marched through the milling throng of curious soldiers, Romero slipped past the two manacled chiefs, whispering among them.

He came back with Tsalante, who had accompanied the party of eleven chiefs that had arrived. He spoke to the little soldier chief Sheridan, then waited while the Indian-talker Romero translated.

"General, he says they've come to tell you the village is on its way, just like you asked—"

"Whoa!" Sheridan barked. "I didn't ask the bastards to

be on their way at sunrise. I told them to be here at sunrise!"

"Romero," Custer said as he stepped forward, "ask how long it will take."

"He says the village will be here late tomorrow."

"What the hell's taking 'em so long?" Sheridan asked.

"Ponies are poor from winter grass, General."

"What goddamned horses are these?" Sheridan yelled, pointing at the twelve ponies.

"The best in two camps. The rest are played out from the long winter and poor grazing."

Sheridan grew exasperated. "How the devil can these twelve get here, and the villages takes so goddamned long?"

"General, these warriors aren't dragging any travois loaded down with children and old ones. They rode fast—just to keep up with Satanta's son."

Sheridan glared flints for a moment, then walked over to the two manacled chiefs. Suddenly he whirled about, slamming one fist down into an open palm. Smiling at Custer.

"By damned, Custer!" he roared. "If you don't always manage to outflank me—like you did Stuart at Gettysburg!"

Custer laughed with him. "Shall I have the prisoners returned to their tent under guard, sir?"

"By all means." Sheridan flung an arm at the rope nooses hanging from the limb above. "But I'm leaving those damned hemp collars right where they are. Might serve as a reminder to the bastards what a chance they're taking. And a reminder of my personal faith in you, Custer."

Custer sensed the weight of Sheridan's faith once more.

"I figured I'd lost much of your faith in the past few weeks, sir."

"Perhaps I've been a little headstrong of late. Should try harder to give an old friend his due . . . especially for old times' sake."

He shook his head. "Hope I don't end up regretting that I didn't hang these miserable bastards." Sheridan's eyes leveled on Custer. "Sadder still if I end up regretting that I believed in you."

"Have I let you down, sir?"

"No, not once."

"Nor will I ever, General."

CHAPTER 20

"So tell me, Romero, is this old man ready for his trip?" Custer asked as the pair walked up to Custer's breakfast fire.

"He is."

Custer appraised the ancient chief with the stature of a stout oak water keg. The Seventh had been camped here at Fort Cobb since the eighteenth of December waiting for the tribes to show. He couldn't send a Kiowa on this delicate mission, but Romero had found this ancient Apache chief spending the winter in Satanta's villages. Iron Shirt's face was as chiseled as the roughened bark of the blackjack oak dotting their camp.

"Problem is, General, Iron Shirt don't trust the old she-bitch."

"Mahwissa?"

"Way he sees it, she'd just as soon slit his throat as talk."

"You tell him it's not his to like her or not. She's going along to help him find the Cheyenne and Arapaho. Tell them to come in to Fort Cobb before the soldiers destroy their villages. Mahwissa saw first-hand what my troops can do to an enemy camp."

Iron Shirt waved his hands energetically, jabbering in his toothless Apache generously laced with Kiowa and sign.

"Old man says he'd tell the tribes what your soldiers did at the Washita. Says you are the strong arm. He'll tell the other tribes of your mighty power."

"And tell Iron Shirt not to worry about the woman. She'll cause him no trouble." Custer nodded toward the four women walking up, Monaseetah among them.

Romero chattered at Mahwissa, then turned back to Custer. "Says she wants to take the old Sioux along, Stingy Woman."

Custer shook his head. "She's a regular pain in the neck, this one."

"I figured her to pain a man a lot lower, like where he sits his saddle!" Romero chuckled.

"Pray she isn't a nuisance to Iron Shirt. And inform her the chief is her only companion. She needs no other."

"She ain't gonna—"

"Just tell her what I said, Romero."

As Romero translated, Mahwissa's eyes stabbed at Custer like bone awls. Stingy Woman crossed her arms, glaring haughtily at Romero.

When Mahwissa finally spoke, her words burst like a furious dam breaking. She stomped up to Custer, one fist balled on a wide hip, the other hand shaking a scarred and battered finger at him, reminding him of his mother wagging her finger at a naughty young Autie.

"Says you're giving her to the old Apache—to warm his robes each night."

"Giving her to Iron Shirt? Where'd she come up with that idea?"

"She figures that 'cause she knows about you and Monaseetah. Says the soldier chief uses the young squaw for his pleasure, so you're giving her to the old man for his robes."

"That's the most preposterous thing I've ever heard! You'd better change her mind about things!" Custer snapped, watching Monaseetah not taking her eyes from the ground. "Tell Mahwissa it's time to show me that her words are straight. I remember when she told me she would help with her people. Now she can prove it."

As Romero translated, Mahwissa's chin jutted proudly. She glared at the Apache, as if to say, *Keep your hands to yourself, old man.*

"She understands, General."

"About time. I could have negotiated a cease-fire with the Army of Northern Virginia in less time! Moylan, bring up the horses."

Romero pointed out the animals three soldiers brought up: two horses decked with McClellan saddles, a pair of blankets lashed at the cantle, and a young pack mule swaying beneath more blankets and burlap sacks.

"They have provisions for fifteen days. A kettle and some fire-making gear in that greased pouch there." Custer stepped up to Iron Shirt. "Tell the old chief I trust him with this mission. On the mule are presents of food, clothing, and blankets. I don't want Mahwissa returning to her people empty-handed. Tell the Cheyenne I'm sending these gifts because I want peace. I don't want another village destroyed."

When Romero concluded, Mahwissa hugged Stingy

Woman, then leapt atop the horse she chose to ride, regally peering down on those gathered to watch the departure. She nudged her animal close to Custer.

After she patted the belt that tied an old blanket coat about her waist and finished a short speech, the scout translated.

"She says she'll do what you ask. You'll hear from her people very soon. And she wants me to tell you that the soldier chief is sending her on this journey without a weapon. Important to a Cheyenne squaw to have a weapon. A knife's such a small thing, she says."

"A knife?"

"What they call a *mutch-ka*. May not be a big thing to you but mighty important to her."

With the way the old woman stared at his belt, Custer realized Mahwissa wasn't after just any knife. She had her heart set on his own hunting knife.

Custer slid the sheath off his belt. He refused to let it go as he held it up to her, waiting for Romero to translate his instructions. "Tell her I want the knife back the next time we meet. When she comes back before the moon changes. My favorite knife—I'll let her use it on this important journey to talk of peace with her people."

As quickly as Romero finished, Mahwissa yanked the knife from Custer's hand and jammed it in her belt. Patting the knife, she gazed into the distance, refusing to utter any thanks or even acknowledge the soldier chief.

Iron Shirt raised his wrinkled hand in farewell, then signaled the woman to follow. Jerking on the mule's rope, the old Apache set off through the cold mist hanging in the trees like frosty cotton. Neither he nor the old woman ever looked back.

★   ★   ★

Custer jerked awake—frightened.

He was reassured only when he gazed down at her sleeping face nestled beside him in the gray of army wool. He'd been afraid she wasn't there. Afraid Libbie had found out and—

It washed back over him. Monaseetah had remained all night, falling asleep while he scratched nib and ink across paper. A letter to Libbie, then one to his half-sister back in Monroe, and finally the official work: reports and catching up on those never-ending journal entries. He recalled the sound of her gentle, childlike snoring as he had slipped beneath the covers a handful of hours ago.

The first night they hadn't coupled beneath his heavy blankets and robes.

A smile crossed his lips, recalling how she loved licking the sweat off him, tasting it with the delicate tip of her tongue as the beads glistened down his neck, along his shoulder, and across his chest. Tracing the pink tip of her tongue over his heated flesh whenever they lay exhausted in the joy of one another.

"General?"

He'd wait a minute, breathing shallow and slow. Maybe the soldier would go away.

"General? It's Sergeant Lucas."

He wasn't going away. Not this one. Sergeant Gregory Lucas believed it was his duty to awaken Custer when any need arose. Good soldiers never let their commanders sleep in.

"What in tarnal blazes is it, Lucas?"

"The scout Romero is here."

"What's he want?"

"He's here with the old Apache."

Custer bolted upright in bed.

"Iron Shirt, General," the interpreter spoke up.

"Very well, Romero. Get both the Indians something to eat. I'll be out shortly."

"Both, General? Iron Shirt came back alone."

Custer kicked his feet out of the blankets. "Where's the woman?"

"Says she stayed behind at the—"

"Behind!" Custer pulled on his long-handles, yanking dirty stockings over his feet.

"Says she was ordered by the chiefs not to come back."

"Ordered, was she?" His boots on, Custer rose. His breath fogged the tent as he slipped his arms into the wool tunic, angrily jamming buttons through their holes. He noticed Monaseetah watching him from behind her blankets.

"See that he has some coffee and breakfast. I'll be right there."

"Something else he says."

"Sounds like bad news. Spit it out."

"Iron Shirt says after the Cheyenne chiefs talked it over, they decided their ponies couldn't make the trip right now."

"Don't they understand I'll track them down and destroy their villages?"

"Two of 'em wanna come talk with you," Romero said.

"Only two?"

"Little Robe—a Cheyenne chief. And old Yellow Bear, Arapaho. They told Iron Shirt to tell *Hiestzi* they were coming in to talk with him."

"That's more like it!" Custer cheered, bursting through the tent flaps. "More like Christmas greetings!"

"It is Christmas Day, ain't it, General?" Lucas said.

"Merry Christmas! Now, be off, Romero—get some breakfast in Iron Shirt's belly."

He listened as their steps worried across the old snow before he ducked back in his warm tent.

Christmas Day. Custer felt guilty for not even missing Fort Hays, much less Christmas back home in Monroe with his family. Home: glowing candles and fragrant spruce garlands draped along every wall, wrapping every banister; smells of fresh-baked goods from the kitchen as the door swung open to the huge dining parlor.

Soon enough would come the new year, 1869. What it held for him, Custer dared not ask. All that concerned him at this moment was a young creature of the wilderness who pulled back the covers for him, exposing one breast as firm and round as a ripe melon.

Monaseetah patted the blankets beside her and cocked her head, coy as always. Her eyes invited him back into the garden. Dark, liquid eyes shy behind the long, raven-black lashes. She invited him.

"Why not?" he asked. He swallowed hard, his breathing quickly labored, shallow. His nostrils filling with the heated woman-musk of her. His mate.

As his shadow crawled over her, Custer realized deep in the very being of him that every man deserved at least one Christmas like this.

"Happy New Year, Angel Face!"

Custer toasted his young brother, holding a cup filled with nothing stronger than black coffee.

"A very happy New Year to you, Autie!"

Tom had been toasting one and all with whiskey he had brought from Fort Dodge in small flasks. At twenty-three, the young captain loved revelry. There was a lust for life flowing in his veins that in some way, for some reason, had always seemed diluted in his older brother.

Up and down officers' row on this night of celebration men danced with one another to tunes pumped out by the regimental band. Bright fires leapt into the inky darkness of the late night as a soft snow drifted down upon Fort Cobb. General Hazen and his staff had come down to pay their respects, celebrating at Sheridan's quarters.

Here at Custer's camp his officers had gathered: Myers, Yates, Thompson, Benteen, along with Godfrey, Cooke, and Moylan. Young Tom Custer had dragged along the reporter Keim, with everyone well on his way to seeing in the new year in uproarious style.

Since leaving Camp Supply three weeks ago, Monaseetah had genuinely come to enjoy the company of these white men. Not only because they showed her a consideration she had never known among Cheyenne males, but because these white men knew how to have fun. Their joy was like that of a young Cheyenne warrior celebrating a victory with his young friends.

From time to time, she gazed up at Custer. Studying the fine cut of his face, that sharp angle of his Teutonic nose as it blended into his cheek. Or the clean line of his thin lips nearly lost beneath the bristling mustache and beard tinted red-gold with dancing firelight. He let the snow fall on his long, combed curls, scented with cinnamon. She studied the eyes—clear as the glasslike surface of a prairie pond at sunrise, as yet unruffled by the breeze of day.

She was wondering again now, why for close to a week he had not pressed himself on her, contenting himself to lie with her as they fell asleep together, entwined without passion. To her repeated question, he merely patted her swollen belly.

She sipped at her steaming coffee mixed generously with sugar. A treat, this, rarely found in a Cheyenne winter camp. Sugar or coffee. Together they were a magical potion fit for the Everywhere Spirit. A delicate dance upon her tongue.

So much like this *Hiestzi*. Brave and strong, unafraid of the unknown. A man so alive and unconcerned in riding headlong toward the mysteries of time beyond . . . and through it all this soldier chief smiled at his enemies. His joys must be genuine.

He caught her staring at him. Monaseetah smiled and gazed into the fire. She sensed him moving around the others, stepping up behind her.

"Here, Autie!" Tom Custer leapt up, shoving his tin cup into Custer's hand. "Take this!"

"I don't drink!"

"Dear brother," Tom replied, sweeping the ground in a grand bow, "I wish the honor of a dance with Sally Ann!"

"You've had quite enough to drink tonight, Tom."

"Not near enough, Autie, ol' boy!"

Tom wrapped one of Monaseetah's hands gently in his. Her eyes searched Custer's for approval.

"I ask only that you dance . . ." Custer paused.

"Civilized, Autie?" Tom brought Monaseetah from her perch. "I'd do anything for a dance with this dark-eyed beauty!"

In time to a tune played by the regimental musicians

seated beneath a canvas awning among the trees yonder at
Sheridan's camp, Tom swept Monaseetah side to side. A
light, airy waltz, Tom slowly circling the Indian princess.
Turning her ever so slowly as he swung, side to side,
circling the fire. Eventually she swayed with him, absorb-
ing his rythmn, gazing now and then at Custer, her smile
childlike with the novelty of it.

All around them the others clapped in time. Yates
stepped up, tapping Tom on the shoulder. Confused and
scared, Monaseetah turned to dash back to her seat as Tom
released her. But Yates swept her up in his arms, gliding
gaily with her around the fire. Joining in the fun, Myers and
Thompson cut in for their dances with the Cheyenne
maiden. Then Godfrey and Benteen, a chorus of laughter
when Monaseetah giggled at each change of partners. Tom
cut in again.

"Sally Ann . . . Sally Ann!" He spun her a bit too
wildly, frightening her as his toes caught, stumbling, almost
falling.

"Tom."

Custer was at Tom's shoulder. A strong hand clamped on
his shoulder, slowing his drunken waltz. "You've had
enough . . . she's had enough for now, little brother."

"But I'm not done dancing with Sally Ann."

"I think you're quite done for the night, Tom," Custer
whispered, sensing the eyes of the others between his
shoulders.

"Done . . . for the night? Whatever do you mean,
dearest brother?"

"Let me take you to your tent."

"Damn you, Autie!" he cried. "It's New Year's

Eve . . . I want my dance with the most beautiful woman in the world—to hell with George Armstrong Custer!"

"Please, Tom," Custer soothed. "Don't embarrass yourself. Come, let me get you tucked away so you sleep it off."

"Dear, dear brother." Tom tried to focus on Custer's face, swaying, letting Monaseetah go. "Always was worried 'bout your little brother, weren't you?"

Without struggling, Tom leaned into Custer, belching on the sour whiskey. "Back to the days we were boys in Ohio . . . Michigan. I was always the one raising hell. Always getting licks at school with those oak paddles. You know I even chewed back then? When the older boys dared not."

Tom pushed himself to arm's-length from his older brother. "But you, Autie? You never raised hell. Oh, you always played jokes on others, but never raised hundred-proof hell like me!"

"C'mon, Tom—"

"Why, can't you see you got the only woman at the ball—and the most beautiful . . . oh, goddamn you, Autie! You always had the prettiest ones! You got Libbie and now you're wenching with this girl."

·"Tom!"

The sudden slap of Custer's voice silenced them all. "You're drunk, but that gives you no right—"

"General,"—George Yates stepped in—"I don't think he—"

"Don't think what, Lieutenant?" Custer demanded.

"You're right, Autie," Tom said. "Always right, big brother. You've got a proper army wife back east. And here in the Territories you've got your army whore to keep you warm. What gave you the right to all the whores in the world, big brother?"

Custer savagely wrenched his brother around. In that moment his right hand drew back, open and ready to strike the babbling, drunken mouth.

"General Custer!"

With that foreign voice, Custer turned, watching two figures approaching: one a picket guard, his rifle across his chest, the other, Romero.

"What is it?" Custer asked, his hand dropping as Yates and Moylan steadied Tom on his feet.

"Indians, sir. Lots of 'em."

"Indians?"

"Just come in. Cheyenne. Arapaho. Congratulations, General! Down at Sheridan's headquarters, they're all saying you got the head men to come in without a goddamned shot fired!"

"Where are they?"

"At Sheridan's party."

"He hasn't served them whiskey, has he?"

"None I know of."

"Good. Can't have them getting drunk . . . no hang-overs while we parley." He turned. "Moylan, see that Tom's bedded down. I'll look in on him in a bit."

"Awww, Autie," Tom murmured. "Be a lot warmer you get me a beautiful squaw to snuggle down with."

"Goodnight, Tom. That whiskey in your belly is doing all your talking for you. Moylan, please."

"Well, boys!" Custer turned back to the others at the fire. "Looks like this'll be a grand new year for us all."

"No mere bunghole tooting in the wind there!" Myers cheered.

"C'mon, Romero—smile!" Custer cried. "Why, for most of last year, they had me in exile. So this new year can be nothing but an improvement!"

An impressive delegation of Arapaho and Cheyenne leaders greeted Custer two days later when he held council at Sheridan's camp. What amazed Tom Custer the most was that they had been frightened enough to come on foot to meet with the renowned Yellow Hair.

Looking at the poor shape of the chiefs, it was easy enough to believe their ponies were too weak to allow the villages to journey across the winter wilderness. The tribes hadn't located buffalo for better than two moons. For a time they had survived on pemmican. Once that staple was gone, they were driven to eating their camp dogs. The chiefs admitted a man would be hard pressed to find a dog in any of their camps.

Tom Custer attended the council chaired by General Hazen. What had begun in the morning hours lasted past dusk, replete with the usual smoking and eating, the presentation of gifts before the negotiations could start. By midday, the younger Custer found himself liking the Cheyenne chief Little Robe. With a quick wit, the stocky leader often let himself bear the brunt of his humor. What appealed to Tom most was that Little Robe appeared to recognize that his people must find accommodation with the white soldiers and settlers crowding onto the southern plains.

Long after dark the army and tribes reached an agreement. In return for a resumption of their annuities and a guarantee the army would not destroy their villages, the Indians agreed to maintain peace with the government.

Custer insisted that this meant their villages must return to the reservations—immediately.

With the next sunrise the tribes dispatched runners carrying word of the new agreement, expressing the urgency of coming in to the reservation as soon as the camps could be put on the trail. Sheridan instructed the chiefs to bring their people to the new post he would construct in the shadow of the Wichita Mountains, a short ride to the south.

Over the next two days, wagon trains of badly needed provisions reached Fort Cobb. From those wagons Sheridan and Custer presented more gifts to the head men of each band in recognition of their new peace agreement.

Two days later, Custer pointed both his Seventh Cavalry and the Nineteenth Kansas volunteers south. By January 8 the entire command arrived at the juncture of Medicine Bluff and Cache creeks flowing at the base of the Wichita Mountains some forty miles south of Fort Cobb. Sheridan selected an ideal site offering enough grass, timber, and stone for construction of a permanent post, in addition to a good supply of water and game found in the surrounding hills. He announced he was naming the post in honor of his West Point classmate and Civil War comrade, Joshua W. Sill.

As the weary troops erected tents and teamsters removed stiffened harness from the mules, the wind swept out of the north, forewarning of yet another winter storm. Within an hour, that storm slashed down on the Medicine Bluff Creek camp with a vengeance, driving rain and sleet before it. Winds blew with such a fury that no man dared step out to seek firewood. Enough wind for every man to hunker in his tent, making the best of it.

Still, try as they might, two soldiers ordered by Surgeon

Lippincott to build a fire and boil some water failed in their every attempt to shelter the sputtering flames from the wind.

"Keep trying, boys," Lippincott growled. "Gonna need that fire for heat if not for sterilizing."

"Damned Injun squaw," one of the soldiers grumped. His head was wrapped in a worn woolen scarf, and he blew on his frozen, cramped fingers.

Again the soldiers bent over the sparks nursed in the lee of Lippincott's hospital tent. A raw wind drummed over the rattling canvas, sweeping all sides with a fury as it clapped like two huge hands, roaring in laughter at the feeble efforts of these men. Yet their perseverance paid off and flames licked along the firewood, sputtering beneath the icy sleet and tobacco-wad raindrops.

"By damn, boys!" Lippincott cheered. "Soon enough two lives may depend on your fire."

Well enough did Tom Custer understand that Lippincott held those two lives in the palm of his hand at this very hour. Through the stormy evening he had followed his older brother as Custer made his rounds of camp. Checking on everything like a mother hen ready to nest. Fighting one of his frequent bouts of insomnia. Perhaps only Tom knew why.

Late that night, a few of the Custer circle lay sleeping in the headquarter's tent, driven to their blankets by the potent combination of their long winter trail, the incessant storm, and Tom's patent whiskey.

Tom had sat up with his older brother into the wee hours, sipping his whiskey as Custer nursed his coffee, still unable to admit he was afraid to be alone. Then, while Tom dozed, Custer penned a long and sentimental letter home to Libbie. Almost three and a half months had passed since kissing her goodbye on that railroad platform in Monroe. Yet, in listening now to a brutal wind hurling itself against his tent, Custer sensed that more than mere time and miles had come between them. In some way he hoped his words would reassure her across that gap of days and distance, touch her.

There it came again. That sound like no other.

At first Custer believed it was the keening wind. Slashed through the trees, circled around the humps of the Wichita. Yet the cry refused to rise and fall like the wind. If anything, it grew stronger.

Shaky, Tom rose to one elbow, his eyes reddened and gummy from whiskey and lack of sleep.

Moylan stirred next. One by one they each poked their heads from their blankets like hibernating bears, hoary breath like ghostly halos dancing in the pale lamplight.

"What the Sam Hill is that?" Cooke asked, half-corked still.

"If I didn't know better. I'd call it a baby's cry," Moylan replied, the sober one in the lot.

"Sally Ann's baby!" Tom cried.

"She ain't Sally Ann!" Cooke growled, flinging a limp arm at Tom.

"Both of you hush!" Moylan barked, watching Custer push up from his stool, stepping over the bodies strewn across the tent floor, and stop at the door.

"Monaseetah's baby," he whispered.

As the wind sighed, the unmistakable wail of a newborn rang clear as a prairie starburst.

Custer flung back the flaps, letting the night and wind and sleet batter him.

The water stung his face, the ice slashing at his eyes. Another cry raised the hairs at the back of his neck.

Tom gazed at his brother's face, realizing Autie was weeping. For one of the few times in his life, Custer shed tears.

"Monaseetah's baby is here at last!"

CHAPTER 21

CUSTER made certain every last man of them fidgeted, cold and anxious as they waited in his tent.

He had had Moylan summon his officers to an unexpected conference. His flair for the dramatic coupled with his trembling rage dictated he wait until they had gathered before making his grand entrance.

Tearing the flaps apart, Custer yanked their attention to him as surely as if he had slapped them with the back of his hand. Pausing, he let each man suffer the silent, icy impact of his eyes. Fred Benteen stared at the rawhide quirt Custer slapped monotonously against a muddy boot.

"Gentle-men." Custer made it sound profane, something he was loath to speak. "As most of you are aware, yesterday, the twenty-third of January, a post express arrived from Camp Supply with mail from Fort Dodge, letters from home."

Custer paused. "Including some traitorous news for me!" he roared.

From his tunic Custer wrenched a crumpled newspaper page. He shook it before their faces.

"An old friend from my Michigan days sent me a copy of the St. Louis *Democrat*. Most of you get clippings and news items from your hometown papers, but my friend thought I should read an article written about me by a St. Louis man: a most scandalous story about our recent campaign against the Washita village of Black Kettle."

Custer's eyes, now steel blue, sliced toward the officers, accusing every man. Some shifted from boot to boot. Others cleared throats or wiped hands across lips gone dry.

Benteen swallowed hard. He watched Custer tense his jaws, struggling to control his anger.

"This St. Louis journalist couldn't know a bloody thing of our campaign! But the language he used says that it was written by someone who knew what went on—an officer of this regiment! That wording, the detail, these veiled implications—all of it means some officer of this regiment wrote this filth to ruin me!"

"Read 'em some of it, Autie!" Tom Custer prodded, his own eyes scolding the others.

Amused in a way, Benteen watched as the Custer family closed ranks.

"Listen to these words a traitor uses," Custer said. "Reviling me before the American public!"

And now, to learn why the anxiously-looked for succor did not come, let us view the scene in the captured village, scarce two short miles away. Light skirmishing is going on all around. Savages on flying steeds, with shields and feathers gay, are circling everywhere, riding like devils incarnate. The troops are on all sides of the village, looking

on and seizing every opportunity of picking off some of
those daring riders with their carbines. But does no one
think of the welfare of Maj. Elliott and party? It seems not.
But, yes! a squadron of cavalry is in motion. They trot; they
gallop. Now they charge! The cowardly redskins flee the
coming shock and scatter here and there among the hills to
scurry away. But it is the true line—will the cavalry keep it?
No! No! They turn! Ah, 'tis only to intercept the wily foe.
See! a gray troop goes on in the direction again. One more
short mile and they will be saved. Oh, for a mother's
prayers!

Will not some good angel prompt them? . . . There is
no hope for that brave little band, the death doom is theirs,
for the cavalry halt and rest their panting steeds . . .

And now return with me to the village. Officers and
soldiers are watching, resting, eating and sleeping. In an
hour or so they will be refreshed, and then scour the hills
and plains for their missing comrades. In a short time we
shall be far from the scene of their daring dash, and night
will have thrown her dark mantle over the scene. But surely
some search will be made for our missing comrades. No,
they are forgotten. Over them and the poor ponies the
wolves will hold high carnival, and their howlings will be
their only requiem.

Custer let the officers suffer his fury in silence as he
paced before them.

"This tells the public that we didn't do everything we
could to rescue Elliott." Tom was the first to speak,
protective, even combative in defense of his older brother.
"It says the Seventh gave up searching while Elliott was

butchered. We didn't know, dammit! Who was it? Which one of you gutless bastards wrote this—"

"As surely as I'm standing here," Custer interrupted, pushing Tom back a step, "I know this was penned by one of you. If I ever find out who's guilty—" He slapped the rawhide quirt against his boot for emphasis, "why, I'll give him a sound thrashing he'll never forget!"

His threat hung like stale cigar smoke in the silent tent. The silence was punctuated only by the slap of that quirt he drummed against his boot.

Benteen took a step forward. "May I look at the paper?"

Stunned and speechless, Custer shoved the article toward Benteen, like some loathsome thing contaminated with pox.

For breathless moments, the captain scanned the page, listening as Custer's breath rose and fell in labored wheezes. The Missourian handed the article back to Custer. He adjusted his holster, freeing the mule-ear from its brass stud, a gesture not lost on a single man in that tent. Least of all George Armstrong Custer. Benteen blinked anxiously, steeling himself for what might come, raking the tip of a pink tongue across his dry lips.

"Colonel," Benteen began, "you threatened a sound thrashing for the man who wrote that letter." His eyes flicked to the rawhide quirt, returning dead-level with Custer's. "Well, sir—be about it, and now. Appears I'm the author of that article you hold in your hand."

A dangerous electricity sparked between the two men. Tom Custer bolted, lunging at Benteen. His older brother restrained him, struggling to bridle his own anger.

"You wrote this filth?" Custer spat.

Benteen sensed every eye on his back. "No. I wrote a

letter to a friend in St. Louis. He has contacts in the newspaper business . . . St. Louis, Chicago, even the New York *Times*."

As he watched the color drain from Custer's face, Benteen straightened himself. "I had no idea my letter would ever wind up on the front page of any paper."

"You knew damned well it would—you goddamned, two-faced traitor!" Tom Custer shrieked. "Better you resign your commission. It's unhealthy for you to stay on in this outfit, you lying bastard!"

Having taken about all he could from the younger Custer, Benteen's eyes snapped to Tom, eyes filled with white fire. "You're going to make it unhealthy for me to stay on—*you?*"

If his meaning was not clear enough, he slipped his hand beneath the mule-ear so it rested loosely on the butt of his pistol.

"Benteen?" Custer said savagely. "You wrote this about me, about my regiment?"

"I did."

"I had no idea," Custer stammered, confused, not knowing what to say. "No idea any man would step forward to confess . . ."

Benteen figured Custer had intended to use the article to bully them all, not expecting the real author to announce his guilt. He watched as Custer swallowed hard, his nostrils flaring above that bushy mustache, before his eyes climbed to Benteen's again.

"I'll deal with you later, Benteen." His face turned crimson as he struggled to maintain his composure.

Those gritty words hung in the close, sweaty air as

Custer shoved his officers aside and tore from the tent, disappearing as quickly as he had entered.

"You frigging sunuvabitch!" Tom Custer flung his words at Benteen, restrained by two officers.

"Your brother's feelings are far less precious than a soldier's life, Lieutenant. Don't forget that—ever." Benteen stepped forward. He wasn't any taller than the younger Custer, but he loomed with the bulk of an ox over the whipcord-lean lieutenant from Michigan. "Damn Custer's feelings, I say! Your brother can go off on a sulk and suck his thumb, for all I care! Lives are at stake here! His poor judgment is to blame—not that bloody letter I wrote."

"I understand you all too well, Captain. Mind you, he might forgive you someday. But I never will!"

Benteen stood in the fury of Tom's rage a moment longer before the lieutenant shoved past the Missourian, blasting from the tent. It was quiet enough to hear boots scraping on the hard ground or a nervous cough. Captain Samuel Robbins came beside Benteen.

"You've tackled yourself a real handful there."

"I can handle either one of 'em," Benteen growled.

"A real hornet's nest you've stirred up, old boy!" Myers snorted.

"Figured on making some waves," Benteen admitted. "Want to save some lives next time out."

"What'll you do when Custer wants to deal with you later?" Thompson inquired.

"I'm not afraid of him or his horsewhip. I'll beat Custer at his own bully game. Before he can confront me in private, I'll force his hand in public."

"Never advisable to bait that man," Myers said.

"He's right," George Yates agreed. "I staffed for him in the war. Let it blow over, by God. He's hurt enough."

"Enough?" Benteen snapped, glaring at Yates. "You Monroe boys stick together, don't you, Yates?" He glanced out the tent flaps. "I'll fetch that reporter, Keim. Take him with me when I see Custer. We'll have it out, once and for all. Keim'll be my witness. Not like you, Yates—someone Custer can bluff and bully."

Benteen glared at them all. "I'll break that arrogant bastard yet—see that never again does he send men off on suicidal attacks then refuses support to those soldiers in their tragic moment of struggle!"

"Captain's pardon," Yates said, "but Custer's not the sort to be cowed by anybody. He'll never forget your insults."

"I bloody well hope he doesn't!" Benteen shouted. "We're talking about saving lives, stopping Custer from sending men to their deaths to further his career. Can't any of you see that? When Custer will send any man to his death to further his hunger for promotion and glory, none of us matters anymore."

Benteen was certain none of them understood a thing he tried to say. At the tent flap he stopped, sickened with bile at the back of his throat. He sucked a deep breath of the cold to still the nausea. He wheeled on them, his passion bubbling, his voice thick with mockery. "Mankind's just dust in the wind to him. Custer plans his glory and fame to last the eons. Who are we mere mortals to try stopping a man destined to etch his name across those stone walls of eternity itself?"

Benteen jammed the cap down on his head and dove into the cold.

★ ★ ★

"Allow me one final sweep of the Territories, General!" Custer demanded, banging his fist on the table in Sheridan's tent, scattering some coffee-stained maps. "By God, I'll march south and west from here. You can't deny me this! If I can't be in Federal City for Grant's inauguration—"

"Neither one of us. There's not enough time," Sheridan said. "We haven't finished our task here."

"So I'll put our homebound march to good use before calling it quits on your campaign."

"Use the march for what, Custer?" Sheridan asked.

"Find the most troublesome, bloodthirsty band—the Cheyenne Dog Soldiers under Medicine Arrow."

"Damn that red bastard!" As much as he hated to admit to preferring another man's idea to his own, Sheridan had liked Custer's proposal from the start. "Here's to your success." He held up the sterling silver hip flask that was never far from his side. "More then ever—may you find the Indians you're so desperately seeking."

"Thank you for your continued faith in me, General."

"Truth of it is, Custer, I'm very pleased by the progress you've made this winter. If you concern yourself strictly with your job here you won't find time to worry about the lives of a few miserable savages."

Sheridan waved a hand, silencing Custer as he continued. "Just the way you did things in the war. You pressed on, doing a soldier's work. Do that now! Be a soldier before anything else!"

Last night on the eve of his departure, Sheridan had grappled with the fear that his winter campaign had become a grand failure. So this morning the whiskey tasted better than breakfast, what with having to leave the Territories with much undone, called back to department headquarters and the desk that awaited him. Whiskey and cigars, better than the best breakfast salt pork and hardtack. For an old warhorse like Phil Sheridan, whiskey and cigars made a fighting man's diet.

Sheridan appraised Custer. "I've seen a handful of your kind before. Not only in the army, but in public life. You're after the brass ring! Something no amount of money can buy—power."

"Sir, if I may—"

"That's no disgrace." Sheridan lifted his hand. "Truth is, every great military commander hungers for power."

Custer sank to a leather trunk as soldiers loaded the wagons around he and Sheridan, a late February sun just poking its head over the hills.

"Why the hell you think I sent Sully packing back east?" Sheridan watched Custer's expression narrow.

"That's right," Sheridan said. "You're commander of the Seventh Cavalry. I ordered him back to Kansas."

"I never—"

"'Course you never knew, Armstrong." Sheridan sipped at the flask. "Got rid of that old pussy-footer so this campaign would be *your* show and *your* show only."

He waved the flask under Custer's nose, a finger pointing. "Don't frig this up, Custer! I can put you in the right place at the right time—like I did through the Shenandoah campaign. But I can't fight your battles for you."

"I had no idea that's what became of Colonel Sully."

"When I first got to Camp Supply, you two were arguing like yard dogs over who would lead the attack on the hostiles. The old slogger wanted me to ship you back, send you off to some other regiment. You believe that? By damned, you should've seen the look on his face when I told him he was the one packing!

"The rest of the campaign's in your hands alone, dear boy," Sheridan finished. "I've sent Sully home to pound sand. So it's yours to find the Indians. Do what you've always done best: Find the enemy and make him bleed."

Custer leapt to his feet. "By all means, General!"

"Don't dally with the chiefs. Those old bastards just waste your time. Show 'em how you made a name for yourself on the James and the Rappahannock! All those red sonsabitches understand is toughness anyway. They'll sneer at your kindness as a mark of something weak and womanly."

"Yes, General."

"I ought to know, dammit. I strung up some of those Yakima bastards back in '56 up in the Oregon country. The hostiles will remember you only for the pain you dealt them on the Washita. Not a goddamned soul—white or red—will remember you for any kindness you show an Indian. Not those two old Kiowa in the shadow of Fort Cobb. And certainly not those Cheyenne running to save their miserable hides."

Sheridan sipped at the whiskey that warmed his gut as few things could. "Hell, history will treat you kindly only when you act in a decisive manner and strike with a firm hand! Damn those peacemakers in Washington City! Let them tend to their knitting while we get on being soldiers!"

Sheridan wiped the back of his hand across his thin lips, stepping close to Custer. "Years from now you won't find the name of one of those politicians in the schoolbooks, Custer. Only the generals and those like you—destined to ride a shooting star—will be cloaked in printer's ink. So don't be dismayed that the tribes have not come in! This only proves your greatest opportunity yet! Greater than the Shenandoah campaign."

"That would take some doing, General."

"Blast it, son! Don't sit on your record. Make 'em stand up and take notice of you back east. The only way you'll wear these goddamned stars again is with your butt in the saddle. Not resting on your laurels."

He slapped a gloved hand on Custer's shoulder, leaning close to confide. "You teach a hound by rewarding it, don't you? That's what we tried with these savages at first. Reward them. It didn't work, so now we punish them. Just the way you'd do with your hound. Reward doesn't work! Sherman knows that. Even Grant's come to the light. As sure as you're sitting before me, *you* can be the instrument of our pacification on this frontier. The choice is yours. Will you obey not only that direction I give you, but what history demands of you? Dammit, some soldier's name will be written in the annals of this western land, a name repeated over and over on the lips of every schoolboy down through all eternity. Will it be George Armstrong Custer?"

On 2 March, Custer led the full command of his Seventh Cavalry and Nineteenth Kansas out of Fort Sill, bound for Fort Hays via Camp Supply. To garrison the new post Sheridan had erected deep in the heart of Indian Territory, he left behind a complement of the all-Negro Cavalry, those called "buffalo soldiers."

Winter still gripped the plains—cold, blustery weather battering the soldiers daily. Every man nursed frostbite— ears, noses, cheeks, fingers, or toes. For seven days

Custer's troops plodded west by south. Every morning his scouts stuffed a day's supply of jerky and hardtack in their saddlebags before setting out on their dawn-to dusk march, fanning through the countryside ahead of the blue columns.

Come the morning of the ninth, Custer's scouts hurried back with news that, while not exactly to Custer's taste, was nonetheless not without flavor. They had located a trail no more than a month old.

"How many lodges?" Custer asked eagerly.

"One travois, General," replied Moses Milner.

"One." Custer sighed. "Not to worry, fellas. Something tells me that one travois will lead me to bigger game."

"Your itch same as mine. Got a hunch we'll run those brownskins down yet."

"Keep your scouts fanned wide, Joe," Custer instructed.

"Your itch the same as mine, General. We'll make a scout out of you yet."

Custer's faith in his hunch paid off the next afternoon. Eleven more lodges had joined the first. He dropped from the saddle beside his scouts on the bank of a small bubbling spring.

"Camp ain't that old," Milner said.

"We're finally gaining on 'em?" Custer piped excitedly.

"Got a couple weeks' lead at the most."

Custer patted his chest, "Remember, boys—I've got another hundred dollars for the scout who leads me to the village where the white girls are held. Moylan, pass word we're camping here for the night. When you're done, have Romero bring Monaseetah to my fire."

Milner turned to Hard Rope. "Say, old fella—that'll be my hundred dollars this time! Best you make camp. I'll boil coffee."

"Good. Hard Rope and Little Beaver tired of your white chin-music. You make better coffee than talk, Joe California."

Custer watched Milner lead the Osages into the trees, laughing. Two old Indians hunkered under their blankets coats and one jerky-tough scout pounding their backs with his every joke, chasing after his hundred-dollar dream.

By the time Moylan returned with Romero and the young Cheyenne mother, soldiers had unsaddled horses and raised canvas along the creek.

"Have Monaseetah look over the Indians' camp, Romero," Custer ordered.

Without replying to the interpreter, Monaseetah slipped off to an old campfire with the infant tied at her back. Monaseetah knelt, raking the old ashes, examining everything that caught her eye. She walked every inch of the Indian camp, picking up a bit of cloth or a scrap of old hide. Sniffing at old bones, she broke each one apart, examining the age of the marrow. Custer watched her repeatedly place her palm against the ground, as if testing for the warmth of some print left by man, beast, or lodge pole.

Romero interpreted her conclusions. "Twelve lodges camped here, a small band of some petty chief. Says the village broke up to hunt some time back, but seems they're gathering for something important. Left here less than two weeks ago."

"Were they scared off? Know of our coming?"

"She says no—they packed and rode off in no particular hurry."

"How far will they travel each day?"

Monaseetah gazed thoughtfully across the merry stream before her hands danced as gracefully as two birds fluttering

in courtship. "When the Cheyenne travel in late winter—
when the grass is scarce—they make short trips each day.
Moving from one stream to the next. Where they know
there'll be water," she signed, and Romero interpreted for
Custer.

One ability no one had ever questioned was Custer's
memory for detail, like the topography of the old maps he
studied every night by lamplight. His command had already
crossed Elm Fork, at times called the Middle Fork of the
Red River. Several miles to the east, that Elm Fork joined
a sizable prairie river called the Sweetwater.

"By glory, the bands are heading north by east!" Custer
exclaimed. "Marching to the Sweetwater."

Romero shook his head. "Cheyenne head south this
time of year. Especially when they're hungry. They're
moving toward the buffalo with empty bellies, General."

Monaseetah broke in, wagging her head, her chatter
quick and hands flying.

"What did she say?"

"Funny thing," Romero admitted, his dark brow fur-
rowed. "Says she can't make sense of it either—seems the
bands are moving backward for the season. Gotta be
something important for them—"

"What do you mean *backward?*"

"I'll be damned but she claims the bands are marching
north and east, just like you figured."

Custer couldn't help smiling now. He had drawn a card
few men would have pulled from the deck, winning a big
hand of the game. But by no means the last hand of the
night.

"I'll soon have my Indians, Romero—the ones I've
wanted since last fall."

"Dog Soldiers now, General." Romero eased himself down on a stump.

"Ask her what's so important to the Cheyenne for their bands to move backward now."

When her hands came to a stop, Romero looked at Custer, his dark eyes brooding. "To join with many others, to come together to fight Yellow Hair."

The news she had given *Hiestzi* had saddened Monaseetah. She remembered how hopeful she had been at first, thinking she would have him forever. Now, that girlish dream seemed cold as yesterday's fire.

Each night since the baby had come, she yearned for him anew. Yet more and more he made himself too busy with the other soldier chiefs and that young brother who called her Sally Ann. Monaseetah hadn't bled for days now. No longer did she wear the rope and blanket scrap that absorbed her flow. Healed at long last.

Why will he not come to me? she wondered.

Of late Custer seemed obsessed with finding the Cheyenne bands she knew were gathering for a great war council. Once Yellow Hair found and destroyed their camps as he had done on the Washita, Monaseetah knew the soldier chief would leave her.

Even if the Cheyenne surrendered, as he had conquered the Kiowa without a shot fired, Yellow Hair would leave her. With victory complete, the soldier chief would ride far to the north.

Back to his other woman.

Up and down this creekside camp she listened to soldiers excited at finding the trail of the hostiles warming. But

Monaseetah sank into a wallow of despair. Beside her, the infant wailed, his belly empty.

She sensed the keening of her heart signaled a deeper hunger still.

Hot tears slipped down her cheeks. Never before had she felt for any man as she did for him, and never before had Monaseetah felt so abandoned, knowing that Yellow Hair was slipping from her life already . . . as surely as the spring tore itself from the winter.

A long, long winter gone.

CHAPTER 22

STILL more lodges joined the trail early the next day. By late morning Custer's scouts ran across a second and larger campground. The number of fire pits indicated the village had grown to twenty-five lodges.

More surprising still, by the next day, 12 March, Jack Corbin tallied better than a hundred sets of travois poles scratching the earth, joining the northbound march of the Cheyenne war camps.

"By glory, Jack!" Custer cheered at the news, happier than he had been in weeks. "We've flushed 'em like a covey of prairie hens now. We'll herd them on ahead of us until they're gathered up."

"And you're ready to strike." Corbin picked something off the trail. "We're right behind 'em. Trail's warm."

"Horse apples?"

"Though they ain't steaming, they're still warm to the touch." Corbin crumbled one in his threadbare mitten.

"How far ahead of us?"

"Two, maybe three days, the way they're lollygagging

along." It was Milner who answered this time. "Don't seem they know we're fixing to run up their backsides neither."

"If you don't want them Cheyenne to know you're coming, best keep your flankers and skirmishers in close, General," Corbin advised.

"All right. Bring them in. Let Pepoon's trackers know too. Saints preserve the man who lets the Indians discover us now!"

"Should I take word to the commands, sir?" Moylan flung a thumb back along the columns.

"By all means. No bugle calls, no more hunting. No firing of guns for any reason. See that Captain Myers posts sentries with the wagons and the herd, and deploys a perimeter guard tonight. Small fires, for cooking only. Fires out after supper, before dark. I've gotten this close—"

"You don't want a damn thing spoiling it now!" Moylan agreed.

A half hour later Custer sat with his scouts at a small fire, brewing coffee, discussing the country ahead, when a young soldier approached.

"General Custer?"

Custer looked up. "Private Reed, isn't it?"

"Yessir. Ellison Reed."

"What have you there?"

"Salt, sir."

"Where'd you find salt?"

"Down by the river, General. There's a salt stream, yonder by the spring. Banks piled high with salt cakes like this. A natural lick drawing critters from all 'round. Thick with tracks down at the spring. Figured we gone without salt for too long now. This here's for you, sir."

"That's kind of you, Private. How do you figure to grind it?"

"Have a coffee mill, General?" Corbin interrupted. "I'll show you how we grind salt back to home."

"Splendid, Jack! Not only have you tracked the end of the trail for these Cheyenne we've been following, but you have a way to grind the salt Reed's discovered."

"A treat for any man likes the taste of red meat, General," Milner added.

"Man needs a treat," Custer said, "before he likely heads into battle."

Before winter's dusk had swallowed the encampment, Custer called his officers together and issued marching orders. Tom Custer listened as his brother stated that any item of personal gear such as blankets or tents or clothing which could not be loaded in the wagons was to be burned.

"I'll allow each man one blanket," Custer said.

Every worn-out horse and mule was shot by the rear guard. Already suffering from many days without proper rations, the soldiers would at least fill their bellies on the stringy horse or mule meat as they readied for battle once more.

That next morning, Tom Custer's company covered their smoky fires with sodden earth, resuming their march before first light. Before the sun climbed a hand above the horizon, the scouts rode in with the stirring report of finding a recent encampment of some four hundred lodges just ahead.

"Fire pits warm enough to take the chill off a man's bones," Milner repeated after Tom waved him over, anxious to hear the news. "Damn big herd of ponies. Them Cheyenne gathering up, young Custer."

"I bet Autie cheered your news."

"Part that made him happy was to hear them Cheyenne don't even know we're on their tails. He's sneaking his blue army right up their red asses!"

"How soon?" Tom asked.

"Hard Rope and old Little Beaver told your brother he'd not sleep this night before seeing many Cheyenne."

"That's grand news, Joe!"

"Itchy for a fight?"

"You bet I am, you old bastard! Got a score to even with them red bastards for butchering Elliott's men at the Washita."

Milner led his old mule back toward the commissary wagons, where he might wangle a mouthful or two of food from the sergeant.

Around noon Custer sent Hard Rope up the trail to a nearby knoll. He was to signal the columns to proceed if the countryside beyond was clear.

"Little Beaver says that's got to be the valley of the Sweetwater," Romero said to Custer as they watched Hard Rope scramble up the hill. "Man points his nose northeast, he'd run into the Washita, not far from where Black Kettle was camped."

"I'll find those Cheyenne soon, or my name isn't—"

"*Custer!*" Hard Rope had whirled, racing downhill, weaving through the hackberry brush. He slid to a stop beside Custer's horse.

"Come see. Many horses. Big village. Your eyes see, this time."

"Moylan, you stay here. I'll see what Hard Rope's spotted."

At the top of the knoll Custer dropped on his belly

alongside the Osage, crawling the last few yards to the crest. In the valley of the Sweetwater below grazed a far-reaching herd of ponies, watched over by several young herders.

Hard Rope nudged Custer, pointing out the extent of the herd's pasture. "Big herd, chief. Means big village."

Adrenaline warmed Custer's blood. Nothing like that feeling of impending action. He was ready to have it out with the Cheyenne, done with their lying. Their ponies were nowhere near as poor as they'd claimed. His shrinking net had snared them. Now all he had to do was present them the choice. Give him the girls and return to the reservation—or go to war.

Custer's attention was yanked to the southeast, down the valley where a young herder burst from the trees, riding bareback atop a spotted pony, whistling his shrill alarm.

"Eagle wingbone!" Hard Rope muttered angrily.

"What's going on?"

"See yourself, Chief." Hard Rope pointed. "Your soldiers get spotted by a pony boy."

Custer caught a glimpse of the head of the blue columns snaking their way up the Sweetwater. The boy rode to warn the villages.

Other herders wheeled, kicking their ponies furiously. Waving blankets ripped from their backs, the boys roused the ponies, starting them for the river, where they forced the leaders down the slippery bank and into the icy water. Screeching their alarm, the herders whirled through the herd, driving the leaders up the north bank, escaping the cavalry's advance.

Custer spun, dashing downhill under a full head of steam. "Moylan!"

"Sir?"

"Head back to the columns, that direction. Tell them we've been discovered. Order them up on the double! I need support for a possible attack!"

Romero eased up. "They can't tear that village down quick enough to escape, General."

"But the warriors will come out to engage us while their women dismantle the lodges and retreat. A staying action while the village slips away, then the warriors themselves will disappear."

"You're learning 'bout these Indians," Romero said.

"I know they won't fight if they can run," Custer replied as he slipped his boot into an oxbow stirrup. "This is one time we're going to surround them and take the fight to 'em. You coming, Romero?"

"Hell, this is one ride I wouldn't miss for all the vermilion in China!"

"Ride with us, Little Beaver," Custer shouted.

"No." He wagged his head. "Little Beaver go back, paint his face now. Tie feathers in my hair. Bring out my war shirt before I fight those squaw killers. I want those Cheyenne to see how many Cheyenne scalps decorate my war shirt."

"Be about, then, old man! There'll be plenty of fighting for you soon enough." Custer put spurs to his stallion's flanks.

Romero rode boot to boot with Custer for better than two miles, racing around the base of a hill, heading for a treeless ridge. For miles in all directions the countryside lay free of ravines and timber which could conceal Indian ambush.

"Ho, General!" Romero grabbed Custer's wrist, yanking back on his own reins.

"Look 'head of you." Romero pointed.

Atop a rocky, sandstone formation more than a dozen feathered heads peered at the lonely pair of riders. While Custer brooded on what to do next, Romero counted more than fifty skylined heads.

"Best we get our tails high behind—get out of here while the getting's good," Romero suggested anxiously.

Custer twisted in the saddle, squinting into the bright, winter light reflected off the snow and splintering through frost-rimed trees. No sign of his columns yet. He turned, watched the warriors grow braver, milling about, studying the brace of horsemen below.

"We aren't running, Romero." Custer said it with the flat sound of a hammer pounding an anvil.

"You're crazy! These are Cheyenne Dog Soldiers, if I ever saw one! They'd love to pick their teeth with your bones!"

"Stand your ground," Custer ordered as the scout turned to go. "I'll have you shot for desertion," he growled as his pistol cleared its holster, "if I don't shoot you myself."

Romero stared into the bore of the hand cannon Custer aimed at him.

"Doesn't take long for the sight of a muzzle to take the starch out of any man," Custer said.

"Hell, General. Don't know what's the better way to die. Them bloodthirsty bucks up there—or you."

Custer stuffed the pistol away, grinning. "C'mon, Romero. I'm not about to shoot you. Our days aren't over yet."

"Sooner'n you think," Romero replied. He pointed as a couple dozen warriors mounted and started down the slope.

"I bloody well don't care if they're not coming to welcome us with open arms," Custer said. "What matters is I've found the camp where the white girls are held." He drew a deep breath, checking over his shoulder for his troops. "You remember the bodies of that young woman and her little boy we found in the Kiowa camp on the Washita?"

Romero nodded.

"They were butchered soon as the camps learned soldiers were on the way. I've vowed that won't happen this time. The first shot fired by us will kill those two girls, as surely as I put a gun to their heads myself. I've got to think of them above all."

"You got any ideas to save our hides—yours and mine?"

"Go tell those warriors we want to parley with 'em."

"Parley?" Romero squeaked like a dry buggy wheel in need of tallow.

"You've got to convince them we want a truce—no fighting. It's the only way we keep the girls alive. If they think we're about to attack, those two lives will be blood on my hands."

"Here's hoping your plan works, General." Romero tapped heels and zigzagged forward, heading for the snowy bluff. Halfway there he drew up, loping in a tight circle, signing his desire to parley. From the twenty-odd emerged three warriors. As the trio set across the snowy meadow, the others followed.

Starting to sweat, Romero wheeled his horse in a spray of snow. He raced back, sliding to a halt beside Custer, who stood in the stirrups, eyes flicking to the rear.

"Can they see my troops now?" Custer asked.

"From that hill, you damn bet they can."

"They won't try anything stupid, will they?"

"Wouldn't put a thing past a Dog Soldier, General."

"Then by all means, Romero, tell those warriors to halt where they are."

Despite Romero's signs, the three kept coming. Worse yet, the twenty behind them galloped to catch up. The interpreter watched Custer yank his pistol free. With the weapon in the air for the Cheyenne to see, he brought up his empty right hand to show the warriors they had the choice: either heed the warning of the empty hand, or deal with the consequences of the loaded one.

The Cheyenne understood without translation. They finally brought their ponies to a halt.

"Tell one to come forward to talk," Custer instructed.

After a momentary conference, a tall, imposing figure urged his war pony forward, smiling as if he were on some afternoon lark.

Stalling tense minutes while the soldiers advanced toward the clearing, Custer and Romero parleyed with the solitary warrior called Bad Tooth. From him the interpreter learned much about the enemy. The tribe was indeed Cheyenne, under Chief Medicine Arrow, who was himself in that larger group of riders watching the parley. Their village of three hundred lodges was camped at the mouth of a stream emptying into the Sweetwater. Nearby stood a village of two hundred lodges under Chief Little Robe.

"The soldier chief knows of Little Robe," Romero explained to Bad Tooth. "He is a good friend to the soldiers. It would please the soldier chief to meet the great Medicine Arrow."

"Who brings pony soldiers to our village of women and children?" asked Bad Tooth. "The powerful Medicine

Arrow will not stoop to talk to soldiers like those who butcher helpless ones or burn the villages of the frail and sickly ones."

"Black Kettle?"

"He was a weak old man. Medicine Arrow is the mighty leader of the Southern Cheyenne. Not some tired old man waiting to die wearing the white man's bacon grease on his lips."

"I've heard about all I'm going to take of this one's surly mouth, Romero," Custer said. "I'd love to knock the smile off that face. Tell this loudmouthed one he looks upon the Yellow Hair. Tell him I want peace, but only if Medicine Arrow wants peace. Will there be peace, or war? Yellow Hair waits for Medicine Arrow's answer."

"Yellow Hair is with you?" Bad Tooth demanded.

"I am *Hiestzi!*" Custer shouted in Cheyenne, startling both Romero and the warrior.

The warrior swallowed, gave the soldier a harsh once-over.

Custer removed the buffalo-fur cap, running his fingers through his long curls. Beneath the midday winter sun, his hair was burnished gold.

"Yellow Hair! *Aiyeee!*" Bad Tooth ordered another of the trio to dash back to the growing line of mounted warriors easing down the slope into the meadow.

"They're getting a bit too close, General," Romero cautioned.

Custer glanced toward the rear. "They'll have us surrounded before the troops show."

"Surrounded—" Romero gulped, "or worse."

Custer raised his pistol, pointing the muzzle at Bad Tooth's chest while nudging his own stallion forward. "Stay close, Romero. If there's any gunplay, this big one will be our shield."

Custer halted beside the astonished warrior staring at the gaping bore pointed at him.

"Ask him if he speaks with one tongue, Romero."

"I speak with one tongue, Yellow Hair," Bad Tooth replied.

"Why do your friends creep up on me? Do they want to see your blood?"

The Cheyenne's anxious eyes flicked over both shoulders, seeing the warriors easing along the sides of the meadow, hoping not to attract the soldier's attention.

"Tell your friends to stop where they stand, or *your* blood will be spilled on this ground!"

Bad Tooth's Adam's apple bobbed as he stared into the muzzle.

"That's right. You will be first, my faithless friend. I will blow a hole in your heart big enough there will be nothing left of it for your dogs! I do not trust a man who tells me he wants to parley while others sneak up to take my hair."

"No!" Bad Tooth shook his head, hypnotized by the pistol bore.

"None of you will wear the scalp of Yellow Hair. Many want it. None is brave enough to take it. Today is a good day for you to die."

With the Cheyenne's angry, frightened warning, the rest of the warriors withdrew, flinging gritty threats and curses. Then they fell silent as they parted for an old warrior leading a band of some forty others who loped right up before the pony soldier.

"I know this one," the old warrior sneered, pointing to Romero. "He lived with Cheyenne."

"Who's this, Romero?" Custer whispered.

"The old boy himself. Medicine Arrow. Always been a treacherous snake. Years back his name was Rock Forehead. Now among the Cheyenne he's called Medicine Arrow because he's keeper of the tribe's sacred bundle of arrows—big medicine going back before the grandfather of any man now alive."

"Medicine Arrow," Custer muttered, assessing his enemy.

"But the red bastard hasn't changed," Romero added. "Rock Forehead always was a bloodthirsty scorpion."

"You!" The old chief whirled on Custer. "You are the Yellow Hair who defeated the sleeping village of Black Kettle?"

"I am." Custer bowed his head to the whispers and mutterings, murmurs of awe and respect, hearing also the growls and yelps for his scalp.

"You bring many soldiers with you, Yellow Hair?"

Custer considered that question before answering. "I bring enough to show the Cheyenne that my word is strong."

Medicine Arrow's eyes darkened. He hadn't heard the answer he wanted. "With so many horses, there will be little grazing for Cheyenne ponies. How many horses ride with Yellow Hair?"

Custer turned to Romero, whispering, "Cagey old reprobate, this one. Treacherous snake would love to kill us all."

"How'll he do that?"

"I think this old bat figures we're a small expedition. Most likely, word reached him of a small party of soldiers roaming the countryside last month—a scouting party I led from our camp on Medicine Bluff Creek."

"Could be, General. Suppose he did get wind of a small outfit—Medicine Arrow might figure to wipe us all out quick."

"You bet your cold backside he would!"

"Want me to give him the bad news?"

"No," Custer answered. "I'll break it to him in my own way . . . in my own time."

"Can't wait to see it, General. This old boy's done his share of evil—and then some. Some claim he's an evil wizard. Can perform magic—even tell the future. Heard tales of some he's cursed in years gone by, ones died in strange mysterious ways. Be a pleasure to watch you take the starch outta him."

Custer studied Medicine Arrow. "Let's see if he can predict the future when he sees how many soldiers ride with me."

"You white men talk too much!" Medicine Arrow grunted as he signed angrily. "Yellow Hair mixes courage with foolishness, coming to see the Cheyenne with only this Mexican dog at his side. A dangerous mistake for the man who destroyed a weak village on the Washita."

"Medicine Arrow!" Custer shouted, surprising all with his precise Cheyenne. "You anger me with such bold talk. I come to you in peace—but you growl like a dog snapping for a fight! If that is what you want"—and he glanced over his shoulder—"then behold—war is what Medicine Arrow will get!"

Custer flung his arm at the advancing columns heaving into view at the far edge of the meadow. "Romero, tell this old bag of wind how many soldiers march with Yellow Hair. Tell him!"

Romero grinned. "Happy to, General." It was his turn to sneer at Medicine Arrow. "You have no more than a hundred warriors in this meadow. Yellow Hair has many times more. He can crush you like a wolf spider."

"It will take many soldiers to crush our warriors."

"Old man!" Romero barked. "See how many march against you!"

Medicine Arrow studied the blue shapes bursting from the timber at the far side of the meadow. He whirled on Romero. "You turn against your people, dark one, bringing soldiers down on us to kill children and the old ones."

"Old man, your warriors have done evil. Yellow Hair comes to fight only if you want war. It is your choice. Yellow Hair demands your warriors stop their raids, and demands your villages return to the reservations."

"We can find no buffalo to hunt on this reservation."

"You must return," Romero repeated. "If you do not do what Yellow Hair tells you, you will suffer as Black Kettle's village suffered."

"Is this the word of Yellow Hair?"

Romero turned to Custer. "General, the old one wants to know if I speak for you when I say we will attack if need be."

Custer glared at the chief, then nodded. No word spoken.

Medicine Arrow's eyes flicked to Romero. "Ask Yellow Hair if he intends to wipe our villages from the breast of our Mother of All Things as he did to Black Kettle."

After a moment, Custer thoughtfully replied, "I will not destroy your villages—unless you want war. The choice is up to you. You must make that choice now."

The old chief fumed a moment, listening to the angry vows of his young warriors, gazing at the swelling strength of the soldier columns led into the snowy meadow.

"I want Yellow Hair to show me you want peace with the Cheyenne. So many soldiers come, they will frighten our women and children. My people will wail when they hear it is Yellow Hair come to surround their village. It is for Yellow Hair alone to assure my people that what happened to Black Kettle will not happen to them. We must hurry, Yellow Hair—before my people run to the hills and Medicine Arrow has no one to lead back to the reservation with him."

When the translation was completed, Custer whispered to Romero, "Why, that sly old fox. He wants me to come with him to his village—alone."

"Be quick, Yellow Hair." The chief motioned with an arm. "Come to my village with me now. Show my people you talk straight. They will know you mean them no harm if you ride into my village at my side."

"Why alone?"

"Haven't a clue. Can't be a good reason, whatever it is. Always been a treacherous snake." Romero sighed, eyeing the old chief. "Years back, his name was Rock Forehead. Now he's called Medicine Arrow because he's keeper of the Cheyenne's sacred bundle of arrows—a sacred object going back before the grandfather of any man now alive. But, he hasn't changed. Rock Forehead always was a bloodthirsty bastard."

Custer turned at the sound of hooves beating the winter-hardened earth, watching Moylan gallop up. "Well, I'd best find out what this sly fox is up to." He called to his adjutant. "Mr. Moylan! What the Hades took you so long?"

"It's one thing for you to get the columns moving."

Moylan sounded breathless. "It's quite another for me to do it."

"Lieutenant, this here's the great Cheyenne chief, Medicine Arrow. And he wants us to have a talk with him." Custer turned to Romero. "You head back. Find Myers. Have him assume command of the troops in my absence."

"You're riding into that village alone, General?" Romero asked.

"Not alone, Romero." And Custer smiled. "I'm taking Mr. Moylan with me."

"M-me . . . with you?" Moylan squeaked.

"That's right. We're accepting this cutthroat's invitation to dine in his lodge."

"Tonight, General?"

"No, Lieutenant. Right now."

Moylan glanced back at the swelling columns of blue. "Shouldn't we wait until the troops come up and they can go to the hostile camp with us? Hard Rope says there's bound to be more warriors than you can count."

"Mr. Moylan, the Seventh Cavalry will never be intimidated by a large force of warriors. Mere numbers are meaningless. To your grave I want you to remember it takes only one Indian to kill a soldier who's lost his courage."

"Yessir."

"Romero, give my message to Myers, and stay with him."

Custer watched the interpreter wheel and gallop off into the sparkling, frosty light of midday. He turned to the Cheyenne chief.

"Medicine Arrow, we will go with you to your lodge now—to talk of peace, or war . . . between our peoples."

CHAPTER 23

Lieutenant Myles Moylan watched Medicine Arrow wheel his pony about, parting the warriors in a V like a beaver's nose breaking the glassy surface of a high-country pond. Moylan gulped, not sure what he was following Custer into.

An eleven-year veteran from Massachusetts, Moylan had first served with the Second Dragoons where he had risen to rank of sergeant by 1863. Later that year when he had been transferred to the Fifth Cavalry and been given a commission, the young Yankee was dismissed from the service for some unnamed and impetuous act. Under a false name, Moylan turned around and reenlisted in the Fourth Massachusetts Cavalry, where he fought out the rest of the war, earning a brevet major for heroism. When the Seventh Cavalry was formed in 1866, Moylan was appointed its first sergeant major. Custer soon took a liking to the scrappy Irishman and commissioned Moylan as first lieutenant. While the rest of the officers did not appreciate Moylan's "left-hand" promotion, Custer himself took young Myles

under his wing, where with Tom Custer and Billy Cooke he
became part of Custer's first inner circle.

As the warriors parted for Medicine Arrow, Moylan
recognized the old Cheyenne woman, the one called
Mahwissa. Wrapped in a leaf-green blanket atop her gray
pony, Mahwissa intently watched the parley in the
meadow.

Custer halted at her side, a forced smile on his lips. "You
have fared well with your people."

"You have learned some Cheyenne talk," she replied.

"I have a good teacher."

"How is Monaseetah?" she asked.

"She is well. Monaseetah rides with us." Custer threw a
thumb to indicate the advancing cavalry and wagons.

"She has a child?"

"A son. Born the first week of the Moon of the Seven
Cold Nights."

"Will he have a brother, Yellow Hair? Will you give
Monaseetah a child of your own? She is your woman."

"Monaseetah is not my woman," he stammered, his eyes
searching the faces of the curious warriors.

Mahwissa's wrinkled lips curled. "It is true no black-robe
waved his hand over your marriage. Yet the Everywhere
Spirit knows you took Monaseetah as your wife. She is
fertile like the prairie soil in spring. It is not yours to decide,
Yellow Hair. The Everywhere Spirit will use you in His
way. Not even the great *Hiestzi* can change that."

Agitated, Custer glanced at her belt, anxious to change
the subject of this conversation. "You have my knife. The
knife I let you carry to visit your people."

"Yes." She giggled, pulling aside her blanket to expose

the scabbard at her belt. Mahwissa had trimmed it with small, tinkling tin cones and strips of red cloth.

"You decorated it for me. I thank you." Custer extended his hand.

"No longer is this your knife." She closed her blanket.

For a moment Custer was speechless. "I see," he finally replied, straightening in the saddle. Custer gazed at the old chief. "Tell me, is Medicine Arrow like you, Mahwissa? Is he a liar too? I gave you warm food to fill your belly. A blanket for your back. Yet now you steal my knife. Is the word of the Cheyenne an empty sound?"

Mahwissa threw her head back, cackling. "Do not talk to me of lies between our people, Yellow Hair. You offered food and I ate. You gave me a blanket and I slept. You gave me a pony and sent me back to my people. I stayed. Would you not remain with your people?"

"I asked you to help—"

"Yellow Hair, hear me! I would sooner starve in freedom with my people than live with a full stomach as your prisoner. Though I would shiver at night without your blankets, I would sooner let my bones freeze and my flesh rot in freedom than live my years beneath your warm blankets."

Moylan watched Custer draw in his shoulders at the tone of her words as if flinching at a painful wound. Without knowing what was said, he sensed the air sour between Custer and the woman. And Moylan knew as few others would exactly how shame stung Custer like a slap in the face.

"I will remember, Mahwissa," he whispered. "You spit in my outstretched hand, like an ungrateful dog."

"No longer will you treat me like a dog, Yellow Hair," she said with a sneer.

Custer gazed at the amused faces of the onlookers. "Sadly, it will not be you, nor this Medicine Arrow, who will suffer. Instead, the Cheyenne of the future will pay for your stupidity here today. Listen! You can hear the Cheyenne of winters to come—hear their keening on the prairie winds. Listen! I hear Cheyenne children crying, growing weak with empty stomachs. Fathers killed by soldiers. Mothers chased into the wilderness to starve. Listen to the winds of the future!"

Custer straightened in the saddle, signaling Moylan to follow. Medicine Arrow studied the renowned Yellow Hair as he rode up, as if appraising the portent of the moment.

Written on both faces Moylan saw the realization that they were about to play out a drama neither one had the power to stop. Two men brought here to confront each other, setting in motion the gears of some machinery that would grind inexorably for eight more years.

Something in the haughty way the old chief sat on his horse told Myles that Medicine Arrow had made his choice—to defend his people and their ancient nomadic way of life.

Moylan studied Custer as he and the commander drew closer to the Cheyenne villages on the Sweetwater, wondering if Custer had learned that all his kindness had gone for naught. Moylan sensed something tighten, shrivel and die in Custer back there when Mahwissa shamed him.

With the set to his commander's jaw, Moylan realized George Armstrong Custer finally accepted the fact that the Indian respected only a pony soldier who was tough and fearless, a soldier as possessed in following his own vision of personal glory as were the Indian warriors who rode against him. Near the center of the sprawling, bustling village, Medicine Arrow halted in the midst of a large crowd come to see the great Yellow Hair.

Boys stepped up to take the reins from Medicine Arrow as he slid from his pony. Others came to lead the soldier horses away. The war chief ducked into his lodge. At the front stood two short tripods. The first held a war shield. From the second hung a bow and quiver stuffed with arrows.

Custer ducked into the close warmth of the lodge, the adjutant on his heels. The chief gestured for Moylan to have a seat on the robes by the door.

Medicine Arrow settled at the rear of the lodge, showing Custer to sit at his right hand. He muttered briefly to the gray-headed woman busy at the fire. Without a word she scurried like a gray spider from the lodge.

"My woman is told to bring the camp crier. He will walk the circle of our camps, calling the chiefs and counselors to join us in our talk. The fire warms our cold bones while we wait. When all are here, we listen to what lies in each other's hearts."

Custer turned to Moylan. "Myles, see how they've placed me at the right hand of the chief himself, the seat of honor."

One by one the chiefs, and counselors entered, taking their respective seats in the circle. Each plopped down on the dark robes like winter owls around the cozy warmth of the fire.

"Myles," Custer whispered, "you see this ancient one here?" He gestured to the wizened Indian at his right, his face carved with the passing of many winters. "Probably a

medicine man among these people. One of their feared
shamans. Seems I'm flanked by two powerful men among
the Cheyenne. You're privy to a momentous occasion, Mr.
Moylan. The tribe is about to pay me a great honor."

Custer swept his arm about. "Crude paintings on the
buffalo-hide wall. Figures representing the stories of Medicine Arrow's life. Deeds in peace and war. Rawhide parcels
hung from the poles. Some hold articles of dress. Others
might contain rock and feathers, ashes or bone—all part of
Medicine Arrow's personal magic."

Directly behind his head, Custer pointed out a long
bundle wrapped in the skin of a coyote's winter hide. From
it hung fringe. Porcupine quillwork decorated both red and
blue trade cloth wrapping the ends of the bundle. "This
must be some magical container—something signifying the
chief's rank among his people. An esteemed honor for a
man to sit beneath the bundle."

What Custer could not know was just how wrong he
could be.

For a man to be given a seat at the right hand of the chief
was disgrace enough. Yet it was a mild rebuke compared to
the Cheyenne giving him this place beneath the sacred
bundle. Its presence over his head during this council
marked how momentously serious these proceedings were
viewed by the Cheyenne.

Years before, when Rock Forehead had been chosen as
the keeper of that sacred bundle by the Southern Cheyenne, he had taken his new name. Legend had it the
bundle's Medicine Arrows had been presented by the
Everywhere Spirit to a Cheyenne man in the long before as
a gift to a chosen people. Wrapped in a wide strip of
winter-gray fur lay the four arrows: two shafts painted

crimson, symbolizing a continued abundance of food for the Cheyenne people, the second pair painted black to signify the tribe's continued victory in war.

By placing the soldier chief they called Yellow Hair beneath their sacred arrows, the Cheyenne had placed George Armstrong Custer on trial.

While Custer admired the red-and-black-dyed forked stick from which the sacred bundle hung, the last guests stooped into the lodge. The elkskin flap slid over the doorway.

The old man to Custer's right drew a long buckskin bag into his lap. From this beaded bag he pulled a pipestem as big around as a walking stick, from which hung a decorative array of war-eagle feathers and winter-white ermine skins. To the end of this stem the chief attached a crimson pipestone bowl, inlaid with pewter and rubbed with bear grease to reflect every dancing flame of the fire.

At the old man's waist hung a smaller pouch. From it he drew a handful of willow bark and tobacco mixture, which he poured on a square piece of red cloth on the ground before him. Herbs and leaves were added, then stuffed into the huge pipe bowl. During the ritual, the old one droned an ancient prayer, asking that with the smoking of the pipe this day would come truth from every tongue.

The old medicine man surprised Custer, grabbing his wrist. The old man closed his rheumy eyes and turned his face toward the smoke hole above, placing the soldier chief's hand over his heart while he murmured his toothless prayers.

Finished, he dropped Custer's hand, next presenting the long pipestem to the heavens and earth, then to the four winds of life. With no warning, the old man placed the mouthpiece against Custer's lips as he held a coal over the pipe bowl. The soldier chief drew in a mouthful of the fragrant smoke, steeling himself against the waves of nauseau rolling over him. Never had he used tobacco. Even the smell of it on a man's breath could turn him green.

The shaman pulled the mouthpiece from Custer's lips, once again placing the soldier chief's hand over his heart. Muttering another prayer, he raised Custer's hand aloft, shaking it while the others repeated his prayer.

Over the next quarter-hour the soldier chief smoked alone, emptying the entire bowl. Through it all, the Cheyenne studied him for any sign of weakness. Medicine Arrow himself held the yard-long pipestem while the shaman cradled the bowl. The chief explained why Custer smoked alone.

"Yellow Hair, you stand before the Cheyenne people to speak the truth—or all your soldiers will be killed for your deceit. If your tongue is not straight, if your words do not show what truly rests in your heart, Yellow Hair and all his soldiers will die together, left for the buzzards to pick their bones clean beneath the winds of summers yet to come."

At Medicine Arrow's signal, the shaman refilled and lit the huge pipe bowl, starting it on its journey around the lodge. Four times it passed each man. With four prayers, every man smoked. With its last circle, Medicine Arrow held the pipe bowl against Custer's dusty boots, the long stem pointed heavenward.

"The wise counselors of the Southern Cheyenne have smoked this pipe. Their breath is like their prayers, forever on the winds to touch the heart of the Everywhere Spirit."

Custer smiled through the speech, wishing he had Romero at his side. From the start of their council, the Cheyenne had refused to use sign language. The soldier chief contented himself with catching a word here and there.

How he ached to ask about the white girls, though he decided not to press the subject for the moment. There would be time when the villages were surrounded. When there was no chance for the Cheyenne to kill their captives. One ill-timed word now, and it would spell a death sentence for those women.

"Our prayers to the Everywhere Winds ask that the soldier chief speak the truth to us," Medicine Arrow explained. "Evil will follow you all your days, that evil will fall to your sons, and to the sons of your sons, if your tongue does not speak true."

Custer ran a raw tongue around his foul-tasting mouth.

"You are a most treacherous one, oh Creeping Panther. You slink in the night to surround a winter village of sleeping women and children. Hear me, white man!" Medicine Arrow took a thin willow twig, with it loosening the dead ash in the pipe bowl.

"This deadly curse I lay on you and your sons, and on all the sons of your sons, a curse made powerful many times over from the lips of this council."

Medicine Arrow turned over the tall red pipe bowl, slowly pouring the ashes onto the soldier chief's muddy boots.

Custer froze, frightened. *Are they anointing me for some reason? Giving me this place of honor beneath the coyote bundle . . . spreading ashes on my boots as other cultures anoint with oil?*

With no way to know for certain, he nodded at each chief. Just as ignorant of white men as Custer was of them, the council believed he understood the seriousness of Medicine Arrow's curse.

"Hear us, Yellow Hair! Should you ever approach a Cheyenne camp with evil purpose, to destroy as you did the helpless ones of Black Kettle on the Washita, you will one day be killed, your soldiers lying broken like the brittle grasses of winter. Your white bodies left to rot beneath the all-seeing eye of the sun above. Cheyenne spirits will determine your fate. My curse rides your shoulders, till the end of your days."

Medicine Arrow took the pipe bowl from Custer's boots, passing it to the medicine man.

Custer dragged a freckled hand across his dry lips, worried. With the shaman putting the pipe away, it appeared the council had drawn to a close—and he hadn't had the chance to speak.

"Medicine Arrow." Custer began to move his hands in the ancient language of the prairies. "I thank you for the honor of your lodge."

He studied the chief's face, searching for some sign of agreement, some flicker of good intention.

"I come to speak of peace with the Cheyenne. No more can your young men ride north to the settlements of the white farmers to carry off their women and children. No longer can you wander off your reservation for hunting or for raids."

Lord, did he wish for something to drink, to soothe his scorched throat.

"If the Cheyenne want peace, you must return to the reservation. If you want war, Yellow Hair will bring sorrow to the door of every Cheyenne lodge."

Custer pointed toward the tent flap. "Do not force me to

use the soldiers who surround your village. Do not force me to destroy those you hold most dear—your families, sons, and daughters. Return to the land given you by the Grandfather back east, return before it is too late for either of us to stop the killing."

For a long time after Custer's hands fell silent, the Cheyenne elders considered the words of Yellow Hair, ruminating as a buffalo cow would chew and rechew something hard to swallow.

"Hiestzi," the old chief eventually whispered, "we will consider your words. It is a hard thing you ask—for the Cheyenne have always been a strong people. We do not like the choices you give us. Each choice means an end to our way. Your bullets are an easy answer. Bullets kill Cheyenne warriors. But soldier bullets will never kill the spirit of the Cheyenne."

He paused while the murmurs of approval faded.

"Hear me, Yellow Hair—as long as there are Cheyenne women, there will be Cheyenne warriors. You may have enough bullets to kill Cheyenne warriors today, but as long as there are Cheyenne wombs, there will always be Cheyenne sons! The spirit of our people lives with the hills and the sky. Everlasting!"

Custer politely waited as he considered the chief's words. "You have spoken well, Medicine Arrow. My heart is small . . . it lies on the ground this day to know we both are warriors driven to fight each other. Never will it be said Yellow Hair questions the courage of the Cheyenne."

Medicine Arrow nodded, the doubting scowl beginning to soften.

"Hear me, Cheyenne," Custer continued. "You say that you cannot trust that my tongue is straight. You will know me by my actions. For what I do will stand much longer than what I say."

"Yellow Hair has spoken well," Medicine Arrow replied. "We will judge you by your actions. If you deal with our people with one heart, you will live. If you prove to have two hearts . . . then you and your soldiers will be wiped out to the last man. Our Everywhere Spirit will crush your faithless bodies after driving your minds mad with fear. Hear me! Fear that evil you bring upon yourself, Yellow Hair."

"Like you, I am searching for an honest tongue—among the Cheyenne," Custer signed. "I hope to find that tongue among those in this lodge. In the days to come, we will talk of peace, as we blaze a new road for the Cheyenne to travel."

Medicine Arrow's dark eyes slewed around the lodge. "We will talk, Yellow Hair—of many things."

Custer shifted anxiously, knees aching from sitting for so long. "Will Medicine Arrow tell me where I can find the most suitable ground for my soldier camp?"

The old chief studied the shocked faces of those around him before he answered, gesturing for the soldier chief to rise. "Come, I will show you myself where your soldiers can camp. You will have the swift-flowing river, and timber for your fires. Plenty of grass for your horses. Come, Yellow Hair."

While their leaders conferred in Medicine Arrow's lodge, both the Cheyenne and the soldiers engaged in an uneasy standoff.

Myers had his officers deploy the troopers around the villages like Joshua encircling Jericho, as a number of mounted warriors dodged in and out of the trees, taunting and shouting at the soldiers. Anxious troopers warily watched the timber. Nervous, but itching for a chance to even the score for Elliott's men. Back and forth the officers rode, trying to keep a lid on things, knowing one wrong move by either side would blow the cork on a powder keg.

By the time Custer and Medicine Arrow emerged from the lodge into midday winter brightness, a flurry of noise and frantic motion swirled about them. Both leaders realized the situation must be diffused.

"I do not hold these young ones much longer, Yellow Hair," the Cheyenne chief growled. "I told you what the sight of your soldiers would do to our villages."

"You *will* hold your young men!" Custer snapped, his hands flying angrily. "And I will withdraw my soldiers to our camp for the night. Now show me!"

Custer and Moylan mounted and were led by the Cheyenne chief to a campsite three-quarters of a mile above the villages. Only then did the warriors drift away from the timber, resigned that there would be no fight this day.

As his troops pitched their camp along the Sweetwater, Custer had a chance to really study the faces of his haggard soldiers. Skin sagged beneath sunken cheeks. Eyes without brightness peered back at him as he rode through their ranks. Smudge from countless fires caked their faces. Teeth stood out as if all were grinning skulls. He began to realize to what extent the long and hard winter had exacted its toll on his men. No soldier had come this far unscathed. They had had more than five months of freezing, too little to eat, and still had untold miles yet to go.

Something deep within Custer tugged, unlike anything he had felt since the days of the Shenandoah. A warm knot of sentiment rose in his throat as he gazed at these young soldiers—his Seventh Cavalry. While they grumbled and complained as soldiers always had from the time of Alexander and Caesar, still these boys in blue had followed. Wherever Custer led, soldiers followed. Talk around the campfires had it that glory awaited Custer at every turn. Honor would surely come to every soldier who followed in Custer's wake.

"Monaseetah." Custer showed her a stump to sit on. Moylan had brought her from one of Lieutenant Bell's ambulances. Custer signed for her, "I need your help freeing the girls. I think they're in these camps."

"I will help." She removed the infant from the folds of blanket at her back, rocking him in her arms.

"We have found the village of Rock Forehead. He is the one your people call—"

"Medicine Arrow. A wild and wicked man. Black Kettle did not respect his counsel. Said he had too much power— power he gained through fear."

"Fear can be a great ruler, Monaseetah. It controls as few things do."

"An evil man. There are stories he has killed men with his curses."

"Romero said the same thing. Don't tell me you believe those stories too!"

"Yes, *Hiestzi*. Many have told me."

"He's an old man! Flesh and blood—like me! Old dogs like him have worn teeth. I'm more worried about his young warriors—they have the sharp teeth."

She hid her face.

"Monaseetah? Is this old man so evil that he will hold the

white girls in his village, while saying he knows nothing of them?"

Monaseetah's eyes darted this way and that, like the sudden flight of frightened hummingbirds. "Yes," she whispered.

"You are afraid of something?"

"Yes."

"Of Medicine Arrow."

"Not afraid of him. Afraid of something I cannot see. The evil he can do. If it were something I could see, I would use my knife to kill it. We can fight what we can see. It is only what I cannot see or touch . . ."

"There is no evil here," he soothed, slipping an arm around her shoulders. "You are safe with us here. No man can hurt you."

Her head sank against his shoulder. For a long time they sat staring into the flames before Custer spoke.

"Are the two white girls in Medicine Arrow's village?"

"They are here, Yellow Hair. I will help you free them from the evil one whose curses kill his enemies."

Custer smiled down at her. "I welcome your help, little one. But there is no danger from that old man."

Monaseetah straightened, her eyes narrowing, her lips drawn in a thin line of determination. "Yellow Hair, he brings a curse upon many. If you sat in his lodge, he has probably cursed you. Medicine Arrow must be defeated so the good men of my people can rule once more."

"With your help, Monaseetah, we will free the two white girls." Custer helped her to her feet, enfolding her in his arms. "Then we can end the reign of this evil one over your people."

CHAPTER 24

CUSTER wasn't at all surprised the next day when Medicine Arrow and most of his head men showed up in the soldier camp, announcing they came in friendship, wanting to talk with Yellow Hair.

"Medicine Arrow," Romero translated Custer's greeting, "it is an honor to have you visit our camp. Make yourselves warm by our fire."

"Tell Yellow Hair we thank him for his kindness," Medicine Arrow replied, settling on a wooden hardtack box.

"Are you hungry?" Romero inquired.

"No. Tell Yellow Hair there is no need for food now. We come as a gesture of friendship. In that spirit, I have asked some of our young men to come with me to perform for you. Following some riding tricks, you will enjoy a serenade of singers with flutes and hand drums."

The old chief signaled one of his young warriors, who rode back to the edge of the camp where he gave word that the performance could begin. In colorful dress and paint, a dozen horsemen charged single file into camp, each one dropping off his pony to one side or the other, striking the ground with his heels before vaulting once more onto the animal's back. Around and around the large gathering of soldiers they rode, performing their tricks.

"General Custer?"

Custer eyed Moylan, suspiciously. "What is it, mister? You seem agitated."

"Can't really talk here, sir. About the Indians."

"No need to worry. They don't understand English. Besides, we'd surely draw their suspicions by walking away to talk. Why not just say what you need to say—wearing a smile? Like you're watching the riding. Move your eyes around some as you talk, not focusing all your attention on me."

Custer pulled back laughing as a rider swept by him, making a valiant try for the soldier chief's buffalo-fur cap. "Out with it, Moylan."

"Watch commander brought word from our pickets. Wanted you to know they've spotted some unusual activity in the villages."

"What seems to be going on with our Cheyenne friends?"

"They've brought their pony herd into the village."

"Perhaps they're moving them to another pasture."

"Not this time, General," Moylan said.

"Then spill it."

"They're loading the horses. The village is preparing to take flight." Moylan blurted it out like a man shedding himself of a hot potato, anxious to watch someone else juggle it.

Custer's eyes narrowed as he watched a sudden, drawn

look cross the face of Romero, who was standing at his side. Then he threw an icy look in Medicine Arrow's direction. "Romero, looks like you'll have some translating to do here shortly."

"Damn that cutthroat bastard!" Romero growled.

"Tell you what, Lieutenant," Custer said as he slapped Moylan on the back, "keep that best Sunday-courtship-supper smile of yours as you stroll off to find Tom and Captain Yates. Fetch Myers and Dr. Renick. Thompson and Robbins too. Tell them all."

"And when I've told 'em?"

"Have them select some steady hands from their units. Those men should pack their pistols and wander back here in pairs. No more than three together. It must seem casual. Don't alarm the chiefs."

"What'll they come here for?"

"Tell them to be ready to act at an instant's notice—but not until I give the order personally. You understand everything I've told you?"

"I'm off, General!"

"Be gone! Quickly!" Custer's blue eyes twinkled as he watched Moylan amble away. Then he looked over at his interpreter. "Smile, Romero."

Romero tried, then snarled, "Don't feel like smiling."

"Best we put on airs—so they don't realize we know they're playing us false. Stay close to me, now."

The riders finished their performance and the singers began their serenade. At the same time, Custer watched the first soldiers ease up among the ring of spectators.

"General," Romero whispered behind his smile, "aren't you worried about the village leaving? They've got the two girls!"

"I'm not worried. Because if things go right, in the next few minutes I'll have something these faithless Cheyenne value even more highly."

"What's that?"

"Hush, Romero. We're about to play our hand."

Counting heads quickly, Custer estimated he had enough of his soldiers mingled in with the Cheyenne, something over a hundred troopers. He studied each of the copper faces. Still the Indians showed no suspicions. It irritated him that they must all be laughing at him. Yet his was the trap ready to spring.

"Tom!" he called across the circle, grinning like they were about to play a boyhood prank on someone, "there are four of these fellows I want worse than the others. If any are to escape our noose, the four I point out must not."

"Count on it, Autie!"

"Men!" Custer announced. "As I stroll through the warriors, I'll stop briefly in front of the four I don't want to escape under any circumstances. They're the ones to sit on if you have to."

Minutes later Custer stopped alongside Romero, waiting for his right moment. When the serenade ended and the musicians turned to leave, Custer stepped to the center of the circle.

"Romero, tell the chiefs what I'm about to say is of great importance."

"Warriors of the mighty Cheyenne Nation," Romero began, waiting until the Indians gave him their attention, "you must pay heed to the words of Yellow Hair."

"Have them see I'm removing my gun belt," Custer instructed as he unbuckled the heavy canvas belt, allowing it to dangle from his fingertips. "I want them to see that I throw my weapons on the ground as proof that in what I'm about to do I don't want to shed any man's blood—unless they force me to."

As Romero translated, Custer watched the change come over the copper-colored faces. Through the crowd ran an unsettling murmur when the interpreter mentioned bloodshed.

"Have our guests count the number of armed soldiers here to cut off their escape. Tell them I'm angry with what they tried to pull—coming here under the pretense of a friendly visit while their village escaped. They can see their plan has failed and they're my prisoners."

As the words fell from Romero's lips, the warriors grew agitated. Those seated at the fire leapt to their feet, snatching hidden revolvers from robes and blankets. The young warriors mounted on horseback nocked arrows on bowstrings. One by one, the riders dashed to freedom, galloping from camp.

Strident, angry chatter broke out among the rest of the Cheyenne. Younger voices cried for resistance at any cost. Older ones counseled reason and prudence. Tension boiled like an angry kettle. Pandemonium and threats, bold gestures and snarling defiance threw itself against the blue wall.

In the midst of the storm, Custer kept his eye on one of the four he had selected. A tall, gray-headed chief calmly entreated his brothers to act wisely before any shots were fired in haste. From the folds of his wool blanket he yanked a cocked revolver.

Nearby stood another. A formidable opponent in any battle. With no firearm, the warrior placidly brandished a bow strung with an arrow in one hand, while the other inspected arrow after arrow, testing the sharpness of each barbed head. When he had selected a half-dozen of his best, the warrior gazed about him, as cool as any war-hardened veteran in blue.

"No man shoots unless I give the order!" Custer hollered into the melee, figuring he had two soldiers for every warrior. For his plan to work, the Cheyenne must believe Yellow Hair didn't want any bloodshed.

"Don't shoot!" he shouted over the hubbub again.

In the excitement most of the warriors twisted free and fled through the soldier's lines into the thick timber. Until only four chiefs remained captive, surrounded by a hundred armed troopers.

"Good work, gentlemen! We have the four," Custer cried.

Tom Custer led the troops in a cheer as Romero had the chiefs sit by the fire.

"Myers, put the camp on full alert!" Custer bellowed. "Yates, take Tom and alert the Kansans. Tell them the village is preparing to flee and that I hold four chiefs as ransom for the two girls!"

"Damn right, Autie!" Tom roared. "'Bout time we show these bastards a taste of their own treachery!"

Another cheer thundered from the throats of soldiers too long on the trail of hostiles they weren't allowed to fight.

"Go back to your stations, men. Each company has its orders. Consider our camp under attack at any moment."

Custer waited while Myers detailed a twelve-man guard for the prisoners, then he settled on a cottonwood trunk before the chiefs.

"Romero, tell these prisoners I know what they tried to do, coming here with lies on their tongues!"

The chiefs didn't need to know a word of English to see that Yellow Hair was as mad as a wet hornet.

"Tell them I know they hold two white girls, captured in the Kansas settlements last fall. I'm here to get those girls back. As soon as I have the girls back, the tribes must return to their reservations and abandon the warpath for good."

"Yellow Hair!" Medicine Arrow shouted.

Custer shook a finger at the Cheyenne. "And you tell this lying dog that he and his friends can return to their people only when I have the girls and his tribe is on its reservation."

"Yellow Hair!"

Custer leapt to his feet, ready to lunge at Medicine Arrow, surprising not only Romero with his anger but the chiefs as well. Flecks of spittle clung to his lips like cottonwood down.

"Tell him, Romero! Tell him now, or I might choke the lying bastard myself!"

A change came over the Cheyenne chief as Romero translated. No longer arrogant, he shrank at the sting of the soldier chief's words.

"Yellow Hair," Medicine Arrow began, barely whispering, "I am Rock Forehead. Keeper of the Sacred Arrows of my people. Do not hold me here. I am of no worth to you. I am an old man. You bring a curse on yourself by your deceit. You offer us the hospitality of your camp, then take us hostage. One day ago you sat in my lodge. Were you not given freedom to leave?"

The chief creaked to his feet, scuffling forward to warm his hands over the fire. "We could have held you prisoner, but did not. You grow angry with what you think are our falsehoods—but are blinded by your own!"

Custer replied and Romero translated. "You did not give me back my freedom yesterday. My troops surrounded your village, old man. Even more important is that I came to you on an errand of peace. Unlike what you came here to do, to deceive me while your village took flight! Your heart bears the black stain of deceit, Medicine Arrow."

Custer repeatedly clenched his fists, fighting down his gall. Finally he turned to the chiefs. "As a show of my good intentions to find peace between us, I will allow you four to choose one of your number to return to your people as a messenger."

"Autie!" Tom Custer loped up to the fire. "Autie, the village is leaving."

"They're moving already?"

"Yeah, heading north."

Custer wheeled on the chiefs, smiling. "There, you see? Your evil plan goes on without you! Your village is moving farther and farther away as we speak. Abandoning you! Decide now who will carry my message to your village."

Custer stalked away while the chiefs whispered between themselves, angrily gesturing, beating their chests, shoving each other.

"Yates!" Custer sang out, watching his Monroe friend ride up.

"Kansas boys on the alert, General. We're securing all livestock in the middle of the compound so the Indians can't run 'em off."

"Good, but I don't think we'll be attacked. That village is on the run. They're too busy making good their escape. I think they realized we're just too big an outfit to attack . . . even to hit us and run like Mosby's raiders in the Shenandoah."

"We hung some of those Johnny bastards!" Tom Custer growled.

"Times are, I think on stretching the neck of lying dog Medicine Arrow," Custer snarled.

"Damn, Autie," Tom grumbled, wringing his hands. "I was looking forward to a good scrap with these Cheyenne."

"Just remember one thing, little brother," Custer said, the twinkle gone from his azure eyes, "we've never fought the Cheyenne before."

"What about the Washita?"

"We didn't fight any Cheyenne warriors there. We attacked a small village with a few old men."

"You make it sound like you don't know who'd come out on the better end of it if we did fight Cheyenne."

When Custer glanced at his younger brother, his eyes were as cold as the winter sky overhead. "Whether we can defeat Cheyenne warriors, that remains for the future. But you're right—I'm not sure who'd come out on top if we had your scrap with 'em. Would it be the Cheyenne warrior who believes with all his heart in what he's fighting to protect— his home, family and his way of life? Or would it be the soldier who's getting pay to do his job until something better comes along and he can desert? You tell me which one makes a better warrior."

Tom watched his brother turn, stride away purposefully, his eyes fixed on the ground.

"Hey, Autie! Which one, eh?" Tom's voice trailed after Custer.

Custer stopped, turned slowly. "You don't really want me to tell you, Tom."

Custer shook his head. "Imagine how those poor girls must feel—hearing of troops nearby as they're tied, thrown on ponies, and spirited away with the fleeing village. With no apparent effort made by those soldiers to rescue them! God in heaven—what am I to do?"

His eyes climbed from the coals at his feet, beseeching. "Romero, will the Cheyenne keep their prisoners alive long enough to exchange for the chiefs?"

The scout sighed. "Can't say, General. Only thing I'm sure of is that you're lucky Medicine Arrow isn't in that camp right now. He'd have them girls gutted, scalped, and skewered, left behind as a little surprise for your soldiers to find."

"With him here, what will the village do?"

"They'll get as far away as their skinny ponies will take 'em. Then they'll sit down to figure out what to do next. And while they're sitting, you can creep back up on 'em."

"To have them pull away again. That cat-and-mouse would go on until . . . No. We're sitting tight, right here. I may not have the best hand in the deck, but I'm going to play out the hand I've been dealt. C'mon, Cheyenne-talker. Let's go bust one of those four loose."

Custer glared down at the four bronze faces. "See which one's the messenger."

Romero turned to Custer a moment later. "You're not going to believe it—the old bastard himself."

"Medicine Arrow?" Custer replied, grinding a fist into an open palm. "I should've known! All right. Tell him when the girls are freed and Medicine Arrow takes his people back to the reservation, I'll send these three warriors to him."

As Romero translated, Medicine Arrow's head bobbed eagerly.

"That's not all—you tell him that if he doesn't release those girls, I'll level his villages—like Black Kettle's. Then

I'm going to hang every last warrior I can lay my hands on until the trees are filled with Cheyenne flesh for the buzzards!"

Custer watched all four sets of eyes stay with his hands as he slowly curled them into fists as if he were choking a man standing before him.

"Tom, go requisition a tin of hardtack from Bell. And a small sack of parched corn and a couple pounds of coffee. Better bring a pound of sugar. Go on."

When Tom had returned with the gifts and Romero led up a captured Cheyenne pony, Custer instructed his interpreter, "Tell Medicine Arrow these gifts are to show his people I can be as kind as I can be brutal."

"Sending presents back with this old bastard," Romero clucked. "Good idea. You're learning 'bout Indians, General."

"All I know is that I'm gambling the whole pot on those Cheyenne believing my word. They don't believe me and I lose that gamble—those two girls are dead."

"Appears you put the scare of God in this bastard." Romero flung a thumb at Medicine Arrow.

Custer waved his hand, irritated. "Get him out of here before I change my mind and do something I'll regret!" He turned on his heel and headed back to his tent, seething with anger.

More and more of late he wondered what white women were doing out here on this frontier anyway. Seemed the Indians never captured any men. The white women served only to lure the young warriors who lusted for conquest, and more. He brooded on the type of woman who would venture into an unknown, dangerous land, standing shoulder to shoulder with her man—assuming every risk the land threw at them both.

Warriors hungering for white women. *But am I all that different? A white man who's bedded a captured Cheyenne girl?* he thought.

It'll be years before this land can be safe for the likes of Libbie. Women of her cut—all lace curtains and china and out-of-tune piano. Forever blushing behind their hands at the coarse humor of frontier scouts and career soldiers.

When this land is frontier no longer, Libbie can share a home with me here in my wilderness. When Monaseetah no longer belongs to me.

"What's the ruckus?" Custer hollered, stepping from his tent the next morning.

"Indians spotted, General!" shouted a young guard rushing up.

"How many?"

"Fifty. Maybe more."

"Good. Fetch Romero for me, Lieutenant!" He clapped his hands, wheeling back into his tent, where he strapped on his pistol and tugged on the buffalo cap. By the time he reached the northernmost picket line, a large crowd of troopers and Kansas volunteers had gathered to watch the approach of the Cheyenne.

Less than a mile off the Indians dismounted, put their ponies out to graze under the care of two young herders, and began their walk into the soldier camp behind two older men.

"You've got visitors, General."

Custer turned, watching Romero slide up. "Those two in front. Chiefs?"

Beneath a shading hand, Romero squinted, studying the pair. "Can't say. Don't see feathers."

"Whoever that bunch is," Custer grumbled, "they aren't coming like beggars. Every one is loaded for bear."

Beneath a bright winter sun it was plain enough to see every weapon carried by the warriors following the two leaders. Besides a bow, most carried an old rifle or musket. And many had a pistol or two at their waists. The delegation stopped a quarter-mile off, conferring among themselves.

"Romero, take a good look," Custer instructed. "That Little Robe out there?"

"The short one? By God, it might be!"

Custer turned to his brother. "Tom! Tell me that doesn't look like Little Robe."

"Goddamned, Autie—that's him! I'd recognized the rascal anywhere. Good sign, him coming to see us."

"You bet your freckled hide on that." Custer lunged past the pickets. "We just might get those girls back in one piece now!"

"Where the hell you going, Autie?" Tom got no answer from his brother. He glanced at Romero, who shrugged his shoulders.

"Sergeant Lucas!" Tom called. "Get a squad together—move out to protect the general! Left flank!"

The crowd buzzed with alarm as they recognized Custer striding across the icy, windblown prairie alone.

"Johnson! Grab a squad and cover Autie's right flank! Jump to it, man!" Tom yelled.

Romero eased behind Tom to whisper in an ear. "If that is Little Robe out there, the general has nothing to fear."

"Why? 'Cause he was such a good guest of ours?" Tom snarled. "Doesn't mean the rest of those bastards won't take

Autie prisoner, maybe even slit his throat if they get the chance."

"Little Robe's an honorable man."

"He may not have much say about it, what with them sonsabitches ready to guy any one of us!" Tom shouldered Romero aside. "That's not *your* brother out there. Damn, but Autie's always made it hard for me to keep up with him!"

Out on the frosty prairie, Custer stopped, waiting for the chiefs to walk the last few yards between them. Wearing his famous smile, he made sign. "Little Robe! It is good to see you!"

"Yellow Hair! They told me you lead the soldiers. It brings my heart joy to see you!"

They shook hands, touched each other's breast. Little Robe gestured to the warrior beside him. "This is my friend, Slips Away. He came to meet the Yellow Hair. He is a wise and honorable man."

The tall warrior presented his hand. At the same time, Little Robe turned, announcing to the rest of the warriors gathering behind him, "My brothers! This is truly a day of rejoicing. Here stands the great soldier chief, Yellow Hair!"

That name sent a shock wave through the fifty, each straining for a glimpse at the destroyer of Black Kettle's village.

"I invite Little Robe and his warriors to eat at Yellow Hair's lodge!" Custer said.

The old chief stood dumbfounded. He smiled. "You speak Cheyenne now!"

"Yes, I have a very good teacher."

"The girl?"

"Monaseetah."

"Daughter of Little Rock," the old chief replied. "I remember her as a skinny girl, all bone and legs. She has grown much?"

Custer chuckled. "Yes. She has grown much in those summers since last you saw her. She has a son, born two moons ago."

"Lo, the winters pass so quickly when you are an old man—with only dreams to warm you at night!"

"Come, Little Robe. There is much for old friends to talk over."

The chief's finely chisled face lost its smile. "Let us go to your lodge to discuss these matters as friends."

By the time Custer led the delegation to his tent, everything was in order as he had sent Tom ahead to prepare. The tent flaps were tied back so the entire interior was exposed. Several cottonwood trunks had been dragged up for seating. Little Robe selected twelve of his number to accompany him into the tent itself while the rest arranged themselves outside, where they could observe the council.

"Moylan, see that the mess sergeant gets the rest of last night's venison and turkey over here on the double. Fire the coffeepots and bring lots of sugar. We have important guests to feed!"

After the introductions came a meal supplemented with Custer's favorite, wild onions, then the lengthy smoking of the pipe among the thirteen Cheyenne in his tent, and finally Custer's council got under way.

"My soldiers stare eye to eye with Cheyenne warriors, Little Robe. This is dangerous. Tell me how we can help each other, old friend."

"Once more Yellow Hair comes to the heart of the matter without delay. It is good to hear you talk of helping our people. I want to put an end to this trouble, so my people can return to the way we have lived for a long, long time."

Custer said, "Life for us both is changing. Never will it be the same again. We can't stop the flow of history. It is as the river. No dam will ever hold the rushing waters of destiny."

"Does Yellow Hair tell his old friend that honorable men have no say in the writing of history?"

"That is not what I'm saying. We can change the course of history—move the river a little this way, perhaps a little the other way. But we cannot stop the flow of destiny."

"Yes, Yellow Hair. We both know men who have used that river of time for their own selfish ends."

"It is my wish that we can put this talk of war to rest. History will remember us for that, old friend."

"Sadly, I disagree with you, Yellow Hair. History remembers only the wars. History forgets those who work for peace. They are ground underfoot."

Custer fell silent. Then he said grimly, "I understand. All too well. Because you believe in the cause of peace, you must answer to Medicine Arrow. But together, you and I are stronger than he. You must help me help your people. I ask you now for the sake of the Cheyenne nation—do you have the two white girls in your camp?"

Little Robe's eyes never flinched, nor wavered from Custer's steady gaze. Around the old chief ignited an electricity as the other Cheyenne resented Yellow Hair's challenge.

"Yes," Little Robe answered. "They are in my camp."

"Above all Cheyenne, Little Robe is an honorable man. I expect no less than the truth from a friend. My respect grows for your courage in the face of enemies!" Custer's eyes slewed over the hostile warriors.

"Cheyenne!" Custer flung his voice at the angry crowd. "It is a brave man who speaks the truth when all about him are afraid of his words."

While many young warriors murmured haughtily, Custer turned back to Little Robe. "Tell me how I am to get the girls back alive and not be forced to use my mighty hand against your people."

Little Robe shook his gray head. "It is a question I have asked myself many times. Before the first snows of last winter came to this land, I tried to buy the girls from their owner, the one who captured them in the land to the north. Once they were mine, I could take them to soldier chief Hazen. Many times I offered to buy them. As I raised the price I would pay, so too he increased his resistance to me."

"Little Robe sees justice in freeing the girls to Yellow Hair?"

"One man cannot own another," the chief answered. "Other tribes own slaves. Even you white men buy many black-white men. My heart tells me that when we possess another man, does that not make us a little less worthy before the eyes of the Everywhere Spirit?"

"You speak true of the white men, old friend. One reason the men from the south pulled their council fires away from our Grandfather in Washington City was they did not want to give up their slaves. Across four summers I fought those men who believed it right to own another human. Now I am prepared to fight your warriors who believe it's right to enslave these two women."

"You are just in asking for them. We should return the women to their families. Likewise, the Washita captives belong with the Cheyenne people. When will you free them?"

Custer was shocked at the surprise question. "I will tell you what rests in my heart. The captives stay with me only until the white women are freed and your people return to the reservation."

"I will trust to the word of Yellow Hair."

"Yellow Hair is honored by that trust, Little Robe. It is rare for a man to trust his enemy before he pays heed to the council of his own people."

"As long as there is breath in my body, I will work to release the captives to you. Know, too, that there are many in the villages who object to giving the women back to the soldiers without paying the owner for their loss. But I have given my word."

"I am here to do what is right," Custer said. "Yellow Hair would be without honor to pay for the two girls. It would show that one man can buy another. No, Little Robe. You tell your chiefs that Yellow Hair will pay only with blood—his own, if he has to—but only with blood if he pays anything for the lives of the girls. Go to your camps and tell those who would not return the captives they should begin their death songs now. Tell them to think of the wailing in their lodges. Children without fathers. Wives without husbands."

Little Robe creaked to his feet as Custer rose.

Custer looked down at the chief. "Tell your people that there will be much crying and wailing in Cheyenne lodges if your young men test the might of my hand."

Little Robe nodded. "Yellow Hair has spoken what rests in his heart. Now, this old man must go change the hearts of those who would see this land run red before they would give up the prisoners. I only pray I can say the right words to shift the rush of history."

The chief turned to go, accompanied by a crush of feathers and paint, rifles and bows.

"Little Robe, wait!" Custer pressed a hand to the old one's shoulder. "Yellow Hair prays for you too. May you find the strength our people require of you at this moment in history."

"What rests in your heart is good, Yellow Hair. Together we will find that strength."

Like a stone quickly swallowed by a still pond, disappearing beneath a corona of silent ripples, so too was Little Robe swallowed up by the fifty warriors who followed him back to the icy meadow where waited their winter-gaunt ponies.

CHAPTER 25

Two more days passed. The stalemate continued.

Then, unexpectedly, the chief who had accompanied Little Robe's delegation now visited Custer alone.

The soldier chief fumed at Slips Away, stuttering his limited Cheyenne. "You tell me again your chiefs have decided not to release the girls!"

"Yellow Hair holds our three chiefs. Too, you hold fifty more from Black Kettle's camp. I am sent to tell you—release the chiefs, then we can talk of freeing the white prisoners."

His teeth on edge and close to boiling, hands clenching in fists, Custer shook with rage.

"Hell, no!" he shouted in English. "Your people don't understand. I hold my soldiers back. Many in this camp come from the land where you captured the women. They hunger to spill Cheyenne blood! Go back and tell them Yellow Hair sees the Cheyenne are worse than squaws—cowards! It takes no brave warrior to kidnap a woman.

Remember—were it not for those two captives, I would level your village!"

"Many stand ready to answer your guns, Yellow Hair."

Custer leapt up, almost upon the warrior's toes, his cheeks flushed. "Silence! Go tell them Yellow Hair makes ready to wipe the Southern Cheyenne from the breast of their mother! Every man, woman, and child!"

He turned away, afraid of what he might do if he glared into that Cheyenne face much longer. His heart eventually calmed. "Little Robe did not come today, for he is ashamed. Still, I know what course I must take."

Slowly, he turned back to the tall warrior, crossing his arms. Custer's sunburned face clouded. "Take my word back to your people. I grow weary. No more talk. If you do not come to me by noon tomorrow to tell me when you will release the white captives, I will follow your villages. Each time you move, we will follow. Now, go!"

He shoved past the warrior, angrily flailing his arms. "Moylan! Have Sergeant Lucas get this Indian out of my camp! Before I do something I'll regret!"

Custer disappeared into his tent, furious and fuming, collapsing onto his bed, his head propped between his hands. The only thing that helped was Monaseetah's fingertips rubbing across his shoulders, up the tense cords at the back of his neck.

Seeking those places only she knew . . . the calming places.

Noon came and went the following day. And with it, Custer's patience.

"Moylan, there'll be no more quibbling with these Cheyenne—I'm about to force their hand."

"You've been more patient than most, General."

"Those days are over," he spat. "They squat in their villages, laughing at me. I'll not be treated like some treaty diplomat! I'm a soldier.

"We'll force their hand or I'll chop it off in the process. Have Romero take a detail of troops to the village and inform those Cheyenne they must send their chiefs to me at sunrise tomorrow. Not noon. *Sunrise!*"

"Yessir."

"And when Romero's on his way, inform the companies this camp's about to move. We'll sit on the Cheyenne's doorstep before nightfall!"

By six A.M., before the next sun had crept into the east, Custer was up and about, anxious to see matters forced off dead center. Once more this warrior, this cavalry officer who had become known in the Shenandoah as "Sheridan's firebrand," found himself preparing for that to which he had been born—to fight.

By the time the morning frost began to burn off, Custer had fifteen Cheyenne chiefs seated before him.

"You will hold your tongues," he began without preliminaries. "No food. No pipe. I'll leave that to the treaty makers you laugh at. Yellow Hair is a warrior. You will listen without speaking a word. The time for discussion has gone."

Custer pointed at his three prisoners seated nearby. "These men are your leaders. What stupidity to want me to kill them."

He paced in front of the fifteen, reminding them how patient he had been with the slow progress in freeing the white women. Then Custer dropped the other boot.

"Upon your heads rest the responsibility for war!"

Rhythmically, he slapped the rawhide quirt against his muddy boot top for emphasis, like ticking off the seconds until releasing his mighty army on the Cheyenne villages.

"You hold the women. We came to get them back. If you won't release them peacefully, we're prepared to pay for their lives with our own. I'll lay waste to your villages—leaving them a smoking ruin for all Indian nations to know of Cheyenne stupidity!"

Custer stepped close to the fifteen now, assured of their rapt attention. "If you harm one of the women, I will kill ten Cheyenne. And if one of the captives is killed, I will put two hundred of your own to the sword myself! I'm prepared to keep on killing until no more Cheyenne walk the face of this earth! No more wombs to carry Cheyenne warriors!" He said to his interpreter angrily, "See that they understand that, Romero!"

Custer and the other officers gathered with him watched the chiefs eventually indicate their understanding.

"Now, Romero—have Dull Knife join me."

The tall, stately chief, one of the three held captive, followed the pony soldier to a nearby cottonwood. From one of the overhanging branches dangled a length of hemp rope at the end of which hung a noose. Custer signaled Sergeant Lucas.

Two soldiers immediately seized Dull Knife, binding his hands behind him. The warriors shouted furiously. Quickly the soldier guard around them leveled rifles at the delegates. Angrily, the Cheyenne fell silent as the noose fell over the chief's head, tightened at the base of his skull. The rope was raised until the chief was on tiptoe.

Big Head's dark eyes glared flinty hatred at Custer. Yet not a muscle in his face betrayed any emotion.

"See your mighty chief now!" Custer cried, flush with anger. "Listen carefully, for you'll no longer play me the fool. Release the two girls by sunset tomorrow, or you will watch your chiefs hang—one at a time!"

Custer turned to the sergeant. "Lucas, ease the chief down."

When he could stand flat-footed once more, his neck no longer stretched and his hands released, Dull Knife joined the other captives. He sat rubbing his wrists and raw neck.

"None of you'll be so brave tomorrow when I have your bodies hanging from this tree!" Custer roared at the Cheyenne. "I'll watch the magpies feast upon that flesh left on your bones when the buzzards have had their fill!"

In two steps he stood before his interpreter. "Romero, tell our visitors they have five minutes to talk with their chiefs. For if the girls are not freed by sunset tomorrow, this is the last time they'll see their chiefs alive!"

Throughout the next long, fateful day, a hushed tension wound itself through camp like a watch spring; every man was fearful it would get one rough twist too many and the whole thing would snap. Not a soldier could fail to know this was the day the Seventh Cavalry would go back to war with the Cheyenne.

With its pale, milky light, the winter sun had sunk halfway out of midsky, falling steadily toward sunset. Still no tidings heard from the hostile villages.

"You want to see me?" Custer stepped up to the three captives with Romero.

"Yellow Hair will hang us if our people do not release the white girls?" Fat Bear asked.

Custer flicked his eyes to Dull Knife. "The fat one here thinks my words are hollow. No one believes Yellow Hair. You will hang before I destroy your villages! This I say before your Everywhere Spirit!"

Dull Knife nodded. "I believe."

"I too," Fat Bear agreed, quaking. "I am a chief of consequence among my people. They need my counsel. Yellow Hair must release me so I can hasten to my village, speak to the owner of the girls so they can be released in time. I will bring the captives here to save the lives of Dull Knife and Big Head. Hear me—I must hurry!"

"Romero, tell Fat Bear that I want to laugh, if he weren't so sad. A brave one when surrounded by his warriors. But he has no heart when he's alone and staring death in the face."

"Too bad Medicine Arrow himself isn't here to hang with him," Romero growled.

"Make this Fat Bear dangle awhile longer—on a rope of his own making. Tell him this: If you're so important to your people, then you're just the man I want to hold on to. You're worth far more to me here than in your village."

Custer waited as Romero translated, watching the Indian's eyes widen in fear, his chin sag in failure. "By your own words, Fat Bear—like your lying friend, Medicine Arrow—you've tightened the noose around your neck."

Custer left the prisoners' tent before he grew angrier. With a fresh cup of coffee in hand, he climbed a low hill where he joined others maintaining an anxious vigil, watching for any sign from the Cheyenne.

When the pale sun hung two hands above the western

horizon, with less than an hour of daylight remaining before sunset, the breeze kicked up, whining through the naked trees like a squaw's death song.

"General!"

Custer wheeled at the frantic cry from his left. Several soldiers pointed.

"By Jehovah himself!" Moylan roared. "See there on the hill!"

"Believe me, mister—I see it!" Custer cried.

Tom leapt to his side. "What is it? Don't see a god-damned thing but some riders on that hill yonder. You don't even know they're Indians."

"Maybe Tom's right," Yates agreed sourly. "Best we don't get our hopes up."

"Even if it is them Injuns," Lucas said, "who's to say it ain't some trick to buy more time? I say we hang the frigging bastards and be done with it!"

"That's the stuff, Lucas!" Tom spat.

"Hush!" Custer whispered, paying little attention to the angry mutterings of those on the hilltop.

Word reached the three chiefs that riders had been spotted on a hill a mile distant. In their prison tent they sang their thanksgiving, an eerie backdrop for the tense vignette on the hill.

"Moylan!" Custer lunged for his adjutant. "We're acting like headless shavetails! Give me the glass—quick!"

He yanked the brass telescope from its oiled saddle-leather case. He spent anxious, long seconds focusing on the distant knoll. "All I can tell is that they're Indians," he concluded.

"I told you!" Tom shouted, cocky. "Here to pull a fast shuffle on us again, Autie!"

"How many are there, General?" Yates asked.

"Could be a couple dozen. I'll count. See what we're dealing with." He began his tally, slowly swinging the glass from right to left."

". . . eighteen . . . nineteen and twenty—"

He suddenly pulled the glass down, rubbing the eye-piece with his dusty sleeve. "It can't be!"

Custer felt the others press close as he looked again. "Yes, gentlemen! There are two figures on one pony up there."

"Could it be the girls?" Thompson asked.

Custer turned to answer, seeing Daniel Brewster scramble up the long slope toward the officers.

"You spotted the girls?" Brewster rasped.

"We don't know yet. No sense getting excited until we're certain."

"Lemme see for myself!" Brewster lunged awkwardly for the glass.

"You will not!" Custer replied, holding the youth off. "You can remain here as long as you obey orders and remain calm. Otherwise"—he put the glass back to his eye—"I'll have you dragged back to camp before you can say—"

"Good God!" Yates cried.

"What is it?" Brewster shrieked.

"Look there!" a soldier shouted.

"They're dropping off the horse!" another yelled.

"Goddamn—gotta be the girls!" Tom cheered.

"God in heaven, Tom!" Thompson growled, slapping him on the back.

"Yes!" Custer's voice climbed. "It's two women!"

"Anna Belle!" Tears of joy shimmered down Brewster's stubbled cheeks.

"Get hold of yourself, Brewster!" Custer said. "We don't know who they are at this distance."

"It's my Anna Belle! I know it is. Little Robe told me. He didn't lie."

"They're headed this way now!" Myers sang out.

"Thompson!" Custer ordered. "Bring me a squad of Kansas volunteers. Quick, man!"

Custer watched the captain lope downhill into the bustling Kansas camp, then put the glass to his eye once more.

"Yes . . . yes!" he repeated, studying the two figures hobbling through the brittle grasses skiffed with icy sleet, snow dotting the hillside and meadows in huge sodden patches.

"One appears to have a short, heavy figure," he muttered. "The other is considerably taller and more slender."

"You said tall?" Brewster sleeved the moisture from his eyes. "Gotta be Anna Belle, General! Bless her heart!"

The mule-strong, hard-callused settler could fight those tears of joy no longer.

Custer sensed a foreign, salty sting in his own eyes, turning away before it betrayed him. The sensations rushed him all at once: the bittersweet pangs of Brewster's reunion, the happiness of the others witnessing the captives' release, his own success snatched from the claws of defeat. Yet . . .

Someday, too, I must return Monaseetah to her own people, he realized. *Someday I'll watch her return to the Cheyenne as surely as these two young women are hurrying across the frozen ground toward the U.S. Cavalry.*

Brewster darted off the brow of the hill, but was grabbed by a ring of soldiers and dragged, kicking, back to Custer.

"She's waiting for me!" Brewster shrieked. "Dear God in his heaven, lemme go to her!"

"Control yourself!"

"General?"

Custer turned at the unfamiliar voice, watching a squad of Kansas volunteers climb the hill.

"Captain Royce Wenzel, sir!" one man announced, saluting. "You have good news for us?"

"Believe I do, Captain." Custer pointed into the meadow. "Appears the Cheyennes just released the two girls."

The Kansas men scrambled forward, muttering, swearing, straining to see the figures stumbling across the meadow below.

"Lord of Divine Grace!" Wenzel gulped, his voice thick with emotion.

"Captain"—Custer took hold of Wenzel's arm—"Brewster here may prove to be the brother of one of the girls. But I'm not convinced he should be the first to go out there—for his sake and the girl's."

"Lemme go to her!" Brewster shouted, yanking away from the soldier holding him.

"Understandable," Wenzel replied.

"I think your men are more detached from the raw emotions of the moment," Custer explained. "And yet every one of you left homes and families, your livelihoods to accomplish this release."

"Yes we did—"

"Seems fitting your men should be the first to welcome those girls back to the bosom of friends and freedom."

"Bless you, General Custer!" Wenzel sang out.

"Hip, hip, hooray!" the Kansans cheered, slapping backs.

"C'mon, men!" Wenzel strode out. "Let's welcome those Kansas girls back to freedom!" Suddenly he stopped, wheeling around in the midst of his squad, and saluted. "Thank you from the bottom of our hearts, General!"

In the meadow below stumbled two pitiful figures, clawing their way through bare brush and slushy snow, fighting their way back to freedom.

When Wenzel's squad had marched half the distance to the captives, the volunteers began to wave. Desperate and delirious in joy, the women—for the men could see now that they were not just girls—waved back.

"Gentlemen, that's a sight not many will ever witness," Custer said quietly. "We're party to one of the signal successes on this frontier."

"C'mere, you!"

Custer whirled at Lucas's cry. Brewster had torn free, dashing downhill, four soldiers on his heels. A dozen more leaping strides and it was clear as crystal to any man the civilian had the soldiers beat.

"Sergeant, call your men back!"

At Custer's order, Lucas skidded to a halt, staring back in disbelief. He called to his detail; the soldiers slowed and ground to a stop. Brewster raced on at full tilt, arms pumping under an inspired head of steam as he burst past the smartly marching column of bewildered Kansas volunteers.

Seconds later he skidded to a snowy halt before the women, flinging his oxbow arms around the taller of the two. Anna Belle fell into this strong embrace, crying for joy, her big tears streaking the dirt caked across her ruddy cheeks.

They both held out an arm to welcome Judith White into

their warm embrace of homecoming. All three skipped around and around, giddy and childlike, wrapped arm in arm in the frozen meadow as if it were May Day.

As the volunteers caught up, the air filled with rejoicing and shouts heard back on Custer's knoll. Whoops, screams, and squeals of happiness climbed into the dusk-gray skies overhead. The first stain of sunset streaked the pewter underbelly of the clouds as some of the Kansas boys tore off their coats and draped them around the women's shoulders. Wenzel urged his men back to the safety of the soldier's lines.

Halfway down the slope, Custer met them. Shaking their hands, he found himself unable to utter a single words. All about the girls, soldiers and volunteers jumped and cheered, everyone flinging a hand in to touch the freed captives, welcoming them.

Through it all the women kept their own teary eyes on the ground, out of fear and embarrassment. Their faces sparkled damply with joy. They glanced at one another as if to ask, *Is this real? Are we actually going home at last?*

With a full heart, Custer stepped back from the crush, taking it all in, still unable to speak. A knot of sentiment clogged his throat as he studied their deplorable condition, realizing both were pregnant and nearly starved.

"Three cheers for General Custer!"

His eyes swam as Moylan pressed before him. Suddenly there were more Seventh Cavalry and Kansas volunteers.

"Hear! Hear! Three cheers!" Wenzel shouted above the din.

That lump in Custer's throat didn't dissolve until the Kansas men escorted the women downhill to camp and the sun disappeared behind the trees atop the western hills.

"Huzzah for Custer!" Cooke shouted.

"Huzzah!" the hundreds answered. "Huzzah for George Armstrong Custer!"

CHAPTER 26

In closing, Dear Heart—I wanted to tell you of the deplorable condition of the two girls when they were presented to me. Clothed in some sort of short dress made from flour sacks, the brand of the mills plainly visible. This bears witness that the kidnappers of these young women were the same Indians taking our generous annuities of flour from Fort Larned or Fort Cobb.

Their entire dress was nearly Indian: both wore leggings and moccasins, their hair tied in braids. As if to propitiate us, the Indians gave the women rude ornaments like those worn by Cheyenne squaws. Wrists wrapped with coils of brass wire. Rings on fingers. Round their necks hung colored beads.

Young Brewster was heard to say: "Sister, do take those hateful things off."

How to tell you of their joy when they found they weren't the only white women in the territory! You should have seen their faces when Mrs. McNeil stepped from her cook-tent, wiping her plump hands in her apron, grinning like a cat just eating the canary.

Her arms opened wide as she pressed both girls against her ample bosom. Mrs. McNeil is truly one of a kind, Libbie! Besides baking them the best pies and cornbreads, that old woman allowed those girls to choose something from her personal wardrobe, until she could fashion something better. From a bundle I had given Mrs. McNeil after we had cornered a single lodge of hostiles, she drew calico, thread, and needles—to sew frontier dresses for our new guests. For shoes, I'm sorry they had to wear their crude moccasins and leggings. They feel more comfortable sleeping in my "A" tent next to Mrs. McNeil's.

It moves me to once again think of Daniel's poor sister, Anna Belle. Married but a month before she was brutally wrenched from the arms of her wounded husband.

The second captive is Miss Judith White, a year younger than Mrs. Morgan, and taken a month before Anna Belle's capture.

Every evening round the fire at Mrs. McNeil's tent, hundreds of young soldiers and volunteers gather to hear their distressing stories. Traded among the Indians. Beaten by jealous Cheyenne harpies. Countless abuses. And an ill-fated attempt to escape.

No eye was found dry when the two described their first meeting in the hostile camp. How great must have been their joy amid such suffering, fear, and outrage. When one owner grew tired of dallying with his captive, he sold her to another, who misused the women in the most unspeakable manner.

From the moment of their first meeting, the two laid plans for escape. So, trusting to Providence one night, they traveled for hours in a northerly direction. They had reached the ruts of a wagon road and were congratulating themselves when a bullet whistled past their heads. To their horror, their late captor rode up in pursuit.

That very next day he separated them by selling one. From that moment the two have been apart, until brought together on the back of a single pony and sent out to freedom.

What victories we win in this war seem so small—they pale in comparison—before this sweet victory of securing freedom for these citizens!

It had not been dark long that first evening of freedom when the Cheyenne sent a delegation to me, demanding the release of their three chiefs. I reminded them I would not free their leaders until the tribe returned to the reservation near Camp Supply.

The delegation left my quarters quite upset, reminding Romero of some curse one of their evil, old wizards of the tribe had laid about my shoulders. One should only fear such poppycock if one believes in poppycock!

Seems I've fallen victim to one Medicine Arrow, the culprit who has (they claim) cursed my command with total annihilation. Romero himself became agitated, saying I should take it seriously. I find such primitive beliefs amusing at best.

With our camp grown quiet, a second delegation called for Yellow Hair. Seeing I would not bend my demands, they finally promised that as soon as their ponies were fit to travel, their villages would proceed to Camp Supply, abandoning the warpath forever.

With this happy termination to our struggles here, we set out in the morning for Camp Supply. If I were to bring a true peace to this southern frontier, it would prove more than a mere feather in my cap, Libbie. Our friend Philip is seeing to promotion and a regiment of my own with President Grant himself!

Lt. Moylan calls me now for some duty, so I scribble as fast as possible. As always, my prayers are with you, sweet Libbie. May God Himself watch over you. Please remember me in your prayers too, Dear Heart. Perhaps I am in all the more need of your prayers.

Pray you forgive me of my past indiscretions, to forever hold your Bo dearest in your heart.

This wilderness lures me as seductively as any siren.

I will not fail you, dear one.

By midmorning of 22 March, Custer marched his troops north, following the Sweetwater.

After but three miles, they reached the meadow where the Cheyenne villages had stood until evacuated in fear of attack. Another scene of frantic, hasty departure. Stuffed in the forks of the skeletal trees stood enough lodge poles to outfit more than two hundred lodges. These the soldiers set afire, feeding the blazes with the other property left behind—bows, axes, robes, and blankets abandoned in the rush.

Climbing into the hills north of the Sweetwater, Custer turned to watch the leaden, oily smoke claw at the leaden sky. Once again, Yellow Hair left behind only the charred, smoking ruins of a village, and the scattered, bloody carcasses of those ponies abandoned by the fleeing Cheyenne.

As the jangle of saddle gear and wagon harness faded to the north, a wilderness silence returned to the Sweetwater.

The stream's happy chatter mingled with the drone of green bottle flies buzzing over the bloating carcasses abandoned by both races of escaping warriors.

Two days later, Custer's advance guard rounded a point of timber in a wide bend of the Washita, bumping into a sprawling camp of horses, wagons, and soldiers. Assigned by Sheridan to await the Seventh's return, these two companies had fared far better than those who had marched into the wilderness behind Custer.

To Custer's weary cavalry, these commissary troops appeared strange to the eye. Their bodies looked puffy, even swollen. Rosy cheeks chubby. Eyes bulging in clean faces. To top if off, Captain Henry Inman's troops even wore bright blue uniforms.

Custer's cavalry finally realized the strange malady afflicting the Washita troops: Inman's soldiers hadn't been starved and used to the quick.

Since leaving Camp Supply last December, the men of the Seventh Cavalry had undergone subtle changes that no man among them had noticed. Months of busting trails through the wilderness, poor rations, and medical infirmities had taken their toll. Faces gone skeletal. Uniforms now greasy rags.

While some of Custer's troops ran, most limped painfully into that Washita campground. What a sight were those rows of cheery mess fires, each banked by clean utensils and sides of bacon. Everywhere lay half-empty hardtack boxes, each one surrounded by Custer's men. Ravenous soldiers ripped at half-cooked sides of bacon, grease dripping down their dirty, bearded chins.

"General Custer!"

Custer turned slowly. Striding his way came the stout
quartermaster corps' captain. Custer presented his hand.

"Inman! Dear God, it's good to see you!"

"From the looks of it, you've had a deuce of a time!"
Inman rattled Custer's arm like a water pump handle.

"Nowhere near what it might've been," Custer replied
"had the Cheyenne decided to run, forcing us to pursue.
see you've fared well."

"Most of us, General."

"Most?"

"Yes," Inman answered, sighting his duty sergeant
"Lewis! Coffee here, quick!"

"Sit here, sir," Inman directed, indicating a downed
cottonwood trunk. "We'll have your animal watered and
fed. Oats."

"Oats?" Custer moaned. "It's been so long since our
stock had grain."

"You've been through the grinder, sir."

"Yes," Custer murmured. "This does feel good. Getting
out of that blasted saddle. Feels like I've lost most of my
natural padding the last few months!"

"I'm amazed you still have your spirits about you
General. We'll put some meat on those bones of yours soon
enough. Ah, here comes your coffee. Drink it while I have
some hardtack and salt pork brought over."

Custer watched the sergeant scurry off to a mess fire
while he sipped at the scalding, heady potion an army man
generously called coffee.

"I lost four couriers," Inman explained. "Two were
civilian scouts Sheridan left here on his way north. The
other two were our enlisted."

Custer squinted into the middle distance. "Couriers?"

"Not sure what happened to three of them. Found only one body."

"Assume the worst."

"One of my patrols found a pair of ripped pantaloons. Civilian pants covered with blood. Savages had themselves quite a field day with that boy. My patrol searched the area, coming up with a bullet-riddled mackinaw, a coat one of our riders wore."

"That's all you found?"

Inman shook his head. "Wasn't long before the men spotted a flock of crows and turkey buzzards squawking over their bloody meal and half a dozen wolves."

Custer stared at him vacantly. "The bodies?"

"By following a line of spent cartridges, we figured the scout had his horse shot out from under him. Made a dash for it on foot, into the thick timber, where he made a stand. Found his courier pouch riddled with holes. Blood on everything. Letters scattered through the buckbrush. Even scraps of the reporter's stories."

"Did you save those?"

"Saved everything we found."

"Good. We'll take the letters back to Hays. And Keim's stories will reach the New York *Herald*. More than ever, now, I want the world to know these men have gone through more than four months of hell."

Inman coughed, rising, "I suggest you and your men rest here for a few days. Eat decent meals. Sleep in tents again, beneath clean blankets. Before we push on to Camp Supply, then the final leg of our return."

"Fort Hays. Perhaps you're right."

To Custer, all that seemed so far away, Kansas and the new headquarters for his Seventh Cavalry.

And . . . Libbie.

When should I have her come west? To Hays? With reddened, gritty eyes, he stared into the distance. *Should I delay her departure from Monroe until I settle matters with Monaseetah?*

"What say you, General? Rest for the men, sir?"

"Of course, Captain. Two days—then back on the trail." Custer rose unsteadily from the cottonwood stump. "Two days should prove about right."

Inman watched Custer wander off, stopping here and there to shake hands with his bony troops, joking now of their endurance and privation, congratulating all for a job well done in the wilderness. Thanking them for those sacrifices and burdens borne as cheerfully as any soldier in any war had ever marched through a winter of hell, and returned.

On he walked, talking to all, teasing those who would laugh, consoling those who couldn't.

And at every fire, he reminded his men exactly how he felt to ride at the head of the best horse soldiers the world had ever known, or was likely to know—the U.S. Seventh Cavalry.

On the morning of the twenty-seventh, Custer led his troops out of the valley of the Washita for the last time, on their way home.

Five days later, when the columns were still a few miles from Camp Supply, Custer was greeted by a courier dispatched by Sheridan, with word that Grant and Sherman had summoned the general to Washington City, and giving full command of the base camp over to George Armstrong Custer.

As the last few miles were crossed, he devoured the

dispatches Sheridan left for his return: orders, disburse-
ments, assignments—all quite boring and routine until he
came across two items, the first from Washington City
itself, dated months ago.

War Department, Washington City
2 December, 1868

LIEUTENANT—GENERAL SHERMAN
St. Louis, Mo.

I congratulate you, Sheridan, and Custer on the splendid
success with which your campaign is begun. Ask Sheridan
to send forward the names of officers and men deserving of
special mention.

J. M. SCHOFIELD
Secretary of War

Bitter tears welled in his eyes.
Who the hell does this pompous ass think he is, Custer
thought, *singling men out for special mention over and above
others who've suffered just as much as any? Damn his bloody hide!
Damn every one of those puffed-up Washington poltroons who
wave their magic wands over the army's head, pulling strings,
making the generals jump!*
He swiped at his dribbling nose, staring into the bright
sun.
*To make heros of some . . . leaving the rest as common
soldiers. There's not a man riding out of the wilderness behind me
who can't be called a hero! Not a single man of these who can't ride
up the hill to the halls of Congress to receive his medal for valor in
the face of the enemy, while those reeky bureaucrats tremble and
quake in the face of any criticism.*

He crumbled Schofield's telegram, stuffing it inside his coat. Then he found a sealed envelope with his name written on it, in Sheridan's familiar scrawl, dated the 2 of March.

. . . Though we did not make our trip to Federal City and the seats of power, my friend, rest assured all is not lost! We will—we must—continued to wrench your promotion from Grant's desk, with Chandler's support on the Hill.

We have only begun our work on the frontier. More than ever I need a regiment I can call upon to go where needed. To do what is asked. Once again, I need what you gave me in the Shenandoah. Once again, I need George Armstrong Custer at the head of his own regiment of firebrands!

Don't be disappointed about the promotion. It does not lie a'moldering in a grave yet! Trust me. I will push your claims on the subject of promotion as soon as I get to Washington, and, if anything can be done, you may rely on me to look out for your interests.

Custer's eyes smarted as he sensed the kinship he shared with Sheridan. Knowing Sheridan would not let him down. Knowing, one day, he would command his own regiment.

Washington City needs strong men . . . able men . . . men unafraid of taking a stand for what's right and just, he told himself. *Someone who'll bring some sense and order to the frontier, instead of fanning the flames of war from afar. Someone who'll do more than line the pockets of family and friends with trading contracts on the reservations . . . while the tribes starve, or wander off their lands in search of food for the empty bellies of their children.*

A spring breeze nudged the dirty, unkempt beard he had

worn all winter. He scratched it, thinking he'd shave, once warm weather arrived.

Custer realized there would long be a need for good soldiers, officers, thinking men. *More than ever, this Republic needs a man of vision*, he thought. *A man of action. Someone who will bring about a change on the frontier.*

Custer stuffed Sheridan's letter inside his tunic and raised his face to the warming sun of a new season. A sun that would bring rebirth to the land.

My days aren't numbered . . . far from it! My efforts here have only begun to bear fruit.

From the crest of that hill overlooking Camp Supply, Custer stared down into the valley of the Beaver and Wolf Creeks, both shimmering like a pair of silver ribbons beneath a dazzling sun—a sun that shone no less brightly on George Armstrong Custer.

BOOK III

MONASEETAH

CHAPTER 27

A STEADY spring rain fell on the Smoky Hill country of Kansas, drenching everything the soldiers hadn't dragged into a tent last night when the dark underbelly of the prairie sky had opened up. Some eleven hours later, the storm persisted, forming creeks in the wagon ruts carved between the rows of company tents that dotted the boggy meadows like prairie wildflowers in bloom.

Custer had selected this summer home for his regiment where Big Creek dumped into the Smoky Hill River. Fort Hays stood some two miles to the west, on the same south bank of the Smoky Hill along the tracks of the Kansas-Pacific Railroad. For better than four months the small stockade of Fort Hays had bustled with the prisoners from Black Kettle's Washita village, sent north under escort long before Custer led his winter-weary troops back home to Kansas Territory. Custer promptly reported to the new commander of Fort Hays, Colonel Nelson A. Miles.

Here at the Big Creek camp the Seventh Cavalry would stay the summer, until the weather turned autumn cold and sleety. Then Custer would lead his men back to the fort for the prairie winter. For now, he would put up with these soggy skies and wait for the dog days of summer to belly-crawl across the scorched undergut of the plains.

Over his head tapped a steady staccato of rain. It beat not only the roof of his sidewall erected beneath a wide-branched cottonwood, but also the oiled canvas awning stretched in front of his tent. If the weather would ever break, he had the regimental carpenters ready to hammer together a wood gallery surrounding the tent and the base of the tree itself—with railing—like the porch on the family home back in Monroe.

Monroe.

Oh, for spring in the north country! A little shower and things would cool off. Here the spring smothered a man. Nowhere near as muggy, however, as that summer of '64 in the Shenandoah. Chasing Mosby's raiders. Hanging some. Shooting the rest.

Custer sighed, turned back into the tent, deciding he'd wait till tomorrow to write Libbie again.

"General Custer?"

Moylan slogged up between Keim and Sergeant William Johnson. All three were soaked through, their coats no longer any protection from the incessant rain, their wide-brimmed hats soppy, drooping like a beekeeper's under the weight of a good soaking.

"What is it?"

"I have someone I want you to meet," Moylan began, then turned and signaled someone who waited outside the tent. Across the sticky gumbo crabbed a young man, carefully positioning himself on two canes with every step.

The newcomer shuddered to a halt, then placed the

right cane with its brother in his left hand so he could hold
out a big, callused paw to Custer.

"My name's John Morgan, General," he spoke clear and
strong.

"Mr. Morgan," Custer replied.

"I'm looking for my wife. Anna Belle Morgan. Her name
used to be Brewster. I understand she's here with your
regiment." His dark, hooded eyes darted off again.

"General"—Moylan inched forward—"John has come to
take the girl and young Brewster home. To what they have
left in Kansas."

"I plan on raising another house and barn, soon as I'm
fit," Morgan explained. "But for now, it'll be enough just to
take my family with me."

Custer silently regarded this courageous man.

"I figured anyone in camp could lead me to my wife,"
Morgan went on. "But told 'em I wanted to meet you first
off, to shake hands with the man who saved my bride from
the Indians."

"Dan told me you were seriously wounded."

"Was, General. On the mend now. Be back in the fields
behind them mules by fall."

"Your leg?"

"No. Took a bullet in the hip."

"It pains you to move around?"

"Less every day. I laid there that first night, thinking
about Anna Belle. Couldn't move to help when they pulled
her up on one of their ponies. Then had to watch 'em put
the torch to my place. Some neighbors come to look things
over the day after the raid. Found me in the field."

"You'll start over?"

"That land's all I got. That and Anna Belle. Laid on a cot

all fall in Solomon City, nursing my hip. Didn't get no better, so they took me up to Minneapolis. Finally healed up 'bout as good as I'm gonna be for a while. Spent all winter praying I'd get Anna Belle back. All the time part of me said to forget her—savages had her and likely they'd use her up."

Custer saw the tears welling in the big man's eyes, the quiver at his lip.

"Mr. Morgan, your wife's safe and very sound. She's been through an ordeal of unspeakable horror, but she's a strong woman." He turned to his adjutant. "Moylan, take our guest down to Mrs. McNeil's tent. The women are with her, waiting for family to fetch them." Then he turned back to Morgan. "How was it you knew your wife was here?"

"Knew before your regiment got back to Hays. I'd heard talk of your winter campaign to free white prisoners of the Indians. Rode down the Smoky Hill line, past Fort Harker and up to Hays City. Never rode a train before." He rocked uneasily on the homemade oak canes. "Up to Hays City they been posting stories 'bout your Seventh Cavalry."

"Stories?" Custer asked.

"Heard Colonel Miles wanted the whole territory to know what a success you'd made of the winter campaign against them damned Indians. So he had the papers all across Kansas print up stories from your dispatches."

"From what John tells me," Moylan said, "you're quite the hero to Kansas folk."

"No doubt of that, sir." Morgan gave him a big-toothed smile. "All over, folks say you're the man who made this country safe for 'em to farm. They say General Custer's the one who makes 'em sleep easy at night. After they've said their prayers for the Seventh Cavalry, that is."

Custer straightened. "Good to know our winter's efforts are appreciated. Suppose you go with Moylan down to the officers' mess while he fetches your wife. I have a feeling she'll want to freshen up before she sees you. It's been quite a spell, hasn't it?"

"More'n half a year. Some eight months now."

"May I offer a word? Some advice?"

"Of course, General."

"With all the time that's passed, I want you to realize that your wife may have . . . changed some."

"Sir?"

"When you see her for the first time, just remember what a horrifying ordeal she's been through. If she didn't do what was demanded of her, they'd kill her. Remember that when you want to touch her, Mr. Morgan."

"While I was laid up for the shank of the winter I had a lotta time to think. I know the Indians had their way with Anna Belle—any white woman, I 'spect. But Anna Belle's prettier than most."

"A very striking woman," Custer said.

"At first I wanted to forget her. Tell myself it was over. Then I got to brooding on what she'd be thinking, what she was feeling. All of what happened was no fault of her own. Laying on that cot in Solomon City, I asked God to bring my wife back to me, no matter what. Just bring Anna Belle back."

"She's what's most important to you now."

Morgan wiped a hand across his eyes. "Her, and the home we'll rebuild up on the Solomon. Raise some kids."

"I bet that's what Anna Belle wants more than anything too. To go home where she can forget what's happened. To start over."

"May I say something, General?" Moylan inquired.

"Of course."

"Last winter when Dan Brewster came down to Camp Supply, telling us that the Morgans been burned out of everything, well . . . Mr. Keim here came up with a deuce of an idea. I think he should tell you about it, General."

Keim cleared his throat. "Several of your officers and I got to talking while we spent those two days beside the Washita on the trail back. Started taking up a small collection so we could help the two women. Maybe go some toward replacing what they lost in the way of clothing, household goods. The idea just took off on its own, with donations pouring in. Even the Kansas soldiers. Why, we've got over six hundred dollars to divide between Mrs. Morgan and Miss White!"

"Three hundred dollars apiece?" John Morgan whistled low.

Keim said, "I've never seen such an outpouring."

Morgan wagged his head. "Can't believe it. Thank God for you all! For your kindness and your bravery. God bless the Seventh Cavalry!"

Custer felt embarassed as he watched the big man shed tears too long held back. Moylan, Johnson, and Keim looked away, sniffling a bit themselves.

"Moylan," Custer said, "I think Mr. Morgan would like to see his bride now."

"Bless you, General Custer," Morgan blurted like an adoring schoolboy, holding out a big hand once more. "Bless you for the job you've done for us."

"It's what I've been sent here to do, Mr. Morgan."

They turned from his tent and slogged away through

he mud and gumbo along the wagon road, dodging puddles
nd horse droppings.

Nothing like rain to make a man feel lonely. More than the
old of a winter storm. A long, endless rain isolated him.

Custer hurt for her return.

He glanced at his pocket watch again, setting it on his
ield desk.

He had given Monaseetah full run of the Big Creek
amp. His regiment made her welcome, watched her
protectively.

Once a day she would leap atop her pony, galloping west
o visit Cheyenne friends in the Fort Hays stockade.
Among her people, she told stories of the soldiers' winter
march to Fort Cobb, or their come-spring chase of Medicine
Arrow's Sweetwater villages. Each time she returned to
him, Custer found Monaseetah more animated and cheer-
ful, ready to jabber with him, relating the condition of every
oul in the stockade.

Everyone except the three chiefs Custer had captured on
he Sweetwater.

"They are haughty, Yellow Hair," she had grumped one
night. "They won't speak to me."

Even with a lot of coaxing, for the longest time Monaseetah would not tell him why the chiefs would not speak
o her. Her face eventually reddened with shame, her eyes
efusing to touch his, she explained. "Cheyenne warriors do
not talk to women dishonored by white men."

"Dishonored?"

"Yes," she had whispered. "I am disgraced, they say—
because I am Yellow Hair's *whore*."

Custer remembered how that had angered him. Still did,

remembering that cold rock in h is gut when he watched her lips speak those words.

He sipped his coffee, now cold, then stepped to the flaps where he flung the coffee into the muddy company street.

The Nineteenth Kansas would pull out tomorrow. Some to march east to Fort Riley, while others would push south to Fort Zarah and Fort Larned. Fewer still would ride west to Fort Wallace and Fort Dodge. They were citizen soldiers, mustered out from that army post closest to their homes and fields and families.

He'd been in camp less than a month and already Custer yearned for the thrill of the campaign trail. It was in the march itself that he felt full of purpose. Now he waited out the spring thunderstorms, fighting mosquitoes and boredom—worrying about the decision he'd long since made.

Custer turned and sat on a crude wooden bench that slid under the long plank table in his tent. Beside his rope prairie bed stuffed with a grass-filled tick squatted a low stool and a tripod where his tin washbasin sat. On a cord from the ceiling over the basin hung a small shaving glass. Still he had put off shaving the beard that had grown full and red during the winter.

From the ashwood water bucket he raised a dipper and walked to the tent flaps, sipping at the cool water, gazing west toward Fort Hays in the shimmering distance. These days he tried to keep her close. Her tent beside his, where she stayed with her infant son.

He hurt. Wondering when she'd be coming back.

Is it this way with a parent and child? he brooded.

He glanced at the calendar poking out beneath the dispatches and maps on his table. A week from Thursday

Libbie would arrive with their Negro maid, Eliza, by train from Monroe.

Since last September too much had passed between them: not only time, but distance too. . . .

Custer watched the rain batter the puddle in front of his door, mesmerized into a half-dream, recalling the winter he thought would never end, wanting her musky flesh beside him all the more.

How am I to tell him?

Her reflection danced upon the surface of Big Creek, rippling like a prairie storm, staring back at her without an answer.

Monaseetah knelt on the grassy bank, enjoying this shady sanctuary from the muggy heat. She remembered how, as a young girl, she had escaped to river or creek in the heat of the day to find there a private place to think on important things.

I must find a way to tell him.

How could she, when he had grown so angry that time she confessed her love for him? Then she had promised herself she would never utter that word again in his hearing. *Love.*

As desperately as she clung to life itself she loved this man. She had left her people, her way of life—left everything she was for him.

And now I'm afraid.

Scared of what he might say, of what he might do if she told him. Scared of losing him forever.

Somewhere nearby a pony snorted. Her body tensed as she peered from the brush, seeing no one coming. Her body relaxed, taut vigilance gone, like raindrops from greased rawhide.

She must think of the words to use. For what she had to say was not something so simple that it could be said, then forgotten. Such matters of the heart resisted her understanding as easily as pond water slipped from a crane's back.

Another moon come and gone.

She could not deny it. Eighteen summers now—no longer easy to fool herself. Instead of thinking on what should bring great joy, Monaseetah ached with dread.

She dropped her head against the cool, fragrant grass, listening to the water lap against the bank. Its merry chatter eased some of the pain in her uncertainty.

Until something deep within the dark part of her gripped her—knowing he would send her away. With the news she had to tell him, Yellow Hair would send her away.

Monaseetah realized she was crying, finding out at last what it meant to be a woman in love.

"Look at me," he begged, gripping her shoulders. "Tell me you understand."

Monaseetah sensed the plea in Custer's voice. A sound not heard often from Yellow Hair. And every time, it pulled the anger from her heart, making her soft in his hands, like the mud of the riverbank. She gazed into his eyes.

"That's better," he said. "Tell me you understand why you must live at the fort."

Instead, she dropped her eyes and shook free of his grasp. Monaseetah sat upon the prairie bed, staring at the side of the tent. Custer stroked her hair while she pouted.

"I don't know what to say to you, Monaseetah. Can't seem to make you understand that nothing's changed."

She turned back to him, her eyes flicking like wounded birds before she sunk her head in his lap.

"This wife of mine comes tomorrow. To spend the summer with me. Seven moons is a very long time for me to be apart from her. She will expect me to be very happy to see her."

"Aren't you, Yellow Hair?" Monaseetah asked boldly. "And happy to throw me away?"

"No," he whispered. "I will never throw you away. No matter what the years bring."

She believed him. As sure as the sun rose each day, Monaseetah knew he would never throw her away. Time and again he grew angry with her, telling her to go, sending her away. Yet each time he called her back, sent for her, or came to her himself. So certain of it now, she realized he must love her. Even though he was mortally afraid of telling her.

Her knowing made this tearing apart no easier.

"Come times when you make me feel like a used-up, worn-out moccasin you throw aside."

He cradled her head against him. "She comes only to visit me. Come winter, there is no place for her to stay."

She looked up into his eyes. Not sure if it was the truth she read there. Not really wanting to know if what he told her was a lie.

"When will you free my people from your prison at the fort? Send them back to their homes?"

His face registered surprise at her question. "When the villages return to the reservation. Do you wish to go home with them, Monaseetah?"

More than thinking, she concentrated on his fingertips stroking the side of her face.

"I wish to stay with you, Yellow Hair. Wherever you tell me to stay. To be near you."

He pulled her against him tightly. "I thank your Everywhere Spirit for letting you to stay with me for the time we have left."

One of the hounds poked its muzzle through the tent flaps, then leapt onto the bed as a second dog loped in. Their wet noses dove for Monaseetah's face. Custer's pets had formed a special attachment for this Cheyenne girl.

Both of them laughed, wrestling with the hounds, feeling once more the freedom to savor what time they had left. After a few minutes of play, the bitch nipped her male companion and darted from the tent. With his tongue lolling, the male joyously leapt from the bed and followed.

Alone again in the early twilight of a spring evening, Monaseetah cupped her tiny hand along Custer's smooth cheek, still not sure if she liked his bare face. Then she pulled him down to her parting lips.

Resisting a moment, Custer whispered, eyes darting to the cradleboard by the stove, "What about the child?"

"He sleeps, Yellow Hair," Monaseetah answered, pulling him down on top of her as the little life within her belly tumbled.

"The child sleeps."

Nuzzling a warm place for his cheek on the pillow, Custer feigned sleep as she slipped from the covers and padded barefoot to the trunk where her dress lay.

He had to admit, the view from this direction was mighty appealing. His half-sleepy eyes slid from the nape of her neck, across the little wings of her shoulder blades, on down to the slimness of her waist as it molded into the roundness of her heart-shaped buttocks. He'd nearly forgotten how good she looked.

And, until last night, how good she felt beside him in bed. With nothing else touching him but her heated flesh.

"Good morning, my little sunbeam!"

Whirling at the sound of his voice, Libbie swept up the flowing crinoline dress she had worn on the train from Monroe, clutching it before her to hide her nakedness.

"Why, Autie!" she squealed. "Why ever did you want to scare me like that?"

"Scare you?"

"Watching me with no clothes—not a single stitch at all. While your eyes get their fill!"

"Come now," he replied, smiling. "I haven't near seen my fill!"

She let him have it with those amber eyes of hers, eyes that could claim only to be half-mad with him for studying her body in wide-eyed admiration.

"Gracious lady, will you accept my apology?"

He slipped from the blankets, standing before Libbie without shame.

Her eyes widened before she thought to hold a hand over them. "You're terrible, Autie! Horrible to me!"

"Come, now—you've seen all of me before!"

"Not on purpose, I haven't!"

He reared back, amused at the sight of her hiding her face behind one hand while the other struggled to hold the dress over her own nakedness, nonetheless exposing her small, fine breasts.

"Here, Libbie. Let me help you get dressed."

"You'll do nothing of the kind!"

"You white women are such silly prudes."

"White women? What would you know about—" she began, then pulled her hand from her eyes, fuming suddenly. "Autie Custer, if the Good Lord intended people to be naked, he'd not invented clothing for us to wear!"

"The Lord didn't invent clothes, Rosebud! Man covers his own shame."

"And you certainly should be ashamed of yourself, Bo!" she said. "Treating a proper lady so shabbily."

"Lady! For God's sake, you're my wife!"

"You ought to treat your wife better than a common harlot."

He stopped laughing. "You didn't mind me treating you like a harlot last night."

She turned from his probing eyes, then realized in her turning he saw all the more of her. Her lips pressed into a thin, pouting line of anger, realizing he had gone and said it. What she had hoped they would never talk of again.

"Such a long time . . . for us both, husband."

"Too long, Libbie."

"Will you put your trousers on, please?"

"Can't you talk to a naked cavalry officer?"

"Not until he has his britches buttoned. While you do it, you can turn around so I can put my things on."

"All right." He sighed.

Custer plopped on the bed, pulling the gray pants over his feet. "Libbie, there's been so much time since we . . . I only thought we owed it to ourselves to try again."

"I was afraid you were going to say that this morning." She wrenched up the deep blue dress, shook it angrily, and stepped among its ample folds. "I don't want last night to become a habit with us."

"A habit?" He gulped. "A man and his wife can't enjoy each other?"

"Such activity should be preserved for the creation of God's greatest gift, a child."

"There you go with that Presbyterian drivel again!"

"A child, Autie. A child!"

"Stop right now before you get yourself worked up again. I've heard it all many times before. Isn't that why we both just stopped trying?"

"If not to create a child, what's the purpose of our intimacies?"

"Purpose? My God, Libbie—in case you haven't noticed lately, I'm a man and you're still every inch a woman! You made no complaints last night."

"That was last night." She stared solemnly at the tent wall. "I'd grown so lonely for you. Missing you."

"Do you remember the last time we made love?" he asked, stepping toward her.

She shook her head.

"Me neither. You can bet it was a long time before I left Monroe. But last night—that was as good as we've ever been together."

"I was so lonely for you, Autie." She whimpered like a wounded animal.

He clutched her shoulders. "We can grow close once more. Sharing our bodies again as we—"

"We don't need that!"

Custer's hands slipped from her shoulders. "No, I suppose we don't." He was weary of it already. He turned away, defeated. "I had hoped—"

"I quit hoping long ago, Autie." She swept one of his hands up in hers. "Quit hoping for a child that would draw us even closer together. Please," she begged. "The kindest, most loving thing you can do for me is to forget being intimate with me. You must understand how cruel it is—the guilt I suffer this morning—for what I did last night."

"For making love to me? With everything you are as a woman?"

"Yes," she answered firmly. "I can't have a child. *We* can't have a child. And each time we make love, I'm reminded that I'm just a little less as a woman, a little less as a wife to you." She gazed up at him as he brushed a strand of chestnut hair from her eyes.

"Autie, you can't want to remind me of the horror and revulsion I feel for my own body's failure to bear your children!"

Libbie collapsed against him, tears boiling up from some incomplete place down in her being. He stroked her long chestnut hair.

Soon she'll pin it up around her face, he knew. But for now, it flows over her shoulders, rumpled from our night together. Hair long and flowing like—

He tried to shove the other out of his mind. Feeling like a sham dodger, holding Libbie, thinking of Monaseetah.

"All right," he whispered, beaten. Such a hard thing to do, this drawing back from the woman he had fallen in love with when he was ten years old. Too painful for him to dredge up all those hopes and dreams any longer—those prayers that Libbie would be all things to him.

"It's settled, Libbie."

He felt her arms squeeze about him reassuringly. Lord, but he loved this frail, insecure woman so much at times. And others, he wanted her gone from his life. Her and the

constant reminder that she believed he was at fault. That
he was the reason she was barren.

"I promise, Libbie."

Custer gazed out through the narrow slit in the tent
flaps, mesmerized by the line of gold and brown prairie
melting in a haze against the cornflower blue sky. A land
much bigger than any man. Surely bigger than any problem
that might threaten to overwhelm him.

Looking at that shimmering horizon where the green and
gold of the shortgrass rising from the brown flesh of the
prairie to meet the caress of the morning sky just like a
woman's breasts rose to her lover, Custer knew he had
fallen in love with another.

CHAPTER 28

"Is this the place the Injins is kep', Ginnel?"

Custer smiled, bouncing on the seat of the freight wagon he had borrowed for this trip to Fort Hays from the Big Creek camp. *Dear Eliza*.

Keeping much of her childlike and beguiling innocence down through their years together since that first autumn of '64. A freed Virginia slave, she was only seventeen then. His cook ever since. Now housekeeper for Libbie. Custer couldn't imagine doing without her.

"Yes, Eliza. *Wild* Indians."

As Eliza glanced away, Custer winked at Libbie.

"'Cain't wait, Ginnel. Able to tell all I know that Eliza see'd a real live blood-tastin' Cheyenne warrior!"

"Not the warriors you have to keep an eye on," he whispered mysteriously with another wink at Libbie. "It's the women-folk who're the sneakiest of all. Why, you don't know when they might slip up behind you"—he slapped both reins into one hand—"and poke a knife right atween your ribs!"

With the empty hand he jabbed his imaginary knife at Eliza. Gasping in horror, she clutched a hand to her breast and tumbled back against the sideboard of Lieutenant Bell's freight wagon he had borrowed for their trip to Fort Hays.

"Autie!" Libbie yelped, giggling. "You're so cruel to Eliza! Scaring her witless!"

"You scared witless, Eliza?" he asked.

"Me, Ginnel?" She sat straight, flashing teeth yellowed like old ivory set within her ebony cheeks. "No, the Ginnel's quite the kidder, Miz Libbie," Eliza said. "Never know when he mean it, and when he don't. Anythin' at'all . . . he might'n be pullin' my leg."

"But I've never pulled hard enough to pull it off," Custer added.

"Why, Ginnel—there you go at me again!" she exclaimed.

"Yes," Libbie said with a sigh. "We just don't know what to expect of him next, do we?"

Custer watched something strange cross Libbie's face, before she gazed down the road once more. Whatever it was, it had made him cold. Here beneath a bright June sun. Clouds like tiny sailing ships adrift upon the expanse of a blue-domed sea. And her putting this cold knot in his gut.

"There it is," he announced as they neared the outskirts of the buildings. "Now, Eliza, you best be careful around those squaws. I don't want to lose my Black-Eyed Pea."

"Black-Eyed Pea?" Libbie asked.

"The Ginnel called me that back in the war, Miz Libbie. When he was just a freckle-faced soldier boy."

"Not a boy any longer, Eliza." He flashed her his grin. "You just watch yourself, 'cause I may hand you over to them Cheyenne squaws myself—let them find out just how good darkie meat can taste slow-broiled!"

Eliza yelped in mock pain as he pinched her cheek. "Oh, Ginnel! You are a one!"

"Thank you, Eliza," he answered. "At least you're happy you came to Kansas to see me."

Libbie tired hard, but couldn't suppress her giggle behind the gloved fingers she held to her lips. "From the impression I got my first night in camp, Mr. Custer"—and she winked at him wickedly—"I was led to believe you were really happy to see me!"

He felt like a schoolboy propped stiffly on a park bench beside a young schoolgirl named Elizabeth Bacon, who persisted in prodding him to admit that he really did like her best of all.

"You did show me, Autie," she whispered. "Despite everything that's troubling us, I still know you're truly happy to have me with you again."

Libbie slipped an arm through his. Custer steered the wagon past the post entrance, saluting the guards as he passed.

On the east side of the huge open compound that formed Fort Hays stood a large fenced stockade where several large wall tents squatted in the sun like ugly toads. From the open-air prison rose the sound of children's laughter. Several brown youngsters, naked save for breechclouts, chased one another in play.

"The Injins over there, Ginnel?"

Custer eased back on the reins. "We don't dare let them out to roam the fort, I'm afraid. They'd finish off all the dogs we have once they devour every old horse we butcher for them. I'm warning you, 'Liza—keep your eyes open for any old harpy carrying a knife your way!"

"Nawww!" she giggled. "I'm way too old for them Cheyennes to eat, Ginnel. Way too tough, and stringy too!"

This time he laughed aloud.

Yes, he thought, *feels good to laugh with Libbie and Eliza again. Like the good old days.*

Something raised the hairs at the back of Libbie's neck. Downright scared, she stuck to Custer like horse glue once they had left the wagon behind. On the other hand, Eliza seemed more curious than frightened, strolling ahead of the young couple, rambling here and there to see everything and everybody.

The squaws pressed close when the trio had walked past the guards at the gate. Both Libbie and Eliza had huddled behind Custer like buffalo calves in a wolf attack, until he scolded the Indian women, backing them off. One by one the squaws inched up, touching Custer's cheek lovingly, crooning their songs and murmuring their soft sentiments.

Before Custer could begin the tour, an old woman with skin wrinkled like puckered rawhide stopped squarely in front of him. With cloudy, rheumy eyes she studied Libbie's face, then cocked her head to assess Eliza.

"These women belong to you, Yellow Hair?"

"They do not belong to me, old one. On my arm is my wife," Custer grappled to speak with his limited Cheyenne.

"The other? She is your left-hand woman?"

"No. She is helper to my wife." Custer watched Libbie's face, knowing she did not understand their talk.

"Like a left-hand woman helps in Cheyenne lodges."

"No," he cut her off. "Not my left-hand woman."

"It is good," the nearly toothless mouth replied. "Monaseetah remains your second wife."

"Monaseetah is not my wife. She does not live with me as a woman lives with her husband."

The old one wagged her head and smiled. "Fool others, Yellow Hair. Monaseetah rode the long winter trail with you, warming your robes each night. As a woman does for her man."

Custer's eyes bounced over the gathering crowd of prisoners. "She is special to me, yes. But Monaseetah is not married to me. I am married to this woman."

Rolling her cracked lips across her old gums, the wrinkled squaw mulled that over like she would chew toothless on a stringy strand of horse haunch. "Yellow Hair likes having two wives. When one offends, he can throw her away—still having a wife for his robes. You use too much wind saying Monaseetah is not your wife. We know she warmed your robes all winter gone. If you do not want her, give her away to some man who will love her."

"She is not mine to give away."

"Why not throw this one away?" The old woman pointed a bony finger at Libbie. "She is too skinny! She is not full and rounded like Monaseetah. And she looks mean, Yellow Hair. She must surely have a rock beneath her breast instead of a heart. Yellow Hair, this one is not for you."

Custer shoved past the old woman abruptly, pulling Libbie with him.

"Yellow Hair!" the old one shrieked. "Throw this skinny white woman away and finish all the seasons of your life with a real woman—Monaseetah!"

Custer shoved through the crowd, Libbie straining at his arm.

"What's this all about, Autie?" Libbie whispered, peering up at him with frightened, birdlike eyes.

"Nothing," he answered abruptly. "She just wants to know when her people are going home."

"Are they going home soon?"

"As soon as possible," he answered, sweat rolling down his spine.

"Ginnel!"

Custer turned to find Eliza surrounded by children and women. A few of the bravest youngsters licked and rubbed their fingers across Eliza's cheeks, neck, and hands. She stood paralyzed, afraid to move.

"Just relax," Custer said.

"But . . . they lickin' on me!"

Custer waded into the crowd alone, chattering in Cheyenne, shaming the Indians for their rudeness with his guests. Eliza was shaking by the time he reached her.

"What they wanna skeer 'Liza for? Only talkin' to the lil' chirrun, Ginnel!"

"You're a wonder to 'em. They've never seen a Negro before."

"What they rubbin' on me for?"

"They were trying to rub the black off."

"Cain't rub that off, Ginnel!" She grinned big as Sunday.

"I realize that, but they paint themselves black to celebrate victory in war. They think you're wearing paint."

He turned to those who passed close. "Go on, now. It is not paint."

The women and children began to turn away, staring at their fingertips as if searching for a reason no paint rubbed off the strange woman who had come with Yellow Hair.

When Custer turned, Libbie was nowhere to be found.

With his heart in his throat, he caught a glimpse of her, twenty yards away at the center of a small group of women cloaked in their army blankets.

"Libbie!" He scurried over. "You had me worried, there—"

At his voice, the women around Libbie turned. One set of eyes fluttered up to his. Monaseetah's.

"Bo!" Libbie greeted him. "This young woman's just given me this beautiful bag."

"Which one?"

"This one," Libbie pointed out a middle-aged squaw, "she says the pretty young one wants me to have it."

He watched Monaseetah scurrying to a tent before he asked the woman, "Do you give the pouch to my wife?"

"It is a gift," the woman answered in Cheyenne. "To the first wife of Yellow Hair. I give it since Monaseetah herself has nothing to give *Hiestzi*'s first wife."

"It's a gift for you, Libbie," he stammered.

"Everything Monaseetah had is gone now," the woman explained. "Pony soldiers burned everything she owned."

"Thank you for the gift," he stammered.

Monaseetah emerged from the tent, her hair brushed, the dull army blanket traded for her favorite red blanket. She pressed close to the couple, gazing into Custer's eyes.

"Libbie . . ." He gulped, sweat trickling down his spine. "This is the young squaw I wrote you about. Monaseetah—The Young Grass that Shoots Up in Spring."

"The woman who helped guide your last campaign?" Libbie asked, appraising Monaseetah.

"The same."

"She's more beautiful than you described in your letter." Libbie gave her husband a sidelong glance that would have made even an innocent man shudder. "Everything you described—the high color of her cheeks, those pearl-like teeth. But where is her child?"

Custer turned to Monaseetah. "Please bring your child to us."

Instead of going herself, she had one of the older women bring the child to her. Monaseetah gently drew back the blanket from the infant's face.

Libbie smiled, cooing. Straightening, she held her arms out, showing Monaseetah her desire to hold the infant. "With that black hair and those dark eyes, make no mistake about it—he's a little Indian!" she gushed.

Custer watched Monaseetah push through the crowd, headed for the tents.

"His father was a Cheyenne warrior?" Libbie asked.

"Yes. He escaped my noose at the Washita."

Monaseetah swirled back, holding a small sepia-toned daguerreotype she presented for Custer's inspection.

"A photographer visited the post several weeks ago," he explained. "Evidently the fellow became so entranced with Monaseetah that he shot her without a fee."

Libbie studied him. "Make no mistake, Autie. She is an extremely attractive, highly provocative woman." Then Libbie appraised the Cheyenne mother. "I'm getting quite tired now. Will you drive us back to Big Creek, where I can nap before supper?"

"Of course. Give the child to its mother, Libbie."

Monaseetah shook her head and smiled, holding the tintype close to her breast. "Tell her she can keep the child."

"Keep him?" Custer squeaked.

"Yes, Yellow Hair," Monaseetah answered as if it were

the most natural thing in the world for her to offer. "Your
first wife has no child. She can keep my son until I return
to my people."

"But she can't do that! He's not her child."

"Does she not want a child?" Monaseetah inquired.
"Some Cheyenne men will take another wife when one
can't give them sons. Is this not the way with your people?"

"No. It is not the wish of Yellow Hair." He took the child
from Libbie's arms and placed the boy in Monaseetah's,
seeing something wounded cross her dark eyes.

"I am sorry. I want to return to you," he explained. "To
tell you why she cannot keep your baby."

"Come back, Yellow Hair," she whispered. "I must talk
with you soon."

"I'll return." Custer shoved through the crowd, pulling
Libbie to his side, looking over his shoulder at Monaseetah.

"Custer!"

Having swept the two women out of the stockade and
across the parade, then into the freight wagon, Custer
turned. He saw a big man stepping off the porch in front of
headquarters.

"Colonel Miles. A genuine surprise, sir." He saluted.

Nelson A. Miles, commander of the Fifth Infantry,
stepped into the dust and hardened ruts of the parade.
"Ladies." He nodded courteously at the women in the
wagon, tipping his hat. "Can I assign you an escort for your
trip back to Big Creek?"

"No need for that, Colonel. I appreciate your offer."

"Truth is—" Miles leaned in close to the near side of the
wagon so that he might whisper in private to Custer, "Mary
would skin me two ways of Sunday if she found out I hadn't

made a point of offering you an escort for your Elizabeth. Seems my wife's quite taken with your bride."

Custer glanced at Libbie. Just beyond, his eyes focused on the prisoner compound. At the stockade wall a young woman held an infant to her breast. A warm breeze tugged at her hair like the tall stalks of buffalo grass beneath a summer sky.

"Please pass my compliments on to your wife," Custer said, leaping onto the seat beside Libbie.

Miles stepped back from the wagon. His eyes narrowed as he appraised the hero of the Washita. "I will, Armstrong."

Custer snapped the team into motion, quartering the mules in a wide arc around the parade, pointing them east.

"Autie?" Libbie scooted closer as they wheeled past the stockade, slipping her arm beneath his. "Why did those women make such a fuss over my hat?"

He glanced up, studying the hat, set at a jaunty tilt atop her curls. "The bird, dear."

"What of it?"

"Going into battle, a warrior will often wear a stuffed bird tied to his head. As his special medicine helper. Perhaps they thought your bird served the same purpose."

"A medicine helper, Eliza. I'm a Cheyenne warrior!"

Eliza threw her head back and wailed like a wild, hard-riding warrior. "Aiyii-yii-yii!" She and Libbie fell against one another laughing as Custer steered the wagon onto the prairie.

"They liked my boots, too, Autie."

He looked at the strain perhaps only he could read in her eyes. *Perhaps the whole encounter was a bit much for her*, he thought.

This further confirmed his belief that Libbie didn't belong out here in the wilderness. She had married an army officer, but she was the sort of army wife who belonged at some eastern duty station. *The wilderness will take Libbie's kind of woman, gobble her up, and spit her right out.*

"Dear, Rosebud—they'd trade many pair of moccasins for those high-button boots wrapped around your perfect little feet."

"You think my feet are attractive, Autie?" She lifted her skirt and petticoats, turning her boots this way, then that.

"Yes, dear. Very."

"Every bit as pretty as Monaseetah's feet?"

He was sure his expression did not betray him. "Every bit as pretty. If not more so."

Libbie snuggled against him.

After some minutes, he said, "They admire you."

"Admire Miz Libbie for what, Ginnel?" Eliza asked.

"The women take pity on her as my only wife." He turned to Libbie. "Meaning they think you do all the work yourself."

"Did you tell them I had Eliza to help?"

"I told them since you weren't any good at chopping wood and hauling water, tanning hides or making dogmeat stew, I had to take Eliza as my second wife!"

Eliza's hand flew to her mouth in astonishment. Libbie drew back, wall-eyed, regarding him. On cue, they both beat him with their fists, giggling merrily, getting in their licks for his constant teasing.

Custer cowered beneath an arm, laughing. For the moment he was happy just as he was, not wanting anything to change, to disturb this delicate, precarious balance long maintained in his life.

He gazed across the hills, sienna beneath the late afternoon light, looking at that hazy, ever-distant line no man could ever touch . . . and wondered just what happiness a man could find out there.

No man had ever touched that place where this land met the never-ending sky: a place so far away, yet as close as the crest of the next hill.

"Colonel Custer. One of the prisoners wants a word with you, sir."

Custer turned from his horse, watching one of the stockade guards trot in his direction. The soldier's blue tunic was blotched with coronas of sweat salt, a damp necklace staining his chest.

"One of the chiefs?"

"No, sir. A woman."

That almost stopped Custer dead in his tracks. "A woman, you say."

"Young'un. That'un, sir."

Where the soldier pointed, Custer found her waiting for him behind the stockade fence, peering between the rough-hewn planks.

"Open the gate," Custer ordered. He slipped inside, listening as the huge wooden gate slammed shut behind him. She ran to his side. Beneath the summer sun, Monaseetah wore only the doeskin dress, now smudged and greasy. His heart hurt for her, finding her treated no better than a common prisoner.

For a moment he studied her as he would appraise something new. Then he realized it was the long braids rolled on either side of her head.

"Your hair," he gestured.

"Yes," she answered. "The soldier cook showed me last robe season."

"Mrs. McNeil."

"Mac-Neil, yes," she answered.

There was a long, nervous moment as she fell silent, staring into his eyes. How he wanted to sweep her into his arms, wipe the soot from her cheeks, and kiss her neck. He fought the impulse. His breath came harder and his heart pounded faster.

"Come," she whispered. "We find a quiet place to talk. Some shade."

In a little corner of the stockade, tucked beneath a bastion of the compound, they found privacy. Here Custer swept Monaseetah into his arms, hungrily crushing her to him, as if never to let her go.

"I've missed you, Yellow Hair," she sobbed against his chest.

He sensed the delicate tremble of her shoulder blades, like the fluttering wings of a small, helpless bird attempting flight.

"Many times have I wanted to come to you, Monaseetah."

She pressed two fingertips against his lips. "This first wife of yours—she keeps you happy?"

"She gives me what she can of herself."

"So many times since that day she was here, I have thought . . . she is going to have a child for you."

He smiled down at her. "No. She is not to have my child." He watched the smile widen on her lips, brightening her whole face. When the tears rolled down her cheeks, he understood.

What relief she must feel that I'm not having a child with

Libbie, to leave Monaseetah like some discarded distraction who filled some otherwise empty hours.

"You are happy she is not carrying my child?" Custer asked.

She could only nod, choking on a sob.

"You believed I would throw you away?"

Monaseetah reached up, clamping her arms around his neck as would a drowning person. Not daring to let go.

He pulled her down beside him against the wall, holding her as if she were a young child seeking shelter in his arms.

"She and I," he explained, "cannot have children. Long have we tried. It is not to be."

She gazed up at his sunburned face, his bushy eyebrows burnished red-gold like the summer-burned grasses before the first autumn frost. Already little wrinkles marked the corners of his eyes like heron tracks on the wet sands of a riverbank. She wanted their child to have his eyes.

"Perhaps, because this wife of yours cannot have children, Yellow Hair thinks *he* cannot have children."

"We have tried for so long."

"This woman with the pale skin—she is the one who cannot bear a child."

He looked at her strangely. "How can you be so sure of this?"

Instead of speaking, Monaseetah took his rough hand and guided it to her soft, rounded hip, gliding it across to the mound of her belly. The little life within kicked against its father's touch.

He yanked his hand away, afraid. Shaking his head. Refusing to believe.

"It is true, Yellow Hair. This is your child. He moves for you now—to show you."

"This cannot be my child."

"Your wife cannot bear a child, Yellow Hair—but your loins are strong. Her body is dead inside, shriveled like a dry, brittle flower—hardened against the coming of winter. My body is made to give life to children. Your children, Yellow Hair."

She took his hand, placed it on her belly. "I am meant to carry your child. My body is dark and fertile, like the soil. Many times you dropped your seed on that fertile ground."

"Stop it!"

As he said it, he knew she told the truth. The many times he had crawled atop her young body, taking his pleasure there. Now, it was all jumbled inside him: the relief of knowing he could have a child, the fear of having a child of his own, the fear of Libbie finding out. Always the fear . . .

He looked at her. Afraid most of all of losing Monaseetah.

"I wanted Yellow Hair happy with this news," she pleaded.

"Happy? Yes, I am happy. You are sure? I am the child's father?" As he said it, he saw the wounded fawn in her eyes.

"There is no doubt in my heart, Yellow Hair. You have been the only one. No other seed but Yellow Hair's grows within me."

He ran his palm over her belly, feeling it tumble in response to his touch. "It moves . . . so much."

"More than my first child," she replied. "It could have no other father. This little one moves as you do."

"Like his father."

"Your child will be born in the Moon of Black Calves.

The moon when the buffalo born in spring finally shed their coats of red."

"Fall?"

"Before *Hoimaha* comes to lay a blanket of white across the prairie with his vengeance upon the land." She laid her hand atop his. "I am five moons now. This child is halfway to greeting its father, Yellow Hair."

"It comes so soon."

His brow knitted as he paused, considering, brooding. He must find some way to return her to the Cheyenne reservation before she grew so large there would be questions. *Besides*, he told himself, *she will be much safer there among her own people.* And he would be safer with her having their child away from white eyes.

"I must find a way to return you to your people," he told her.

"But I am with my people. And you are here. I will stay."

"No, it is for the best. This child cannot be born among the white men. I fear for its safety."

"Someone would harm our child?"

"Perhaps." Custer sighed. "Among the Cheyenne, children of many colors are adopted all the time. As Romero was when he was a child."

"Yes, I understand that."

"But it is different among whites. To them, our child would be nothing more than a half-breed." He did not like the taste of that word on his tongue.

"He would not live well in your world, Yellow Hair?"

"Far better that he grow up Indian, among those who will accept him."

"Your people would harm our child?" Her eyes filled with fear.

"He might be a curiosity for a time. The half-breed child of Yellow Hair, the great Indian fighter."

"If the child is a girl?"

"She would be treated poorly. Perhaps used by some man, then discarded."

"If our child is Yellow Hair's son . . ."

"Worse yet. He would not be allowed to be his own man. He would always be threatened by men who thought less of him because of his Indian blood. Especially those who wanted to attack me by attacking my son. He would never be his own person, but instead a spirit without a home."

There was but one choice. Monaseetah had to leave for the reservation and raised their child among the Cheyenne.

"Monaseetah, it rests with you to see that our child grows strong."

He clutched her shoulders more tightly than ever before. She winced in pain beneath the iron of his grip.

"What of you, Yellow Hair? Will you come see your child?"

Custer sensed something more painful than fear in her voice. "I will come see my child. Before he grows to be a man."

"When will I see you next?"

"I will come soon. I must hurry, to plan the return of your people to their reservation. Sooner than I had hoped. I did not want you to go."

At the gate, she looked for prying eyes before taking Custer's freckled hand in hers, again pressing his palm against her belly.

"See?" she giggled softly. "The little one kicks for you."

"This second child, Monaseetah—*will* it be a boy?"

She closed her eyes, as if heeding some mystical voice within her. "Yes, Yellow Hair will have a son."

CHAPTER 29

"Hey, Autie!" Tom Custer stood with several other young officers, waving him over. "You gotta hear this story Yates is telling."

"Good to have you back from furlough, George," Custer said to Yates. "How was Monroe?"

"Perfect as ever, General. No better hometown in all this great land."

"What's this story you were recounting for the boys?"

"I was telling about California Joe. Soon as you mustered him out, he was determined to have a ride on a train. Bought a ticket east to Leavenworth. Watched him sitting at his window seat like a boy handed some penny candy, eyes big as a schoolhouse clock when that steam whistle blew and they dumped sand under the wheels. He must've figured that was about the grandest thing he'd ever done— getting pulled along without mule nor horse."

"You rode east with him?"

"Not exactly. Bumped onto him in Hays City when I laid over for an hour of switching engines. Found him right in front of Drum's Saloon—or maybe it was John Bitter's place."

The staccato of pounding hooves drew their attention down company row.

"General Custer!"

Three horsemen galloped up to the group, horses lathered.

The sergeant among them saluted. "Danged happy to catch up with you. Begging pardon, sir."

The mounts snorted and stamped, prancing sideways, fractious with the closeness of so many men on foot.

"What is it, Sergeant?"

"There's been a disturbance among the prisoners, sir."

"Prisoners?"

The sergeant nodded, catching his breath. "The three chiefs calling for *Ouchess*. Colonel Miles says they mean you."

Tom stepped up. "That's Cheyenne for Creeping Panther."

"What about the prisoners?" Custer asked.

"Them three bucks you brought from the Sweetwater, sir. Fat Bear, Big Head, and Dull Knife. Been some stabbings. A little shooting too. Colonel Miles sent me to fetch you, sir."

"Moylan! Someone, bring me a fresh mount. Saddled or not—just bring me a horse!" He asked the sergeant, "Any other casualties?"

"Can tell for sure, sir. Time I left, no one gone in the stockade. Injuns running all about in there. No soldier would be safe to check on them Cheyenne, you see."

A horse was led to him. Custer lunged to the saddle in a fluid motion, pivoting the animal into the company street between rows of tents. With a leap, the horse wheeled and galloped away, followed by the sergeant, caught by surprise at Custer's sudden departure.

Clouds of yellow dust burst from the hooves as Custer haunch-slid the animal to a halt on the sun-baked parade near the prisoner stockade. His pale eyes scanned the milling captives for some sign of Monaseetah. Tossing the reins to a nearby trooper, he started to dart away when Miles called out "Custer!"

"Colonel! What in tunket's going on here?"

"The prisoners—"

"Anyone killed?" Custer stammered, anxious.

"Don't know for sure."

"How the devil did it start?"

"Near as we make out, for days now the prisoners have been led to believe there were other Cheyenne in the area who've come up to rescue them from the stockade."

"Why, there's not a bloody Cheyenne within a hundred miles of here!"

"We know that! But the goddamned prisoners didn't." Miles ground his teeth a moment, watching Custer seethe. "Seems one of our Indian scouts thought he'd have some fun with the captives, so he started the rumor."

"Did the prisoners attempt to break out?"

Miles shook his head. "When I learned of the goddamned rumor, I thought I should put the chiefs in the guardhouse, until things simmered down a bit."

Custer glanced over to the raw-boarded building. "You got them locked up?"

"We didn't get that far."

"What the blazes you mean?"

"My sergeant who was escorting the chiefs never learned

a word of Cheyenne, so he couldn't explain things to the chiefs."

"What difference does that make?"

"Goddammit, Custer! The chiefs thought we were taking them out to a hanging!"

Custer shook his head. "So they decided to die like warriors rather than at the end of a rope. What happened?"

"All hell broke loose. Squaws came up, surrounding the sergeant's men and the chiefs. One of the soldiers put a bayonet against Dull Knife's ribs, to prod him to the gate. But the old chief just stood there like a stone. They all watched as that bayonet pushed through the blanket into his ribs. As soon as the squaws saw blood on the old man's blanket, the knives came out."

"Where'd they get weapons?"

"Hell if I know. We didn't search a damned one after they were brought north from Camp Supply. Could be they were mess knives sharpened on stones."

"Any of our men dead?"

"Not yet. One sergeant gutted pretty bad. Lippincott tells me he may not see the morning."

"Any others?"

"The lieutenant—officer of the day. He heard the commotion and came running. Got a knife in his neck for his trouble. Blood gushing over his tunic. All hell broke out. The troops fired across the compound."

"Dear God!"

"In all the excitement, I'm glad no more than the one was killed."

"Killed? Who?" Custer grabbed Miles's tunic.

"A chief. Big Head, we believe. A bullet through the heart."

"But you don't know if anyone else in there is bleeding or dead."

"No, that's why I sent for you. Way they're worked up, you're the only one can go in there now."

"What about Fat Bear?"

"Knocked out cold—a rifle butt to the jaw."

Custer dashed to the stockade gate. "Open up!" he called to the guards.

"But General. I ain't got orders—"

"Open those gates or I'll open up the side of your head!" He shoved aside the sergeant's rifle. "The rest of you brave soldiers . . .   What can those Cheyenne in there do to you boys out here—penned up as they are, like cattle for the slaughter?"

The gate opened slightly at the sergeant's urging. Custer dove through, hearing the clunk of wood on wood as the gate clattered shut behind him.

"Custer!"

He turned, finding Miles at the wall. "For God's sake, come out until things simmer down."

"Things won't simmer down on their own."

"Watch out, Custer!"

Custer whirled at Miles's warning. Cheyenne squaws crept toward him from all sides like sheep, their eyes wary, watchful of the soldiers at the stockade walls. Fear and panic glistened in every eye. Like the eyes of trapped animals.

Two dozen ringed him, jabbering excitedly. He waved them quiet. "Monaseetah?"

"She comes, Yellow Hair," said one old woman, her earlobes tattered from earrings pulled out across the years.

"She is hurt?"

"No one saw her hurt," another squaw answered.

"Will the soldiers shoot us, Yellow Hair?"

"We only protected our chiefs," another explained.

He said. "The soldiers will not kill you."

"It is true," one old woman exhorted the others. "These soldiers will not shoot women down in cold blood like buffalo caught in a narrow valley."

"They came to hang our chiefs!" an old one shrieked.

"No." Custer pointed to the guardhouse across the parade. "They were taking your men to the little house."

He saw Monaseetah hurrying to him across the sun-baked compound. The women parted for her respectfully, as Yellow Hair's woman.

"You are safe?" he asked, clutching her shoulders.

"I am not harmed." A hand went to her belly. "Bullets close." She pulled aside a flap of her blanket, the red one she had worn since that freezing morning beside the Washita.

In a fold of the crimson wool he saw a shabby beam of sunlight pour through the bullet hole. Anger scraped across his bowels. Now, more than ever, he had to get her out of Hays. Far from here.

An old woman shoved her way through the crowd, showing him three bullet holes in her blanket. With a gnarled finger she made a pistol, imitating the whistling bullets zinging around her during the fracus. "Ping! Ping!"

"Yes," he replied. "No more shooting now. No more—ever."

Monaseetah pressed against him. There were no easy answers to any of this. Yet, as a man hopes for spring in the cold heart of winter, he realized this tragedy held the solution he had been seeking. Now he could send her south.

"There are no Indians coming to rescue you," he explained. "Yellow Hair made you his prisoner. Only Yellow Hair can free you."

He gestured to Monaseetah. "Even she will tell you how Yellow Hair rode alone into the camp of the great Medicine Arrow. Yet no warrior touched a hair on my head."

Monaseetah nodded in agreement. Her gesture set the women wailing and keening. Tears slid down the deep crevices of their old faces. There was no escape.

"Yellow Hair is mightier than all our warriors!" one old woman shrieked.

"Mightier than our chiefs!" another wailed, ripping at her hair in mourning.

One by one they wandered off to begin their self-mutilation for the dead and wounded. Slashing arms and legs, blood oozing into the sticky, red mud at their feet. They hacked at their hair and chopped off fingertips. Above it all hung a keening wail like a winter wind through dead and dying trees.

"Where is the body of Big Head?" Custer asked her.

"He is with Dull Knife," Monaseetah said. "Come."

She pulled aside the flaps of the weather-grayed canvas wall tent for him. As his eyes adjusted to the light, he saw women huddled on the floor, quietly sobbing. Blinking in the dust, Custer made out two chiefs laid upon blankets. Around each body was a cluster of old squaws.

Custer knelt beside Big Head—this tall, gray-headed warrior he had determined to hold at all costs beside the Sweetwater. A winter day, so long ago. Bringing Big Head here, far from his people's land . . . and for what?

He cursed himself for the foolishness of others.

If a man is to die, shouldn't he fall as he's lived? As a warrior, protecting his homeland and the weak ones?

This was the irony of Big Head's death. *Falling with no glory. A victim of folly and stupidity.*

Custer bent, touched Big Head's brow where the women had painted his face with bear grease pigments. That touch was the closest thing to a Cheyenne prayer he could offer.

With a sigh, he turned to Dull Knife.

The old chief opened his thick-lidded, glazed eyes. Feebly, he waved, moving the old women back.

"I am not dead yet," he whispered with a fluid rasp.

Custer recognized that unmistakable rattle in the old man's chest, those flecks of pink foam dotting the Indian's tongue. Death itself etched the old man's weathered face.

"We only wanted to—" Dull Knife hacked up bits of lung and blood, spitting them into a smelly rag an old woman held beside his wet lips. "Yellow Hair . . . we wanted to be guarded by your pony soldiers."

"Dull Knife must not work so hard," Custer replied.

The old Indian's strength faded with every breath. The war chief smiled weakly. "The walk-a-heap soldiers did not know the signs to talk with us. These who have killed us this day will never know the sadness I feel for them."

Dull Knife hacked up more bits of lung into the red rag. "I feel more pity for the young soldiers who killed us than for my old friend Big Head. We were children together. We stole our first ponies together. Now these walk-a-heaps, mere children, have killed two old Dog Soldiers by accident."

"I promise you will be guarded by pony soldiers now."

"Yellow Hair promises this?" His glazed eyes narrowed.

"Yes. I promise."

"Your word is worthless, Yellow Hair. You have cursed yourself. Medicine Arrow . . . all of us were there in his lodge when you cursed yourself."

"There is no curse!"

Dull Knife tried to focus on those winter-blue eyes. Recalling a winter none of them had believed would ever end. . . .

"Remember, Yellow Hair—attack a village of women and children, then you and all your children will die."

"We did not attack you today!" Custer argued.

"I do not speak of this day," Dull Knife answered, his eyelids drooping. "Come a time, soldier folly will bring your end. Just as my time comes before the sun leaves the sky."

"No, Dull Knife!" Custer shouted at the body sagging in his arms. "You cannot die. I will see you returned to the homeland of your people!"

The black-cherry eyes peered into an unseen distance. Down the long, last trail.

"I will never see my home again, Yellow Hair. Already I am on the road to the other side. I will not see my people again. Only the ones who have gone before. There I will be with Big Head, where he already rides a strong pony. Once more we will raid for sleek horses. And drink clear, sweet water so cold it makes my mouth hurt. Not this warm, bitter water your soldiers give us to drink in this stinking hole of death."

Custer heard the rattle, saw it shake the Indian's huge frame.

"This hole, Yellow Hair—where we Cheyenne cannot travel beneath the sky, across the breast of the Mother of Us All as Cheyenne were meant to journey. You make us live on reservations, and soon that place begins to stink with our being there too long, like this prison. Yellow Hair, I would rather die a free man than live in a stinking hole like you white men.

"Everywhere I look in that land where I go, my people are happy. They do not have to look upon the face of the white man, who breaks all promises. I no longer live with a sad heart."

With the quickness of a swallow's wings, Dull Knife's eyelids fluttered and closed. Pink froth oozed from his lips.

An old woman bent her head to his chest. She brought her eyes to Custer, wrinkling them behind the smoky incense of burning sweetgrass braids the women offered in prayer. She raised her face and voice to the heavens. High and eerie, her melancholy song rose from the tent.

Grappling with his own rage, Custer scooped the dead chief into his arms. Clutching the limp frame to his breast as he rocked back and forth. Spitting his words while salty tears scorched his eyes.

"They were going home! With God's next breath, these men were going home! Why . . . ?"

Something inside Custer told him more than just an old Indian had died. Something more precious than any one man's life.

"By all that's holy—these Cheyenne will go home now!"

As he stared into Dull Knife's face, peaceful now in death, Custer came to believe that a flickering hope had been extinguished. A hope he had long hidden.

Nine days later, on 11 June, fifty-four Cheyenne prisoners were herded together and told they would leave for their homeland in the south at dawn the next day.

Speaking through an interpreter, Colonel Nelson A. Miles was disappointed to find less than celebration from the Cheyenne with his announcement—until he realized this journey to freedom had come a few days late.

Too late for Big Head and Dull Knife, too late for the others who would return south whole of body but weak in spirit. South to the reservations, where the bands of Medicine Arrow and Little Robe awaited them. Fifty-three had marched north from the Washita. Three more were captured on the Sweetwater.

Two bodies, bound in blankets and rawhide strips, lay putrefying in the steamy shade beneath the west wall of the stockade. Two old chiefs heading home for burial in the old way, in the homeland of ages past.

Romero had appealed to Custer, who sent him on to Miles with his blessings. The Fort Hays commandant had immediately agreed that the intepreter could take himself a Cheyenne wife who had fallen in love with him. To Miles's way of thinking, the squaw would have a better life with Romero than she could ever have on that parched reservation of the Cheyenne.

That evening before the rest of the prisoners would start south, Romero waited, as anxious as a virgin on her wedding night, at the stockade gate for his bride. As a purple band of twilight streaked the warm land, she was freed. Romero tramped west and north with his woman, Fort Hays disappearing behind them. Neither one ever looked back.

Custer watched sadly from the guardhouse along the western wall of the stockade as the pair rode straight for the sinking, red sun. Like beetles scurrying from the light, they disappeared into the hills of gold and brown, brittle-red earth and creeks of lazy blue-green. A pair of riders reaching for that place where the great beckoning land touched the sky . . . out there far, far beyond.

Somewhere between earth and sky.

At last Custer realized the ache upon his own heart was for the coming loneliness. An ache in their parting. A cruel tearing of flesh from flesh as painful as any gaping, bleeding wound—an agony he had no way of healing.

CHAPTER 30

For days he vowed he wouldn't make a fool of himself at her leaving.

Yet here Custer stood like some moonstruck young warrior, watching for a last glimpse of Monaseetah among the prisoners milling anxiously about in the stockade.

Beneath that dawn-pale light of a thumbnail moon hung limp in the western sky, the Cheyenne had taken Colonel Miles at his word. They were ready to leave at sunrise.

Custer had killed time in the officers' mess, drinking coffee, waiting on something he wanted to be gone and done with, something he had hoped would never come to pass.

Saturday. A working day, 12 June. The sun spread its first crimson tendrils across those dark, eastern hills through which the Smoky Hill had cut its way for ages long, long gone. That haze already lingering over the trees at the river's banks testified to a hot and muggy day a'birthing. Summer had come to the southern plains at last, with as

much vengeance as the past winter had come: a long winter
gone.

Custer moseyed outside to watch the comings and goings
of Captain Myers and his E Troop, cavalry escort for
Pepoon's civilian scouts on this journey south to Camp
Supply. There the Cheyenne would be turned out and the
army would roll back to Fort Hays, their mission complete—the Cheyennes home at last.

By the time the Cheyenne reached Camp Supply, seven
months would have passed since any of the women had
enjoyed freedom. Any, except for Monaseetah. For much
of her captivity at the hands of the Seventh Cavalry, she had
come and gone as she pleased, belonging more to the
Yellow Hair than she had ever belonged to her people.

With the rising of a cold, winter-pale sun, she had come
into his life. Now, with the coming of a festering bone-
yellow summer sun, he sent her away.

Custer swallowed against the painful knot in his throat.
Not since that awful moment of drunkenness played out in
front of the Bacon house in Monroe a decade ago had he
suffered such anguish. Never this sort of fear.

That's what it was, after all—fear. He had to admit he
was scared . . . frightened he would never see her again.
Knowing already he had to.

With the groan of axles, a train of sidewalled freighters
wheeled free of the wagon yard, some already loaded with
supplies and foodstuffs for the prisoners and escort. The
remaining empty wagons would haul copper people: big
and small, wide and thin, young and old; even the dead.
Copper people transferred, from the Department of the
Platte to the Indian Bureau, Fort Cobb, Indian Territory.

While Myers's company stood rigidly by their horses and

off-duty soldiers looked on with passing interest, Fifth Infantry guards opened the stockade gates one last time. A faceless interpreter barked orders for the Cheyenne to march through the gate in single file, one prisoner at a time. Each prisoner was checked off on some clerk's official list.

Custer shook his head. A pitiful farewell for a proud people taken prisoner in winter battle, freighted home while ink dried on a meaningless scrap of paper that would find rest in someone's useless file in Washington City. Given a final Indian Department burial by someone to whom the Cheyenne had never been human beings—only prisoners, names, numbers . . . requisitions, blankets, tents . . . bullets and bayonets.

"At goddamn last, the sonsabitches are going home and out of our hair!" an infantryman blared down on the parade.

Funny to think about it now, Custer brooded, watching the prisoners peeling through the stockade gate the way he would take layer after layer from a prairie onion. *The Cheyenne are taking more than they had when we pulled them out of the valley of the Washita. Then they had only what they wore on their backs, leaving behind a smoking ruin of Black Kettle's village.*

"Farewell, old Cardigan!"

Surprised, Custer glanced at the stockade. Some of the soldiers shouted farewell to Fat Bear, the last surviving Sweetwater prisoner. The old chief ambled through the gate, nodding here, smiling there.

"Happy hunting, Cardigan!"

The soldiers cheered Fat Bear using the name they had given him for the worsted mackinaw coat he had taken to wearing. A gift from the army.

When he reached his assigned wagon, Fat Bear stopped,

turned, smiling his wrinkled, cherubic best, and waved to the men in blue. A new cheer erupted, punctuated by applause. No reason for sadness.

"Goodbye, Sally Ann!"

Custer recognized Tom's joy-filled voice among the soldiers lining the gauntlet each prisoner walked through from stockade to wagons. Once inside the high-walled freighters, the captives thrust their heads around the canvas tops to wave and chatter at the soldiers like schoolchildren setting off on a spring outing. So unlike their solemn arrival at Fort Hays, this merry leave-taking.

"Cheer up, Sally Ann!"

Custer found her in the crowd, waving to Tom, bravely wearing that beautiful smile of hers. Again her eyes searched the shadows along porches or under the eaves of the buildings squaring the fort parade. Hoping, though her heart knew he would not show.

Her brave smile disappeared as she reached a wagon and passed her infant up to the waiting arms of an older squaw.

She couldn't go. Not yet.

Monaseetah turned, shading her eyes to the new morning light streaming out of the eastern hills. One last time she searched for him among the others. To hear once more the vow he had made to her and their child.

"Aren't you going to say farewell to the young one?"

Custer whirled, confronted by the bulk of Colonel Miles. "I hadn't considered it."

"Dammit, Armstrong. You haven't much time left to consider it."

Gazing back across the compound, Custer watched the young woman drop her hand from her brow, looking up into the wagon.

"Yes, Nelson." Lord, did he want to go. But he was too damned scared.

"Not a man could blame you for saying goodbye to that woman."

Miles stepped closer to Custer and whispered, "Hell's fire, I'd be skinned alive by Mother Miles if she found out I'd suggested you say goodbye to an Indian girl when you're married to Elizabeth. But Armstrong—Mother Miles has never been a man far from home fighting a no-win war for the chair polishers back east. Still—" he smiled beneath his shaggy mustache, "Mary isn't awake yet, so I'm ordering you to say your farewells and pay your respects to that woman."

With a shove of his bearlike paw, Miles nudged Custer down the wide steps, showing off a broad row of teeth beneath his Prussian mustache.

"But Nelson—"

"Get!"

"Yessir!"

Suddenly that famous grin flashed, almost as much a trademark as were those long, red-gold curls streaming across his shoulders.

As she slipped a foot on the iron helper, ready to swing herself up to the wagon bed, Monaseetah sighted him—a man in buckskin and blue, racing across the compound, stirring up the dry dust of the parade, loping her way with his arm beating the air.

She resisted her first impulse to dash toward him. Waiting instead, she dropped her eyes. For she was Cheyenne—her lover and husband came for her.

Yet in her heart, she knew she could wait no longer.

Flinging her body against him, Monaseetah clung to

Custer like ivy to an oak as he carried her the last few steps back to the wagon. By the time he set her down, she was weeping, birdlike sobs choked back in her chest.

Custer rubbed her cheeks, smearing tears across the copper-colored skin. Then he tugged her chin up so she would look into his eyes.

She blinked, then blinked again, not sure of what she saw. She had never seen him cry.

No man had ever shed tears for her . . . no man until Yellow Hair. Among her people, tears were a sign of weakness. Yet *Hiestzi* was strong enough to cry without being weak.

"I will not go," she sobbed, fighting back the boiling knot of fear in her throat.

"You must go, little one." He swiped angrily at his own tears, knowing no one must see his freckled cheeks moist. "It is the only way."

"I cannot leave you," she protested.

"For a short time, you must. I will see you . . . be with you again."

She stared at the ground, feeling the babe kick in her belly. "I understand. I must have our child among my people."

Custer gathered her against him once more, caressing the side of her cheek with his callused fingers. "The little one cannot be born here among the white men. I fear for the child's safety. A life of suffering, forever roaming, looking for peace, searching for his own spirit. Lost on the winds, as my spirit roams."

He embraced her, listening to the familiar sounds of the parade—teamsters adjusting harness and brake, soldiers checking cinches and bits, stirrups and belts. Creaky leather, the way his own guts churned.

"Promise me the white man will never know of our child, Monaseetah!"

She nodded, tears streaming.

"If any of my people learn that Yellow Hair has a child," he continued, "there will never be peace in that child's life. Like a curse I had passed onto the blood of my body. Promise me."

"I do, on all that my heart feels for you."

"See he grows straight and true."

"As his father."

"A warrior of power and honor, Monaseetah. With mighty medicine no man can dim or shame."

She had waited long enough and could wait no longer to ask the question. "When will I see you again?"

Behind her the old women called out, shouted for her to board quickly.

Custer glanced up nervously. Myers's company clambered into their black McClellans, settling their rumps for a sweaty ride into the land of summer.

"I promise I will come when I can."

"Tell me! Give me some dream to hold, though I cannot hold you!" She caressed the back of his freckled hand.

The squaws yelled for her to join them before the wagons rolled.

Custer jerked his head in sudden desperation. He wanted to say he would come soon—yet he could not lie to her.

"I don't know, Monaseetah. If I am not there before our child is born, then I may come while the child still suckles at your breast. If not then, when the child walks. With the help of the Cheyenne, he will become a mighty warrior."

Monaseetah's full lips trembled. She grew afraid to speak again. The tears flowed as if some river long dammed had burst. She reached for his hand, bringing it to her lips, holding it there. Knowing no hands had caressed her as these hands had . . . as no man would ever touch her again.

"Monaseetah—" he licked his dry lips, "you are the woman I have waited for—like waiting for the breath of spring after too long a winter on the land. You are the spring for my heart. I will come for you."

She pulled away as the wagons creaked into motion, the shouts for her growing insistent, hands reaching for her. Imploring her to hurry.

Yells and curses reached the sky as horses and mules were jabbed and kicked and prodded into motion. Saddle gear jangle and brassy braying, shouts and curses and whinnying. No one could overhear his final words to her.

Custer shouted it here at the last. "I will come to you, Monaseetah. To be with you for all time. When I come, I will never leave you again."

She scrambled frantically to pull herself aboard the wagon, yanked up with the help of three old squaws who waved to the soldiers as Monaseetah leaned out the back of the wagon. From between her swollen breasts she took that red bandanna he had given her a long time ago, when she had been crying over something of little consequence. Yet, instead of drying her eyes with it now, she waved the bright bandanna to him as the wagons circled the parade, then pointed west and south toward Indian Territory.

Custer stood frozen in the center of the emptying

parade, dust settling on his shiny boots, smudging his fresh blue tunic with its gold braid shimmering in the new-orange light of summer morn. He held his hand high and still, as if in prayer to what spirits there might be to watch over the future. What gods might guard that future and bring things to pass.

From her place in the wagon she gazed at that solitary figure standing tall as a mighty, wind-battered oak in the middle of that empty parade, his hand outstretched as if in prayer to her Everywhere Spirit.

"Yes, Yellow Hair," she murmured, knowing he heard her with only his heart now, "I know of your promise—to come for me one day in the Moon of Fat Horses."

She laid a hand across her swollen belly, the other held aloft waving that bright red bandanna for him to see as the wagons lurched past the last dull-gray cluster of Fort Hays buildings.

"Your son will know of your coming," she promised. "In that Moon of Fat Horses when Yellow Hair comes, the son of Yellow Hair will finally know his father."

Her black-cherry eyes glazed and she could no longer see him for the dust, for her tears.

FROM THE AUTHOR

I was born on the first day of 1947 in a small town on the plains of Kansas. That great rolling homeland of the nomadic buffalo has remained in my marrow across the years of my wandering.

From Nebraska to Kansas and on to Oklahoma, I've spent a full third of my life on those Great Plains. Another third growing up in the desert Southwest an arrow's shot from the wild Apache domain of Cochise and Victorio. The most recent third of my life has passed among the majestic splendor of the Rocky Mountains—from Colorado and on to Washington state. In less than a year, I am back in Montana, here in the valley of the great Yellowstone River, in the veritable heart of the historic West. The plains and prairies at my feet, the great Rockies as my backrest.

The Great Plains and all its history run in my blood. I suppose they always will. More than merely growing up there, my roots go deep in the land that over the last hundred-odd years soaked up about as much blood and sweat as it did rain.

My maternal grandfather came from working-class stock in St. Joseph, Missouri, where he first became a carriage-riding sawbones doctor who as a young man moved to Oklahoma Territory, finding it necessary to pack two small thirty-six-caliber pistols for his own protection while practicing his medical arts from his horse-drawn buggy. In later years he would be proud to say he never stepped foot in a motorized vehicle.

It wasn't long before Dr. David Yates met and fell in love with the schoolmarm teaching there in Osage country, Pearl Hinkle. My grandmother had bounced into The Strip, formerly called "Indian Territory" or "The Nations," in her parents' wagon in June of 1889 during the great land rush that settled what is now the state of Oklahoma. With immense pride I tell you I go back five generations homesteading on the plains of Kansas—Hinkles, simple folk with rigid backbones and a belief in the Almighty, folk who witnessed the coming of the Kansas Pacific Railroad along with the terrifying raids of Cheyenne and Kiowa as the Plains tribes found themselves shoved south and west by the slow-moving tide of white migration.

My father's father wandered over to the territory from the vicinity of Batesville, Arkansas, when he first learned of the riches to be found in what would one day become south-central Oklahoma. It was an era of the "boomers"—when oil money ran local governments and bought law-enforcement officers both. Yet in that violent and lawless epoch, Oklahoma history notes a few brave men who stood the test of that time. I'm very proud to have coursing in my veins the blood of a grandfather who had the itchy feet of a homesteader turned justice of the peace in that ofttimes rowdy, violent, and unsettled frontier.

Still, it was more than what Scotch-Irish heritage ran in

their veins that both my parents passed on to me—more so the character of those sturdy, austere folk who settled the Great Plains. From my father I believe I inherited the virtue of hard work and perseverance. And from my mother, besides her abiding love and reverence for the land, I have inherited a stamina to endure all the travesties that life can throw at simple folk. Those traits she has given me, along with a belief in the Almighty—the selfsame belief that helped those hardy settlers endure through hailstorms and locust plagues, drought and barrel-bottom crop prices.

Brought up in the fifties during the era of Saturday matinees and some twenty hours of prime-time westerns on these small boxes we fondly called TV, early on I found myself bitten by the seductive lure of the West. Yet it was not until 1965, during my freshman year in college in Oklahoma, where I was studying to become a history teacher, that I was finally able to separate the history of the West from the *Myth of the West*. Over the intervening twenty-five years I have happily found the historic West every bit as fascinating as the mythic frontier.

You would be hard pressed to find a man happier than I—still teaching as I am thousands of readers outside the confines of the classroom about a magical epoch of expansion that roared rowdy and rambunctious across the plains and mountains of our Western frontier. A man is a success when he can put food on his family's table doing what he loves most to do.

Over the years I've been cursed with the itchiest of feet, moving on frequently as did the rounders and roamers of this mountain West more than a hundred-odd years before me. In the last three years we have been nomads, moving from Colorado to Montana to Washington, and now to these windswept foothills of the Prescott valley. My wife, Rhonda, hopes we can stay put for awhile, here in Billings along the Yellowstone, under the sun hung in that Big Sky, while we raise our two children, son Noah and daughter Erinn.

There'll be time enough to move on, time enough for me to see what's over the next hill. Time enough still to follow the seductive lure of tomorrow and the next valley across the years to come . . .

The legend of George A. Custer continues in this novel filled with Indian lore—a fascinating and authoritative look at the frontier military at the time of Little Big Horn.

SEIZE THE SKY
by Terry C. Johnston
Volume 2 in the Son of the Plains Trilogy

Turn the page for the tale George A. Custer and his son, Yellow Bird as told by a master frontier storyteller, Terry C. Johnston. SEIZE THE SKY will be published in April 1991 and available wherever Bantam Books are sold.

The Hillside

Clouds of black powder smudged the late-afternoon ridges like yesterday's coal-oil smoke. Yellow dust stived up into the broiling air beneath the countless unshod pony hoofs and moccasined feet scurrying through the gray sage and stunted grasses beneath a relentless summer sun. There weren't many of the big, weary, iron-shod army horses left on the hillside now. A few carcasses lay stiffening, their four-legs rigid and bloated. But most of the big, iron-shod horses had clattered down to water.

He cried out. Not wanting to go up that hill. Terrified of what he saw. More terrified of what he heard.

Wailing, screeching, and hideous cries assaulted the ears. So many keened in mourning. Still others cried out their songs of victory. Many more lips screeched bowel-puckering shouts of vengeance as they attended their deadly labors of conquest. The side of the hill ran dark with blood.

He dared not look, covered his eyes. But just as quickly his mother jerked his hand away from his dirty face. She wanted him to see, to remember.

The parched, sandy slope was littered with the stinking refuse of battle: Bodies pale and lifeless, scattered across the dusty sage and brown grasses. Their dark blood soaked into the eager, thirsty soil that stretched all the way up to those mule-spine ridges far to the east where the sun, now into its western quadrant, glared down like a cruel, unblinking eye.

He tripped, stumbling to his knees. He cried out as he was dragged to his feet again, as his spindly, copper-skinned legs bled. Quickly he cut off his own yelp. Long ago he had been taught that a boy of the People does not cry out in pain.

There were several women and men clustered around each of the pale bodies on this knoll. Mostly it was the women, hunched over their crude handiwork. These bodies were as white as fish bellies—except for bloodied, leathery faces, necks, and hands.

What hairy creatures these fish-bellied men are.

Some of these browned-hide faces were almost coppery enough to belong to the People. Had it not been for all the hair on their faces that made him shudder with the sharp memory of childhood nightmares—he would not have believed these bodies were what the neighbor tribes called the dreaded *wasichus.*

His mother halted near the crest of the hill. There she knelt and enclosed him within her arms. At first her teary eyes moved about before gazing at last into her son's face. She instructed him to stay by her side. Fearfully his own dark-cherry eyes darted about the hillside and he understood why she admonished him not to wander. Here in this place existed a mad fury he had never seen in his few summers of life.

Women, children, old men—running about carrying knives and axes, stone mallets and tomahawks, lances and bows, pistol butts and rifle barrels . . . cutting, slashing, clubbing, tearing and gouging.

The little boy huddled against his mother. Fear formed a hard, hot knot in his belly.

She bent, putting her face right next to his so she would not have to speak so loudly. Instead, she began to sob again before any words could come out.

Another woman of their tribe came up beside the mother and son, kneeling in the blood-soaked soil. She was a good friend of his mother and her name was Bighead Woman. He called her *aunt* because he had no real blood relatives among the People. His aunt smiled down at him, brushing the tears from one of his dirty cheeks. When she looked into his wide, frightened, small-animal eyes, he saw in hers a sorrow he had never before seen on her face.

"Monaseetah," the older woman whispered hoarsely, like a trickle of water running over a drought-parched creek-bed, "you must be quick about this now. I wish to leave and go with the others across the hills. To touch these pale men who came with such foolish hearts to strike our camps of women and children again. Always they come to strike the women and children first—"

Her words snapped off like dry kindling in mid-sentence as Monaseetah, the boy's mother, lifted her face, a mask of utter sadness and despair. Bighead Woman understood that despair and hopelessness immediately.

"This, I did for you, Monaseetah." Her gnarled, scarred hand pointed down at the three bodies crumpled on the ground nearby. "I watched so that none would touch his body. Many came here to mutilate him . . . as they do now with the others who rode against us when the sun was high in the sky. But, I told them your story. Most left without a word to find other bodies they could revenge themselves upon. Some said a small prayer for you before they turned to go. My heart shares how you must feel. Long ago I lost a man in battle—in a time of cold when the Winter Man's breath blew white out of the northlands. My man was killed in a battle just like this with the pony soldiers. It was the time you lost your father. You will remember . . . must remember—that time those cowardly white warriors of winter followed their chief . . . this one!"

Bighead Woman gestured violently toward the naked corpse beside them in the dust. She waited for Monaseetah to speak.

"I thank you for your care this day, sister. I will stay here now. My son and I will stay to watch over the body until dark fills the sky. We will see that no harm comes to this man. You need wait no longer. Leave us now."

The older woman reached into a small quilled pouch hung at her belt and removed a bone awl, its point hardened in fire and sharpened for punching holes in the thickest of bull hides. With that awl clasped in her right hand, Bighead Woman twisted the white soldier's head to the side so that he slumped over one of his forearms. Monaseetah grabbed the woman's hand to still it.

For a long moment they stared at one another, the older woman able to read what lay within the liquid depths of the young mother's eyes.

"What I do now is not for you, my young friend," Bighead Woman explained softly. "This I do for him. *Hiestzi* did not heed the words told him long ago during his days in those lands to the south. Eight winters it has been now since the elders of our tribe warned him not to attack the women and children and villages of the People. Yet, Yellow Hair did not hear our clear, strong words. This I do for him. So that Yellow Hair may hear better in the life to come—I wish to open his ears up to the songs he should have heard long ago."

Eventually Monaseetah's fingers loosened their frantic grip on the older woman's brown wrist. "It is understood," she replied as she pulled her hand away in resignation.

Cautiously, Bighead Woman inserted the point of the bone awl into the left ear canal then suddenly rammed it all the harder when she encountered resistance. She brought the bone spindle out accompanied with a slight trickle of blood. When she had twisted the man's head to the left, she punctured the right ear as well. Finally she wiped the bone awl on her dusty buckskin dress and dropped it back into her pouch.

"It is right, this that you do," Monaseetah sighed. Her voice was like a dry wind that scours the distant prairie home of her Southern Cheyenne people.

"Yes, it is right, little sister." The older woman shakily rose to her feet. "Perhaps you will be granted another time together with *Hiestzi*. In another place, in some dream yet to come."

"Perhaps." Monaseetah did not look up to see her friend walk away to join the others scurrying like maddened red ants across the yellow hillsides where the heat rose in shimmering waves to the bone-white sky.

Frightened still, her son looked down the slope. Here and there warriors had turned the fish-belly bodies of their white victims face-down after mutilation and desecration. He remembered the Cheyenne belief taught him by the old ones: it was bad luck to leave an enemy facing the sky because his soul could more easily escape the earthly plane.

Many of the hairy, tanned heads had been smashed to jelly. The congealing ooze was already attracting both crawling and flying insects. Some heads had been severed from the bodies. Among the sage and yellow dust lay other body-parts: hands, feet, penises, legs and arms. Practically every man's back bristled like a porcupine with a score or more arrows, most fired into the dead bodies by eager young boys or infuriated, wrinkled old men who could not remember ever celebrating such a resounding victory. Truly, this was a day for joy and singing the old songs.

Farther down the slope two older youths played a game of shinny-ball with a soldier's head, batting the bloody trophy back and forth with discarded rifles that could be found beside every dead soldier. The bearded head rolled into the sticky entrails that had tumbled from another soldier's belly wound. Suddenly the two youths had a new game to play. They yanked and pulled, tore and ripped the warm, snake-like intestines from the man's belly.

The little boy turned away, his mind already numb to the shrieking, crimson spectacle all around him. Even here at his feet he could not escape the gore. Here lay three of the white-bellies, looking like helpless fish flopped on the creek-bank. All three had been stripped by the women. Yet, for the first time he noticed—while two had been desecrated and horribly mutilated, their genitals hacked off and tossed aside, their thighs gashed, a hand gone or foot cleaved off, heads scalped and pummelled to a sticky jelly—the hairy-face in the middle remained untouched.

Why had his aunt protected this one from desecration? Why had she stood guard while his mother hauled him up the hillside to view this body? Why would they want this one, solitary soldier out of all the others to hear better in *Seyan*—his people's Life After Crossing Over?

This soldier's face bore a look of peace.

The boy felt something very different boiling inside his own belly. In summer all he ever wore was the little breechclout and his buffalo-hide moccasins. The sun's scorching fingers raked his naked back. Trickles of sweat coursed down his heaving chest. It seemed the sun's rays grew hotter, the stench more suffocating. He imagined the white-belly corpses inching in on him here where he sat near the crest of the hill.

"Aiyeeee!"

He jerked up, his nose inches from the frightening glare of an ancient, shriveled woman. The skin on her face sagged, as did the wrinkled pair of old dugs he saw as he peered down the loose neckline of her ill-fitting skin dress. The boy swallowed sickly.

Her wild eyes darted like accusing black marbles from him, to the white soldier, to Monaseetah, and back to the soldier's body again.

"You have not touched this one yet!" Her teeth showed black gaps from which burst a hideous odor.

"No." Monaseetah placed a hand on the dead soldier's chest, over his heart just above the bloody wound. "He is a . . . my relative."

"*Aieee!*" Her head fell back as she laughed crazily, and the boy feared it would fall off the old harpy's shoulders. "A *relative*, sister?"

"You are Sioux? Yes?" Monaseetah did not remove her hand from the soldier's heart.

"Minniconjou."

"I am *Tsistsistas*. I know this soldier from long ago. Several winters now. In my land to the south. This one, he was foolish to come north. But, he is my relative."

Slowly the old one bent forward, studying the young mother's face with a rheumy eye. "You see to him, Cheyenne sister." The old hag peered at him closely a long moment before he pulled away, hiding behind his mother. "I want his boots, *Tsistsistas*. Only his boots!"

She cackled once more as Monaseetah scooped up the knee-high, dusty black boots she had set aside for herself. The scuffed cavalry boots belonging to two other soldiers were nowhere near as tall as these. Running her hands over the soft, pliant, black leather, the wrinkled one smiled now that the precious treasure belonged to her.

"These, little sister, will make fine bullet pouches . . . perhaps a quiver for some man's arrows. Maybe a hiding place for a man's love charms or war medicine. So very soft—"

"Take them and go, old one!" Monaseetah snapped. "Just go!"

Her fiery words caught the boy by surprise. He rarely heard his mother bark at others. She almost never shouted at him or his older brother—only when they had really deserved it.

"He is your relative, you say?" She squinted the cloudy eye again, stooping close to the young Cheyenne mother, glaring with suspicion and disbelief at Monaseetah.

"He is."

With a bony finger the old one brushed a lock of the boy's light hair out of his eye before she took that same finger and dipped some of the drying blood from the massive, oozing wound at the soldier's left side. With that blood she smeared something on the man's left cheek. Again she dipped and painted, dipped and painted until she had enough of a symbol brushed dark against the sun-burnished skin and reddish-blonde whisker stubble.

"I leave this here to tell all Sioux they must leave this body alone." The old woman's face softened. Perhaps she remembered years without number gone by, remembered little ones at her breasts, remembered a man she had loved long before there were too many years to count any longer. "My people will not bother him seeing this sign on his body, little sister. Do not worry your heart."

Monaseetah was stunned, not at all sure what she should say. "Thank you . . . for your great kindness." She dropped her gaze, ashamed of her tears.

"Little niece, it is always better to grieve. Later you can heal from that mourning for those who have gone before us to the Other Side. It is always better to forget after some time has passed . . . and you go on into the days granted you by the Father of us all."

"But, I do not want to forget. I will never forget."

Monaseetah's words turned the old woman around after a

few hobbling steps. She looked at the tall, dusty cavalry boots clutched securely beneath her withered arms like a rare treasure.

"I will always remember this day, little one. Remember for all the time that is left me. I too can never forget. Sometimes, it might be better to carry the hurt inside . . . and remember what happened here beneath this sun."

The wrinkled one turned away and was gone.

More frightened now, the boy clung to the back of his mother's buckskin dress. Monaseetah pulled free a butcher knife and set to work with its sharp blade.

He could not see what she was cutting until stepping around her shoulder. His wide, wondering eyes watched as she finished hacking off one of the pale man's fingertips. Monaseetah let the soldier's right hand fall before she dropped the fingertip into a small pouch hung round her neck.

Why would she take part of this soldier's body to keep when everywhere else on the hillside all the others hacked at the white bodies with pure, unfettered blood-lust?

He studied the soldier's head and saw that it would truly make for a very poor scalp. The short, reddish-blonde bristles were thinning, the hairline receding. *No wonder no one had torn this skimpy head of hair from the white man's skull.*

"Here, my son." Monaseetah gave him an elk-horn ladle she had pulled from her wide belt. "Bring me water from the river. Take it. Go now."

She nudged him down the hill toward the river that lay like a silver ribbon beneath the wide, white sky. At least it would be cool beside the water, he thought.

Dodging the huge bloating horses and gleaming soldier corpses, he went to the river and scooped water into the ladle. Mounted warriors screeched past him as they rode to the south. Shaking, the boy spilled half of the cool water on his lonely, frightening climb back up the long hillside. He slid to a halt beside his mother and choked back the sudden, foul taste of bile washing his throat.

It surprised him. For the first time this afternoon he wanted to vomit. He gulped and swallowed, fighting down the urge to rid himself of that breakfast eaten so long ago.

As his mother began to wash the white man's head and face, the boy turned away.

She used a strip of dirty, stiffened, white cloth—one of the dead soldier's stockings. If only these white men wore moccasins instead of the clumsy black boots that made their feet hot and sweaty. With moccasins the white men would not need to wear these silly stockings. He smiled and began to feel better for it.

This was his seventh summer. He was too old to act like a child, the boy decided.

Finally he turned back to his mother and knelt to help her with her chore. Monaseetah scrubbed the last of the black, grainy smudges from the edges of the bullet hole in the soldier's left temple. Little blood had oozed from the wound.

Perhaps this pale man had already been dying from that messy bullet wound in his side. The boy had seen enough deer and elk, antelope and buffalo brought down with bullets. And he knew no man could live long after suffering a wound in the chest as terrible as this. *This soldier had been dying and he was shot in the head to assure his death.* Someone had wanted to make certain that this soldier was not taken alive. Someone had saved this pale-skinned soldier from the possibility of torture by issuing a bullet to the brain.

Strange. As the boy looked about the hillside, he could see that the warriors had taken no prisoners. As far as his young eyes could see along the ridges of shimmering heat and yellow dust and black smoke and red death—none of these pony soldiers had lived for longer than it took the sun to move from one lodgepole to the next.

The boy sat quietly and watched his mother at work. With care she washed the white man's entire face, scrubbing the dirty sock dipped in river water over the bristling stubble of red gold sprouting on the burnished cheeks and strong chin. The lips were cracked, peeling, and bloody from days in the sun and from drinking alkali water.

The boy's eyes wandered down the pony soldier's frame until they froze on the wound in the man's left side, just two of his little hands below the white man's heart. An ugly, gaping wound; he imagined the exit wound had to be even bigger. Surely the warrior who had shot this pony soldier had been no more than one arrow flight away when he fired his gun—no more than fifteen of his own short, little-boy strides. A shot fired far enough away not to bring instant death—but close enough to insure that death would be come eventually.

He wondered: *In his last moments had this soldier gazed down this slope, seeing all the lodges and wickiups where slept the young, unmarried warriors along the bank? Hadn't the soldier seen the great village stretched for miles along the Greasy Grass? Or, had he seen, and refused to believe his own pale-blue eyes now staring in death at the summer sky of the same robin's-egg hue? Had he plunged on down toward the villages and his own death?*

How could his mother treat this soldier as she would a member of her family? They had no relatives. Monaseetah and her two sons were alone in this world. It had been twelve winters since Monaseetah's mother was killed by pony soldiers far to the south along the Little Dried River. Eight winters now since Monaseetah's father had suffered the same fate at the hand of other soldiers in a similar dawn attack. His thoughts and fears tumbled: Why had his mother told the old Minniconjou woman this white-bellied soldier was a relative?

The stench of dried blood and putrefying gore clung strong on the breeze. He rubbed his nose and fidgeted, wanting to be gone. His mother's hand quieted his nervousness.

"I am finished at last, my son." She pulled him round to her gently. "I want you to listen to my words with all your heart. Listen to me with your soul, son of my body."

The boy nodded, wanting only to be gone from this hillside.

Monaseetah tossed aside the dirty stocking she had used to bathe the dead soldier. When he studied her eyes for some answer to his confusion, the boy discovered tears glistening her dark eyes, streaming down her coppery cheeks. He thought, *She is the prettiest woman I have ever seen*.

With a tiny, dirty finger he touched her cheek, wiping away a single tear. Without a word Monaseetah took his tiny hand, directing him to touch the white soldier's hair.

"The red-gold of a winter's sunrise," his mother whispered as she touched the soldier's hair.

Monaseetah guided his hand to stroke her own dark, silky hair falling unfettered in the hot breezes across her quaking shoulders.

"Black, my son. Sleek as the raven's shiny wing when it snags the sun's rays in high flight."

She took the boy's hand and brought it up to touch his own head. She held some of his own long hair before his eyes.

"Your hair is not like your mother's."

"I do not understand," he said, quivering.

Again, Monaseetah took his hand to touch first the soldier's thinning, close-cropped hair. Then her own long, loose hair. Finally his own. Looking at it perhaps for the first time in his young life, the boy found himself growing scared, with a cold creeping right down to his toes.

"I named you Yellow Bird because of the color of your hair, my son."

He watched her choke back a sob that made his mother shudder. She swiped at her wet cheeks before he worked up courage to ask.

"You are my mother, aren't you?"

"Yes." She smiled through the haze. "I am your mother."

Anxiously, Yellow Bird wrung his hands through his hair, not understanding, afraid to accept what his mother had told him. He did not like the feeling at all. He had been scared before, he remembered. Like last summer when his pony had been spooked by a rattler, bolting into the hills as he clung to its mane in desperation. Yet, right now he was more frightened than he had ever been.

Yellow Bird bolted to his feet. As quickly his mother snagged his wrist and yanked him down beside her. He fell to his knees, sprawling over the naked pony soldier.

He cried out as his face brushed the pony soldier's cold, bristling cheek.

Fiercely he clamped his eyes to shut off the flow of hot tears. In a flood, he figured out what she wanted to tell him. But Yellow Bird knew his mother wanted him to say the words himself.

Desperately he hungered for escape. The hillside filled his nostrils with the stench of blood and bowels released in death, gore scattered across the gray-backed sage and yellow dirt and dry red-brown grasses in savage, sudden, welcome death. At once Yellow Bird could not breathe.

"No!" he shouted. It scared him to hear the unbridled fear in his own voice.

"Yes," his mother cooed. She cradled his little hands within hers, holding him in this place of terror.

"No-o-o-o-o!" Yellow Bird whimpered like a wounded animal caught in a snare.

Again and again he whipped his head from side to side, whimpering his word of denial.

"It is so, my son."

Suddenly he let his tense, cold muscles go, like a dam releasing. Yellow Bird stopped fighting his mother. Instead he collapsed against her, sobbing as he stared down at the soldier. Once again he took up some long strands of his own loose, unbraided hair, lifting it into the bright, truthful sunlight. There before his eyes it shimmered, each strand much lighter than the dark, coarse hair of any other Cheyenne he had ever known in his few summers of life.

After what seemed like another lifetime, Yellow Bird brought his face away from his mother's soft breast where his tears had soaked through her soft, buckskin dress. Already the sun had begun to cast long shadows in its relentless march to the west.

"Yes, Yellow Bird," Monaseetah said quietly. "This is your father."